Ryan could feel the poison start to seep into his mind

The one-eyed man's willpower was always strong, but his mind was distracted by the need to take in air. He didn't have the immediate strength to break eye contact, and by the time he was able to breathe evenly, and devote his full attention to Ethan, the tentacles of hate were already beginning to take hold. Jak was his friend and comrade-in-arms, sure...but if they took out Jak, then J.B. would be freed.... No, he knew that wasn't the case, but why the hell should Jak escape this torture? What made him so special?

"Chill him." The words escaped from Ryan's lips before he even knew it was what he felt.

Ethan stepped back and looked across the line at the three companions who were now fully under his influence. Then he caught Jak's baleful glare.

The baron threw back his head and laughed, long and loud. This was going to be one hell of a hunt.

**Other titles in the
Deathlands saga:**

JAMES AXLER

DEATH LANDS®

Death Hunt

A GOLD EAGLE BOOK FROM
WORLDWIDE®

TORONTO • NEW YORK • LONDON
AMSTERDAM • PARIS • SYDNEY • HAMBURG
STOCKHOLM • ATHENS • TOKYO • MILAN
MADRID • WARSAW • BUDAPEST • AUCKLAND

First edition September 2004

ISBN 0-373-62577-4

DEATH HUNT

Printed in U.S.A.

...if we shrink from the hard contests where men must win at the hazard of their lives and at the risk of all they hold dear, then bolder and stronger peoples will pass us by, and win for themselves the domination of the world.

—Theodore Roosevelt,
1858–1919

THE DEATHLANDS SAGA

This world is their legacy, a world born in the violent nuclear spasm of 2001 that was the bitter outcome of a struggle for global dominance.

There is no real escape from this shockscape where life always hangs in the balance, vulnerable to newly demonic nature, barbarism, lawlessness.

But they are the warrior survivalists, and they endure—in the way of the lion, the hawk and the tiger, true to nature's heart despite its ruination.

Ryan Cawdor: The privileged son of an East Coast baron. Acquainted with betrayal from a tender age, he is a master of the hard realities.

Krysty Wroth: Harmony ville's own Titian-haired beauty, a woman with the strength of tempered steel. Her premonitions and Gaia powers have been fostered by her Mother Sonja.

J. B. Dix, the Armorer: Weapons master and Ryan's close ally, he, too, honed his skills traversing the Deathlands with the legendary Trader.

Doctor Theophilus Tanner: Torn from his family and a gentler life in 1896, Doc has been thrown into a future he couldn't have imagined.

Dr. Mildred Wyeth: Her father was killed by the Ku Klux Klan, but her fate is not much lighter. Restored from predark cryogenic suspension, she brings twentieth-century healing skills to a nightmare.

Jak Lauren: A true child of the wastelands, reared on adversity, loss and danger, the albino teenager is a fierce fighter and loyal friend.

Dean Cawdor: Ryan's young son by Sharona accepts the only world he knows, and yet he is the seedling bearing the promise of tomorrow.

In a world where all was lost, they are humanity's last hope....

Chapter One

"'It's a mighty long way down the dusty trail…'"

"Don't—"

"'Where the sun bursts hot on the…' By the Three Kennedys, the next line has completely escaped me!" Doc exclaimed.

"That's a blessing, if nothing else," Mildred murmured. She'd been pleading with Doc to stop quoting half-remembered lines, which she found more irritating than if he had been able to quote whole stanzas, for what seemed to be hours. It couldn't really have been that long, but time was beginning to drag.

The companions were seated in the kitchen area of a redoubt, the last of the dried and still-edible frozen goods in pots on top of the stove. The self-heats had been securely stowed for their journey ahead; they'd leave when their chrons told them it was daylight up above.

A pall of gloom hung over the six friends, caused by the fact that there were only, now, the six. Ryan had veered between raging anger and deep sorrow in the time following the discovery that Sharona had jumped and taken Dean with her.

Although all of the companions had been shocked at the sudden departure of the boy, and hadn't known what to make of the circumstances, it seemed that Cawdor had been hit on a deeper level—from which a scar had formed that was more pronounced than any physical reminder of his hard, raging life. Questions consumed Ryan's mind. Had she tricked the boy? Or had he left of his own accord, without a word to his father and friends? Where were they now? What was to become of them? He had withdrawn into himself, not even wishing to share his anger, pain and confusion with Krysty. For several days he had been little more than a spectral presence, haunting the corridors of the redoubt where they were now resting.

He finally emerged into their midst, and spoken, his tone grim, resigned. But it was the dulled quality of his one good eye that was the biggest sign of his pain, its hard glitter and diamond-hardness temporarily gone.

"Wherever that bitch has jumped, and wherever they both are, there's no way we can follow. And she knows that…" He didn't add that it was Dean who would have told her or that this was the hardest thing of all to bear. "But even if we can't follow, we can still hope…I can still hope," he added after a pause. "All we can do is carry on. I want us to get out of here as soon as we can."

There were no arguments from the others. To jump from this redoubt would remove Ryan from the source. To move on in physical space would make the moving on within him that little bit easier to initiate.

The companions scoured the redoubt, stripping the place of anything useful. No one spoke much, and the task was achieved in triple-quick time. They were soon entering the mat-trans chamber, settling into positions that would reduce the stress and agony that came with every jump.

It was the one-eyed man himself who closed the chamber door, folding his length into a sitting position, knees drawn up protectively as the chamber air began to crackle as a white mist whirled wisplike from the metallic disks on the floor and ceiling.

The obliquity of the jump was something Ryan welcomed.

The deviation, however, didn't last long.

He was haunted by dreams, not the surreal nightmares of a mat-trans jump, the effect of every atom being broken, twisted and turned into an electron stream shot from one unit to another before being painfully reassembled. Those kinds of nightmares, at least, had shape to them. They were sickening, and exposed every fear and loathing contained within the human brain. But they were just nightmares, just the subconscious dredging up the detritus and spewing it out in protest of the battering it was taking from the jump.

These hauntings were worse. They weren't nightmares. They weren't even dreams: neither in the sense of having coherence nor in having narrative; not even the distorted logic of most dreams. Instead, they were fragments: wisps as much as the white mist that had swirled around him before he'd finally passed out, with as much substance and with as much seemingly benign malevolence.

A succession of images and memories passed through his brain like a cavalcade; Dean as a small boy—absurd, this, as Ryan hadn't known of Dean until the boy was nine—Sharona as she was before the rad sickness; the Brody school in which he had enrolled the lad when he had found him again. The circumstances of his rejoining their party the last time, after being used as a gladiator in a sport of barons. What had happened since: snatching him from Jenna, the twisted wife of Baron Alien, who had mixed old-occult practices and the old tech nuke to make her own new way of promulgating a master race... Fireblast, but Ryan had thought Dean had been lost forever.

The last image ripped from his head and held up in front of him was of Dean as he had last seen him: at rest in the redoubt, with plans for the next day. Plans to explore the underground base, to join his father and friends in stripping it before moving on to their next location, the next step in their search for...

Well, for what? What was there now, beyond survival? Twice before Ryan had found his son and then lost him. Was there to be a third chance?

Ryan opened his eye with the feeling that, should he part his lips, his intestines would vomit themselves out through his mouth and the pressure would blow his brains down through his nose.

Except, this time, he wouldn't fight it and he wouldn't care.

But he did. The nausea and sense of being turned inside out, the pounding in his skull, as some kind of consciousness returned...served to kick in his sense of survival. Operating on instinct rather than intellect, he pulled himself together, battling to regain the full use of all his senses as rapidly as possibly, lest the mat-trans chamber be vulnerable in any way, leaving them open to attack. He was first on his feet and the first to organize the six companions into a party capable of securing the immediate area.

As always, it was Jak and Doc who took longest to recover from the jump. Doc's body and mind had been through too much to withstand the jumps, but still the seemingly old man's stubbornness pulled him through. As for Jak, he was tough, but there was something in him that didn't respond to the jumps. The albino was always the last to come around, puking painfully as his body readjusted.

J.B. and Mildred exchanged concerned glances as they secured the area. Ryan, perfunctory about the operation, made himself go through the motions, seemingly not as sharp as usual. Fortunately, Krysty could feel the darkness coming off him, which had nothing to do with her doomie sense and everything to do with her feelings for the one-eyed man, and was able to cover and compensate.

A thorough recce determined that the redoubt was secure, so they settled in for some rest before heading into the outside world. In itself, the redoubt had been no problem. Deserted, it had remained untouched since the advent of skydark. The only signs of passing time were the layer of dust that had gathered where the gently wheezing air-conditioners had slowly begun to wind down without continuous maintenance. The air was slightly stale and some of the comps had cut out where transistors and fuses had died of age.

As with most of the redoubts they had visited, there was no sign of life. Unlike many of those other redoubts, there was little sign that the land around the installation had suffered much upheaval. The levels they explored showed little other than minor cracks in the re-inforced walls and ceilings.

And unlike other bases, this one hadn't been com-pletely stripped. The armory would replenish their ammo supply and the clothes stores would provide much-needed new underwear, T-shirts and fatigues for those who wanted them.

The companions rested, then spent a whole day tak-ing inventory and planning their next move. Another good night's sleep refreshed them enough to tackle the unknown that lay beyond the redoubt. They knew from preliminary recces that the levels were intact up to the surface, that the maps and charts on the walls of some of the offices and comp rooms suggested they were in the northwest of the Deathlands, an area prone to erratic climatic and temperate conditions. All levels to the final exit door were known territory: what lay beyond was in question.

Which was how they found themselves gathered in the kitchen area, waiting for their last meal, Doc's impatience and anxiety expressed in the way he once again sang old snatches of half-remembered songs and poems.

"How long before we eat? I'm getting antsy waiting down here," J.B. muttered.

"Yeah—get going. See what face," Jak agreed.

"It'll be ready when it's ready, like everything is," Ryan commented flatly.

"It's not like you to get all philosophical on us," Mildred said with a note of surprise she couldn't quite disguise.

Ryan shrugged. "Had some time to think, and I've

had a lot to think about. But, fuck it, you just have to keep on, right?"

"If you say so, lover," Krysty said gently. "But it doesn't mean we should give up."

"Give up what?" Ryan asked. The clearness of his good eye as he fixed it on her betrayed that he was genuinely confused as to her meaning. Was she saying to never give up on looking for Dean, or did she mean never give up on their quest? But what use was looking for the promised land when he would never be settled inside?

"Give up on anything…on each other," Krysty said.

There was little else to say. Ryan knew she was right. If nothing else, the companions had to look out for one another. They had been through too much together and lost too many friends along the way for it to be any other way.

He nodded. Brief, but enough. "You're right. Let's eat, get ourselves together and get out there."

Within an hour they were ready to go. At least an hour remained until, by their estimation of the time zone, the light would be good enough to call it daybreak.

"Dark night, let's not leave it any longer. Even if it means watching the sunrise, I need to get out of this pesthole," J.B. said irritably.

They used the elevators to move them through the base, unwilling to expend unnecessary energy now that they were laden for the journey ahead. There was a silence over the group as they entered the elevator that would take them to the top level. Mildred, looking around at the companions, felt that it would benefit them to get out of the redoubt and into whatever was outside. Action would break the torpor that hung over them.

However, whatever was outside, in fact, was their next problem.

Knowing they were in the northwest, and that the earth and rock around the redoubt hadn't suffered from shock waves and tremors, they knew little about what was beyond the exit door. As they left the elevator and moved up the gentle incline toward the thick, reinforced exit door, the unknown began to assume importance. Would the exit be blocked by a rockfall? Were they in a valley, or up the side of a hill where the scree may have eroded and thus leave them stranded? Was the redoubt entrance under water? What was waiting on the outside?

There was no way of knowing until the lever was pressed, and the door began to rise. There were outside sec cams, but they had long since ceased to function as a result of the nuclear winter following skydark.

Ryan waited by the lever to the main door as the last set of interior sec doors ground shut. When they had closed, the companions were standing within a shallow channel of space. The reasoning was simple. If there was danger, they could defend the channel until the outer sec door was closed again, thus eliminating any risk of an enemy gaining access to the labyrinthine redoubt, indefensible with the small force they had at their disposal. Natural dangers were another matter.

"You realize that if there's water out there, you're going to have to be pretty damn quick," Mildred said as Ryan prepared to open the door. "The pressure if we're below sea level will shoot it through the gap..."

Ryan agreed. "We should have enough time to get the door closed before this fills up," he said flatly. "Anyway, chances are it won't be under water. The tunnels would be fucked with that much pressure, and there's no sign of dampness or leakage."

Mildred nodded. Ryan was right. There hadn't been signs usual of a high water table and they had rarely seen a redoubt with less stress damage or water infiltration. Nonetheless, there was a worry nagging at her that Ryan wasn't one hundred percent on the ball right now.

"Okay, triple-red and in position," Ryan said as he moved to press the lever, which they all knew was usually Dean's job.

The companions fanned out on either side of the sec door. Krysty and Jak lined up behind Ryan. The one-eyed man had unholstered his SIG-Sauer, which he held in his left hand as he pressed the lever with his right. Jak had his .357 Magnum Colt Python to hand, while Krysty had her .38-caliber Smith & Wesson ready for action.

On the far side of the channel, J.B. took the front position, choosing to shoulder his M-4000, which, with its load of barbed-metal fléchettes, would wreak havoc on any flesh-and-blood enemy who may be lying in wait. Behind him, Mildred was ready with her Czech-made ZKR 551 target pistol. It wouldn't cause as wide a range of damage as J.B.'s blaster, but with Mildred's crack-shot ability it was just as effective. Doc took the rear. The most vulnerable of the companions because of the mental and physical battering he had taken, he nonetheless had a streak of sheer granite will within him that would always make him a formidable opponent. If nothing else, he had his LeMat percussion pistol, which had the ability to inflict maximum damage on anything hostile that approached.

Ryan pressed hard on the lever and the outer door began to grind and open slowly. There was no inrush of water. Neither was there a trickle of rock and gravel to presage a landfall to indicate they were blocked in by rock.

As the door opened wider, the light from the redoubt tunnel flooded onto the land beyond. Dawn hadn't yet broken, and Ryan cursed under his breath, knowing that the light streaming from the redoubt made them an easy target. He released the lever and flattened himself against the wall, motioning to the others to do likewise.

From what he had seen before pulling back, the land beyond the redoubt entrance was barren and flat, and there was a track that led from the door to the level ground. It was a shallow incline, and the dust on the track was undisturbed, suggesting that no one had been sniffing around the redoubt entrance for a long time.

He tried to still his breathing and to listen, straining for any noises that may betray anyone waiting in ambush, but he could hear nothing. He looked at Jak. The albino youth's hunting senses were so finely honed that he had an almost preternatural grasp of the natural world around him. Jak shook his head briefly. He could neither hear nor smell anything dangerous out there. Ryan then looked at Krysty. With her doomie sense, her sentient hair would curl tightly and protectively to her scalp if there was imminent danger. The Titian mane was free-flowing.

The one-eyed man signaled across to the Armorer. They would move out, covered by their companions, and recce the area. He counted to three and signaled.

The two men rolled under the partly open door and hit the dirt outside the redoubt at the same moment, temporarily blind to the area beyond the arc of light as their eyes adjusted to the surrounding gloom. Ryan went left, J.B. right. Both held their blasters ready to fire at the least provocation.

Ryan felt the ground give beneath his feet. It was hard-packed dirt, suggesting that the area was dry, but there was a soft top layer, almost like dust, which made him feel that the place in which they had landed was like a desert. The impression was reinforced by the sparse trees and vegetation that loomed as darker shadows against the earth and sky as dawn approached.

His eye scanned the immediate area for cover and saw only a small cluster of rocks barely large enough to shelter one person. He made for the rocks, ready for an enemy to spring into view or to open fire. There was nothing to suggest the rocks were being used in such a manner. He skidded to a halt, hunkering down by them and pausing to look around.

All remained quiet.

He looked across to where the Armorer lay flat against the ground, one hand clutching the M-4000, the other clamping his battered fedora to his head. Their movements had thrown up a cloud of dust that shone in the approaching dawn as the first rays of the sun hit the motes.

J.B. shook his head. All was clear on his side of the track.

Ryan turned to signal the others to follow, then realized that they wouldn't be able to see him. It was too dark outside the redoubt.

He rose to his feet and looked around. As the sun began to crawl above the horizon, he could see that the redoubt had been built into a hillside that had long since eroded, leaving the roof of the reinforced concrete tunnel almost exposed. The track had obviously, at some time, led down into the lee of the hill, but the weather conditions over the past century or so had virtually leveled the ground for as far as he could see. Which suggested that there were harsh storms—possibly chem storms—and that the desert wind was potentially deadly. They would have to get moving and try to find their way into a more hospitable terrain as soon as possible.

"Come on out. It's clear," he called as he walked back toward the entrance, waving J.B. back to the light as he did so. By the time he was within the pool of light, the Armorer was at his side and the others had emerged from the entrance.

"It looks bleak," Mildred murmured.

"No animals. Bad sign," Jak added.

Ryan had to agree. If the terrain could support little in the way of wildlife, then it was unlikely to welcome the companions.

"We need to move as soon as the sun's up. Mebbe we'll get a better look around in the light. And once it's up, we can get a direction. Right, J.B.?"

The Armorer nodded, already searching his capacious pockets and baggage for his minisextant.

"What do you think caused that?" Mildred asked,

facing the entrance and noticing the way the hill had eroded.

"Chem storms," Krysty replied. "They could strip anything down if it's stuck in them long enough."

"Then I would venture to hope that we are not that unlucky," Doc commented. "Although…"

J.B. had turned and was looking toward the horizon. The rising sun looked bloated and purple through the shimmering haze of cloud that hung sluggishly in the sky. Purple clouds—the sign of toxic chem—seemed to hover malevolently above the desert floor. As the light spread over the land, he could see that the foliage that had struggled to survive was stunted and twisted where years of chem-soaked rains had affected plant DNA structures. The earth had a faint purple-brown tinge in its dry constituency where the chemicals had infected the soil.

J.B. took a reading and pointed to the south-southwest.

"Sea's over that way, I reckon. Depends how far north we are in the first place, though. Guess the sea should keep the land cleaner over there," he added, unable to keep the uncertainty from his voice.

"Only one way to find out. And we sure as hell can't stay here," Ryan said simply.

They struck out in the direction indicated by J.B. once he'd consulted his minisextant and his old plasticized map. Ryan led the way, with J.B. bringing up the rear. Between them, Krysty and Mildred were followed by Doc and Jak, the albino mutie changing his position in the line to cover Doc's back now that Dean was gone. It was a small thing, not even spoken of among them, but it was indicative of the changes they would have to make. Without the younger Cawdor, the dynamic of group security and battle plans had changed: regardless of personal feelings, to adapt for their survival they would have to almost forget that he had ever been among them.

The arid landscape that stretched around them was revealed in its immensity as the sun fully rose and cast its light over the land. As far as they could see, in every direction, the layer of dusty soil covered hard-packed earth that was streaked with the purple of the chem clouds above. It wasn't desert. This was definitely soil rather than sand, but it seemed all the more desolate because of this. The few grasses that were spread in sparse croppings were tough, spiked blades that threatened to cut anyone who brushed against them. Few plants could survive in the nutrient-drained, chem-raddled soil, but those that did were sickly specimens that seemed to wither under the hot sun.

And a hot sun it was. The chem clouds, sparse purple and yellow wisps across the sky like a malevolent gauze, offered no protection from the harsh rays. Rather, they seemed to rap and to magnify the intensity of the heat, giving off a humid and fetid odor, with an underlying and poisonous sweetness that made breathing an effort.

As they marched, the companions were grateful the redoubt had given them plentiful supplies of water, since anything they would find—if at all—in this wasteland would be tainted and possibly deadly.

Grateful, also, for the salt tablets that Mildred had looted from the pharmacy in the redoubt and for the protective clothing that they had been able to find. The jackets Mildred, Doc, Jak and J.B. had chosen had been made for the old Pacific northwest weather, and so were thick and heavy. They also had hoods and visors that kept off the worst excesses of sunstroke, even if they made you sweat heavily underneath.

A whole day's marching was slow and painful. Doc's breath rasped painfully in time to their footsteps, and Jak stumbled and fell a couple of times, needing water and salt tablets more than the others. His small, slight frame had a surface area to mass ratio that made him lose water and salt quicker than any of the others, especially beneath the heavy protective jacket.

Mildred looked back at the pair several times as they marched, concern evident in her face.

The barren land seemed to stretch endlessly on all sides of them. Should they have struck out and tried to find life of some kind? Should they have taken another day or two's rest—the ancient air-conditioning system could possibly have coped—and then made another jump, rather than risk being fried out here? Ryan had seemed to be motivated by more than just his survival instincts this time. It was a desire to escape the confines of a redoubt, and to just do something…anything. Or was she just reading that into the situation because she was tired, hot and cranky?

They stopped a couple of times on the first day, taking advantage of the sparse shade offered by a few stunted trees. The shallow root systems of the twisted trunks spread over a long distance before petering out, suggesting that they took whatever sustenance they could from the rain as it fell. It was likely that there was no water table unless a person dug deep—something that the lack of damage to the redoubt had earlier suggested—and that the only viable source for survival were the rains. Considering the dryness of the topsoil, it was likely there was little in the way of rainfall on anything approaching a regular basis. Looking at the deadly chem clouds floating above them, and the vast expanse of nothingness around them, the companions were glad for these signs: to be caught in a chem storm with no shelter would potentially be deadly.

Still, they trudged on in the heat, moving at a pace that seemed to deteriorate as the sun moved painfully slowly across the sky. Covering nowhere near the distance they usually would in such a time, the fall of twilight was promising. The temperature dropped rapidly, and although they all knew that before long it would be bone-chillingly cold, the sudden descent to a lower temperature was welcome after the stultifying heat of the day.

They continued until they came to the shelter of a stunted copse of trees. Ryan signaled for them to stop and, using the wood around them, they set about building a fire. The arid wasteland seemed deserted, but the light and heat was for protection as much as their own warmth. It would enable them to keep a lookout for any marauding nocturnal creatures. There had been no sign of any kind of life so far, but that wasn't surprising considering the intense heat of the day. Anything that could live in such conditions would have to be hardy, and also nocturnal. The night, when they were trying to rest before the rigor of the next day, would be the dangerous time.

The companions organized themselves into watches and tried to rest. But, despite the clothes and thermal blankets they had taken from the redoubt stores, the cold seeped into their bones. When the time came to be roused for watch, none of them could safely say that they had gotten much rest.

As the sun rose the next morning, the companions were out of sorts and tired. Not one of them had had a good night's rest.

"Gaia, but I hope this changes soon," Krysty said as she stretched, looking up to the green-purple sky and making the most of that brief period between the chill of night and the heat of day.

"It can't stretch like this for much farther. We should hit the coast soon," J.B. stated.

"Trouble is, what kind of condition are we going to be in when we do?" Mildred commented. "The salt tablets won't last forever and neither will the water."

"We press on. Can't turn back," Ryan said simply.

Doc fixed Ryan with a stare. His blue eyes, sometimes clouded with troubled visions that only he could see, were today startlingly clear. He could almost see into Ryan's heart, see the pain. But at what cost to the rest of them? He chose to say nothing—this wasn't the time—and handed out self-heats to the other companions, leaving Ryan to last. The one-eyed man gestured that he wasn't hungry.

"My dear boy, I do not care whether you are or not. You have to eat, keep up your strength. We are relying on you, do not forget," he added with emphasis. "You are of little use to us if you do not have the energy re-

serves to march or to fight…and of little use to yourself in such a case, I should not wonder."

Ryan frowned and studied the old man intently. He
was right, of course, he was. The one-eyed man took the
food. It was bland and chemical-tasting, as self-heats
usually were, but it was energy. That was all that mattered.

"J.B., you reckon we're still headed in the right direction?" he asked. The Armorer checked his minisextant with the sun and confirmed that they were still on
south-southwest. "Then I figure we keep going. We've
come too far to turn back. It has to get better…"

"More out there," Jak commented. "Smell it, hear it.
Mebbe not much, but something survives on more than
this." He bent and took a handful of the dry soil, letting
it run through his fingers.

"Then let's go," Ryan decided. "Sooner we move,
sooner we get the hell out of this."

They broke camp and set off once more. Mildred
wondered if she was the only one to detect the double
entendre in Ryan's choice of words. From the way that
Krysty was looking at the one-eyed man, she suspected
not.

Jak had been correct. It was a subtle change, and it
took some while for them to notice, but the Gila monster that sprung across the line as they marched brought
it home. The conditions were improving. The air was
still stifling and the heat from the sun was still intense,
but there was a lessening in the humidity. Looking up,
they could see that the cloud cover was spare, the chem
clouds allowing more of the sky to show through un-
tainted. The soil around was still dry, but there were

signs of lichen and fern. The grasses looked less stark. They were softer clumps, thicker and more lush. The trees appeared to twist less, the root systems seemingly able to burrow a little deeper into the earth.

Stopping to take note, Jak could tell that there was more wildlife. He could hear birds, see a few in the distance. Obviously poor, scrawny creatures, they were there, nonetheless. As were the reptiles and insects—more than that Gila monster or the dung beetle that now crawled across his combat boot. Even the presence of a dung beetle suggested mammals from which it could scavenge. Small one, mebbe, no more. The albino could sense no danger in the shape of larger predators.

Jak allowed himself a small smile. "More life—mebbe food and water and not so much heat," he said to the others.

"Mebbe. Press on some more before we rest, see if we can find out what," Ryan replied. For the first time in days, a smile creased his seemingly ever-grim visage.

They moved forward with a renewed sense of purpose and a pace quickened by expectation. And as they moved, so the landscape around them seemed to improve with every half mile they traversed. The dusty top layer of soil gave way to hard-packed ground beneath, which became that much softer beneath the trampling of their feet. The patches of grass and lichen spread out so that the exposed soil became an exception rather than the rule. And the musk of animal life grew stronger around them, becoming almost tangible.

Which should have been a warning.

The farther from the redoubt, the more the landscape

began to resemble something that could feasibly support life. It was almost as if the redoubt itself had somehow acted as the epicenter for the desert area. Perhaps it had. Although the toxicity would have abated within the area itself, it was possible that the military activity in the redoubt had concentrated on chemical warfare, which was reflected in the desolation. The thought crossed Mildred's mind and she made a note to check herself and the others for any signs of contamination that may occur in the next few days. Assuming that the next few days would be quiet enough to allow for such a check.

It seemed as though quiet might be the case as the day slowly faded into twilight and they put distance between themselves and the barren land. It was still stiflingly hot, but even so the temperature had dropped a few degrees and the lusher vegetation allowed for more shelter from the direct heat of the sun.

It also provided hiding places for the wildlife that became more prevalent.

Jak slowed and focused his attention on a clump of turquoise-berried shrubbery wild with red and yellow leaves among the green.

"What?" Ryan questioned briefly, stopping as he noticed the albino hunter slow down.

Jak answered him with an almost imperceptible nod, not bothering to shift the glare of his red eyes from his target. In a smooth, fluid motion he palmed a leaf-bladed throwing knife from within his patched camou jacket. The knife left his hand with minimal effort, flashing through the air and into the clump of vegetation.

There was a squeal—fear and pain mixed on a

screeching note—and the bush seemed to take on a life of its own, exploding as two creatures shot outward in a blur of motion. They were moving away from the companions, fleeing in fear, but the death rattle from the shrub suggested that there had been a third creature and that Jak's aim had been true.

Ryan moved toward the vegetation, the SIG-Sauer in his hand, ready to blast anything that may present the merest hint of a threat. He used his heavy combat boot, raised tentatively, to open up the dense foliage. It would take an incredibly strong bite or claw to go through the toughened leather, and he was unwilling to risk a more vulnerable hand or arm to the task.

"Fireblast! That's not a pretty sight," he breathed as the creature in the shrubbery became visible.

The others joined him.

The creature was some kind of mutie raccoon, larger than any they'd seen before, with a heavily developed back and hindquarter musculature that made it look like some sort of hybrid raccoon-badger. Its snout had been cleaved by the knife, the razor-honed point making short work of the bone and flesh, Jak's unerring arm driving it up and into the frontal lobes of the creature's brain. The mutie lay in the last twitches of death, staring up at them with eyes that could no longer see.

"Shit, that's a mean-looking bastard," Mildred whistled.

"Yeah, and his little friends are going to be pretty pissed at what we've done when they get over the urge to run," Krysty added thoughtfully. "They've been tailing us, right?"

Jak nodded. "Smelled them couple a miles back.

Part of pack, getting closer, bolder when they think we don't know."

"They're pretty quiet for something so big," Krysty stated. "I thought I could feel something, but I didn't hear them."

"Guess we'd better be triple-red, then," Ryan said decisively. "If we're their game, they'll be back. Figure we're probably the biggest, tastiest-looking prey they've seen for a while."

The companions set off once more, keeping closer and staying on the alert. Blasters were drawn in anticipation of an attack. As they became aware, it seemed that there was more noise, more movement. Was it because they had been slack before the chilling or had the scent of blood stirred up the creatures of the woods?

Small rodents scuttled into the undergrowth as they approached, causing J.B. and Ryan to draw beads, fingers tightening on triggers before relaxing as they realized there was no threat.

Doc and Mildred directed their attention to the skies. They were entering an area where there was a denser canopy of leaf and branch cover than before. What kind of birds were sheltering in the cover provided? And not just wildfowl. There was also the possibility of snakes dropping onto them from above.

"Over there," Jak snapped suddenly, gesturing them to halt. He slipped out of line and into the cover of a grassy knoll. He emerged, dragging the corpse of what looked like some kind of wild dog. It had been gnawed at the hindquarters, the stomach and ribs stripped bare. The head and forequarters had been barely touched.

The animal almost had a look of surprise on its muzzle, its glassy eyes seemingly shocked even in the moment of chilling.

"Fresh, mebbe less than day. No flies, maggots, no rotten meat smell. Must be close. Mebbe we stray onto their hunting ground."

He didn't add that the dog looked powerful and that the mutie raccoons were either powerful in a pack or were even more formidable than they had guessed individually.

"Need to stay triple alert now," Ryan said quietly. "They could be close."

"Not all that close, dear boy," Doc said, suddenly sinking to his knees and examining the still intact forequarter of the beast. "I suspect we may be in spitting distance of something approaching a ville."

"Why do you say that?" Ryan asked, puzzled.

Doc smiled grimly and traced a scar line on the joint of the dog's foreleg. "This is no mere scar, and I suspect that this creature may not have been as wild as it was once. Dr. Wyeth, would you confirm my suspicions?"

Mildred came over and hunkered down beside Doc. "This had better be good," she muttered. "It's not my idea of a good time to kneel down and look at a hunk of rotting carcass."

But her imprecations went no further. She squinted, taking a closer look at the scar. Dammit, but the old fool was right.

"Shit, that's been stitched. This is a domestic canine, which means we must be near some kind of settlement. There's no way it would wander far if it was used to living with people, and it doesn't look like it's been dragged that far."

Ryan's face split with a crooked grin. "Signs of life. That's something, right? We'll move on out, keep heading seaward. Who knows how far we are from the coast, but at least we know that there's someone between us and the water."

Spirits lightened by this revelation, the group picked up the pace. If they could find some kind of settlement before darkness fell, it would be safer than making camp out here.

But, as they moved on, Krysty frowned. The strands of Titian hair around her neck and shoulders started to curl, wrapping themselves close to her nape. She shot a glance at Jak and could see that he, too, was in a heightened state of awareness.

"Yeah, approaching from there—" he nodded as his gleaming red eyes caught hers "—and plenty of them."

Even as he spoke, the others became aware of a crashing in the undergrowth that was growing nearer with every second. A pack of the mutie animals was approaching at speed.

Ryan unslung the Steyr, and slammed the bolt. "Triple-red. Fire as soon as you sight," he yelled. Even as he spoke, he was aware that the gloom of twilight under the cover of the trees would make for great pools of shadow that would disguise the movement of the creatures. Hoping the light would hold out long enough, he knew there would be places where he would have to shoot on sound alone, which would be difficult once the firing started, obliterating all else.

The first of the mutie creatures, driven by a lust for

blood and, perhaps, some primeval desire for revenge, appeared from the undergrowth only a few yards from where they stood. It leaped across the intervening space, its powerful haunches propelling it through the air. Ryan raised his rifle and fired a solitary round. The creature's flight was checked, the force of the shell almost changing the mutie's trajectory as it spun sideways, falling to the ground with a hideous cry of pain. A second shell finished it off. The one-eyed man was taking no chances that the wounded animal might fight back.

Rather than retreat, the chilling of the lead creature just made the muties more ferocious. They began to pour out of the undergrowth, reaching double figures with a frightening speed. Mildred, Krysty and Jak, armed with their handblasters, picked off the animals singly, aiming—like Ryan—for accuracy. But there were too many animals and not enough space and time in which to maneuver.

"Doc, take the left hand with shot. I'll deal with the right," J.B. yelled over the bedlam of squealing muties and blasterfire. As he yelled, he unslung his Smith & Wesson M-4000.

"Understood," Doc shouted, for once not wasting words. The Armorer's intention was clear: they were the only two of the companions with the firepower to put a serious dent in the marauding forces. While the others picked off the animals in front of them, it would be up to Doc and J.B. to try to stem the flow from the darkness beyond.

It was no time for subtlety.

Doc used the shotgun chamber of the LeMat, firing into the darkness, the percussion pistol roaring as the shot emerged from the barrel of the old blaster, moving at high velocity into the darkness, spreading out to put deadly pellets through anything that got in its way. The squeals and cries from the darkness suggested it was an effective tactic.

Likewise, J.B. fired off a blast from the M-4000. The normal shot charge from such a blaster would be effective, but the Armorer had loaded barbed-metal fléchette rounds that, when propelled at immense velocity, would turn and twist in the air, ripping chunks out of whatever they came into contact with, causing irreversible internal damage on any carcass they entered.

The twin-pronged attack had the desired effect. The numbers of attacking creatures were immediately lessened; many turned and fled in fear or injury. The rest of the companions had the precious seconds they needed to pick off whatever attackers remained.

In the aftermath, the air stank of blood and cordite, the carnage obvious, even in the encroaching darkness of the night.

"Shit, too late to find a ville now," Ryan murmured. "We need to move on a little, pitch a camp, before the stragglers return to attack again."

"We should be okay," J.B. commented. "There's enough chilled meat here to keep most of the predators for miles around busy until sunrise."

Krysty allowed herself to shiver. "Let's get moving, then, before any of them come out of cover."

Doc smiled. "That would be wise. And, of course, the smell will be awful here."

Jak snorted. "Yeah. Sooner pitch camp better—downwind, right?"

Chapter Two

Jak stayed on watch through the night. Their camp was another five hundred yards from the scene of the slaughter, but even so the albino youth felt a nagging sense that there was still danger in the air. When Ryan asked him, he shrugged. He couldn't say what it was, but that he just had a sense of it. The woods were too alive for the night; something was making the wildlife restless.

Krysty had been unable to shed any light on Jak's unease. She was still running on adrenaline from the battle against the mutie raccoons and couldn't sense anything.

Jak stayed silent, as still as a rock, looking back into the darkness. His red eyes were like coals in the night, burning bright toward the scene of carnage. He refused attempts to relieve him, telling Ryan he wouldn't be able to sleep, anyway. He could smell the blood and the hunger as the smaller scavengers came out of hiding to pick clean the carcasses the companions had left behind. He could hear the sounds of the feeding frenzy, of the crunch of bone and rending of flesh mixed with the squabbles as predators competed for the choicest pieces.

But he could hear more than that. Beyond, and almost hidden beneath the surrounding sounds, he could hear a migration. Smaller animals, birds—these were the vanguard. They were moving toward the area where the raccoon fight had taken place; but they weren't motivated by the need to feed. It was more than that. They weren't carnivorous creatures, and would, in truth, be at risk from the scavengers around the carcasses.

So what was scaring them so much that they were blindly running into trouble? It had to be something big, which was why he felt the need to stay awake, to listen and to try to read the sounds of the night. The sounds were too far off to be an immediate threat, but the group was moving fast enough—if the flight of the creatures he could detect was an indication—to trouble them the following day.

By the time dawn had broken, the companions were all awake. At first light, they struck camp. By this time, the flight of the smaller creatures was obvious to all, so close had it become. Yet what lay behind it…

"It's trouble, no doubt about that," Krysty said softly, her tone betraying the worry that she felt. Her hair was nestled close to her scalp, her doomie sense working overtime now that she had rested.

"Yeah, but what?" J.B. queried. "Is it the kind of trouble where we try and move out of the way, or is it the kind where that'll just get us blasted in the back?"

"A dilemma, my dear John Barrymore, a dichotomy that we must solve if we are to save our skins," Doc whispered.

"Any idea what it is, Jak?" Ryan asked. "It doesn't sound like a sec party of any kind…" The one-eyed man had been speculating to himself that, if they were near a ville, the noise of the previous night's firefight with the mutie raccoons may have carried. And it would be understandable if the ville baron's response to unexpected blasterfire was to send out a party to hunt down the possible threat. But the disturbance seemed to be natural. He couldn't hear men, horses, wags. And there had been no other blasterfire.

Jak didn't answer him at first. His attention was still so focused on the source of the flight that it took a while for him to snap into the space occupied by his companions.

"Not men," he said slowly, shaking his head. "Not just animal."

"What does that mean?" Mildred asked, voicing the confusion they all felt.

"Means not know, not get it," Jak replied. "Ryan, let me recce. Stay here, give half hour," he said, tapping his wrist chron.

Around them, the birds chattered and swooped in and out of the foliage and the grasses rustled as small mammals and reptiles moved past them, taking care only to avoid the companions.

Ryan assented after some thought. "Triple-red, okay?"

Jak flashed Ryan a grin—as if he was ever anything else—and moved off into the jungle, running against the flow of the wildlife.

"Okay, people, get hard," Ryan said to the others, indicating the cover of nearby trees. "Safe to assume we can't outrun it. We need to know what it is. Let's hope Jak finds out."

JAK MOVED THROUGH the woodland like quicksilver, using the clumps of trees as cover, swift and surefooted. This was his natural environment, giving himself over to his finely honed hunting instincts and not thinking consciously, letting his senses tell him what to do. Even through the heavy combat boots his feet seemed as tactile as his hands, searching out the uneven sections of the woodland floor, groping for and avoiding treacherous roots and divots.

He was soon past the mass migration of wildlife, and skirted the clearing where they had defended themselves against the mutie raccoon pack, pausing briefly to note that the scavengers who had followed in their wake had made short work of clearing the carcasses. Few scraps of flesh remained, and there weren't even that many bones left to mark the battle. Only fresh stains where the blood-soaked earth hadn't yet been fully absorbed into the woodland floor.

In the eerily empty zone past the migrating creatures, there was a cone of silence, one that was soon broken by a noise that he recognized immediately. One that had been hidden enough by the other sounds to disguise it sufficiently until now. And the scent, sickly sweet, that was also too familiar.

Stickies…

Jak slowed and moved with more caution. The stench of them filled his nostrils and he could hear their movements—fast, slithering, almost reptilian—as well as the hissing breathing and the wordless mewling of the pack.

Stickies tended to move in packs, like herds of cattle, but not normally this fast. And he had never known a pack to cause such a panic among the wildlife of an area. Something out of the ordinary was occurring here and he needed to find out just exactly what it may be.

His senses told him that the pack was at least thirty strong—he couldn't keep track after counting that many different noises—and moving with speed. They would be on him in a few minutes. He knew he could outrun them once he'd completed the recce, but he needed to get closer, undetected. He jumped for a handhold on a tree limb that was just a foot above his head. He tested its strength, knowing it should hold him easily enough.

Jak pulled himself up into the tree, using the leaf cover to hide himself. He took a good look around. There were enough trees to provide cover for him to circle the pack, always assuming the branches were strong enough to take his weight. Or else he could stay here and wait for the pack to come into view. Unfortunately, from his present position, the trees that provided him with cover also prevented him from getting a good look at the pack.

Jak was patient. He could wait all day and all night for his prey, immobile and focused. But that was when time wasn't such a pressing issue. Right now, he couldn't afford to wait.

Testing each limb as he moved, Jak clambered from tree to tree. He was high enough for any noise to be put down to birds fluttering in the branches. Besides, stickies weren't climbers. As long as he could stay high, he could evade them if he was spotted.

It took only a few trees before he was upon them. He stopped and looked down. The noise they were making had covered any of his own and he felt certain that his presence had not been detected.

They were a heaving mass of mutie flesh, moving almost as one. The black, shining eyes, bereft of intelligence; the fleshless lips over jagged, razor-sharp and yet rotten teeth; the papery, pale skins and the hands with the suckerlike pads on the ends of the fingers. Their very presence seemed to emit an aura of decay. And they were agitated in a way that he had never before seen. As the stickies moved, they tore up anything in their path. The foliage, vegetation and shrubbery that littered the woodlands, even the grasses, were torn from the ground, leaving a churned-up trail in their wake.

Most stickies were mindlessly destructive at the best of times, but this was more than that. It was no wonder that the animals, reptiles and birds had wanted to flee. Anything in their way would be ripped to shreds. Not even for food, but just because it was there.

And the companions were right in their path. Waiting.

Jak turned and moved swiftly through the trees until he was sure he was beyond sight and sound of the pack. He dropped onto the woodland floor and began to run, picking his way nimbly over the roots and the uneven earth. All the while, his mind was racing. By the time he reached the companions, there would be only the slightest of distances between himself and the stickies. Although he was moving fast, the extra distance in circling them would tell. It would be enough time for the group to adopt a defensive position and to try to blast their way out of trouble, but not enough time for them to move out of range and to safety. They couldn't rely on keeping one jump ahead when they didn't know what the terrain in front of them was like.

But this was a large pack, and whatever had stirred them up had made them a savage and vicious enemy that would attack regardless. Stickies were normally cowardly, and a taste of blasterfire would scatter them, fear overcoming rage. However, he felt that this pack had something stronger driving them on.

And that was another problem to weigh—what if the thing that enraged the stickies was hot on their tail? Fighting off such a large and maddened pack would be hard enough. To then have to fight another enemy may be a step too far.

Jak was in sight of the companions, who broke cover as he approached. He was barely breathing hard, despite his exertion, but it still took valuable time for him to spit out everything the recce had told him. As he came to the end of his report, the pack was within hearing.

"Fireblast and fuck it, we stand and fight," Ryan snapped. "Too late to do anything else. They're moving quick." He directed the companions back to the positions they had adopted while awaiting Jak. "Fire on sight—just try to chill the bastards as they come through."

They had one chance to clean this up quickly. Because of their pack mentality, and because the woodlands were becoming more dense, there was a narrow channel through which the stickies would probably try to squeeze. With the companions in cover on either side of this channel, they may just be able to take them out quickly and en masse as they formed a bottleneck to move through. Stickies weren't smart enough to back off and spread out, striking back at an enemy by spreading their attack front.

The companions could smell the muties before they were upon them, the sickly sweet odor of their sweat filled their nostrils and made them gag. Stickies were vile enough in ones, twos or small groups; but this strong, and it was almost enough to make a challenger give up and run. The companions trained their blasters on the narrow channel, waiting for the first of the muties to hove into view. They had to be close. The noise they were making was now deafening, the smell overpowering.

The foliage trembled, shook and finally was ripped asunder as the pack of stickies burst into the clearing. The wait had been so tense that it was almost a shock when they finally broke cover. They were ripping up anything in their path, each almost oblivious to the others around it, their collective state whipped into a rage of fury and fear—fear that seemed to be coming off them in waves, and was driving them onward. The mass of mutie flesh filled the clearing in less than a few seconds.

Fingers had twitched on triggers, tensing and untensing for the moment when they would have to squeeze to unleash a barrage of blasterfire at the optimum moment to cause the most damage.

And now that moment had arrived.

"Fire!" Ryan yelled. "Aim at their heads."

The roar of blasterfire was intense, so loud that it washed over the noise made by the pack, drowning everything in the liquid shout of the pistol and machine-pistol action. The screams of the first stickies to feel the impact were lost in the hurricane of sound, but the reactions of their fellows showed that the initial burst had registered through the ranks.

Jak's Colt Python had the force of a Magnum round.

The slugs he squeezed off ripped through their initial target, the rippling force of the bullets causing fatal damage almost instantaneously, the exit velocity such that the slugs cannoned into the head of the next stickie in line, taking it out at the same time.

Krysty, Mildred and Ryan had blasters that demanded more precision: the Smith & Wesson, the ZKR and Ryan's favored Steyr all taking out one stickie at a time with rapidly delivered single shots that ran true and chilled.

But it was J.B. and Doc who could do the most damage. The LeMat percussion pistol's second chamber, with its heavy ball, could do a similar job as the Colt Python, the heavily charged ball driving through one stickie and taking out the mutie directly behind as it retained enough momentum to cause lethal damage. It was, inevitably, the shot chamber that was the most deadly, the pellets striking home at a number of targets. Those that it didn't chill immediately were either trampled beneath the feet of others as they fell, or turned and lashed out in blind anger and pain, fighting with their own.

However, it took valuable time to reload the LeMat, so it was as well that J.B. could fire repeatedly from his Smith & Wesson M-4000, each cartridge load of barbed-metal fléchettes causing damage to the stickie hordes. The pump action enabled him to fire swiftly, and his natural skill and affinity with weapons made reloading a fluid and fast motion, which seemed to come as second nature.

The channel into the small clearing was soon filling with the chilled and the injured, forming a block to the other muties. That should have been the end of matters. Stickies were normally cowardly and would run if attacked by any kind of superior force.

Not this time. Whatever had frightened and agitated them scared them far more than the prospect of being chilled by weapons fire. Instead of turning back to something that terrified them more than the blasterfire, they continued to advance. And if they couldn't move in a straight line, they would try to find a way through the denser foliage.

Ryan cursed under his breath when he saw them begin to divert. It was always a risk to stand and fight such a large number of stickies simply because of the sheer weight of their numbers. The only advantage that made it even feasible was that the stickies would be likely to follow the same route through the woods and thus would be concentrated in a small area.

The fact that they were now spreading out, moving into areas where it would be hard for the companions to hit them in bulk, and would be able to use the cover of the trees, made it a much more difficult task—one that verged on impossible at the best of times, let alone now. The companions had been marching all day and hadn't had time to recover from the previous night's fight with the mutie raccoons. This had been—they had hoped—a similar situation. Not now.

"Spread out," Ryan yelled.

"There's a lot down, they're thinned out," J.B. shouted. "Watch for them circling… Jak, what can you see?"

"Less half left," the albino mutie replied pithily. "Still moving blind," he added.

"So are we," Krysty yelled at the Armorer and Jak. "Be our eyes."

Down on the forest floor, Krysty was right. The dense foliage echoed with the sounds of chilled and chilling stickies, mingling with the enraged cries of the remaining pack and the rustle of the foliage as it was disturbed. There were sounds from all around, making it hard to pinpoint the danger. The light was poor, the woodland in shadow and it was almost impossible to pick out movement through the density and the dark. She, Ryan, Doc and Mildred were blinded at ground level. But J.B. and Jak were still in position up trees and had a better view of what was going on around.

Better, but still not great.

"Shit, can't see too much," J.B. yelled over the noise. "Three of them to your right, Millie, about three o'clock."

Mildred furrowed her brow, frowning heavily as she tried to pick out one noise from another. At the Armorer's words she turned to her right and squeezed out three shots at the first noises she heard. Screams of pain confirmed that she had found a target with at least two of the shells. But the third hadn't quite finished the job. An enraged stickie, pouring blood from a neck wound, crashed through the undergrowth and was upon her before she had a chance to move. It crashed into her, driving her backward into the bole of a tree and knocking the breath from her. Her lungs ached for oxygen and lights danced in front of her eyes as she was momentarily stunned. She felt the creature's hot, fetid breath on her face and, as the lights cleared, could see the blind hate in its pinprick black eyes, all the more intense for the white and hairless skull surrounding them. The stench from its body made her mouth fill with bile. The feel of the suckers on its fingers made her flesh crawl.

It was the gag response that brought her just enough time to react. The stickie made her so nauseous that she projectile vomited into its face. The hot stream of bile and puke hit it squarely, filling its mouth and nostrils, stinging its eyes. The stickie screamed, suddenly blinded, and released its grip, staggering back and clawing at its face. Dragging air into her lungs with a painful, rasping gasp, Mildred brought up the Czech ZKR so that it was level with the creature's face as it managed to blinkingly clear its eyes. The last thing it would have seen was the barrel and dark maw of the 551 as Mildred squeezed the trigger to release a slug. The exit wound took half of the creature's thin, eggshell skull with it.

Mildred spit onto the ground, trying to clear her head and the bitter taste of bile from her mouth. That had been too close for comfort.

She dragged herself upright from the bole of the tree, shook her head to clear it and entered the fray once more. She was needed....

Doc was having problems. The LeMat was difficult to reload in a hurry and a cry from the Armorer had alerted him to the fact that a couple of stickies were headed in his direction. Realizing that he wouldn't have the time to reload the cumbersome percussion blaster, he rapidly holstered it and withdrew the sword from within the silver lion's-head swordstick that contained the blade tempered and made from the finest Toledo steel. The seemingly old and frail man was deft and quick with the blade, as many had found to their detriment, and he had to use all his skills when one of the stickies burst through the undergrowth and was on him before he had a chance to drag the blade fully from its sheath.

"By the Three Kennedys, I'm not falling that easily," he breathed, putting his weight on his back foot to stabilize himself as he flicked his wrist, the tendons straining as he rolled the blade emerging from the stick, changing its upward trajectory into an arc so that, as the tip cleared the sheath it flew toward the stickie, arcing across its throat and slicing into the thin, pliable flesh. It parted like rotting meat, the carotid artery severed. The creature stopped in its tracks, mutely clutching its torn neck before tumbling to the ground.

Meanwhile, Ryan had shouldered his Steyr and had drawn the SIG-Sauer. The rifle was fine for distance shooting, but close-quarters fighting required a hand-blaster. He started to fire at the sounds coming from the undergrowth, but it was so dense that he couldn't tell if his shots were having any effect in the bedlam.

"Where are they?" Krysty yelled to J.B.

"I don't know. They're getting lost in the woods," he replied, switching from the M-4000 to his Uzi, which he set to single shot as he slipped down to ground level. "Just keep triple-red. Try to pick 'em out."

Picking them out was something that Doc could do only too well. With an instinct that told them he was less dangerous because of his lack of a blaster, the stickies were concentrating on him, somehow communicating with one another in a way that only they could understand. He was holding his own, the sword a flashing blade that sprayed the air with crimson as he claimed victims. But he was outnumbered and having to spin in circles just to keep the weight of the numbers at bay.

Jak, picking off those he could from up in his tree, could see that Doc was being overwhelmed. He smiled. A cold, vulpine grin of expectant bloodlust. Time to help Doc out.

Slipping down the tree after a last look around to take in the positions of both his companions and of those stickies visible in the density, Jak slid the .357 Magnum into its holster. The Colt Python was a formidable blaster, but inappropriate for the kind of fighting he would have to engage. In close quarters, there was always a chance that the Magnum shells would pierce a stickie and go clean through, possibly damaging a compatriot too close to the action. He didn't want to chill Doc while he was trying to save him.

As Jak ghosted through the trees, he could almost taste the stickies as they converged on the old man. Their smell cloyed his sensitive nostrils, sharpening his hunger to thin them out a little.

Doc was fighting hard, fighting well, but he was hugely outnumbered. The stickies came at him from every direction and it was all he could do to thrust, parry and slice a few at a time. His actions drove back those whose blood spilled onto the ground, but they were just replaced by others, equally as intent on ripping Doc to shreds. He was backed up against a tree, holding them at bay on three sides, and praying that none would approach from the rear to pin him to the bough.

"Doc!" Jak yelled by way of warning.

"Thank heavens. I could not wish for any more," Doc gasped breathlessly.

The stickies were so intent on their task that they paid no heed to the shout from behind them. They couldn't ignore the whirlwind that swept into their midst, however, rending them asunder with an attack of staggering and intense ferocity.

Jak had palmed a razor-sharp, leaf-bladed knife from the many hiding places in his patched and tattered camou jacket. He had one in each hand, held loosely to facilitate movement, but firm enough so that they wouldn't drop. His eyes glittered as he focused on the pack in front of him. Some had been cut by Doc; they smelled of blood and fear. It was a sweet smell to him, goading him into action.

The albino teen became a grim-faced chilling machine. Moving quickly, he sliced and chopped, going for vulnerable body areas that would slow and disable first. Many of the stickies he slashed would die from internal injury or loss of blood, the pain preventing them from fighting; to chill every last one of them, one by one, would be too slow a task. Speed was of the essence, here, so unless he was able to strike a chilling blow first time, it was better if he disabled the stickie, returned to it later to finish it off, after Doc was safe.

The blurring form of Jak cutting a swathe through the pack caused enough disturbance for those at the forefront to be distracted, torn between continuing their attack on the old man or turning to face the new enemy.

It was all Doc needed. The distraction Jak caused enabled him to get off his back foot and begin an offensive. He stepped forward, the flashing Toledo steel blade proscribing fatal arcs through the air, striking home chilling blows on the stickies in the front ranks before being swiftly withdrawn and put to the test once more, striking true and removing the enemy from the fray.

Between them, the two companions were able to cut through the muties with ease, turning to deliver chilling blows to those who were still alive and twitching.

It felt as though the tide was beginning to turn. But not, perhaps, for Mildred and Krysty. At shouted cries from both Ryan and J.B., they had all tried to find a central point at which they could converge, a point from which they could fight back-to-back, knowing that they stood no chance of hitting each other if they were the source of noise, directing fire. It would have been a simple enough plan if not for the fact that darkness was descending too rapidly in the already gloomy cover of the forest and the noise was such that it was hard to pick out direction as they exchanged calls, desperately trying to locate one another.

Stickies loomed in and out of the darkness, confused by the shooting, angered by the chilling of their fellow pack members, bloodlust fuelled by the smell of their own dead—and driven almost to distraction by the sound of beating hooves and distant cries that could faintly be heard over the pandemonium.

Whatever had whipped the pack into such a frenzy in the first place was now catching up with them. It would be a case of "shoot first, ask questions after." The four companions, isolated in their search for one another, fighting off stray stickies who stumbled upon them in the darkness, knew that they would also be easy prey for whatever pursued the stickies.

Ryan and J.B. had holstered their blasters, unwilling to indulge in a firefight when there was a good chance of hitting each other in the confusion. Ryan had taken the panga from its thigh sheath; the heavy blade was causing stickie blood to flow copiously. Likewise, J.B. was using his Tekna knife, taking out the mutie attackers as they stumbled across him, or vice versa as he tried to find the others.

For Mildred and Krysty there was no such luxury. The women didn't have knives. Unwilling, like the men, to indulge in hazardous blasterfire, both used their blasters as clubs. It was fortunate that the muties were prone to blindly rush into attack and that the women were trained and practiced in unarmed combat. It was relatively easy for them to use their skills to stop the muties laying hands on them, even though the clammy, sticky-padded fingers clung to their clothing and flesh when the muties were able to lay hands on them—hard to dislodge and repulsive to the touch. Once the creatures had been disarmed and brought to ground, the butts of the handblasters delivered fatal, skull-crunching blows, the thin skulls of the muties caving easily.

But it was the weight of numbers that caused the women to tire rapidly.

Jak and Doc had dispatched their opponents with ease and were about to set out to find their companions when Jak stayed Doc with a hand on his arm.

"Listen," he said simply.

Doc's face screwed and contorted with the effort to distinguish one noise from another in the melee. Then he turned to Jak, an astonished expression on his features.

"Men on horseback? Truly, we are fortunate," he enthused.

"If friendly," Jak commented wryly. "We not trust. Find others."

"I'll certainly agree with that," Doc concurred. "I fear we would be better trusting to your skills in this task than mine, so perhaps you should lead," he added.

Jak smiled, a brief ghost flickering across his white, scarred visage. "Good call," he said wryly.

The two companions plunged into the mayhem. With their blades still firmly grasped, they were able to dispose of any opposition they encountered on their search for the others.

Mildred was their first find. She was in the act of dispatching one stickie with a jackhammer blow to the side of its skull while twisting to evade the sucking grasp of one that had approached from the rear. Doc's sword carved the air and took off the stickie's left ear before slicing down into its neck. With a high-pitched scream of pain, it whirled away from Mildred, releasing her to turn to Doc. Before the old man had a chance to follow through on his attack, Mildred clubbed the back of the mutie's skull, reducing its brains to mush.

"I have never—and I mean, never—been so glad to see you, you old buzzard," she breathed heavily.

"I shall take that as a compliment, my dear Mildred," Doc replied. "We must find the others. Another enemy is almost upon us."

"Aw, shit, this is just going to be one of those nights, isn't it." Mildred spit.

"This way," Jak commanded, leading them off. He could hear Ryan cursing loudly as he hacked at an enemy. He was heading in that direction when Krysty came crashing out of the undergrowth.

"Gaia, but am I glad to see you," she said. "Where—"

"This way. Quick," Jak snapped, interrupting her. He moved toward the sound of Ryan's voice.

The one-eyed warrior pulled his panga from the neck of a chilled stickie. He looked up as he heard them approach.

"Thought that didn't sound like stickies," he noted, eyeing them. "Where's J.B.?"

"Here," came a voice from nearby, followed shortly by the Armorer as he crashed through the trees. "Shit, that was hard work," he panted, pushing his fedora back on his head and wiping his brow with the back of his hand. "We must have been closer than we knew. It's just so fucking dark now."

"Yeah, and we've got more company," Ryan commented, wiping down his panga before sheathing it and unholstering his SIG-Sauer. He checked and reloaded as he said, "Must be what was driving those stickies berserk. Figure we've seen most of them off, and the others are probably running from whoever this is—but I don't know about you, but I'm too tired to run."

"I'll go along with that," J.B. agreed, taking down his Uzi and checking before smoothly clicking it on to rapid bursts.

Jak frowned. "Wait—spreading—trying round up stickies."

Ryan lifted his head and listened intently. Jak was right. He could hear the remnants of the mutie pack being driven back toward them.

"Fireblast! They're coming right through here," he yelled. "Cover, now! Triple-red!"

The companions sought whatever refuge they could in the cover of the trees. They had converged on a natural path formed by an avenue of trees and it seemed that the horsemen were intent on driving the muties back through this path.

The stickies were being encircled and pincered, there was no doubt about that, either, but there was no escape. What was going on?

The few stickies that were left were driven past the companions' cover. Once level with the area where Ryan's people were in hiding, a volley of shots rang out from blasters carried by the horsemen. The few remaining stickies were mowed down in the hail, their bodies jerked by the impact and thrown across the path. They remained still, smelling of death: that unpleasant odor of cordite, blood and excrement.

Ryan could see exactly where all his people were. They would have been hidden to the casual view, but he had noted their cover. In turn, they knew where he was. He signaled them to remain in hiding. Let the horsemen make the next move.

One rider came into view, walking his horse slowly. He had a Remington slung over his shoulder and was clad in animal skins tied over ragged leggings and a jerkin. He had a beard flecked with gray and long hair tied back from his face. He stopped almost directly in front of where Ryan was in cover, and looked around from his mount.

"You might as well come out, people. We know you're here and we've got you surrounded. Chill me, and you'll be as fucked as these mutie bastards."

Chapter Three

Ryan knew from the sounds of horses and men around them that the stickies had been driven and chilled at this spot for a reason. The riders had heard and possibly seen some of the battle that had taken place on their approach, and they were making a point. Now they were all around, and there was no way that the companions could escape.

Casting his eye over the hiding places of his companions, Ryan could see that they were as aware of this as he was and were waiting for a sign.

The bearded rider kissed his teeth. "Come on. You know you're surrounded and you know we could drop you where you hide. It wouldn't be hard. But why haven't we done that? We want to parlay first, see who you are. One thing—you're not stupe. You could chill me now, no prob, but that would just bring the rest of us down on you and you know that's bad move. So I'm still here. And I appreciate that. But we don't have forever."

Ryan signaled to the others, hoping they would see through the gloom, and stepped out, hands loose at his sides, no weapons in view.

"You'd think we did have forever, the way you can't stop talking," he said calmly, stepping into the clearing, avoiding the stickie corpses but still making sure he was out of range of the mounted man's foot. Although his body language bespoke relaxation and compliance, he kept himself alert and ready. Careless meant chilled.

"I only talk so much when I have to wait," the bearded man said. "My name is Ethan, Baron of Pleasantville. Looks like we ran these fuckers right into you. Wasn't the purpose."

"I kind of gathered that," Ryan returned guardedly. "It's not the usual thing to do with them."

Ethan paused, then laughed. It was a loud, hearty laugh and showed no malice at Ryan's comment. "I don't know," he gasped finally, "it could be a kinda new sport, I guess. But it's the last thing you needed, right? After all, I know most what goes on around here and I don't know you—so you're either traveling through or lost from somewhere."

Ryan nodded, almost imperceptibly. "Got that right."

"So why don't you call the rest of your people out, then we can get back to Pleasantville and you can rest."

Ryan smiled, his eye showing that there was no humor in the gesture. "Rest, yeah, that'd be good. But mebbe it'll be a permanent rest, nice and cold…nice and chilled."

"One-eye, I could have had that done right from the start—and you know it," Ethan said in a low voice.

Ryan knew that he was speaking the truth. To root out the companions and chill them wouldn't be much harder than culling the stickies. The riders surrounded them and the companions were fatigued from two extensive firefights. Odds were that the baron of Pleasantville was genuine, and Ryan had little choice but to play the odds right now.

"Okay, you win," he said softly, raising his arm and gesturing.

From their concealment, the companions came forth, until it seemed that Jak, Krysty, Mildred, Doc and J.B. had joined Ryan in forming a circle around the baron. All of them were careful to keep their arms by their sides, hands free of weapons.

Ethan studied them. "That all?" he queried. Ryan nodded and the baron gave a low whistle. "Now that's what I call interesting damage you caused out here," he added almost to himself. Then, seeming to remember where he was and what he was supposed to be doing, he whistled again—this time sharper and harder, the sound piercing the forest.

The foliage began to rustle and ripple as though it were alive with movement. Through the blanket of cover emerged a dozen riders, all clad similarly to their baron. The horses were a mix of squat pony stock and sleeker beasts. Similarly, the compose of the sec party itself was a mix. Short and tall, fat and thin, black, white and all shades between. Whatever kind of a ville Pleasantville may be, it certainly had no problem with ideas of physical difference.

It crossed Mildred's mind that the Pilatu could have done with such an example. But then she remembered that Dean had been with them then and experienced a sense of loss she hadn't felt for a long while. What, she wondered, must Ryan be feeling?

The riders surrounded the companions so that Ethan now sat in the middle of two rings: the inner a possible threat, the outer his protection. In truth, the clearing wasn't large enough to accommodate all the horses and people that were now gathered there, and the companions could quite literally feel the breath of the horses down their necks as the animals jostled, the smell of death unsettling the beasts.

"This really all of them?" Ethan asked his men. Ryan knew that the one who answered would be the second in command. He made a mental note of who that sec chief may be. He was a hook-nosed, craggy man, with long dreadlocks down his back. He looked to be part white, part black and part Native American. But all mean... He had the still, calm air of a born mercie who would have no problem chilling everyone in the clearing—friend or foe—without a second thought.

The man shook his head. "Yeah," he said. "Yeah, ain't no others. They're good, give 'em that."

"Some are a whole lot better than others, if y'ask me," another rider said lasciviously. He was a squat, fat man with one clouded eye and scars across his forehead. He smiled, but looked about as far from the idea of a jolly fat guy as it was possible to get. He nudged the side of his mount with his heel and the horse's head came down, pushing at Krysty's shoulder. "I'm betting this one could be real good, y'know what I'm saying?"

It wasn't just the words, it was the way that they were used. There was something in his tone that couldn't be ignored. Krysty focused on this and forgot that they were surrounded and outnumbered by a hostile group.

"Watch what you're doing, fat boy," she growled, stepping to one side.

"Whoo-hoo. What do we have here?" he jeered. "She's a real feisty one, ain't she?"

"Cut it out, Jonno," the sec chief said wearily. But

there was no real authority in his tone. It was something he was saying for the sake of it, not because he meant it.

"C'mon, Horse, it's just a little fun," the fat man whined before leering at Krysty. "Could be a whole lot more fun, though…"

Krysty backed away from the horse, her body tensing. Her Titian mane had closed around her neck and shoulders protectively, signaling her sense that she was in some kind of danger.

The companions tensed with her. They knew that they were hopelessly outnumbered, but they would always defend one of their own.

Ryan kept his eye fixed on Ethan. The baron was watching the developments with interest. The one-eyed man guessed that he was using this situation as a yardstick for how they would react, how stupe or smart they would be. Imperceptibly, Ryan signaled to the others to stay. They were watching him for a lead, and although they had the desire to fight, they knew that he was playing the odds.

The sec chief—Horse—sighed heavily. "Jonno, cut it out. Do I have to give you more bastard scars than you already got?"

"Shit, you big-haired fucker, it's only some fun. Right, Baron?" the fat man asked, looking across at Ethan. The baron stayed impassive, which the fat man took as a sign of assent. "Yeah, only some fun," he added, almost to himself. He leaned forward over the front of the horse and reached out for Krysty. "Just a little fun, honey. Now you-all ain't gonna do anything with all your friends here about to get chilled if they get in the way, are you?"

He reached out and looped his fingers in her hair, trying to tug her toward him. The strength of the prehensile mane surprised him and a flicker of a frown crossed his face. He allowed it to pass, paused until he thought he had the measure of her strength, and then tried to pull her to him.

At first Krysty held back, making him tug harder, sit farther forward on his saddle. Then she acquiesced, moving a few steps closer and letting him believe that he had the upper hand.

It worked. He was still seated forward on the saddle and was complacent. He would offer little in the way of resistance.

Timing her actions, she waited until he was at the optimum point, then stepped back suddenly, wrenching her head, straining her neck muscles and feeling the hair tug on her scalp. The sentient tresses had encircled his hand to hold it in a viselike grip. It wasn't something she could do consciously, but as a result of the fear and adrenaline that coursed through her body. She felt a searing pain as her neck muscles protested. Her hair, protective of her body and strength, let loose of the fat man's hand.

It was enough. His balance completely thrown, he fell forward with a startled yelp, crashing onto the ground at her feet, landing heavily on a dead stickie. The yelp turned into a yell of disgust as he struggled to his feet, eyes blazing.

The mounted riders reached for their weapons, but a gesture from Horse stopped them. The sec chief could see that the baron was studying this with interest. Likewise, Ryan stayed his people. Krysty would have to deal with this on her own and he had no doubts about her capabilities.

The fat man was facing her. She backed off him to give herself more room to maneuver. He took this as a sign of weakness and a savage grin crossed his features.

"You won't be so pretty—or so keen to fight back— when I've finished with you," he snarled, pulling a long-bladed hunting knife from beneath the layers of skins and furs.

Krysty allowed herself the smallest of grins. He was telegraphing his intentions far too much, and taking him out would be easier than she thought. A fact that became obvious as he lunged at her with all the finesse of a runaway rhino—except that he had none of the danger. She moved aside to allow his arm to thrust past her harmlessly, then caught him at the elbow, snapping his arm backward and at the same time kicking back with the heel of one silver-tipped cowboy boot so that it cracked into his shin and raked down, splitting the cloth and flesh and hammering into the bone.

The fat man howled in pain and toppled over. Krysty took the knife from his hand and dug one knee in the middle of his back, pinning him to the ground. She pulled his head up by his hair with one hand and held the blade of the knife against his throat.

"One good reason," she whispered. "Just one..."

The click of blasters being drawn and beaded answered her. The riders had been still long enough and now their weapons were trained on her. Horse held his hand aloft to stop them firing.

There was a second—so tense it seemed like an hour—before Ethan spoke.

"Seems to me you met your match, Jonno, and you got what you deserved. But don't chill the fucker, lady. He's too good a hunter to lose over his bad manners."

Krysty let the fat man go and stood, stepping out of his immediate range as she did so. She didn't want to give him the slightest chance to strike back. He stood and dusted himself down, shaking his head to clear it, cursing under his breath. He turned and glared at Krysty, then at his knife, which she still held by her side.

"I was only joking, y'know," he said accusingly.

"Well, you're not funny. And no fighter, either," she added with venom.

The uneasy silence was broken by the baron's harsh laugh. "More like you're a better fighter." He chuckled. "Jonno's good, all right, but you're better. All of you, by the look of what you did before we got here."

"You've got to watch your own back," Ryan said, emphasizing the dual meaning of his words with a look at the riders encircling them.

"You'd be as chilled as those stickies if I wanted," Ethan commented, spitting on the nearest corpse for his own emphasis. "You're interesting people, that's for sure."

"I cannot but think that 'interesting' is an unusual epithet for such a situation," Doc mused.

The baron laughed again. "Y'see what I mean? What the fuck are you talking about, old man? You pitch up in the middle of a bunch of rabid stickies, whomp the fuck out of them, face off with a superior force in terms of arms and numbers, and then stand there and discuss the meaning of words... Shit, if that ain't interesting, then you tell me what is."

"A fair point, if a little forcefully delivered." Doc Tanner smiled.

"Good," Ethan said decisively. "Then you come back to our ville and we learn a bit more about you. In return, you get fed and watered, and get to rest."

"And if we say no?" Ryan queried.

Ethan's smile hardened. "Did I say you had a choice?"

The one-eyed man looked at the horsemen surrounding the companions. He didn't like the fact that they were being told what they had to do. Handing over power to another wasn't something that came easily to any of them. On the other hand, they were in no practical position to fight; they could already have been wiped out. The baron seemed open enough to want to learn about them, and any hint of hostility came only when he was apparently crossed. That was worth remembering. What was also worthy of consideration was that the companions needed rest and food and it would be stupe to turn up the chance of this. Any problems could be dealt with as they arose, when they were rested and in a better condition. Looking at his friends, Ryan could see that they were all bruised, dusty, tired. Some had cuts that needed attention and their postures were slumped, tired.

"Okay, we'll come with you," Ryan said slowly, testing the baron with his choice of words.

Ethan allowed himself a small, tight smile, acknowledging that he understood the one-eyed man and that he, too, would play the game.

"Good," he said finally. "Now we wouldn't expect you to walk, as it's some way. You have any objection to sharing our horses?"

Ryan looked around at the riders. Some of the horses looked as though they wouldn't support more than one man, but others seemed sturdy enough. He looked back to Ethan and shook his head briefly.

"Okay. As for you, Jonno," he directed to the fat man, who was still standing where he had fallen, " you can take the lady with you. But she gets to keep that knife of yours for now. A trophy," he added to Krysty. "Make sure the fat bastard doesn't try anything else on the way back."

The fat man said nothing, but his expression betrayed his less than charitable feelings about the baron's decision. The ripple of laughter that spread through the other riders did little to improve his disposition and he looked sullen as he climbed back onto his horse, grudgingly holding his hand out for Krysty. The Titian-haired beauty made a point of ignoring this and mounted behind him without acknowledging his gesture.

Horse, the sec chief, took over, assigning a rider to each of the five companions, taking Ryan on his own mount. It was obviously a gesture of respect. Next to the baron, he was the highest-ranking rider, and he was acknowledging Ryan's leadership. The one-eyed man took this in the spirit it was intended and nodded his thanks as he mounted the stallion that carried the sec chief.

When they were in position, Ethan held up his hand. "We go back the same way. Take it easy. The horses must be exhausted after the chase and some have extra loads. Keep alert, but I don't figure on there being trouble, do you?" he asked of his sec chief. Horse gave a brief shake of his head, his dreadlocks brushing against

Ryan, as hard and wiry as his body. Ethan nodded, pleased. "Let's go…"

The hunting party started back through the forest, taking the path that had been carved by the pack of stickies as they had rampaged, tearing their way through the foliage and trees. It was only by taking this path that the companions became aware of the extent of the damage caused by the pack.

"What the fuck were they doing?" Ryan whistled, looking at the churned-up earth and devastation left in their wake. "I've seen a shitload of stickies in my time, but I've never known them to act like this. And to stay and fight like they did to us. Usually they run…"

Horse grunted. "Your guess is as good as mine. They attacked some farmers on the edge of the ville and we set out after them. Expected an easy hunt, chill them, then go home. But I've never seen stickies move at that pace. Something spooked them."

"Figured it might have been you," Ryan said guardedly. "After all, you were at their rear."

"Only 'cause we hadn't yet caught up with them when they ran into you," the sec chief replied.

"Yeah, guess so," Ryan agreed, keeping the hint of doubt out of his voice. Why chase after them when they had already passed by the ville? There was something about the story that didn't quite ring true, but that could wait until later, until Ryan had recce'd the situation a little better. What was important now was to get to the ville and to rest. As the horses trotted gently over the rough earth, the one-eyed man felt every little rut in the ground as a jarring pain. His eye was heavy and he felt his body begin to give in to the fatigue that had been staved off for so long by the adrenaline rush of combat and the need to keep alert.

On their own shared mounts, the other companions were finding that they, too, were falling prey to their tiredness. Krysty kept herself awake by sheer willpower, not trusting herself to so much as doze while she had to ride behind the fat man. For his part, Jonno was trying to make amends for his earlier attitude by keeping up a nonstop stream of banalities.

"Look, I'm really sorry about earlier. I just got carried away. I was only fooling, and I misjudged. You know what it's like in the heat of battle, you kinda find it hard to switch off and get back to being normal. Whatever the fuck that is, y'know. But I don't want us to have got off on the wrong foot. Ethan wouldn't like that, and he's not the kind of dude you screw with, y'know what I'm saying? It's not that he's a bad guy, and he's a great baron, right, but you don't want to get on the wrong side of him, y'know? That's just bad news for everyone involved, right? Hey, are you listening?"

Krysty answered with a grunt, then added, "Look, apology accepted, and I don't care about the rest right now. Just keep your eyes on the path ahead and keep riding, okay?"

Jonno pursed his lips. No one talked to him like that. They all tried but they paid. All the bitches who laughed at him for being fat and ugly and scarred. He would just bide his time and get her when she didn't expect it.

J.B. and Mildred were seated behind riders who said nothing beyond initial hellos. They were glad of it; the last thing they needed was to have to concentrate on conversation after the battle. Particularly, Mildred, who was sure that she would throw up again if the ride was any more rocky.

Doc was behind a large, heavily muscled rider with an ebony skin that seemed to shine in the moonlight that lit the path cleared by the stickies. The old man could feel he was slipping. Nothing seemed real anymore. What was real? A man who had lived his life over three different centuries, with large chunks removed between them, Doc's grasp of reality was always a little loose, and now he was sure that he had descended into madness. In the distance, riding toward him, he could see a Brougham driven by his beloved Emily, the wife he had left behind in the nineteenth century, and who would never have known what happened to him, just that he vanished one day, without trace and forever. Perhaps it was better that she didn't know; that she could never see him as he was now, aged and beaten by the fates. God, but he missed her. And here she was, driving toward them. Seated beside her, he could see Rachel and young Jolyon, the children he had never seen grow to maturity, and who had been dead for longer than he could know—longer, indeed, than he had been alive. How could a father so outlive his children? It wasn't natural. But then, what had happened to him hadn't been natural.

They couldn't see him like this. They couldn't. He turned his head away from them as they approached, tears streaming down his face, his body shuddering in convulsive sobs.

"You okay, man?" the rider asked him, a worried note creeping into his voice.

Doc didn't answer. It took all his effort not to turn to

look at his wife and children as he heard the Brougham approach, gaining with every second. If he could only…if he could just…just wait until the sound was on the wane. If he could only keep his will intact for that long, then surely his sanity would also follow?

It was no good. As the Brougham approached, he felt compelled to turn. It was a force far greater than his meager willpower could cope with—the force of longing, despair and loneliness. Everything he had ever held dear to him had been snatched away—or else he had been snatched away from it. His wife, his children…

Doc gave in to his longing and turned to face the oncoming Brougham. His eyes were wide, tears coursing down his cheeks. As the vehicle passed him, he could see Emily, Rachel and Jolyon turn to look at him. They were the ages they had been when he had last seen them, but changed. Their eyes were empty and their skins were dry and mummified. They were husks. As he, himself, was now…

Doc looked away, crying out in pain and rage. The rider in front tried to keep his eyes fixed on the path ahead. He had heard nothing, seen nothing. There was nothing…

The other riders exchanged glances and shrugs. If they were expecting any of the companions riding with them to explain, they would wait in vain.

Jak had questions of his own. He was riding behind a wide, fat-bellied bald man whose apparent bulk wasn't just due to excess weight. Underneath, there was a lot of muscle, as Jak had found when he had almost fallen from the horse early in the journey, the horse stumbling in a rut and throwing both riders forward. The bald man had moved with the motion, but Jak had been taken unawares and almost thrown. As he'd toppled, the man had shot out an arm and grabbed Jak. The albino youth had, in turn, taken grip of the arm. He had expected soft flesh. Instead he'd gripped muscles and tendons that were like barbed wire wrapped around brick.

"Thanks," he had said simply as he clambered back.

"No problem—name's Stark," the man had replied with an equal simplicity.

Both were men of few words, but had found a respect for each other in that seemingly inconsequential moment. Jak had thought the man a blubber mountain and had found hidden depths. In return, Stark had been impressed by the albino's lightning-quick reaction, and the wiry strength with which he'd flung himself back into the saddle; all the more remarkable after the firefight he had just been through.

Since that moment they had conducted a conversation that had been drawn out not by the lack of things to say, but by the natural manner of both. Jak would ask an elliptical question and Stark would pause for a long while, considering an answer that wasted no words. He would then phrase a question of his own and Jak would reply in kind.

Neither had passed comment on Doc, but Jak chose that moment to ask what he felt was an important question.

"Why you hunt stickies?"

Stark waited for some time, then said, "Like Ethan said."

"So why follow so far when they move on? No sense if they not cause damage. Waste of energy and ammo."

"Mebbe. But like I say, it's as Ethan says."

Jak pondered this. There was a coded message in there, if only he could unlock it. His keen senses were jangling with the rush he always felt when there was danger ahead. It wasn't like Krysty's mutie doomie sense, it was something altogether more instinctual, a preternatural development of his instincts that had been honed by years of survival, years of hunting.

"Ethan always tell how it is?" Jak asked finally.

A long pause. "Ethan always tells it how he sees it."

Jak considered that. Stark picked his words very carefully and he hadn't actually agreed with what Jak had said.

Their conversation lapsed. The pauses lengthened into silence as they rode on through a night that was now approaching dawn. The other companions were having trouble keeping conscious as fatigue and lack of sleep tried to claim them. But Jak, who had spent so many hours in a state of inert awareness waiting for prey, was able to focus and to stay alert.

So it was that he noticed something very strange, something that made his instincts quiver more than ever.

As the mounted party traversed the trail ripped up by the stickies, the ville of Pleasantville became visible in the distance. A shattered metropolis lay beyond, remnants of old skyscrapers and buildings dimly visible in the early-morning haze. But the ville itself seemed to have been constructed in an old suburban area. It was still too dim for him to fully distinguish, even though his red albino eyes found the twilight of evening and dawn more conducive than the bright light of a daytime sun. However, there was something that made no sense if what Ethan had told them was the whole truth. For, to reach the ville, the riders now left the track that had been carved by the pack of stickies. A track that veered off to one side of the farthest outcrop of the ville, past the last buildings and signs of life that Jak could see.

Surely they had been told that the pack had attacked farms on the edge of the ville, which was why they had been chased. But the track, clearly visible because of the devastation it had caused, veered off way past the last sign of tilled land, cutting across an area that could only be described as a wilderness.

Why had Ethan lied? It looked as though the stickies had passed close to the ville, but hadn't actually made contact. So why mount the chase at all?

Jak was sure that the answer to this question would also provide an answer to the churning sense of anxiety gnawing at his guts. They were riding into a danger of some kind, of that he was certain. What it was had to be determined, but as he cast a glance at the rest of the companions, tired and battered on the backs of their mounts, in no condition to fight, he was concerned that they were riding into trouble when they were least capable to deal with it.

The ground was now softer under hoof, less rutted and destroyed. The movement of the horses became more fluid, lulling the already exhausted companions into a stupor, with no bone-jarring ruts to shake them out of their torpor. Jak wondered if any of the others had noticed that they had left the stickies' path, and that it deviated from the ville.

Why? Why had they been lied to? Why had the stickies been hunted so ruthlessly? Was that what had whipped them into a frenzy, or had something else happened to make them that way…perhaps so they could be hunted?

Jak felt the movement of the horse begin to lull him. A sense of fatigue and exhaustion swept over him, making it hard to concentrate.

Shit, whatever faced them, he needed to sleep first. He had no choice.

He jolted awake suddenly. What had caused him to stir? His head was pounding, his heart racing. The last thing he could remember was the ville coming into sight and feeling so, so tired.

Jak raised himself on one elbow and took a look around. First thing to strike him as weird was that he was lying down. How the fuck had that happened without his realizing it? His eyes adjusted easily to the gloom and he could see that the other companions were also in the room with him. There were two windows, with thick hangings that kept out the light, apart from at the very edges where they weren't flush to the windowframe. Through these gaps, Jak could see that it was a bright light, but not the intensity of midday. Probably late afternoon, early evening.

The room itself was plastered and painted in a light color that trapped whatever could get through the hangings and magnified it. In this half light, Jak could see that the others, like himself, were in beds that were covered with blankets and quilts. Their weapons and supplies were by each bed, as though taken off individually and placed by the right bedside. He looked down: he was still fully dressed. He guessed that his friends were, too. The only other furniture in the room was a long wooden table, set against the far wall and bare apart from a pitcher and six cups.

It would seem that the companions had been lifted en masse from the horses when they had reached the ville, then put to bed like children. A gesture of this magnanimity was something that was unknown in the Deathlands, and Jak was curious as to why they had been afforded such respect. No one was that nice unless they expected something in return. But what? He couldn't shake the memory of the track forged by the stickies, veering off away from the ville. It had been such a little, and such a stupid, lie. There was a connection of some kind, but he was too tired to work it out right now.

Jak stood, every muscle in his body aching as he did so, the rigors of the firefight and the ride not yet cured by his rest. He could feel every last blow that he had taken during the battle with the stickies, and was sure that the others would feel the same when they awoke. Tentatively he walked toward the table, testing his strength. He was sore, but still quite supple. His limbs hadn't stiffened with injury as he feared they might. But he could tell that his speed was impaired. Movement was more…not difficult, but awkward. He reached the table and picked up the pitcher, sniffing at the contents. He could smell nothing but the faint aroma of the wood from which the pitcher was made. Jak dipped a finger into the clear liquid and then licked it. No taste other than what you'd expect from water—the faint coppery tang of earth and perhaps a hint of metal from whatever piping had carried it to an outlet.

Figuring it was safe to drink—or at least, as safe as

any water—he poured some into one of the cups and drank deeply. His mouth felt as though someone had held a jolt party in there; it was thick and dry. The water eased it.

Jak put down the cup and turned as he heard stirring from behind him. Ryan was starting to come around, raising himself.

"What the fuck happened?" the one-eyed man asked slowly, looking around him and taking in his surroundings.

"Guess were more tired than thought." Jak shrugged. "Water," he added, pouring another cup.

Ryan got up from his bed and walked slowly to Jak, taking the cup from him. "Thanks," he said after drinking deeply. "So this is Pleasantville. I see they've left us all our stuff," he continued, indicating the packs that had been stowed by their bedsides. "Mighty nice of them. A bit too nice," he added, exchanging a look with Jak. The albino youth nodded.

"Yeah. Triple-red on that," he said simply.

By this time their lowered voices had penetrated the consciousness of the others and they were all beginning to stir. Krysty and J.B. were next up and they shared Jak and Ryan's caution. Mildred pulled herself out of bed, but didn't immediately go to the others. She knelt beside Doc's bed and checked him.

"Old buzzard was hallucinating out there," she said over her shoulder to the others. "Just want to see that he's okay."

Doc opened one eye and fixed her with a baleful glare. "My dear Dr. Wyeth, pray tell me what is hallucination and what is not, when all—either concrete or

fancy—seems so tangible that you can reach out a[...]
touch it. Whether or not 'tis there, does that make the
emotion it causes any the less real?"

"Yeah, you're okay," Mildred muttered. "Now get
the hell up and drink something before you dehydrate."

When all six companions were up and clustered
around the table, the door on the far side of the room
opened and Horse stepped through. The tall, gaunt sec
chief eyed them, then nodded in some private satisfaction.

"So you're all still here and all awake. Good. Ethan
wants to see you. Now."

Chapter Four

With some hesitation, the companions followed the sec chief, leaving their weapons and supplies by the sides of their beds. To attempt to retrieve any of them could easily be construed as hostile action and, until they knew what they were up against, it was best to maintain innocence. Besides, the sec party could easily have taken their weapons away while they'd been unconscious and not have treated them with such respect.

It wasn't as if they were exactly unarmed now. They might not have their blasters, but Ryan still had the panga sheathed at his thigh, and his scarf—a deadly weapon in experienced hands with the lead weights sewn into the ends that turned it into a bolo—around his neck. Doc carried his swordstick with the silver lion's-head, and J.B. was equipped with his Tekna hunting knife. As for Jak, it would have been interesting to see if anyone could have found the number of leaf-bladed throwing knives secreted on his person.

So, if Ethan, baron of Pleasantville, and his sec chief trusted them enough not to do a body search, to take away Jak's jacket and Doc's cane, and to leave their weapons by their bedsides, then why should they feel any suspicion? Not for any reason that could be rationalized. Just their instincts telling them that people in the

Deathlands—particularly barons—were never normally this friendly.

Horse led them along a maze of corridors lined with windows that showed that they were moving through more than one building. Some of the old suburban sprawl of houses that constituted part of Pleasantville had been joined together by stucco-and-brick corridors that made several houses and shacks into one single building. It would be possible to travel almost an entire circuit of the ville without actually setting foot outside into the elements.

It would also make finding the way around more difficult if you weren't familiar with the ville. This was something that always set alarm bells ringing loudly in Ryan's head, and they were certainly deafening right now.

"Why does Ethan want to see us?" he asked the sec chief in as neutral a tone as possible. It was the first time any of them had spoken since leaving their dormitory, and Ryan felt his voice sound unnatural and loud in the quiet corridor. They had passed no one on their journey, and although they could see people outside and through the windows of other buildings, it was almost as though they had been purposely isolated from the ville inhabitants until they had seen the baron. It didn't help their sense of paranoia.

The sec chief seemed to take a long time to answer, leading them through another corridor, not looking back. For a moment, Ryan thought it possible that the man hadn't heard his question, and started to speak again. But Horse finally broke the silence, looking back over his shoulder. His dark skin and sharp features accented his hooded eyes, which stared coldly from under his nest of dreadlocks.

"Ethan just wants to get to know you better, see where you're from, where you reckon to be going. It's not a problem, is it?"

The wording of the second sentence was innocuous enough, but it was the tone of his voice—it carried an undertone of menace, as though he were daring them to say that it was.

Or was it just that customs and manners were different here and the mix of races and accents that had gathered over the generations had produced a strange speech pattern? Certainly, they had heard so many different modes of speech over the years.

Ryan looked over his shoulder at Krysty. She was his barometer of mood—her mutie doomie sense was liable to pick up the slightest tremors, even if she had no conscious idea herself. Her Titian mane was flowing, not tight and coiled, but there was some agitated movement from the strands around her neck.

She noticed Ryan staring at her and gave him a puzzled look. The sense of danger—no, not even that, but rather of caution—was so slight that she wasn't aware of it herself. The one-eyed man returned her look with a slight, crooked grin and turned back to the sec chief.

"No, it's not a problem. Not unless you want it to be. Not at all," Ryan replied.

So there may be no problem right now, but it was a time to be triple-red. That was okay—he could tell from his brief glimpse of the others that they felt entirely the same way, without needing to be told.

Finally they seemed to reach the end of their journey. The corridors, which had been sparse up to now, were becoming more and more decorated. Animal heads mounted on wood, paintings that looked both new and scavenged from predark times and tapestries of bright colors were hung from the walls in an organized fashion, as though someone had applied some thought to their placement. That little fact alone gave Ryan a clue as to the man they were about to meet properly for the first time.

A pair of white-painted double doors—modest but tellingly clean—marked the end of the corridor. Horse stopped in front of them and knocked twice, standing back to wait for a response.

"Come," a voice intoned from the other side, loud enough to be heard, but calm and unhurried.

The sec chief put a hand on each door and opened them. They were on the verge of the baron's lair and each of the companions felt a tightening in the gut. Now they would find out if this was going to be friendly, or if they would have to fight.

They followed Horse into the baronial chamber. Like the corridors outside, it was decorated in a combination of paintings, animal heads and tapestries, tastefully arranged against a brilliant white wall. The floor was polished wood, shiny and slippery underfoot. The furnishings were sparse but comfortable: two sofas and three high chairs covered in a multicolor tapestried material that matched some of those on the walls; two long tables against the walls, with books and papers neatly arranged on the top, along with a wooden bowl of fruit and a pitcher of—presumably—water, and an old, mid-twentieth-century desk in a dark wood, polished and cared for, restored to its original sheen. Behind the desk was a late-twentieth-century swivel chair, carefully restored with animal hide, dyed and colored to resemble the original black leather or PVC covering.

Ethan was standing behind the desk, leaning forward and supporting himself on his knuckles, resting lightly while he perused a document unfurled on the desktop. Behind him, a window onto the outside framed him in a halo of light. If this was the effect he wanted, then it succeeded. It painted him as a man caught in the middle of a busy day running a ville, a man looked up to with a godlike status. If it was chance, then he was lucky. If it was deliberate, then he was a clever manipulator.

Which one was it?

Ethan looked up. "Ah, good," he said lightly, folding the document so that its contents would be concealed before coming round his desk and striding across the room to Ryan, taking the one-eyed man's hand and forearm in his own and grasping them firmly. "You are, I trust, well rested after the rigors of yesterday?"

"It was good of you to look after us," he answered evenly.

Ethan gave a crooked grin. "Not at all, not at all. The pleasure is entirely mine, I assure you. As you may recall, I described you as 'interesting,' and I haven't changed that opinion in the slightest. You fascinate me, and if you wish, you can look on my hospitality as a way of satisfying my own curiosity. Now come, sit down."

Ethan led Ryan toward the sitting area, Horse indicating to the other companions that they should follow. They sat, following Ryan's lead as he and Ethan reached the sofas. They were soft and yielding. Ryan felt a twinge of concern, as they were so soft that springing from them if attacked would be difficult. But why be too concerned when there was only Ethan and Horse in the room, and the baron's attitude was distinctly nonthreatening?

When they were settled, the baron lifted one of the high chairs and placed it so that he was positioned in the middle of the two sofas, able to see all parties. He sat, leaning forward with one elbow on his knee, fist under his chin, the very model of attentiveness.

"You can go, Horse. I'll summon you when I need you," he said to his sec chief without looking up. The dreadlocked sec boss nodded almost imperceptibly and withdrew, closing the doors behind him.

"So," Ethan began when it was certain that they were alone, "I'm thinking that you have a tale to tell. You see, we have regular patrols around the territory, as we have to protect the trade routes to and from this ville. We have a thriving economy from our trade, and we live better than many baronies. But vigilance is the price we pay. You see my drift?"

"I'm not sure," Ryan said guardedly. He was all too aware of what Ethan was saying, but wanted the baron to come out with it himself. Unfortunately, Doc still wasn't as sharp as at his best and took Ryan's words at face value.

"My dear boy, I feel sure that our kind host here means to ascertain how we came to be in his lands without seeming to have passed any of his patrols."

Ethan smiled, noting the flicker of exasperation that flared briefly in Ryan's eye. "Precisely," he said levelly. "I've never known anyone to get past our lines without warning."

"What about stickies?" Jak asked.

Ethan's face darkened and something hard and cold shone through. "We thought they would be no problem, just pass through and then go without even bothering us. Whatever stirred them up, it's an error we won't make again."

It was a plausible enough explanation, but there was a darker undertone to the baron's voice that suggested this wasn't the entire answer. It served to remind them to keep on guard, especially as Ethan picked up his subject again without hesitation.

"Point is, we knew they were coming, as we left them. We didn't know you were here until we stumbled on you and damn near chilled you along with the stickies. Now how does that happen?"

"To tell you the truth, we don't really know. We came from the northeast, across the dry plain. We should have been visible enough," Ryan stated. He would let Ethan work it out from there. He wasn't going to explain anything beyond that.

"My people avoid the plain. Nothing can really live on that shit, and I'm mightily impressed that you got across it. But we circle it with our patrols and we should have sighted you before you hit there. It's not that big a place and there's nothing to conceal you if you're observed from the surrounding territory. My guess is that you're not telling me the whole story, here," he added, eyeing Ryan carefully.

"My guess is that mebbe some of your patrols aren't as thorough as you'd like, or not as observant," Ryan returned coolly.

The baron gave Ryan a cold, hard stare that was difficult to read. It was as though he had deliberately hooded his eyes to block out all his feelings. From what they'd already seen, Ethan didn't take kindly to not having his word instantly obeyed. But weighed against this was the fact that he was fascinated by the companions and could sense that there was some bigger story lurking behind their guarded words.

He spoke again after a long, considered pause. "Okay, if you won't tell me, there's not much I can do. No, that's not true. Actually, there's an awful lot I can do. We have methods of torture that would normally break a man in less than a day—that's if he survived. But you people aren't like that, I can tell. You're not the kind who give anything away, and I figure you'd rather buy the farm than give me the satisfaction. Besides all that, you've proved yourselves to be exceptional fighters, and we can always do with those in Pleasantville."

"Really? You strike me as not having much trouble," Ryan replied.

Ethan gave a small smile that was entirely lacking in warmth. "Why d'you think that is? Because we fight hard for what we've got, and we fight hard to defend it. And people—by which I mean other, lazier barons who would want to take rather than build—know this. So they leave us alone. There's a lot of jack and a lot of goods in this ville, and we wouldn't be able to hang on to it if we didn't know how to. Y'see what I mean?"

Ryan nodded. "So what do you want from us?"

Ethan smiled again. This time, there was a knowingness behind the eyes. "You don't waste words, do you? I like that, although I wish you'd waste a few in telling me where you came from and where you learned to fight like you do. So I figure that mebbe you will if you hang around for a while, get used to us. Mebbe you'll like it enough to stay. We could always do with people like yourselves, who contribute to the well-being of the ville." He leaned forward, so that he was looking Ryan directly in the eye. "I'll tell you what I offer. You can stay in Pleasantville for as long as you like. You'll work for your accommodation and food, but it'll be good work, not crap. I want you to work with Horse and look at our sec strategies, in return for which we learn things about combat from you. If you like it, then you join his men and stay on. If not, you leave and carry on to wherever you were going. And mebbe—and only if you want—you tell me how the fuck you ended up in the middle of that forest."

Ryan looked at the companions. Despite the rest, they were still battered from the firefight with the stickie pack. A few more days or a week in the ville, with good beds and food, would do them a lot of good before they moved on. He didn't trust Ethan one bit, but if they could play along and buy a few days, then that would benefit them. At the moment they were in no state to stand and fight if they said no and Ethan turned on them.

"Yeah, okay," Ryan said with an inclination of his head. "We'll do it."

"Good." Ethan said no more, but had a smug expression as he rose and walked over to his desk. There was a bell-push on one corner, and he depressed it. Wherever the other end of the connection may lay, it wasn't audible, and it had to have been some distance, for they waited a few minutes before the double doors opened and two sec men walked in, their blasters conspicuous from their belts, hands seemingly casual but ready for action.

J.B. noticed this, and he also noticed Ethan indicate with a subtle gesture that relaxed the sec duo.

"These boys will clear you out of last night's dorm and find you regular accommodation. They'll also tell you a bit about the ville as you go. Okay, boys?"

The two sec men grunted. They didn't seem as though they would be garrulous mines of information. Ethan turned away, his audience with the companions over, his attention already focused on the papers on his desk.

Ryan rose, followed by the others, and walked toward the doors where the sec men waited.

"I hope you've figured what we could be getting into here," J.B. muttered as he joined his old friend. "It doesn't feel right."

"With you on that," Ryan returned in an undertone, "but we can't just leave—not yet. Play them along a while, see the lay of the land."

J.B. agreed, but his jaw was set tight. This wasn't like the Ryan he knew. It was as though he were holding back, not sure of a course of action. The Armorer couldn't remember the last time he'd seen Ryan so indecisive.

As the companions walked through the double doors, they noted that one of the sec men held back, so that they were led and followed by an armed man. With no blasters of their own, it was an uncomfortable feeling.

"We'll collect your stuff, then show you where you're staying," the leading sec man said in a deep, coarse voice that seemed out of place with his wiry, shaven-head form. "You've been allocated billets around the ville."

"You mean to say we're being split up? And that Ethan already had it worked out?" Krysty asked suspiciously.

"Course he did, lady," the sec man at the rear piped up—literally, as despite his bulk and the beard that sprouted from his cleft chin, he had a voice that was almost falsetto. "The baron worked out what you do from what you were carrying, and made plans accordingly. He always plans for every eventuality."

"Does he now," Doc murmured. "I wonder what he would have done if Ryan had refused him?"

"Like Track said, the baron plans for every eventuality," the shaven-head sec man at the front of the line replied in a voice that betrayed everything by its very neutrality.

They were led back to the dormitory where they had slept the previous night to collect their blasters and supplies, under the watchful eye of the two sec men. Nothing was said, and no attempt was made to take their weapons from them, but all the companions could feel that the sec men were assessing them and the way they handled the equipment, as if sizing them up as future opponents.

They left the dormitory and marched through yet more corridors. But these were farther away from the baron's residence, and the farther they traveled, the more people they saw. The residents of Pleasantville moved freely inside and outside the tunnels, which linked buildings in a manner that was intended to supply strong defense and could also act as a convenience. There seemed to be nothing sinister about the ville dwellers, who went about their everyday business and looked at the strangers with curiosity.

"Don't they see many outsiders?" Mildred asked at yet another curious gawp.

"None that look like they're going to stay. Only passing through," the man called Track replied enigmatically.

They walked outside of the tunnels and into the harsh sunlight beyond, crossing old roadways bisected by newly hewn paths. The ville was walled off at a visible distance, the forest beyond invisible on the flat landscape as the fortress walls rose. It seemed as though the ville itself was comprised of an old stretch of suburb that had been separated from the remains of the city beyond and added to with a shantytown of shacks as well as some buildings that were sturdier, constructed of salvaged rubble from the ruined city. The smallholdings and farmlands that they had seen on their ride in, before weariness had claimed them, had to have lain outside the walls, which made them an easier target. Unfortunate, but if the land in here couldn't be cultivated, there would be little option.

Farming didn't seem to be their main subsistence, however. The scrub they had seen couldn't support the thriving population that they now encountered. As they were taken into the streets of the ville, they could see that Pleasantville supported a fairly large population, many of whom were trading on the streets or going about their business. Most were pedestrians, but there were some who were using horses—and not just sec men—as well as the occasional old motorcycle or wag, carrying goods from one part of the ville to another or headed out beyond the walls. The fuel and means to run wags and motorcycles didn't come cheap. Ethan had spoken of trade, but it seemed that Pleasantville had something that kept it thriving.

When they found what that may be, perhaps they would have some clues as to why Ethan was keen to find out more about them and to keep them in his ville.

The companions were to be split up and billeted in different places around the ville. This was an obvious ploy by the baron to keep them from forming a force against him by putting physical distance between them and also by placing them where loyal Pleasantville dwellers could keep a close eye on them. But at the same time, he had also chosen to place them where they would be of the most use. J.B. was to stay with the ville's armorer, the notion being that he would add his skills to those of his host. Jak was to be housed with the hunters who foraged the forest for game. Ryan was to stay with Horse, and compare notes on running a sec force with the gaunt dreadlocked sec chief. Mildred— who from her belongings was obviously the healer of the group—was to stay with Pleasantville's healer.

Which left Krysty and Doc. This was a problem, as from their belongings and demeanor it was hard to know what their place in the group may be. It was as interesting for them to see how Ethan had defined them. But perhaps not flattering: Krysty had been placed with a trader who specialized in cloth and jewelry, as though he couldn't see beyond her beauty or put any value on her beyond that. As for Doc—his was, in many ways, the most potentially rewarding as far as Ryan was concerned. For Doc had been sequestered with a man named Bones, who seemed to have no discernible purpose other than as the town scholar. Like Doc, his dress seemed a little eccentric, as he wore an old suit that was patched and mended, giving him the air of an office clerk caught in a predark time loop, worn by age. His eyesight was also bad, and he wore heavy glasses to compensate. But his task in the ville was obviously one that was important to the baron.

This was something that was immediately brought home to Doc when he was led into the man's house, which was one of the old, surviving suburban buildings. It was dusty and crammed full of papers and books. There was also an old comp that was working, blinking away on the man's desk. The house was cluttered with other surviving pieces of old tech, including a camcorder, TVs, old stereo equipment with predark recordings in a variety of formats, books and manuals for the maintenance of this equipment, and a vast library of videotape that took up half of one wall, each tape annotated in Bones's own spidery hand.

Here was the true business of Pleasantville...

Chapter Five

"Remarkable, truly remarkable." Mildred looked up from the stethoscope at the keen-faced woman who stood, hovering, on the opposite side of the bench. She smiled, and it was returned. "So tell me," Mildred continued, "how the hell did you come by this?"

Michaela shrugged. She was small, just over five feet, and had a crop of gingery-brown hair that had been razored so that the long spikes stood on end. Her oval face was open, her brown eyes keen. She looked more like a teenager in a school than an experienced healer.

"That's the weirdest thing," she said in a voice that was as young as her face. "I think that there must be an old hospital in the remains of the predark ville that still has some old tech working in it. One of the hunting parties that was out in there came across it, and brought all this stuff back. It took them a couple of journeys, and to be honest it didn't make much sense to me at first. But Bones has so much stuff, all I had to do was root around until I found books that explained it all."

"Bones?" Mildred queried.

"Yeah. He's the guy your friend Doc is staying with. I hope you don't mind me saying this," she added cautiously, "but they seem well matched."

Mildred bit her cheek to stifle a laugh. "In what way would that be, then?" she asked ingenuously.

Michaela shuffled. She was a heavy-set woman, but light on her feet, and the movement of her feet on the floor of the building used as a hospital was like a light scratching. "Well, it's just that Bones has a reputation for being a bit crazy. Nothing wrong with that, I guess it's a kind of occupational hazard, a bit like me risking getting sick dealing with sick people, what with him having to deal with all that information and try and work out what it means. It's bound to make you a bit strange compared to everyone else."

Mildred couldn't contain herself any longer. She laughed, a hearty belly laugh that made Michaela look at her strangely. "No, maybe I'll explain it to you some-time," Mildred gasped, viewing the healer's baffled ex-pression, "but for different reasons, you couldn't be more right. It's not an insult at all, I just think you've hit it right on the nose. Guess this means that Ethan is pretty slick when it comes to putting people together. Very good at character judgment."

Michaela's pretty face clouded for a moment—only a second, but enough to make Mildred notice. "Yeah," the woman murmured, "he is kinda good at that sort of thing."

It had been so brief that Mildred could almost have assured herself that it was her own imagination at work. But it had been there. She decided to press the matter. "Ethan has it all worked out—getting someone to take on all that old knowledge that you found and try to make sense of it, getting this stuff shipped out here so you can study it. And hell, this is the richest ville that

I've seen for a long, long time. Seems like he wants to drag you all out of the dark ages and into a new age."

Michaela chewed her lip. "In some ways I guess you could say that," she muttered. "In some ways... But let's get back to this. You say you've seen things like this before?"

Mildred scanned the child-woman's face. There was something that she didn't want to let slip right now, that was for sure. But then again, how could Mildred hide her own excitement and not reveal how she had knowledge of what was in front of her: something that she thought she would never see again. Vaccines against smallpox, chicken pox and rubella. Three slides taken from three vials and examined under the 'scope. Viruses and vaccines in a refrigerated cabinet that she had not seen since the days before skydark, when she had been a working hospital doctor.

"I guess I'm kind of like this Bones guy," she said cautiously. "I find something interesting on our travels, and I like to find out more."

"So this has survived elsewhere? We're not alone?" Michaela said with an anxious eagerness.

"Yeah, I've seen it," Mildred said carefully, "but not for a very long time."

"YOU ASK ME, there ain't a finer armory anywhere on this craphole planet," Scar said proudly, chambering a round into a pump-action 12-gauge and taking aim at a distant target. He squeezed and the blaster roared, the target—a wooden representation of a man—splintering under the impact. The recoil had to have been heavy, but there wasn't even the slightest tremor in the man's shoulder muscles. J.B. noted this: Scar Longthorne, the armorer for Pleasantville, was three hundred pounds of muscle, standing at six-two. He made the wiry J.B. look like a scrawny dwarf beside him. And he had an ego to match his size.

All that J.B. had heard about since he'd been dropped off at the armory was how big, how well-equipped, how well-maintained it was. And it was true that the ville had amassed—either through trade, scavenge or plunder—a formidable range of weaponry. They had knives, swords and spears of all descriptions, immaculately oiled and polished. There was a wide range of hand-blasters, rifles, SMGs, and also a few heavy-duty grenade launchers. All of these crated and oiled, stored in oiled paper and rags to protect them until they were required. Grens and plas ex for a wide variety of uses, all stored at the optimum for their maintenance, be it damp, dry, cool or warm. Yes, Scar had done a good job. It was just that J.B. wished he would shut up for once. He hadn't stopped boasting since J.B. had arrived.

Why? He didn't have to: the Armorer would admit that it was a good armory, well-kept. But he had seen better—both bigger and of wider range—during his days with Trader and after. And, much as he admired a man who had a pride in his work, and shared J.B.'s love of inventory, there was something about Scar that didn't ring true. The nonstop barrage of boasting wasn't purely about his work.

The man looked as though he had been a warrior, and a good one. His name came from the multitude of white, crisscrossed lines that covered his otherwise tanned torso. But there was hint of fat around the gut that didn't sit with the muscles on his chest, arms and neck; a slight drag in one leg as he walked. J.B. suspected that Scar felt some kind of resentment at being retired from the fight, felt belittled at being put in charge of the inventory instead of being a user; and this belligerent display was his way of proving that he was still of some use.

Which would make him prickly and possibly dangerous. J.B. would have to tread carefully if he was to learn anything from this man. And learn he had to: if the companions were to work out what Ethan's aim may be and what their chances were of walking away without having to stand and fight.

"Yeah, I must say, it looks pretty impressive. And I doubt if I've ever seen anything kept in a better condition," J.B. said carefully when the echo of the shotgun discharge had blown away on the breeze. "I guess that the baron is pretty keen on amassing a good armory, else you wouldn't have anything like this. Am I right?"

"Sure as shit," Scar replied. He was warming to the stranger who had been thrust upon him. He had the right amount of respect. "But see," he added, gesturing at J.B. with the 12-gauge, which he held loosely in one hand, "it's not just the size of the armory that counts, it's how you keep it. Ethan's keen on getting together a shitload of weapons, but if he didn't have me to look after it…"

"Exactly. It'd just be a pile of junk. And that would be no good to anyone," J.B. said, massaging the big man's ego and watching him visibly preen at his words.

"You got that right. See, I was a fighter and hunter for a long time, but I always had the best weapons, 'cause I looked after them. Then I got hurt—" he went silent, as though the memory were still painful "—and it took a while to heal. Started looking after all this while I was waiting, and when I was fit enough to get back into the fray, Ethan begged me to stay doing this. Said he'd never seen an armory like it, and that it would make the ville stronger. Shit, when your baron makes you an offer like that, how can you say no?"

You can't because he'd have you chilled, J.B. thought, that's how it works. But he said something completely different: "The thing I don't get is, what's Ethan afraid of? We didn't see any other villes in striking distance, and it doesn't seem like you have much trouble—you do too much trade, from what I've seen, to be at war with anyone. Who the fuck do you fight with all this?"

Scar eyed J.B. up and down. The Armorer kept his face blank, not betraying his intense curiosity, making it seem like an innocent question.

Finally, the heavily scarred man said, "Mebbe we don't fight so much as do a lot of hunting. And that's all I can say to you. If Ethan wants us to talk about it, then he'll say. That's all."

The big man turned on his heel and strode off toward the armory building, the 12-gauge over his shoulder. He was suddenly, and obviously, silent, which gave J.B. something to think about as he followed on his heels.

KRYSTY WAS in a house filled with color. From room to room, the air was thick with the musk of scented cloth, the natural smells of the cotton and wool, freshly washed, sun and woven, mingling with the oils and perfumes used to make the cloth more attractive as it was cut into clothing. The scent and the colors were almost overpowering, taking the woman back to her days as a child, with Mother Sonja in the ville of Harmony, where everything was fresh, clean, good and filled with sensations, many of which had been dulled by the grind of survival in the Deathlands.

This entire house was nothing more or less than a warehouse for the cloth sold and traded by Angelika, the woman with whom Krysty had been billeted. She was a tall, thin woman of indeterminate age. Her hair was piled high on her head and interwoven with strands of her own cloth in a multitude of colors that seemed to do nothing less than turn her into a walking rainbow—or a good advertisement of her own wares. And when she spoke, she had a strange accent that Krysty couldn't place.

"How did you come to be here?" Krysty asked her as they moved bales of cloth.

"I trade and I travel." The woman shrugged. "I traverse the seas in boats that are almost sinking… Many the time I could have been chilled, never to see dry land once more. But the fates, they look after me, more than so many others. So I land, and I travel once more, buy and sell, buy and sell. Then I come here with traders and Ethan makes me offer."

"Which was? I mean, it must have been something to stop you after all that travel," Krysty asked, trying to draw the woman out.

"The journeys, they become all as one after a while. Mebbe is time for a change. Mebbe time to stay, make roots. And why not here? Ethan tells me…" She paused, weighing her words. "Well, he give me chance to build finest stock of cloth in the land. Make the best trade. Become first in this, as in all else. This ville become rich, and get richer. Has something few others have."

"What's that?" Krysty tried to make it seem an offhand question, but her curiosity was definitely piqued.

Angelika smiled. "Ambition. Old word. And something—shit, what is word…" She clicked her fingers impatiently. "Ah, unique. Yes, that is it—unique."

Krysty frowned. She wasn't getting the whole story. But before she had a chance to frame a further question, Angelika hurried her with a little gesture.

"Now come, we still have much to do, not to gossip around fire like old women in the evening."

"Is this all you do? Sit around?" Jak was bored. If he was in the middle of stalking prey, he could stay silent and still for hours. But this was intolerable: inaction born of inertia.

"We don't always hunt. It's not that kind of ville. So why don't you just kick back and go with it, Whitey? Fretting about it ain't gonna make things any different." Jonno crossed his fat legs and propped them on the table. He smiled, his scarred face seemingly smug. Complacent and lazy. Jak's dislike of him was even more pronounced than before.

Jak had been given a bed in the fat man's house and had been assigned to learn more about the hunters in Pleasantville. There was no way he was going to learn anything at the moment, as it seemed that they weren't in a hunting mood. There was one thing that made him curious, however. He had believed that the fat man was actually sec rather than hunter, as he had been with the party that had captured them—Jak looked upon it as that, seeing they had been given little choice in their actions—and had answered to Horse, the sec chief. Hunting and working sec were different tasks, and to see a ville working the two in tandem was unusual. It set some alarm bells ringing in the albino's head.

Jak paced up and down the small room, looking out the window at the activity in the street. The air of torpor that permeated the fat man's living quarters was driving him mad. The street outside looked rich: there was a lot of jack, a lot of trade. Also a fairly large population, big enough to require a good quantity of game to support their appetites. Okay, so they made a lot out of their trading. The scrublands around that housed the farms couldn't keep this ville fed, and they had to get through a lot of game, even if they traded foodstuffs. So why weren't they hunting?

"You wondering why we're not out there chasing some mutie skunk to skin it and cook it?" Jonno asked. Jak turned and shot him a sharp glance. Was he some kind of mutie with a sense that could see what he was thinking? The fat man caught the glance and held up his hands. "Hey, ain't that what you and your weirdo friends do to get by out there?"

Jak relaxed. The man was just setting him up for another insult. That he could deal with.

"So when you hunt? Plenty mouths feed, not much work done," Jak replied, ignoring the gibe in the fat man's comments.

Jonno smiled. It was the face only, the eyes remaining dead, scanning Jak to try to get some response from him. "Oh, there's plenty of work gets done, but only when the time is right. You know what I mean?"

"Seasons for game around here? And you hunt then, keep meat preserved?" Jak asked, knowing that wasn't the answer, but trying, in his turn, to lead the fat man on.

Jonno grinned, flicked his tongue over his teeth, relishing some memory that he didn't want to share. "Yeah," he said slowly, "I guess you could say that. A season...a time when it's right and when the stakes are high. Then the hunting begins. And it keeps us fed for a whole lot longer than you'd think."

He laughed. It was low, lascivious and filled with a lust for blood. But not in the sense of being a hunter: Jak had heard that sound before, from the sick and twisted evil they had encountered on their journeys.

Whatever was hunted around Pleasantville, Jak was pretty sure it wasn't game for food.

RYAN CROUCHED, his body leaning slightly forward, weight balanced on the balls of his feet, rocking gently. In one hand he held his panga, the other was free, palm flat, to act as balance. He circled the sec chief, who was just out of arm's reach, also crouching and circling. The ghost of a smile played at the corners of the dark man's mouth, his dreadlocks swaying in rhythm to his body movement.

Suddenly, with the speed of a snake, the sec chief thrust himself forward, his arm twisting so that his knife traveled in a corkscrew movement toward the one-eyed man's gut. Ryan shifted his weight and pulled back, narrowly avoiding the corkscrew motion as he just went beyond reach. At the same time, he brought his empty hand down, the edge of his palm striking just below the elbow, deadening a nerve. The barest grimace crossed Horse's impassive visage as the knife dropped from fingers now nerveless and numb, all feeling killed by the blow. Before he had a chance to recover and use his other arm, Ryan had stepped beneath his guard and had the panga on an upward swing, the lethal blade arcing toward the sec chief's jugular.

Horse brought his free arm up to grab at Ryan's hair and neck, but he knew that it was too little, too late. The blade stopped within a hairbreadth of his neck, the rapid ascent suddenly halted by Ryan's rock-steady arm. The sec chief could feel the rush of air on his throat, could almost taste the cold metal in the fear in his mouth.

Ryan's gritted teeth grinned mirthlessly. "You're not bad, but you've been out of practice. I figure you would have been faster if you hadn't spent so long out of combat."

The one-eyed man dropped the blade and stepped back out of the sec chief's grasp.

Horse exhaled a long breath that said plenty. "Fuck, fuck, fuck," he swore softly, before raising his voice to a normal level. "Shit, Ryan, it doesn't look good for you to do this to me in front of these guys, but it's a good thing. A reminder that we're slack."

Ryan shrugged. "You can't keep a hundred percent if there's no one to fight. It's the old problem. Training only gets you so far—unless you're willing to go the whole way and risk losing men by keeping it real. And that's just stupe. We've had a lot of travels and met a lot of fuckers who'd see us buy the farm. You've got your land so well sewn up that you don't get challenged."

"Yeah, but how do you keep a sec force up to the task if they don't get the chance to fight? Answer me that?"

Ryan shook his head. "Wish I could."

The two men had been talking as though they were alone. In fact, they were being watched by a number of Horse's select sec guard in charge of outlying patrols around the baron's territory. Ethan knew the problem the sec chief faced with no real combat for his men, and also that Horse would welcome input from Ryan, who the sec chief had singled out for attention in his discussions with his baron. So it had been obvious that Ethan would send Ryan to Horse's hospitality.

The first thing the sec chief did was to arrange close-combat practice. The men carried this out, watched by Ryan and Horse. The two men had then staged this little display for the watching guard.

"Okay, men, break now. Take a drink, loosen up. We hike after the sun reaches its height," the sec chief called before leading Ryan toward his shack.

As they walked, Ryan raised a matter that had been giving him some pause for thought. "You probably won't want to answer this, but I've got to ask. Pleasantville is a rich ville, right? And yet you don't seem to get attacked or put under threat from any barons that are either around here or hear about you from traders. I rode convoys, I know how they talk."

Horse paused before answering. "Let me answer you like this. If you were supplying something that no one else could, and if you were wiped out and that would disappear, then wouldn't that give you a kind of security? Make you...I dunno, kind of exclusive?"

"Sure, but what could be that special?"

Horse frowned. "I'm gonna have to stop at that. Ethan will tell you when he's ready. But I like you, Ryan Cawdor, and even saying this much could get me chilled, but keep up your guard, Ryan, and remember that whatever happens, I may not want to have any part of it."

The sec chief strode off, leaving Ryan in his wake. The one-eyed man watched him go, every nerve ending straining with the sense of danger that now coursed through his veins.

"PLEASE, YOU MUST make yourself at home and examine what you will. I have work to do. You're perfectly welcome to join me if you wish."

Bones polished his thick-lensed spectacles and put them back on his nose, peering through them owlishly. He was sitting across the table from Doc Tanner. The table was covered in papers, both printed and handwritten, covered in stains from the strange coffee-type barley brew that the wizened man seemed to exist upon. He had hardly spoken to Doc since the old man had arrived, merely to point out the facilities and where Doc would sleep. He had been engrossed in a series of old manuals, trying to make an old comp work. He had still been working when Doc retired for the night, after examining the contents of several bookcases.

This was their first chance to talk and Doc was determined to make the most of it.

"Tell me, before you become engrossed in your mission, how did you end up becoming the keeper of such a magnificent archive?"

Bones allowed himself a small smirk, taking this as a compliment. "I've always been the one who was interested in the past. I suppose it was because I was quite a weak, ill child, and when we all used to go into the old city, I'd always come back with something about the past. It was just something I did. To be honest with you, I don't know how I survived. Must be hardier than I thought. But when I grew up, and we started to fence off the ville, and less and less people plundered the remains, I would still go, even though I wasn't supposed to. I was useful for working with traders, as I have a better brain for jack and trade than anyone else I've ever met—that's not an idle boast, just an observation. And a truism—it kept me alive, as I would have been a liability otherwise. Physical endeavor isn't my suit, and this made me valuable to past barons."

"And Ethan?" Doc interjected, a little bewildered at the torrent of words that spewed forth from Bones.

"Ethan is different. A planner and a dreamer, but also a pragmatist. He knew I was getting old and, although my brain is still sharp, my eyes weren't at their best anymore. I looked too vulnerable to outside traders. So I trained my successors and he told me to build this archive, to use what I had spent my life amassing as a pleasure. He has plans, you see, and some of them he has been able to put into operation. He is what the old books call an entrepreneur. A unique service, and a unique way to show people what it is, using the old tech that I can use for him. He's quite a man."

"I am sure," Doc murmured, beset by qualms that he couldn't quite pin down.

"Now, if you'll excuse me, I must be getting on with this," Bones said, rising to his feet. "Please, avail yourself of anything here."

"I will," Doc promised. "It has been a long time since I have been able to glory in books."

Bones returned Doc's smile with a genuine pleasure. He was sure he had found a kindred spirit in the old man.

Perhaps... Doc was cautious. He waited sometime, leafing through a couple of old books, before he went over to the wall of videotapes. He read the spidery writing on the labels with care, selecting one that seemed to be recently recorded. He went to the doorway and checked to ensure that Bones was ensconced in a far room. He was running an old tape machine from the mains. A generator outside powered electricity for his work, and Doc idly wondered how much wag fuel he used, and how important Ethan considered his work to allow such a usage.

Discordant music came from the tape machine, and a man with an English accent Doc recognized from his own past was yelling over the music. Something about "please don't take me to the sanatorium..." Doc shivered. This was a sanatorium of sorts, if his suspicions were correct.

Seeing that Bones was immersed in his work, Doc turned and strode across the room to one of the video machines that was connected to an old television set. He tried to put the tape in, but found one already in the machine. Taking it out, he saw that it was, if the title was anything to go by, a pornographic tape. No wonder the old man's sight was so bad, he chuckled to himself.

But the laughter stopped when he placed the tape in the machine, clicked on the TV set and let the video run, being careful to turn down the sound lest Bones should hear what was happening.

As the action unfolded on the screen in a blur of color and motion, Doc realized what this unique service was, and why Ethan would record it to show to visiting traders and barons.

It was violent, nasty and could have only one possible outcome. It couldn't be staged often, but it could command big jack for the ville.

And Doc Tanner had the nastiest feeling that he and his companions were being lined up for Ethan's next big payday.

THEY HAD AGREED to meet as soon as possible to discuss whatever they had learned. But that wasn't to be as easy as they had hoped. The people with whom they had been billeted were keeping a close eye on their activities.

Doc was bursting to tell the others about what he had discovered, but whenever he tried to leave the house, Bones would emerge from his self-imposed exile with his old tech and always have something he wanted to discuss, some ancient tome on which he wished to elicit Doc's opinion.

Ryan found that the sec training would suddenly expand if he wanted to get away; Jak found himself on a hunt when Jonno found him attempting to make his way toward the sec camp. Krysty had to suddenly assist Angelika whenever it seemed downtime would allow her to get away; J.B. found that Scar would find

some piece of his armory that—surprisingly for such an
egotistical man—he would want J.B.'s advice on, mys-
teriously realizing that he'd had this blaster for a while
but still wasn't sure about some of the attachments that
he'd bought in the same consignment.

Distracting the companions had been accomplished
so subtly that the friends only realized in hindsight what
had been happening.

Except for Mildred. It seemed that Michaela, who had
taken a liking to the medic, had found it hard to lie to her.
There was little illness in Pleasantville, thus it took only
a short while to deal with the patients at the hospital.

Mildred sighed as she stripped off the white gown
that Michaela had given her, to match her own.

"I can't remember the last time I wore whites," she
said, placing the gown in a dump bin to be washed.

"Wherever it was, it must have been somewhere that
was able to raid an old city, right?" the healer questioned, her curiosity piqued.

"Something like that," Mildred replied offhand, reminding herself to watch her words—she didn't want
to have to explain too much unless it was necessary. Especially as it would be bound to get back to Ethan and
stir up his curiosity about them even more than it already seemed.

"No, but really, you must have seen a whole load of
really odd stuff out there. I mean, you've traveled. I've
never been more than a day's ride from this ville all my
life. Like being in a cage, really…" Her voice took on
a wistful edge. "I mean, we only really know what's
going on from convoys and hunting parties, and they
might not be telling the truth, might they?"

"Why wouldn't they?" Mildred questioned. The use of the phrase "hunting parties" made her feel uneasy. There wasn't enough wildlife around here to support regular hunts from the ville, let alone any outsiders, but she felt she should play it slow.

Michaela shrugged, gave a vaguely embarrassed grin, as though she knew she had let something slip that she shouldn't. "I dunno, really. It's just that they don't have to be honest, do they? Mebbe there's something out there that would stop us giving them… Well, they wouldn't get what they want," she finished, confused, embarrassed even more, and aware that she was encroaching on dangerous territory.

Mildred came over to the young healer, took her hand and fixed her with an intent stare. "Hey, listen to me. If there's something going on here that I should know about, something that you're not so happy with to judge from what you've just said, then maybe you should talk to me about it. If it's something that puts me and my friends in the firing line, then we deserve to know. You save lives. That means that you feel a certain way about people," she continued, choosing to ignore the fact that she saved lives, as well, but would equally take them if necessary. That was different: that was pragmatism. She continued. "You said something about a hunt, honey. What is there to hunt around here?"

Michaela pulled away, refusing to meet Mildred's gaze. "No, I've already said far too much. I shouldn't have… Where are you going?"

Mildred had turned her back and was walking toward the door that led to the street. "I'm going to find Ryan, maybe the others. I think it's about time we got the hell out of here."

"No!" Michaela chased her, grabbed her by the arm, almost pulling her back. "That would be the worst thing you could do. You wouldn't get more than a couple of miles."

"Then what is it, child? Tell me," Mildred implored, taking the young woman by the shoulders.

Michaela refused to meet her eyes. "I can't. I've told you too much already, without even meaning to... Look, all I know is that we're not supposed to let you all get together and talk until we've found out about you and told Ethan about it."

"You're supposed to spy on us?"

Michaela nodded.

"Then what does Ethan want to know about us? Why?"

"He likes to collect knowledge. He says it's powerful, more so than jack. And he thinks you'd be good material."

"For what?"

Michaela refused to look Mildred in the eye. When she spoke, it was almost a whisper. "For the hunt..."

Mildred let her go, stepped back. Every gut feeling had been telling her this, but now it was confirmed. "He wants to hunt us?"

"Not him, and not exactly hunting you. It's how we live so well. He sells the hunt to other barons for big jack. They watch or take part, depending on what they want. And every hunt is different, no two the same. He uses this word he got from an old book. Com... Com something..."

"Commodity," Mildred whispered. "A unique commodity."

J. B. DIX WAS BORED—bored to tears with hearing about the armory and about Scar, and about how good Scar was at keeping the armory. He had never before thought that he could get bored with inventory, the care, upkeep and use of...but Scar had taken him places he thought he could never go.

He'd had enough. These past few hours had been excruciating. Nothing could ever be this bad again, not being covered in syrup and left to the mercy of razorjawed mutie ants, not being submerged in a sea of slavering stickies, not anything...any or all of it would be preferable to having to listen to this stupe bastard babble on and on and on...

The big man was rambling about an M-16 that he'd recently acquired, and how bad a state it had been in, and what he'd had to do to clean it up. "I'll show you what I mean," he added at the end of his monologue, disappearing into the back room of the armory building to hunt it down from his workroom, where he modified and cleaned inventory.

This was J.B.'s chance. While Scar was out of sight and earshot, he could slip away. He wanted to find out what information, if any, his companions had gleaned during the day. He could report nothing, except how boring Scar could be, but the others may have some information.

J.B. slipped out of the building and hurried across the

impound that housed the target range. He was past the main gate and into the ville before Scar had even found the M-16 in his junkpile workroom.

The Armorer knew where the others were billeted, and decided to try to find Mildred first. The hospital was in an easterly direction and he walked that way, scanning the busy streets. He didn't want to call attention to himself by asking directions, so he walked in silence. The farther he went, the more every nerve ending screamed that he was being followed.

Shit—he knew that Scar would be looking for him by now, but this felt like more than that. As all the companions, he'd seen so much danger that the signs affected him on instinct, without his being able to rationalize how he could feel like this.

An alleyway. J.B. changed direction suddenly and ducked into the fortuitous cover, making for the far end. He scanned the side for anything that would provide a hiding place from which he could observe his pursuers. There was nothing.

And now there were two men at the far end of the alley. J.B. recognized one of them as a sec man who had been in the party that had bought them here. He turned and could see two more entering the alley behind him.

Four to one. Not good odds. Even less so as he only had his Tekna, and they had knives and chains, with blasters at their hips and shoulders.

J.B. unsheathed the knife. He was ready for attack.

But he wasn't ready for what happened next. One of the sec men took an airgun from one of his holsters, leveled it and fired. J.B. tried to move out of the trajectory, but the alley was too narrow. The sec man had aimed a body shot and J.B.'s surprise had made him too slow. A dart pierced his clothing, puncturing the skin. He looked down to see that it was a cylindrical dart with a flight on the end. He felt a hot shiver as something entered his bloodstream. Then nothing.

He looked up, Tekna still in his hand. To his astonishment, the sec men had vanished from each end of the alleyway.

He was alone. Alone with the dart he plucked from his skin and clothing.

What the hell was that about?

Chapter Six

The Armorer came out of the alleyway, looking around cautiously. There was no sign of the sec men who had trailed him, neither was there any indication that anyone on the main street had noticed what was going on. Everything seemed to be as normal, as if nothing had happened.

But what had happened? J.B. rubbed thoughtfully at the area where the dart had pierced cloth and skin. It tingled, a very slight pain where the skin had been broken. And there had been that warm feeling where something had entered his bloodstream. But what?

It was more of an imperative than ever that he get to Mildred, let her take a look at him. Then gather the others. Before, it had been to share intelligence. Now it could be much more serious. It occurred to him that if the sec men had been following him, then it was possible that Scar Longthorne had deliberately given him space to make a run, leaving him out in the open for the sec men. Thoughts whirled around J.B.'s brain as he searched out the hospital. Why was he the one who had been selected? Or was it possible that this was happening to all the others? Had they all been targeted in this manner? And what was the point? Ethan had them at his mercy in many ways, having separated them. Why not just attack them all when they were together rather than have them stalked like wild animals when they made a run?

Shit, there was a kind of logic here that would make sense if they knew Ethan's purpose. But until then, it was a complete mystery. Perhaps the others would be able to come up with some answers, mebbe they'd found out something else...

The ville was still unfamiliar, and J.B. felt hot. It seemed such an effort to try to find the hospital. He looked up at the sky above, squinting through his spectacles at the sun, which was on the wane. It shouldn't be this hot, still... Alarm bells began to ring in his head. This wasn't a natural kind of heat. The sooner he got to Millie, the better...

BUT MILDRED WYETH had left the hospital. She hadn't wanted to hang around after hearing what Michaela had had to say to her. Like J.B., she'd felt a pressing need to consult with the others, to form a plan. They had been forced into a backs-to-the-wall situation without even being aware of it, and it was now time to reunite.

"The hell with this," she'd said to the small healer. "I know you're supposed to keep me here, and I like you, but don't try to stop me." Mildred had glared at the girl. Michaela had backed off; there was something about Mildred's body language that bespoke of an ability to forget she was a healer and to become a hurter.

"The baron has sec men watching all the buildings where you are, do you realize that?" she'd said in a small voice—partly from fear and partly from a desire to avoid being overheard. "You didn't hear that from me."

Mildred's demeanor had softened a little as she'd noticed how scared the girl was and how much it had taken her to speak those words. "Okay. I guess you need to be careful, too. This'll get you out of trouble," she'd said, stepping forward quickly and hitting the girl on the side of the neck with a straight-handed blow learned from the martial arts she'd studied a little of back in the days when she had been young and the world had made sense...of a kind.

Michaela's expression had held a sudden mixture of shock and hurt, passing over in a fraction of a second before she'd fallen to the floor, unconscious. Mildred hadn't wanted to hurt the girl, but at least she could claim she had been overpowered if Mildred was caught. If? Chances were that she would be, but what the hell.

Mildred had left the building in plain sight, not bothering to hide. If there were sec men waiting for her, she was prepared to stand and fight if that as what they wanted. But she suspected that they had a more devious game afoot.

Unbeknownst to her, her thoughts echoed those of a disoriented J.B. as he searched for the hospital. The world was beginning to look as though he were seeing it through a distant heat haze. What the hell was in that damned dart? Dark night, but he needed to find Millie, and quick. It was now obvious that there had been some kind of trank in that dart. Millie might be able to help him, but only if he could stay on his damned feet until he found her.

The hospital came into view. He began to move toward it, feeling as if he were wading in quicksand. The faster he tried to move, the slower he seemed to progress. Finally, after what seemed to be an eternity, he reached the door and crashed into the frame. There, on the floor, he could see a short woman with spiky hair, lying unconscious.

There was no sign of Millie. He leaned heavily on a bench, gasping for breath and cursing to himself.

What the hell had happened to her?

MILDRED WYETH HAD ONLY one thing on her mind: find Ryan, then round up the others. She knew that the one-eyed man had been billeted with Horse and so headed for the sec compound. As she approached, keeping an eye out for any pursuers, she could see the dreadlocked sec chief walking away from Ryan, who was obviously lost in thought about whatever exchange had just taken place.

Mildred looked around. If she was being followed, then the sec orders were to trail her and not to stop her. Which meant that Ethan wanted to see what they would do. Okay, let the bastard play his games for now. It crossed her mind that she preferred barons who liked to flaunt their power in strong-arm tactics. At least you knew exactly where you were with them and didn't have to play ridiculous paranoid mind games, which is how she felt right now.

Ryan was about to turn away to walk from the sec chief's shack when he caught sight of Mildred, running toward the wire that encircled the compound. Her face was set and grim.

Somehow, Ryan had been expecting to see one of the companions like this, and he felt a weight lift from him. The balance had been tipped from reacting to what was around them into acting. Now the first move was made and they could try to set the pace.

Ryan jogged over to meet her. "What's going on?"

Mildred told him all that she had learned from the healer, and how she had left her. She also outlined her suspicions about being followed. Ryan cast his eye over the territory at her back. There were no signs of any sec men, just the residents of Pleasantville going about their business. But he didn't doubt her judgment.

"Fireblast, I'm sick of waiting for something to happen." His voice gritted. "Let's get the others rounded up."

Without pause, the one-eyed man started to scale the wire. If he used the main gate, he may have to try to explain himself to the sec guards, maybe even take them out. This would be quicker, as the wire around the compound was a purely visual barrier, being only ten feet high. He flipped over the top and landed next to Mildred.

"Right, we should stick together now," he said.

"No complaints from me on that score," Mildred agreed. "Who're we going to pick up first?"

Ryan grinned. "Jak would want to hear all this, don't you think?"

JAK LAUREN LOOKED out the window at Jonno's house, feeling bored but still wired, like a coiled spring waiting to explode into action. All his instincts screamed that danger was imminent. The small signs in Jonno's actions and attitudes toward him spoke of a man who was biding his time before going in for the kill.

The fat man was in his kitchen area, frying cured

pork. He seemed to spend most of his time in the house in the kitchen, which explained his huge gut. He was singing—tunelessly—an interminable song about a gaudy house with mutie sluts who could do impossible things. Jak doubted if the fat man ever got to do what he was singing about. The song was about as close as he would get.

But at least he wasn't on Jak's back, taunting him. It was almost as if he wanted to goad him into action. No chance. Jak had more patience than the fat man could ever imagine. It was on that thought that Jak caught sight of Ryan and Millie moving toward the house. They weren't bothering to be cautious and were moving quite openly.

Something had happened. It had to be. No need for caution, then. Jak allowed himself a small smile and moved toward the kitchen. He was so quiet—and the fat man so absorbed in his food—that Jonno didn't hear Jak pick up the skillet. He probably didn't even feel it hit him on the side of the head. He just knew oblivion.

Time for Jak to join his companions.

KRYSTY WAS BORED out of her skull. She had cut, stored and sold cloth until she never wanted to see another roll of material again. The smell from the dye pots at the rear of Angelika's house-cum-warehouse, where she added her own touches to the bales that were brought from traders or woven in Pleasantville, was beginning to catch at the back of the Titian-haired woman's throat, making her want to gag anytime she went near the back of the building. As if this weren't bad enough, she had been unable to find out anything about the real business of the baron, the multicolored merchant staying firmly silent on that point.

She was supposed to be cutting enough material for a dress. Instead, she was looking out the window. She had to blink when she saw Ryan, Jak and Mildred coming toward the house without taking any precautions to disguise their movements.

"Krysty, are you finished with the cutting yet? I have dye pots to empty, and they're too heavy for one," Angelika said as she came into the room. She stopped when she saw Krysty gaping openmouthed out the window. "What is this that is happening?" she asked, coming over to look. She, too, stopped dead when she saw the trio approach. She looked at Krysty. It was a look that asked what were they doing out in the open like that and what was Krysty going to do when she was supposed to stay here?

Krysty shrugged and answered in the only available eloquent manner. She hit Angelika on the point of her jaw with one well-judged punch, rendering her unconscious. Then she ran back to her room, grabbed her weapons and made for the door.

"What in the name of Gaia is going on?" she asked in a bewildered tone as she left the house. "Shouldn't we be playing it triple-red?"

"Mebbe it's not the time for that," Ryan answered. "Mebbe this is the time to goad Ethan into showing his hand. Have you got your blaster?"

Krysty nodded. "You guys?"

Mildred smiled thinly. "Yeah. Guess we always remember that... all of us," she added, not knowing that the Armorer was at large with only his Tekna, having had no opportunity to take his own weapons from the Pleasantville armory before making his break. "And then there were two," she said to Ryan. "Who's next?"

"Doc's nearer than J.B., so I guess he should be our next pickup," the one-eyed man replied. "Let's get him."

DOC TANNER TOOK the tape out of the old video player, slid it into its case and placed it back on the shelf from where he had taken it. He felt sick at what he had seen, and even sicker at what he suspected Ethan had in store for the companions.

"Oh, dear, I do wish you hadn't done that. I may have been able to persuade Ethan that you were too old to take part and that you would be better off here, helping me with the research. Now, I fear I shall have to report you to Horse, and the whole matter will be out of my hands."

Doc turned at the sound of Bones's voice. The bespectacled man was standing in the doorway, still holding the screwdriver and soldering iron with which he had been working on the old comp.

"You knew I would be curious, of course," Doc stated calmly, keeping an eye on the still hot soldering iron. If he had to get past Bones to make a run for it, the iron was the thing he would fear most.

Bones shrugged. "I would have been disappointed if you had been anything but. It's a shame, as I truly thought I had found someone whose thirst for knowledge would keep me company in the years I have left to me. A companion to accompany me on my way. I've never met anyone like you—someone who has the same thirst."

"Same thirst?" Doc questioned, suddenly enraged. "Thirst for what? For the blood that you record on the machines you restore? The senseless slaughter?"

"And are you so innocent?" Bones fired the question back. "You are so without blame, without any stains? You have never killed?"

"Of course I have. We all have. That is the way of things, the way of survival. If there were another way, then it would be different."

"And you think it is gratuitous for us?"

"That is necessary?" Doc asked, flinging an arm out to indicate the videos.

Bones's gaze followed Doc's arm to the racks of videotape. "For survival, as a means of making—"

The sentence was cut short. Doc had deliberately sought to divert the bespectacled man's gaze away from his person and toward the tapes. Figuring that the man's eyesight was so poor that his peripheral vision would be less than zero, Doc had wanted to distract him for long enough to act. So as soon as Bones looked away, Doc seized his swordstick from where it stood against the table and tossed it in the air so that he had hold of the bottom. Swinging it in an arc, the silver lion's head crashed against the side of Bones's head, cracking with a sickening thud against his temple.

The weight of the cane's end was enough to make the blow a telling one. There was no chance for Bones to finish the sentence as consciousness left him. He hit the floor with a thud.

"Oh, dear, I do hope that wasn't too hard," Doc said to himself as he stepped over the prone man. He felt for a pulse. When he found it, he was relieved to find that it was still strong. For, despite his revulsion and the protest he had made, he could in some degree see that Bones was a prisoner of circumstance, especially considering his age and eyesight problem. Would another baron other than Ethan have been so generous?

Still, no matter, it was time for Doc to find Ryan and to round up the others. With a sense of urgency he made his way to the front of the house, making sure he had his LeMat loaded, just in case there were sec men on guard.

The last thing he expected to see, as he opened the door, was the sight that greeted him: Ryan, Jak, Krysty and Mildred coming toward him, with no pretense at stealth.

J.B. FELT SICK. Sick like he was going to puke violently, and sick like he had nothing left in this spinning world that just wouldn't stop moving around him. If it did, just for a moment, he may be able to pull some kind of coherent thought together to work out what the hell he should do next.

Dark night, if only the world would stay still... But if it wasn't going to, then there was little he could do about it except try to make the best of it.

Feeling as if he were going to burn up, J.B. made his way to the door of the hospital. Behind him, on the floor, he could hear Michaela whimper as she began to regain consciousness. She wouldn't be in any fit state to stop him, no matter how weak he felt, so he left her and concentrated on making his way outside. He was acutely aware that he had to look conspicuous, as he was having trouble staying upright or walking in a straight line, but there was nothing he could do about that. He felt as if he were burning up, but there was nothing he could do about that, either. The only thing he could do was try to reach Ryan. Mebbe Millie had gone there. Mebbe the others were trying to link up right now. Mebbe...

The Armorer was aware of the stares he was getting as he staggered down the street. He was also aware of the bizarre fact that no one seemed to be willing to help or to intervene in any way. They were just watching him, as though they had been expecting this.

Had they?

THE FIVE COMPANIONS were headed for the armory when they became aware of a disturbance back on the main street.

"Hold it," Ryan said softly. "Mebbe Ethan's got the sec finally ready to round us up."

"So why haven't they stopped us before now?" Krysty asked. "It's all been a bit too simple, right?"

"Yeah," Mildred stated coldly. "It's like we're rats in a maze." Ryan looked at her questioningly and she shrugged. "Something they used to do in the old days, see how they'd react. I'll explain it sometime. Point is, I feel that's what Ethan's doing...seeing how we'll react."

Ryan agreed. "Whatever, we need to pick up J.B. Jak, make a quick recce of the main street, check out if that's something we should be avoiding before we carry on."

The albino nodded and was gone. The remaining companions took cover and awaited Jak's return. He wasn't long in coming, and he looked even more grim than usual.

"No need look J.B., found him," he said briefly, indicating the main street. "And he not looking good. Come…"

They followed Jak out onto the main street, where they came across a scene that was bizarre in its incongruity. While the crowds went about their everyday business, a small phalanx had formed around J.B., watching him as he attempted to make his way toward the sec camp, struggling with every step. They were watching with curiosity, but making no attempt to intervene or to help.

"What the fuck—" Ryan whispered.

"John! What's wrong?" Mildred yelled, cutting a swathe through the crowd to reach J.B.'s side.

The Armorer looked up at her as he stumbled and fell to his knees. He felt her strong grip take him by the elbow, stopping him from pitching face-forward onto the road. She was appalled to see how pale he was, sweat spangling his brow and running in rivulets down his sallow cheeks. His eyes were pinprick pupils that were struggling to focus.

"Millie…been looking for you…tried to get away from Scar, reach rest of you…chased by sec men… weird thing is, just shot me with a dart…don't know what that was about…" He laughed feebly and shook his head.

Mildred inhaled deeply. She knew what it was about. A dart could carry a culture that would infect J.B. And there were plenty of disease cultures hanging around Pleasantville, pillaged from the remains of the city beyond. That much she knew from what Michaela had shown her.

The others had joined them, the watching crowd dissipating at their arrival. Rapidly, Mildred relayed what the Armorer had just told her and also her suspicions of what had been in the dart.

"What the hell is the point of that?" Ryan snapped.

Mildred shrugged, but Doc looked thoughtful. "I fear I may have an answer," he said slowly. "I suspect that, if I am correct, this would be an action that could qualify as, shall we say, an enticement."

Mildred bit back her inclination to ask Doc to stop pussyfooting and spit it out. That would take longer than letting him get to the point in his own way.

"Why would that be necessary?" Krysty asked gently.

Doc looked at her with disarmingly clear and innocent eyes. "My dear girl, if you had seen what I had seen…why I was endeavoring to join you when… But no, I must try to put this concisely." Doc paused briefly and took a breath. "There is a whole wall of old videotape in the house where I was staying. Curious to find out more, I watched one when I myself was not being watched. The business of this ville, on which their wealth is based, is the staging of hunts for those who can afford to pay—in jack or trade, I assume—in which humans are the prey. I fear that is why Ethan is so interested in us. He sees us as a big attraction, to bring in a lot of jack. And what if we should refuse? He can chill us, but what would that profit him? No, he could make us do it if there was an enticement…such as needing to save the life of one of our own, perhaps."

Ryan had been listening intently to the old man's words. "That makes sense, all right. Too much sense." He fell silent for a moment, then said, "Mildred, do you reckon that you could find out what they've injected into J.B.?"

"If we take him back to the hospital and I take a blood sample. And if it was among the cultures that Michaela showed to me. If I was Ethan, I'd be pretty stupid to let her show me everything."

"Yeah, but mebbe he's underestimated her. Krysty, Doc, you help Mildred take J.B. back to the hospital. Jak, you and me have something to attend to."

While Doc assisted Mildred in helping the stricken Armorer to his feet, and in supporting him, Ryan gestured to Jak. The two friends began to stride purposefully toward the baron's palace.

Krysty watched them go. "There's something odd about this," she said quietly to the others as they began to move J.B. toward the hospital. "Why isn't anyone trying to stop us?"

Mildred and Doc paused, taking in the fact that very few of the passersby were so much as watching them let alone trying to stop them from acting.

"I've got a nasty feeling that this is more complex than we know," Mildred muttered, "but we can worry about that later. First thing is to get J.B. somewhere where I can take a good look at what's wrong with him."

RYAN AND JAK approached the baron's palace, with its maze of corridors linking buildings together, without bothering to disguise their intent. It was obvious that they were being manipulated—or, at least, that Ethan was attempting such—so there was nothing to lose from direct action.

"How take this?" Jak asked.

Ryan shrugged. "I figure the bastard's watching us, waiting. Mebbe he won't expect us to just charge in. If he thinks we're smart, he'll expect us to be cautious. Fuck that, let's hit him before he has a chance to get his sec men on us. No blasters. Let's try to keep it as quiet as possible."

Jak agreed. That would suit him fine.

The corridors and covered walkways that linked the buildings of the baronial palace had doors interspersed at irregular intervals, allowing access to and from the palace. As with their prior journey along the corridors, there were no sec men standing guard. Entry would be simple. Once inside, the problems would begin. First, sec men had to be patrolling the corridors. Second, and perhaps more importantly, how to find their way? All Ryan could recall from their previous visit was how confusing the profusion of corridors had become.

Worry about that later... They reached one of the doors, tried it and found it unlocked. They passed into the corridor with no problems.

"Which way?" Jak asked.

Ryan sighed. "Shit, I can't..."

Jak allowed a small vulpine grin to cross his face. "Kidding, Ryan. Follow me."

Ryan let the albino set off to the left, and followed a pace behind, moving triple-fast. He should have known that Jak's hunter-predator instincts had made him take careful note of the baronial palace that first visit. It was almost as if he'd known it may be useful.

They had moved across two corridors, Jak pausing only to check the layout ahead with the plan in his mind's eye before choosing a direction, when they came across their first sec opposition.

Two men, both heavily built and carrying blasters that looked like H&Ks, were standing talking by a door into one set of buildings. They'd been immersed in their conversation and obviously not expecting to be disturbed. At the sound of running feet approaching, they both turned. The man on the left—a rampant jackal tattooed down one arm—stared openmouthed. The sec man on the right was quicker to react. He raised his weapon.

Jak launched himself forward, thigh and calf muscles straining, into a roll. He came up only a few feet in front of the startled sec man, who was now unsure which of the approaching fighters to aim at. The distance Jak had put between himself and Ryan made a cluster shot impossible. That hesitation would cost the sec man his life. As he stood openmouthed, vacillating, Jak's hand shot out, fingers rigid, jabbing the sec man's windpipe, the cartilage crushed by the force and hardness of the bony fingers. His eyes popped out of his skull as he suddenly found it impossible to breathe, and his fingers, now nerveless, dropped the blaster. Before it had a chance to clatter to the floor, Jak followed the blow with one to the sec man's groin, delivered with his knee. The albino's adversary doubled over, hands dropping to protect his injured groin, pain flaring hot through his lower body to join the agony in his throat.

It left him exposed. Jak took his head between his slim, steel-strong hands, twisting on the muscular neck until the top of the man's spine snapped.

All the while, the albino ignored the other sec man, trusting Ryan to handle him. And the one-eyed warrior had little problem in so doing. Seeing that the sec man who posed a danger was being dealt with, Ryan pulled his panga from the sheath along his thigh, bringing it up with the blade balanced in his hand.

The tattooed sec man was still slack-jawed, but he was showing signs of awakening into action. Almost in slow motion, he began to raise his SMG into firing position. Without slowing, and without breaking stride, Ryan drew back his arm and threw the panga. His aim was swift and true. Before the blaster was leveled at him, and before such an action covered the target area, the panga had cleaved into the chest of the sec man, who looked down with a startled expression at the protruding blade. He coughed and blood bubbled on his lips, dribbled down his chin. As he looked at Ryan again, making a feeble and hopeless attempt to squeeze the trigger of his SMG with fingers that would no longer respond, the light dulled in his eyes and he toppled to his knees. Falling forward, he pitched onto the hilt of the panga as it struck the floor, driving it farther into his chest.

Ryan reached the doors and turned the man onto his back, sightless eyes staring up at him.

"Fireblast, why couldn't the bastard have fallen backward," he grunted as he planted one combat boot on the man's chest to hold him down as he pulled the panga free. It took a mighty heave and the panga slid free, slick with arterial blood, which the one-eyed man wiped clean on the sec man's clothes before sheathing the blade.

"Nearly there," Jak said, indicating the doors. "Next corridor, should be white doors."

"Let's hope we don't have to chill any more of these bastards before we get there. It's taking too much time," Ryan commented. "And that's something J.B. hasn't got."

"LAY HIM DOWN gently," Mildred said as they carried J.B. to a bed. They had made the journey unhindered, but none could shake the feeling that they were being watched. It was unnerving, uncomfortable, and made them each wonder what Ethan's next move would be.

As the companions entered, Michaela, now conscious and on her feet, dabbed at the cut on her head with iodine and winced. She shot Mildred a glance that mixed confusion and fear.

"Don't you worry, lady, you're safe for now," Mildred snapped at her. "But there are a few questions you'd better answer…"

Michaela's glance followed the line of Mildred's vision to where Krysty and Doc had laid J.B. on a bed. She took in his complexion, the sweat that poured from him and his almost delirious state.

"Fuck fuck fuck fuck fuck fuck—" she whispered over and over to herself, lips moving almost inaudibly.

"Yeah, that's right," Mildred cut in, steel in her tone to cast a cold shiver down the spine. "He's been infected with something. And I figure that maybe you know what it is, seeing as you have all these cultures in your care. Now, I can take a blood sample and match whatever's coursing through John's veins with what we've got here, but that will take some time. And it looks to me like there may not be the time, either for John or for us. Or I could ask you nicely…and maybe not so nicely if you won't cooperate." Mildred's brown eyes blazed with barely suppressed fury.

Michaela was in no doubt that Mildred meant what she said. The spiky-haired healer clung to the bench, still not fully recovered from Mildred's earlier blow and unwilling to risk another attack. "Okay, okay," she said quickly. "Look, it's not that simple, Mildred. I didn't want to lie to you, you know that. But I've got to live here."

"Cut the crap, that doesn't matter right now," Mildred snapped. "Just answer the question."

"I'm trying to," Michaela yelled, regretting it as her aching head protested. "Look, I told you that all the diseases and cures were taken from a freezer facility in the old city, right?" She waited for a nod of assent, then continued. "That's okay as far as it goes, that's true. But it's not the whole story. Bones restored the freezer facility we have here, but he also restored another one that Ethan has in his palace. And he had all the records from the old facility in the city. There were some things that Ethan had me look at, and that he wouldn't let me keep here. I wondered why, but I didn't want to ask. I think it's pretty obvious now why that was."

"Shit," Mildred breathed. She was sure that the girl was telling her the truth. Thinking about it, if she was Ethan, there was no way she'd use such a bargaining tool and leave it so easily accessible. "Think, girl," she said anxiously. "Can you remember what it was that Ethan kept with him?" She was hoping that it would be possible to synthesize an antidote from what she had in the lab, or at least alleviate the Armorer's symptoms if she had some idea what had infected him.

Michaela closed her eyes, muttering to herself, trying to recall anything that could help. Despite the fact that Mildred had rendered her unconscious earlier, the spiky-haired healer felt that she would—if their positions had been reversed—have done exactly the same thing. And she was tired of living in fear of Ethan and his regime. Most people didn't give a shit as long as they could eat well and live well, which the hunts enabled them to do. But she had had enough of it all. If there was a time to change sides, it was now. The companions had given her the courage to do this in her head, even if they were hopelessly outnumbered. Of course, she didn't expect any of them to believe her, and she wouldn't have wasted breath in telling them, but she was truly trying to remember what she had seen in the baron's palace.

It wouldn't come. It didn't matter. What happened next rendered her train of thought pointless for now.

The door crashed open and five sec men barged through, shouting at one another. They were led by Horse. Jonno was among the other four. They had handblasters, ready to fire.

"Don't move a fucking muscle," Horse yelled, his dreadlocks still swinging from his momentum, even though he was now standing still in the middle of the room. All eyes turned to him. "You're gonna follow me, now," he said in a quieter voice. "Don't fuck us around and you won't get hurt."

"What about J.B.?" Mildred barked. "He can't be moved. Right, Michaela?"

The young healer looked at her apologetically. "No, but it doesn't matter what I say. They'll move him anyway."

"Too right, bitch," Jonno said with a sneer. "You're a bit too friendly with this bunch for my liking."

"Shut it, fat man," Horse snapped. "No one speaks unless I say so. You two," he directed at Doc and Krysty, "take him and bring him with you. Where the fuck is One-Eye and the white boy?"

"I would not know, to be honest with you," Doc replied with heavy sarcasm. So heavy that it was obvious even to the sec men.

Horse sighed. "Show him what it means to be a smart-ass around here, Jonno," he said wearily.

The fat man smiled sadistically and stepped over to where Doc stood. A backhand swipe with his blaster hand caught Doc across the mouth, splitting his upper lip. Doc grunted in surprise and stumbled, helped to the floor by a blow to the back of his head with the butt of the blaster.

"No! He can't fight back," Michaela yelled, starting toward the old man.

Horse trained his blaster at her. "Guess we know which side you're on now," he mused.

The companions and the young healer stood and watched helplessly while the fat man kicked the prone Doc repeatedly in the ribs before stepping back, breathless and smiling.

"Get up, you old fuck," he snarled. "You've got to carry Four Eyes out of here, yet."

THE WHITE DOUBLE DOORS leading into Baron Ethan's quarters came into view as both Ryan and Jak moved quickly down the corridor. They could see people moving in the daylight beyond the corridor walls, but there was no sign that they had been noticed and marked as hostile, and no sign of any sec men coming to intercept them.

"I'll take the doors, cover you. You recce the room," Ryan snapped, unholstering his SIG-Sauer and chambering a round.

Jak nodded, noting that blasters were now an option and taking out his .357 Magnum Colt Python. He allowed Ryan to get a few steps in front, and prepared to spring as the one-eyed man booted open the doors, the force from his strong thigh muscles ripping the lock from the wood of the doors as they sprang apart. As Ryan advanced, Jak somersaulted into the room, keeping low, moving fast and seeking shelter. He came to rest behind a chair and checked the area while Ryan stayed in the doorway.

It was an absurd situation—the room was empty apart from the baron, who was seated behind his desk, studying yet more papers. He looked up at the intrusion, but seemed to stay impassive.

"Gentlemen, I've been expecting you," he said calmly. "I do hope that you haven't done too much damage to those doors. And, by the way, I also hope that you haven't chilled too many of my sec men."

"Only two, and only because they got in the way," Ryan said, walking into the room and keeping his blaster trained on the baron. "Jak, check that we're alone."

The albino moved to the other doors, opening and checking, ignoring the weary words of Ethan.

"If I wanted to have you chilled, it would have happened by now. But what would I gain from that?"

"What indeed," Ryan mused, walking up to the desk and putting the muzzle of the handblaster under the baron's nose. "But then, profit is the word that matters here, isn't it?"

Ethan shrugged. "Isn't it always? The only way a ville survives and a baron prospers is if it makes jack, trades goods. It has to have something to trade, you must realize that. I'm assuming, of course, that you know what we have to trade or sell."

"Yeah," Ryan said softly. "I know. And I also know that your sec men have infected J.B. You think that'll make us fit in with your plans?"

Ethan calmly raised a hand and pushed the muzzle of the handblaster away from his face. Ryan had to hand it to him. He was cool in the face of a possible chilling. It would be all too easy for Ryan to squeeze the trigger and end his fireblasted life. The baron continued in an even voice. "Unless you want him to buy the farm without putting up some kind of fight, yes. And I don't think you're the sort of people who could do that."

"It won't work," Ryan stated with a confidence that he couldn't feel. "Mildred knows about the sort of shit that you've put into J.B., and she knows how to fix it. Your healer has told her a lot—"

"Yes, I thought she would," Ethan murmured, unfazed by these revelations. "I've suspected for a long time that she isn't what you might call one hundred percent behind my leadership. But doubtless she would also have told your Mildred that not everything that we salvaged from the old city has been stored in the hospital. Don't you think that I would have to be extraordinarily stupe to have infected your friend with something that could be remedied that easily?"

"Mebbe not—but if you don't hand it over, then I'll blow your fucking head clean off your shoulders… and don't think that I won't enjoy it."

"Ryan—sec approaching," Jak snapped, his keen senses picking up oncoming trouble.

Ethan grinned. It was smug and self-satisfied, and for a second Ryan thought it would be worth firing just to see it wiped off and smeared all over the walls. But he couldn't.

Almost as if he could read the one-eyed man's thoughts, Ethan answered his unspoken questions. "You don't know what the infection is, you don't know where I've stored it. Chilling me won't help you—in fact, although you may possibly be able to find the antidote eventually, the time it would take may prove to be fatal. Can you risk that? And that's once you've had to fight off my men, keen to avenge my buying the farm…" Ethan smiled and shook his head. "I don't think so, do you?"

Ryan knew he was right, but still kept the blaster trained on him, unwavering. Jak was facing the door from which the approaching sec could now be clearly heard. He had the Colt Python ready to fire.

"Ryan, take out?" he queried.

"No, this round belongs to him. But it's not the war."

Jak stepped back, lowering his own blaster. "How we

know they not gonna just blow us away?" he snapped at Ethan.

"Wouldn't do me much good if they did, boy," the baron replied before raising his voice. "Come on in. They're not trouble anymore."

The doors opened and a posse of sec men entered the room, led by Horse and Jonno. The fat man was dragging Doc behind him, the old man stumbling and falling. He had lost his silver lion's-head swordstick, and was covered in blood where cuts had opened from the beating he had received at the fat sec man's hands. His face was a mass of puffy and split flesh, and from his stiff and stumbling gait he had been beaten severely about the body. Jonno pushed him forward with a grating laugh and the old man fell to the floor. Jak was beside him in a second, checking him for serious damage. The slightly built albino looked up at the fat sec man, his eyes flashing anger although his face remained impassive.

"Damaged Doc, you pay double, fat man," Jak said with a cold simplicity that left little doubt in the mind of anyone present that, despite the disparity in their sizes, Jak was more than capable of following through on this statement of intent.

Horse ignored the albino and spoke directly to the baron, trying to deflect from the tension between Jak and Jonno.

"Everything okay here now?" he asked mildly, eyeing Ryan, who still had the SIG-Sauer in his hand, although it was now pointed downward.

Ethan nodded, then gazed at Doc. "Why did you beat on the old man?"

Horse shrugged. "He got a little uppity and Jonno got a little carried away."

Ethan pursed his lips and shook his head. "I said that they were to be kept in good condition. Any of the others fucked up in any way?"

Horse shook his head, his dreads moving to a rhythm of their own. "They're okay. They were in the hospital, like you thought, and Mildred had just figured out that she couldn't save Four Eyes without our help."

"That's good. Then I take it that, like our friends here, they know that they must cooperate to help him." When Horse assented, Ethan continued. "That makes beating on the old guy even more stupe. May I have your blaster, Ryan?"

The one-eyed man looked at the baron, surprised. He was in no position to refuse, but the fact was that he would have expected Ethan to just take it, not ask nicely. Confused, he nodded and, temporarily dumbfounded, handed over the SIG-Sauer.

"Thanks," the baron said simply. Weighing the blaster in his hand, he added, "Nice piece of hardware, actually. Good weight." He lifted it up and sighted, as though target shooting. "Yeah, real nice."

Before anyone had a chance to realize what he was about to do, he swiveled, took aim and squeezed, loosing off one shot at the fat sec man. Jonno's face registered astonishment as the shell drilled a neat hole in the center of his forehead, the less than neat exit wound at the back taking a great chunk of skull with it, splattering brain and blood behind him. Still looking mildly bemused, the fat man slumped to the ground.

"Thanks. Shoots real nice, too," Ethan added, handing the SIG-Sauer back to an astounded Ryan. "See, the fat man there broke the cardinal rule. I'm in charge here, and when I say I want something done, I expect my instructions to be carried out exactly. I didn't want any of you to be harmed. Not for any altruistic purpose, but for the simple reason that I want you all in perfect condition for my next hunt. Now clear that fucking corpse away, and get someone to clean the floor before all that blood and brain leaves a stain on my wooden floors," the fastidious tyrant added to his sec chief.

He gestured to some of the sec party who were still standing, astonished, to the rear of where the chilling had taken place. "Bring the old man over to the comfortable seats and put him there. And you and the albino go with him," Ethan added to Ryan. "We have things to discuss."

Ryan and Jak followed the sec men and Doc to the sofas where they had sat less than forty-eight hours before—a lifetime and world of difference away. Ethan sat opposite them and began to speak again.

"You seem a little bemused, and understandably so given what's just happened. Let me put this simply. I work on a rule of supply and demand. The people who give us goods and jack want a good show. They want to hunt or to witness a hunt. And they want blood and variety. The first is easy, the second not so much... So when I come across an interesting bunch like you guys, then I start to think. You're obviously good hunters, and by the same token, would be likely to make good prey. But are you going to do that? No, not without some kind of persuading. And what better than one of your kind being in mortal danger. Your friend J.B. was just unlucky in that he was the first to break cover. It could have been any of you, although mebbe not you two, come to that. You're too valuable.

"So, you see, I get my hunt, the ville gets its jack, and you get to make your friend better if you play along. Sound reasonable?"

"If I say no?" Ryan asked.

Ethan smiled coldly. "Then J.B. buys the farm and you get forced to run or be shot down like jackals. This way you've got a chance. So, no, you're not going to say no. You've got to play the odds, even if you're only doing it in the hope that you'll get a chance to turn it around."

Ryan said nothing. The baron was right, and he knew it.

"Good. I'll take that as a yes, then," Ethan said with a smug satisfaction. "The hunt is in five days, when my paying guests arrive. Until then, Michaela will keep J.B. stable, and will administer the antidote when the hunt is over. Your Mildred will assist, to insure fair play."

Ryan wanted to laugh bitterly. Fair play when J.B. was ill with a mystery disease, Doc was beaten almost to a pulp and the rest of the companions were at the mercy of Ethan's plans for making big jack?

Wait and see. They'd see who was playing fair at the end, thought the one-eyed man.

Chapter Seven

It was always going to be a long five days until the hunt began, but it wasn't made any easier by their being confined to the hospital. The ostensible reason for this was that J.B. was being kept on a level by the ministrations of Michaela and Mildred, with the help of a small dose of vaccine to control the symptoms, administered daily by the spiky-haired healer under the supervision of Ethan himself, who took the precaution of only delivering as much of the vaccine as was necessary, and bringing with him a heavily armed guard.

The companions had been stripped of their weapons before being incarcerated, and this time the sec force under Horse were thorough: blasters were taken, Ryan's scarf with the lead weights, Doc's lion's-head swordstick, the panga and the Tekna knife that Ryan and J.B. used, and even Jak's camou jacket, after the first leaf-bladed knife was found in its concealed position—the subsequent search only proving to Horse that he could spend all day tearing the garment to pieces and still not find every single knife for certain. Unlike the way in which they had been left with their weapons on first arriving, the prevailing atmosphere was now of hostilities in play: no chances were to be taken, even though the companions had agreed to the hunt to try to save J.B.

Ethan may be confident, but this didn't spill over into complacency.

Meanwhile, to keep them fit for the hunt, and to insure that it would present a good spectacle for the expected paying guests, they were allowed to train once a day. Under a heavily armed guard, they were taken from the hospital to the sec compound where, under the gaze of enough hardware to chill a small army, they were allowed to work out and to fight with one another to keep their edge of fitness and to keep their reflexes sharp.

As they fought, they would be watched by a pool of spectators from the ville who, from beyond the wire surrounding the compound, would silently study their form. The citizens of Pleasantville were concerned with the fitness of the companions: the fitter and sharper they were, the more successful the hunt; the more successful the hunt, the greater the jack and trade for the ville. They watched the companions as though they were animals being trained to fight for sport…which is, in a sense, exactly what they were.

Ethan would also come to watch. He had a sizeable investment in the future of his barony tied up in them and he wanted to make sure that he got value for his proffered commodity: the life of their friend.

On the fourth day, he walked through the crowds and into the compound as the companions worked out. Ryan was driving them hard, determined that they would be as sharp as possible for the hunt.

"What he want?" Jak snapped between sit-ups, casting a cold and glittering eye over the approaching baron, who was accompanied by a phalanx of sec men, all heavily armed.

"Don't know," Ryan grunted through the effort of training, "but I figure we're about to find out." The one-eyed man signaled to his people to cease, and rose to his feet in one fluid motion from his sitting position. It was partly so that he could be on an eye-to-eye level with the baron, and partly to press home how fit the companions were—a warning shot for the baron's sec forces.

Ethan gave the one-eyed man a faint grin that suggested he was aware of this.

"You're looking good, there, Ryan. Hope the rest of you are in as good a condition."

The companions were on their feet and around the baron before the sentence had a chance to drift away on the air. They moved so swiftly to surround him that the sec force had no time to react.

Ryan was up against the baron, eyeballing him. He could smell the faint perfumed musk coming off Ethan and could only admire the way that the baron remained calm and showed no fear, even though he was being jostled.

"Back off, there! Back off now!" Horse yelled. The air was filled with the whipcrack of shells being chambered. Ryan turned to see that the sec force had their blasters leveled at the circle.

"Dumb fuck," the one-eyed man said calmly. "You blast us and you blast your baron, as well. That wouldn't be too clever, would it? Should have been faster, Horse."

The dreadlocked sec chief said nothing, but the humiliation and anger blazing in his eyes was a more than eloquent statement.

"On the other hand, what are you going to do to me,

Ryan?" Ethan said softly. "You harm me in any way, and you say goodbye to J.B. getting better. And then you get chilled. So who's so dumb now, then?"

Ryan and the rest of the companions stepped away from the baron, who continued in a calm manner.

"Face it, all you've done is prove to me how fit you are. You've proved that the hunt is going to be a good one and that you'll be worth the jack we're getting. Better, as far as you're concerned, you'll be worth your freedom and the life of J.B."

"Why should we believe you?" Mildred barked. "Why shouldn't we just rip you to fuck right now? At least we'd have the satisfaction of doing to you what you're doing to John."

Ethan shrugged. "Interesting point. It's a simple answer. This ville and the riches we've attracted are based on our word being our bond. If we lie to people about what we're giving them, then we'd be raided and leveled in revenge. No, I always mean what I say. You take part in the hunt, then J.B. will be given the antidote to his sickness, and those of you who survive the hunt— which may be all or may be none, that's up to you— will be set free. You have my word on that."

Mildred spit. "What's that worth?"

"That's your choice," Ethan replied. He gestured to Horse and the sec force surrounded him. "Now I would suggest—and remember, you have the choice—that you keep working. The barons who have paid to see this event will arrive at sunup, and by the middle of the day, the hunt will begin. So if you want to be at your peak…"

He gestured once more and turned on his heel. The

sec men followed suit and Baron Ethan left the companions standing in the center of the sec compound to reflect on their fate.

"HOW'S HE BEEN?" Mildred wearily asked Michaela as they arrived back at the hospital after their training session.

"Same as the last few days," the spiky-haired girl replied, keeping a wary eye on the armed sec man who had been one of the accompanying party and still stood guard in the doorway. This was not so much as a sec measure, but more because he hoped to get a look at Krysty's body as the Titian-haired beauty stripped before using the shower.

"Ethan's been, and has administered the injection for today." She led Mildred out of the guard's hearing and spoke in a whisper. "Look, I've thought of something, but it's a bit of a long shot. It might be the thing we need to tilt everything in our favor…"

"'We'?" Mildred questioned.

Michaela grimaced. "I know you've got no reason to trust me, but the fact of the matter is that I'm up to my neck in the shit. Doesn't matter what does or doesn't happen to you, it's over my head once this hunt is finished. You think Ethan's going to trust me again? I may not have helped you that much, but I did tell you things that I shouldn't have, and I didn't try to stop you. If you buy the farm or go free, it doesn't have a bearing on what's going to happen to me…" She sliced her finger across her throat. "Mebbe that wouldn't be a bad thing, 'cause I'm sick of the shit that goes on here, but I'd rather have the chance to get out in one piece."

"Big speech, sweetie, but what's the point?" Mildred was tired, wanted to shower, and was concerned about J.B. and what the others would have to do on the following day. She was in no mood for grandstanding.

"Point is, I've been thinking, and mebbe there's a way that we can take control of J.B.'s sickness out of Ethan's hands."

Mildred snapped to attention. If they could do that, not only would it be of immeasurable help to the Armorer, but it would also give the rest of the companions an edge that no one else would know.

"Tell me, girl," she urged.

Michaela took a deep breath. "Okay, now I've got to say that it's a long shot, but remember how I told you that all the cultures here—and the ones that Ethan keeps hidden—were taken from a freezer in a hospital in the remains of the city?" When Mildred nodded, she continued. "Well, I don't think that the sec men he sent to clear it out could have really taken everything. I never saw the facility, but from what I was told it was a damn sight bigger than anything Bones has put together here."

"And the point is?"

"The point is that there must be something left there. And chances are that the freezer is still working. If we can isolate what it is that J.B. has, then one of us can make a break for the old city to try to find the antidote."

Mildred kissed her teeth. This was beyond a long shot: it was playing so many odds and possibilities that she couldn't even begin to calculate... On the other hand, it was better than nothing.

"You'll have to go, assuming you know where the old hospital is," Mildred added.

Michaela nodded. "I've been into the old city, and although I haven't been inside, it's been pointed out to me. I can find it."

"Okay. Then we need to find out what it is that J.B. has…"

"I've prepared some slides. I don't recognize anything, but mebbe you will. If not, I can just bring back anything that I know I haven't got here."

Mildred arched an eyebrow. "You've really been thinking about this, haven't you, girl? You must want to get out of here pretty badly."

Michaela shook her head sadly. "You wouldn't believe…"

"I think I might," Mildred said with irony.

Realizing what she had said, the young healer gave a hollow laugh of her own. "Yeah, pretty stupe thing to say. But what d'you think?"

"It sounds worth a try," Mildred mused. "The only thing that could work against us is time."

Michaela sucked in her breath. "That kind of depends on how good your friends are. Most hunts last from the beginning until sundown—some not even that long. If your people are good, and can make it last overnight, then that should be more than enough time, especially if I can get away quickly."

Mildred nodded slowly. "Yeah, sounds good in theory. But what exactly do you get out of it if you do help us?"

"Simple," Michaela said ingenuously. "I get to come with you."

"No way—we don't know that this isn't part of some plan that Ethan has to improve his hunt," Ryan snapped when Mildred laid the plan before the rest of the companions.

"Maybe it is, lover, but maybe we should play along even if it is so," Krysty said softly, toying with her food.

It was now dark outside and the companions were eating after showering and resting from their earlier exertions. There was a sec guard outside the hospital, but a quick recce from Jak had established that it was at enough of a distance that they couldn't be heard if they kept their voices low, which was hard in current circumstances as tempers were short-fused with frustration and exhaustion. A good night's rest was what they needed before the hunt, not an argument like this.

Which is why Krysty was trying to calm the one-eyed man. Since Dean had been taken by Sharona, Ryan had been on the edge. It wasn't that he had made any particularly bad decisions that had landed them up to their necks in shit, it was more that he had been volatile, inclined to explode where previously he had been calm, able to step back and to look at the overall picture before planning action. Now there seemed to be no action, only reaction.

"Why?" he raged. "Why the fuck should we do what this girl says when it may be designed to lead us into trouble?"

Which proved her point...

"Because I fear that we have little other option," Doc mused. He understood only too well the pain of loss—perhaps more so than any of the other companions would hope to know, certainly more than he wished them to ever know—and, like Krysty, he understood, too, that it was imperative to keep Ryan calm. He continued. "It seems to me that, if we are being led in a certain direction, then it would benefit us to try to hoodwink the baron. To let him think that we have fallen for his simple-minded ruse and to lull him into a false sense of security before striking back at the moment that he least expects it."

Ryan gazed at Doc and a slow smile spread across his previously angry and stress-tightened visage. "Fireblast and fuck it, Doc, that's the most sense anyone's spoken to me for a long time, and it's a hell of a lot more sense than I've been thinking for myself. I guess we can't lose that way—if she's genuine, then we've got an ally. And if she's a fraud, then we just string the bastard along until we're in a position to hit back." Ryan looked around his people, as if seeing them for the first time in a long while. "Look, there are no excuses. I've been somewhere else when I should have been with you, and I could have bought us all the farm. Whatever happens now, it's not going to get me any closer to Dean. There's nothing I can do about that except trust to fate that one day I'll see him again. But I've got you people, and you've been with me all the way. Thanks for being there… Now we need to whip this stupe's ass and get away from this pesthole in one piece, and with J.B. Mildred, go get that healer…"

Mildred grinned. "Thank heavens for that. I thought we were never going to get you back, Ryan."

She left the room where they had been talking in hushed tones and fetched Michaela. The spiky-haired girl, who seemed far too young to be involved in a situation like this, had been waiting nervously in a ward at the end of the corridor. As there were rarely any inhabitants who had to stay over to be hospitalized, Baron Ethan had taken the precaution of setting up an alternative clinic for the citizens of Pleasantville, staffed by assistants who had learned their skills from Michaela. This meant that, for the five days leading up to the beginning of the hunt, he had been able to isolate the companions—and most specifically J.B.—from the rest of the ville, and also to isolate Michaela.

She wasn't guilty of being the baron's agent. She knew that, but could understand why the companions were suspicious. After all, until this point she had been careful about concealing her desire to escape Pleasantville to avoid Ethan's wrath, keeping her head down and going about her business without rippling the waters. So of course her sudden desire to help them would seem suspicious: but she was sure that some of her actions had alerted Ethan to her true feelings, which was part of the reason why she had been isolated with the potential prey.

They had to believe her. They were her chance to escape this oppressive ville. If she blew it, then she felt sure that her own life would be short after they had departed.

All this passed through her mind, along with as many scenarios as she could imagine where things went wrong, and she was left to face the wrath of the baron alone. She knew that Horse had always desired her, and that Ethan didn't allow his senior sec men to have relationships with other women in what he termed "executive" positions. If her true desires were known, then it would be big trouble for her. Because Ethan would strip her of her authority as ville healer and hand her over to

Horse to do as he wished. She didn't desire Horse; she desired no man. It was only the awakening of desire for Mildred that had strengthened her resolve to finally act. Not that she would let Mildred know this. She could see the way that the woman looked at J.B. as she tended to him in his sickness. No, it would be enough if she could help them, and also get away herself.

But first they had to believe her.

The door to the ward opened and Michaela looked up, feeling a surge of desire flood through her as Mildred came into the room. She repressed this, as she knew she had to, and tried to read the woman's face.

"Come with me," Mildred said softly, "we've made a decision."

Michaela rose from the bed and followed Mildred to where the companions had discussed her proposal. As she came upon them, she could see immediately that they didn't wholly trust her.

It was Ryan who was the most open and readable: his icy-blue eye was focused on her, his jaw set firm. The long scar puckering his cheekbone and beginning somewhere in the injury covered by his eyepatch seemed whiter than usual against the weatherbeaten tan of the surrounding skin, as if it were the only part of him to reflect the inner tension he felt.

"Sit down," he said evenly.

Michaela chose a position where she could see all of them. She looked around, knowing that her apprehension had to be obvious. As her eyes met Krysty's, the Titian-haired beauty gave her a quizzical stare and her hair relaxed slightly. Ryan noticed this and the two of them exchanged glances, his eyebrow raised in a mute question. Krysty's almost imperceptible nod made up his mind as he began to speak.

"I'm going to be honest with you," he said in a controlled, even tone. "None of us knew whether to believe you. For our own reasons, some of us have had an impaired judgment of late, and where we could always trust our instincts before, it's been a little difficult. And face it, your story could be another plan from Ethan, trying to get someone on the inside of us."

"I understand that," Michaela said hesitantly. "Don't think I hadn't thought of that one myself."

Ryan nodded. "What we were going to do was agree to what you proposed, but not go the whole way with you. We'd play along, but hold back, so we could chill you if you were a spy, and turn the whole thing back on that son of a diseased gaudy slut."

Michaela chewed her lip. "That's as good a name for him as I've ever heard anyone come up with," she commented.

"Mebbe. Point is, we were only going along with you to a certain point, and we weren't going to let you know that—"

"So why has that changed?" she asked, puzzled. She wasn't alone. Jak had noticed the exchange between Ryan and Krysty, but Mildred and Doc hadn't been able to see it, and so were also looking perplexed.

Ryan shrugged. "One of those things. Just something about that way you are right now tells me—tells Krysty—that you mean it. One of those things you can't explain, you just know. And we haven't been listening to those instincts lately. We're going to have to if we're going to get out of this in one piece. All of us," he added meaningly.

"I won't let you down," Michaela said solemnly. "I can't—it'd be letting myself down, too."

"Then we'd better get some rest. You can bet that bastard's going to have us up early in the morning to prepare for his jack fest hunt," Ryan said bitterly. "It might not begin until the sun is high, but if he's got people paying big time, then they're going to want to view the merchandise…and he's going to want to show it off."

RYAN'S WORDS WERE prophetic. It was still early the next morning when the door to the hospital was thrown open and Horse entered, accompanied by a party of five sec men. Included among them were two that Ryan recognized from the hunting party that had initially brought them to the ville. One was the giant who had accompanied Jak. He was the only one who had the grace to look embarrassed about what had happened; the only one who looked on them as anything other than merchandise.

He sought out the albino and spoke in low tones so that they wouldn't be overheard.

"Sorry it has to be this way."

"Not your fault," Jak returned.

"Still sorry," the giant said. "One thing."

"What?"

"The hunt goes through some rough territory, with mutie fuckers. Normally they avoid us, but mebbe if you stir them as you go, they won't be so keen on those following. See?"

Jak nodded, his lips parting in a cold smile of acknowledgment. "Good tip. Thanks."

"Better than nothing." The giant shrugged.

Horse yelled at his men to get the companions out and into the sec compound where they would meet those who were to hunt them. Jak kept his secret to himself—no need to risk any of the other sec overhearing. He could tell Ryan and the others when they were alone. But he was grateful for the comradeship shown by the giant sec man, and he figured that mcbbe Pleasantville could be a good place, if Ethan's influence was removed. Mebbe they could do something about that if they got out of this in one piece.

There was no time for further thought, as the companions were hustled out of the hospital, leaving J.B. behind with Mildred and Michaela. As the door closed on them, leaving a sec guard outside, the two women exchanged glances full of hope for those who had to fight, and full of resolve for the tasks they had to undertake.

Meanwhile, the four companions who would be the prey in this lucrative hunt were marched across the ville to the sec compound, through a throng of ville dwellers who had lined the streets, with stalls and banners, turning the event almost into a carnival. A carnival of carnage, with a scent for blood tainting the air. There was cheering as they approached each section of the crowd, and they were greeted as conquering heroes rather than those about to die.

"Creepy fuckers," Jak mumbled, eyeing the crowds balefully.

"Perhaps." Doc shrugged. "But you have to see that they view this in a completely different way from us... of necessity, in many senses. We can only see that this is some kind of barbaric bloodsport in which we, the unwilling participants, are to be hunted down for the pleasure of a few bloodthirsty and rich barons. Which, I may add, is the way these things seem to have been since time immemorial. Need I mention the Romans, the feudal systems of medieval Europe…" He noticed that Jak and Krysty were giving him blank stares, although Ryan—who had read of such things in books—seemed to know what he referred to.

"The point is that the people of this ville do not see things in that way. To them, we are heroes. Our baiting at the hands of these barons and traders will bring in enough jack and trade to insure that their children eat, and that they are fed, clothed and warmed for another year. Yes, we are heroes in a bizarre manner, and so this procession in which we are treated thus should not be viewed as that incongruous." He nodded emphatically, probably to himself, glad that he had made his point.

The other three—and some of the sec guard who had overheard what the old man had to say—looked at him askance as they continued on their way.

"Hell of long way to say they glad we about to chill," Jak said simply.

"That wasn't actually what I was trying to say," Doc replied testily.

"That's what it sound like to me," Jak responded sullenly.

"Not the point at all—" Doc began, before Krysty interrupted him.

"What is it with you two?" she asked. "We're about to be hunted like wild animals and you're arguing about nothing?"

"It isn't 'nothing,' as you put it, my dear," Doc said hotly, "if we are to understand why this is happening to us—"

It was Ryan's turn to interrupt. "Doc, we don't have to understand why it's happening, we just have to know that it is. Now shut the fuck up and save your energy."

The one-eyed man's attention was suddenly taken by one of the sec escorts, who laughed as Ryan spoke. Cawdor swung around to face the man, who was a blonde with a long, plaited beard and a heavily developed musculature.

"You think something's funny, scum?" he yelled.

"Yeah, I reckon you are," the blonde replied in a lazy, arrogant drawl. "You're about to be chill meat, and all you can do is argue. Now shut up and get moving," he added, prodding Ryan with the muzzle of the Glock he was carrying.

A red mist of rage descended over Ryan, and the Ryan who could be so calm and calculating in these situations, biding his time for revenge, disappeared, replaced by a frustrated man who had reached his breaking point.

Even before a look of shock swept fully over the sec guard's face, Ryan had taken a firm hold of the Glock's muzzle and wrestled it from the man's grasp, wrenching it upward, then driving it backward with as much force as his minimal back lift would allow, the blaster's butt now angled slightly upward from before, so that instead of driving back down into the man's chest, it hit him in the mouth.

It had been too quick, too unexpected, and the sec man had been too slow. The metal of the stock hit him firmly, mashing his lips against his teeth, cutting them so that blood began to flow into his plaited beard, running down the line of the plait as it soaked into strands of hair. Driving through the useless defense of his flesh, the stock splintered his teeth and drove through his gums and jawbone, forcing splinters of tooth into the flesh, breaking the jawbone with a crack.

The red mist evaporated, and Ryan stood calmly, letting the Glock fall to his feet. The force of the blow sent the sec man staggering backward, careering into the man behind, who tried to catch him, the momentum proving too great and also making him veer backward.

Like a line of dominoes, four sec men crashed onto the ground, to the jeers and laughter of the crowd, watched impassively by the companions. Ryan shook his head. It was a suicidal stupe move to make at this time. What the fuck had gone through his head, if anything?

The remaining sec force converged on the one-eyed man, some of them with the stocks of their blasters raised to club him to the ground.

"No!" Horse yelled. "Don't touch him! Ethan wants them unharmed."

The sec guards stared at their dreadlocked boss with a barely simmering resentment. The blonde climbed to his feet, last of all, shaking his head to clear it and spreading droplets of blood around him.

"I'll get you for that, you one-eyed spawn of a shit-eating gaudy slut," he mumbled almost incoherently through the bloody ruin of his mouth. "If you come back from the hunt, then I'll be waiting."

"I'll be back," Ryan murmured, leaving the rest unsaid.

"Come on, let's get these shitters to Ethan before anything else happens," Horse snapped, his dark eyes boring hatred at Ryan. There was nothing he would have liked better than to let his men take out the one-eyed man for that humiliation of one of his men—made all the worse because it was in front of the ville's people—but he knew that he couldn't let that happen. There was much riding on this hunt, and his job was to answer to the baron, who would have been displeased to find his hunt prey a man short.

Despite the grumbling that emanated from the massed sec men now surrounding the companions, the guard backed off and the procession continued until it was in sight of the sec compound.

"What the fuck has he got in store for us now?" Ryan wondered out loud.

"You'll see," Horse replied, turning to eyeball his man. He wasn't supposed to have heard Ryan, but he couldn't resist acknowledging the query with a look that spelled danger. He knew something they didn't, and the odds were short that it was bad.

There was no further time to ponder this, as they entered the compound and were in view of Baron Ethan and his clients, who were looking forward to a good hunt. A stand had been built in the center of what had previously been the training arena, and on this stand stood Ethan, flanked on each side by three men, all of whose clothing suggested that they had wealth, if not taste. The wire encircling the compound was a heaving mass of spectators, waiting to see what would unfold.

Horse and his guard led the companions up to the stand, until they were situated directly in front of the baron and his guests. Ryan cast his eye over the six. All were male, and three of them wore old combat uniforms under their rich brocaded robes. Scavenged jewels and gold dripped from them. Ryan had little doubt that these were traders rather than barons. Their inability to shed the uniforms in which they traversed trade routes in convoys reminded him of Trader, his old mentor, who would have had a similar dislike of shedding familiar garb. These three also looked battle-scarred and tanned by hours of exposure to the chem-addled sun.

By contrast, the other three men on the stand were like Ethan. They were clean, polished and looked as though they no longer had to do a day's work, even if they once had... In fact, one of them looked like a second or third generation baron, with the slightly glassy, vacant look of a bloodline that was a little too in-bred.

The barons wouldn't be too hard to evade, he figured. They probably didn't hunt for themselves, but had others to do their work. No, the real danger would come from the traders, who were still combat-practiced and could prove to be a difficulty.

Ethan held up his hands in a gesture for silence, and the muttering that had buzzed in the background since the companions had entered the arena now ceased. He turned to the men flanking him.

"Gentlemen, these are the hunters and hunted that I told you about. Take a good look at them. Fighters and survivors, ready to do anything to emerge triumphant.

Dangerous prey. Something a little special, a little different from the norm… I know you initially signed up for a stickie hunt, but as I told you, the farm was breached and the bastards escaped."

That explained the wild stickies that had first brought them into contact with the baron and his men. Jak was momentarily angry with himself: his suspicions had been correct and he hadn't put the pieces together. But the flash of annoyance vanished quickly. There were other things to consider, as the baron continued his speech.

"But perhaps this was a good thing. Without it, we wouldn't have found these hunters, who between them cleaned up the herd of creatures you would have been hunting. That was what gave me my next idea, and that, my friends, is why you have had to pay just that little bit more, but it will be worth it."

He gestured to Horse, and before the companions had a chance to move, they were grabbed by two sec men apiece, pinioned so that they couldn't move. At another gesture, they were taken to four stakes that were driven into the ground and tied securely, one to each stake. These wooden monoliths had been carefully situated so that they weren't visible from the entrance to the compound, being obscured by the stand on which the baron and his guests were seated. The companions had no notion that they were there, and no chance to prepare to struggle against the sudden sec movement. As they were tied, the sec guards took pleasure in making their bonds painfully tight; the blonde spit a gob of blood and phlegm into Ryan's face when he had finished securing him.

"You and me, One-eye…if you get back," he said with a sneer before stepping away.

Baron Ethan left the stand and walked over to the stakes, walking up and down in front of the four well-trussed companions before turning to his guests and speaking in a clear, ringing voice.

"I could have sent you out to hunt these people, but if I had done that I wouldn't be fulfilling my role as your host. For, without wishing to insult you, these fighters would probably win the day and chill you to insure their escape. That would be bad business, would it not? Your surviving relatives and sec forces would seek recompense and revenge… However, I have thought of something that would be infinitely more entertaining for you than chasing these people." He paused, then smiled with a vicious evil that ran chills down the companions' collective spines. They had been sold out, and they knew it.

"What if," Ethan began, "they were to hunt each other? Would that not be a fine spectacle? I have watched them, and I consider the albino to be the swiftest and most vicious of them. So what if the other three were to hunt him down? He would have to chill his friends to survive. They would have to chill him to win their freedom, and also to prevent him chilling them. Delicious, is it not?

"You, my friends, can follow and observe this ritual. And, if you wish, you can hunt down the survivors like mad dogs needing to be shot before they can damage anyone else—"

"You are mad, and a fool," Doc yelled. "Do you really think that we would hunt each other like animals for your sport? Death is better than such dishonor."

Ethan nodded. "Wise and noble words, Doc. And truly, I believe that you mean them with sincerity. But consider this…" He produced from a pocket a small crystal, which glittered in the sun, suspended on a leather thong. "What if you had no choice on the matter? What if your free will were taken away, and you truly believed yourselves to be what I told you—each the enemy of the other?"

"Sir, you claim to know of hypnotism?" Doc breathed.

Ethan didn't answer. His cold, vicious smile was answer enough.

Chapter Eight

Jak's red eyes scanned the sec guard and the crowd that stood beyond the baron. In the harsh light, it was difficult for his pigmentless eyes to see clearly, but he could hear all right. There was a muttering among the crowd after Ethan's pronouncement that could be nothing other than shock. Certainly, the sec men he could see—including the giant who he could call friend—looked as astounded as the crowd. This was something that no one had known about.

And it changed everything.

The assumption had been that they would have to outwit the baron, his sec force and the paying guests who wanted to hunt them. That would have been difficult, because of the weight of numbers, but not impossible. Now it was a completely different game. Jak would be set free and then pursued by his friends, who were to hunt him down as though he were a mad dog. He knew what they were capable of, and although he didn't want to chill any of them, his first thought was that this was exactly what he may have to do to insure his own survival.

Jak's eyes adjusted to the sun, and he could see the faces of the sec men clearly. The blood-splattered blonde who Ryan had injured was smiling. To him, there was a certain symmetry to the idea, and he was relishing it. Jak could also make out his giant friend. The bald man was tight-lipped, his eyes hard. He didn't have to say anything to let Jak know that he thought the idea was sick. He'd tried to help by giving Jak a tip about the wild muties in the woods. There was nothing he could do to help his friends now except watch them buy the farm, each for the other.

Even Horse, the supposedly loyal sec chief, seemed to be unamused by what was occurring. His face was set, his large brown eyes dead, his dreads hanging still and framing his high-boned face. The entire set of his body screamed that he was uneasy with this plan. But possibly for different reasons...

Jak had plenty of time to think about what could happen. As the one who wouldn't be hypnotized, he remained tied to the stake, impassive, while Ethan set to work on the other three.

If the baron was as good a hypnotist as his confidence suggested, then Jak would be faced with three fighters who knew him and knew his ways. Conversely, he would know his enemy, and there was always a chance that their edges would be slightly dulled by the hypnotism that clouded their conscious minds. He would be in the wilds, where he felt at home. If he could separate them, he could take them out of the game one by one.

Doc would be the first. The old man had courage, but his body was considerably weaker than Jak's, his skills less honed and his mind inclined to wander. Not easy as such, but the easiest. Then he would take Krysty. She was strong, and had the doomie instincts that gave her an edge when danger was afoot. She would be difficult to best, but he knew her weaknesses. Ryan, he would have to leave to last. The one-eyed man was strong, a good fighter and a good hunter. His weakness was that he wasn't a natural jungle fighter and could be taken by surprise. His strength was that he was bigger than Jak, had more power in those muscles and was tenacious. Jak would be wearier than Ryan, having already eliminated two opponents, but he had an edge of speed that wouldn't be dulled enough to even them up.

It wasn't something that the albino wished to consider. Since he had left the swamps of the bayou, these people had been his friends and family. Even when he had left them temporarily, and his beloved wife and child had been chilled by coldheart bandits, they had returned to help him seek vengeance. He would die protecting them, and now he was tied to a piece of wood, thinking of how he could chill them to insure his own survival.

Jak Lauren's heart hardened as he watched Baron Ethan at his work. If the baron was full of shit, and the hypnotism didn't work, then they would be together and crush him. But if he genuinely knew what he was doing, and Jak had to chill his friends to survive, then he would return to Pleasantville and he would take great pleasure in helping Ethan buy the farm if it was the last thing he was ever to do.

ETHAN HELD THE CRYSTAL in front of Doc's eyes, the light glittering off it as it twirled lazily on the end of the leather thong. The old man tried to look away, but Ethan reached out and snapped his head back so that their eyes met.

"You believe that it is possible, then," the baron stated simply. "That's good. That makes my task a whole lot easier. There will be less resistance..." He fixed his eyes on Doc's, and to the old man it felt as if the baron were looking into his soul. Despite his best efforts, a whimper escaped his lips and a cruel answering smile crossed Ethan's visage. "Look into me, old man, look deep into me..." He held the crystal between them and began to rotate it so that it proscribed a small arc in the confined space between their faces, Ethan's breath hot on Doc's face. The light caught in the facets of the crystal and Doc could feel the colors bite into his retina, breaking up his vision into a rainbow. He was aware of Ethan's voice, crooning to him, but the words became a jumbled mush of sound. He felt an overwhelming resentment begin to grow in his heart. A resentment against Jak. It was his fault that they were in this situation. There would be no problem if it wasn't for him. So Ethan wanted them to hunt the little runt down and buy him the farm. Was that such a bad idea? Think of all the times he'd got them into trouble...him and his so-called hunting skills. More like just another way of putting them in danger. The little fuck...

"I am going to rip your heart out, Jak, do you hear me?" Doc bellowed. He turned away from the baron and strained at his bonds, trying to escape them and head for the albino teen. "You are going to die, and slowly and painfully," Doc roared, his face distorted into a parody of itself by rage and fury.

Ethan stepped back, looking smug and satisfied. "You next," he said, moving toward Krysty. She tried to back off, moving her head to one side, but at the same time keeping the fear out of her eyes. Ethan's hand gripped her jaw and pulled her face around. She found that his grip was surprisingly strong—she had considered that, as a baron who seemed to do little work, he would be soft—and she couldn't stop her head from turning to face him.

"This is going to be interesting," he whispered. "Mebbe I'll plant a few little ideas in there for when you get back—if you do—and mebbe we can have a little fun."

Krysty squirmed. The idea of being Ethan's plaything was repulsive, and yet, even as she thought this, she found a tendril of desire for him creeping into her mind, much to her own disgust. She hocked some phlegm and spit in his face. He calmly wiped it away, still gripping her jaw, and smiled. Somehow, it was much more threatening than if he had hit her. It suggested that he would take his revenge at his leisure, and in his own way.

His eyes bored into her. She called on every reserve, everything she had ever known or been taught.

Meditation and mantras, exercises for the conscious and unconscious, Krysty drew on all of them in her fight against the baron. She could feel his eyes penetrating through her eyes and into her very soul, the tendrils and wisps of hatred that flickered at the corner of her mind. Jak was her friend and had saved her life on more than one occasion. He fought side by side with her, and they stood together. That was the way it had always been. That was the way it had to be. She fought hard to keep that in her mind, but it was forced into an ever smaller space, hemmed in by the hatred that was flooding into her brain.

Ethan was sweating, the crystal twirling in the rays of the sun, the prism of colors bathing their faces. She was difficult; she could resist, and she had an iron-cast will. But he would keep going. He knew he was good at this, and he could sense that she was gradually succumbing to him.

Krysty tried to hold on. Her will was strong; as strong as Ethan's. But there was something that he had over her—he was a free man, and part of her felt constrained by the bonds that tied her to the stake. It was a small difference, but it was there, in her mind. And it was enough to give him the advantage he needed.

Krysty's mind collapsed. She wouldn't have to be going through this if Jak hadn't been the prey. It was all his fault. The better hunter, was he? Why shouldn't he be taking this treatment, as well? Bastard...

"I'll chill you, you little fucker," she murmured to herself.

Ethan stepped back, a smug grin on his face. He took a kerchief and wiped the sweat from his brow. She had finally broken. He looked over to Jak. The albino was watching, but his scarred white visage was impassive. Who could tell what he was thinking behind those red, glittering eyes?

Ethan moved along until he was face-to-face with Ryan Cawdor.

"So, One-eye, that gonna make you easier?" he quipped.

"Funny man," Ryan said calmly. "See how funny you are when I come and rip your fucking heart out and feed it to you."

"Ooh, I'm scared," Ethan mocked. "If you live, I think

I might keep you hypnotized. It could be quite interesting. Now look at me," he said in a more serious tone.

Ryan tried to look away. It was a futile gesture, but he felt he had to make it. Ethan kissed his teeth, shook his head and then drove his fist into Ryan's gut. It was a hard, upward punch that drove the air out of the one-eyed man's lungs. He bent over as far as he could with his bonds, choking and gasping for air. While he was still weakened, Ethan lifted his head up.

"I don't think you're going to be a problem," the baron said softly, lifting the crystal so that it caught the sun, the colors spreading across their faces. Ryan's eye was clouded with pain and, with his resistance weakened, Ethan was able to break through quickly.

Ryan could feel the poison start to seep into his mind. His willpower was always strong, but his mind was distracted by the need to take in air. He didn't have the immediate strength to break eye contact, and by the time he was able to breathe evenly, and devote his full attention to Ethan, the tentacles of hate were already beginning to take hold. Jak was his friend and comrade-in-arms, sure, but if they took out Jak, then J.B. would be freed. No, he knew that wasn't the case, but...why the hell should Jak escape this torture. What made him so special?

"Chill him," escaped from Ryan's lips before he even knew it was what he felt.

Ethan stepped back and looked across the line at the three companions who were now fully under his influence. Then he caught Jak's baleful glare from the end of the line.

Ethan threw back his head and laughed, long and loud. This was going to be one hell of a hunt.

AS THE DOORS SHUT on the hospital, and Mildred and Michaela were left alone with J.B., a sense of complete anticlimax swept over the women. This should be the moment when both of them felt galvanized into action, but instead they stood looking at the closed door, hearing the sounds of the crowd beyond, and felt helpless.

Their eyes met and each knew that the other was thinking the same. J.B. lay there, hovering in some kind of suspended animation. For Michaela to try to escape into the old city to find whatever Ethan was using to keep the Armorer like this was one thing; but it would mean Mildred staying behind and being exposed to immediate danger. For what could she do to protect herself with J.B. like that? It had seemed like a good idea when Michaela had hatched it, but in the harsh light of day, now that it came down to it, it was full of holes.

Mildred shrugged. "Worked with more stupe plans before now, I guess."

Michaela put her head to one side, looking at Mildred and then at the Armorer. "Yeah, but not with one of you in such danger."

Mildred chuckled. "Sweetie, just pray you never know the kind of shit we've been in before now." But then she became serious again. "No, the problem here is that until I know what John's infected with, I won't be happy with chancing discovery. And if you go, we risk discovery every second. Ethan or one of his goons could come in to keep John dosed up at any moment."

Michaela chewed her lip. "Yeah, I've been kind of

wondering about that. He used the infection as a bargaining tool to get you guys to agree to the hunt. But now it's actually under way, just how much do you trust him to keep to his side of the bargain?"

Mildred thought about it. "How about not at all?"

"That's kind of what I was thinking. Which means you'd be left alone, but—"

"Also means that John's on borrowed time," Mildred finished. "I think the best thing I can do is have a look at those slides you prepared, see if I can make head or tail of them."

Checking that the Armorer was comfortable, the two women wasted no time in getting down to their task. Assisted by the young healer, Mildred took the slides and examined them, comparing them to the cultures and viruses that Michaela had in the hospital's freezer. As she already knew, they didn't match: but what she did discover were some points of similarity that led to one conclusion: the virus with which J.B. had been infected at a low level was a variant of meningitis, and if he wasn't treated with the antidote or kept stable, the disease could become full-blown, leading to possible brain damage or buying the farm.

It wasn't the most deadly of diseases back in the day when Mildred had been a practicing doctor, and was certainly treatable and avoidable: but that was then. Now was a completely different matter. In the post-skydark world, it was virtually unknown and could wreak havoc if it took hold. Come to that, it could spread among the population of the ville, and wipe them out. If it reached the stage beyond incubation, where it became transmittable, then they were all running a grave risk and Ethan was playing a very dangerous game.

Mildred tried to explain all this to Michaela without complicating matters about her status as a freezie, explaining her knowledge away as something they had picked up from old archives they had encountered along their journeys.

Michaela seemed to take it all in, and leaned against the lab bench, chewing her fingernails nervously. "I can't believe that Ethan would knowingly put the ville—himself, come to that—in such peril. And, before you ask, he'd be well aware of the risks involved. Bones would have made sure of that: if you'd ever seen his house, and the stuff he'd scavenged from the old city, then you'd know how much old knowledge he's amassed."

"I've heard. Doc was pretty vocal on the subject," Mildred mused. "So if Ethan doesn't really want to administer an antidote to John, and doesn't want the disease to claim him and therefore put everyone at potential risk, then he's just going to chill him. And if he can't be bothered to regulate the meningitis now that the hunt is under way, then he's going to have that done pretty damn quickly."

"Shit," Michaela cursed, "it doesn't sound too good put like that. If I go chasing after the antidote, I could get back to find J.B. already chilled, and you, too, I'd say."

"Damn right," Mildred said softly. "There's only one thing for it, isn't there?"

Michaela's eyes widened. This woman was amazing. "How are we going to do it?" she asked in small voice.

Mildred grinned. "How does 'with great difficulty' grab you?" she asked.

"It doesn't, but it'll have to do, won't it?" Michaela returned with a confidence in her voice that she didn't really feel.

Mildred grabbed the young healer and hugged her, unaware of the feelings she was stirring in the girl's breast. She whispered three words that sealed their course of action.

"Let's do it."

WHILE THE SUN beat down with an intense, dry heat and the fervor of the crowd that watched from around the chain-link fencing reached a fever pitch, Jak felt an icy calm inside. He'd watched the hypnotism of his friends, now turned against him to the degree that they were baying for his blood like a pack of starved hounds. He'd watched the faces of the barons and traders on the stand, eyeing him as if he were a slab of meat ready for slaughter, which he was, as far as they were concerned.

Jak had other ideas. There were a few things he knew that his pursuing companions—now his enemies—wouldn't know. Things that Ethan and his paying guests wouldn't know that he knew. Things that could be turned to his advantage. But only if he centered himself, turned inside and ignored the lust and excitement of the crowds and listened to the instincts that had kept him alive thus far.

He remained impassive when Ethan left the other three tied to their stakes and signaled that the sec guard release Jak. Flanked by the blond sec man Ryan had hit and the bald man he considered enemy only by default—and whose stone-set visage couldn't hide the anger and sorrow in his eyes—Horse stepped forward to free Jak.

While the dreadlocked sec chief loosened his bonds, Jak caught the eye of the bald man. For a fraction of a second, they exchanged glances that communicated many things, not the least of which was Jak's acknowledgment that the sec man wasn't to blame for what had occurred. A good thing to get across, as Jak knew that there was always the possibility that their bond may be necessary if he managed to stay alive and free in the hunt.

The albino stepped away from the stake, massaging his wrists, the white skin reddened and purpled by the tightness of the bonds. Some feeling began to return and, as he rubbed, Jak took a look at the other companions and then at the scum who had paid for this spectacle.

The companions were looking at him with undisguised hate. He had seen those expressions so many times over the course of their travels, but never directed at him. He realized the enormity of his task.

So be it.

The barons and traders who had paid to make them go through this were eyeing Jak with curiosity. They seemed to find it hard to believe that a man so slight should be a match for the other three. No matter: they would soon find out that he was a match for anyone— even the barons and traders themselves. For he would chill them with pleasure.

At another signal from Ethan, Horse and the blond sec guard stepped forward. Jak noticed that the bald man hung back and he refrained from the urge to grin.

"Come on, Whitey," the blond guard said in a voice dripping with malice. "Time for us to take you out to where you get yours." He reached to grab Jak's arm.

"Don't," the albino said impassively.

The blonde gave a short, barking laugh and made a grab for Jak's upper left arm, his fingers encircling the biceps—or at least that's what he intended. A strangely comical, eyes-wide expression came over his face as he realized that Jak had evaded him without actually seeming to move, and he was trying to take hold of thin air.

Jak shimmied out of the grab, pivoted and brought up his heavy combat boot so that the toe and outside edge of his foot connected with the blonde's jawbone. It was the second time in less than an hour that he had been hit in the face, and he lost more teeth as Jak's expert kick crashed his jaws together, grinding tooth against tooth, reducing the inside of his mouth to even more of a bloody pulp than it had been previously. The force of the kick knocked him to one side and lifted him almost off his feet, so that he seemed to be balancing on his toes before the momentum of Jak's foot transferred to his legs and he twisted before falling to the dirt floor of the training ground, raising a cloud of dust.

Horse reached for the Glock that he had holstered at the hip, but was stayed by the hand of the bald sec guard.

"Baron wouldn't want you to chill the little guy and fuck up the hunt, boss. It's Riley's own fault for being so stupe and pissed," he said in a slow, gentle voice.

The dreadlocked sec chief looked around at his man, brown eyes blazing with anger. Then he looked at Jak, who was standing impassively, waiting, and at Ethan, who was eyeing him with interest.

Horse grunted. "Yeah, guess so," he said grudgingly. "But I don't like my men made to look stupe."

"Then they—we—shouldn't act it," the bald man said simply.

Horse's eyes met with Jak's. The albino was bland, unreadable: that was what made him so dangerous.

"Okay, Whitey, I guess you get away with that one, for obvious reasons. But don't fuck with me on the way out to the hunt, or I might be tempted to forget myself."

Jak gestured his assent, not wasting words. He waited until the sec chief had signaled for two more of his men to drag away the unconscious blonde, and then started to walk toward a horse that had been saddled for him.

"We're going to take you out to where the hunt begins, and then give you a half hour head start before we let the other fuckers go," Horse explained. "The paying guests will be with us, and Ethan will follow with the sec that accompanies your friends," he finished with an ironic lilt on the last word.

But Jak wasn't listening. His attention was turned to the barons and traders who were on the stand, readying themselves to join him. His acute hearing was able to pick out at least some of what they were saying to each other.

"Boy's got no chance…" one of the barons said dismissively.

"I'm not so sure. He looks too scarred to have no chance," one of the traders countered with a wise shake of the head.

"Meaning?" the baron queried.

"Meaning that you don't get that scarred if you lose

fights," another of the barons added. "You just get chilled."

They all laughed. Then the shortest and ugliest of the barons proposed a wager: "I'll bet you that no matter how many scars the little runt has, he won't be able to get past those ex-friends of his. They want him chilled, and they know him. He might be tough, but he's outnumbered."

"I'll take you on that," one of the traders piped up enthusiastically. "He's a tough little mutie—seen 'em down in the south. You can fill the shitters full of ammo, and they'll still come running after your hide."

"You, sir, are on—what do you want to wager?" the ugly, short baron asked enthusiastically as they began to leave the stand to take their mounts and follow Jak and the sec guard, so that they would be in position for the beginning of the hunt.

Jak's horse took him out of earshot. But the words of the barons and traders echoed around his head. They were treating this like a sport: fair enough, that's what it was to them. But it was more to him. And he was sure that he would make great sport out of chilling all of them if he got out of this alive.

Horse and Riley rode in line, keeping Jak in the middle. They rode at a steady pace, and in silence. A silence that Jak felt no need to breach. He knew that the blond sec man was looking forward to seeing the companions rip one another apart, but he still wasn't sure about Horse. The lean, dreadlocked sec chief seemed a decent man, a man of some principle. It was probable that there were things about this hunt that stuck in his craw, but his first duty was to his baron, and he would stick to that. But if Jak chilled the coldhearted bastard Ethan, what then?

No matter, that was only idle speculation at this point, something to fill his mind while they rode.

As they approached the edge of the ville, the crowds grew sparse. The majority of the population had gathered in the area between the hospital and the chain-linked compound to view the companions as they were prepared for the hunt. Was it also to make the paying guests feel good? Jak wondered idly. Out here, there were only a few people, going about their everyday business. They didn't even stop from their tasks to watch the sec guard and Jak ride by. As the crowd noise grew more and more distant, the albino hunter could hear the horses carrying Ethan, the barons and the traders, and their own personal guard.

The buildings grew sparse. They passed beyond the walled limits of Pleasantville and out through the small holdings and sparse farmland that surrounded the ville, forming the flatlands that stood between the forest and what passed for civilization. They passed the tracks made by the wild stickie pack less than two weeks ago, and Jak wondered in passing what Ethan had done to the caged creatures to make them act in a way that was so contrary to usual stickie behavior.

The man was scum. Dangerous scum.

They traversed the flatland easily, and within an hour were into the forest. At what seemed like an arbitrary point about a hundred yards into the woods, Horse stopped Jak and Riley.

"Wait here for the baron and his customers...your audience," he added to Jak. "Remember, you have all your weapons, but don't get any smart ideas about trying to chill them. You've got your ex-friends on your ass, and the four-eyed guy and Mildred waiting on you back in the ville. You wouldn't want any more of your people to be fucked over than necessary, would you?"

"Could be fun," Riley muttered, but said no more as Horse's glare silenced him.

Ethan and the hunt audience rode up.

"You ready, boy?" Ethan asked.

"Have to be," Jak replied coldly.

"Insolent little fuck, isn't he?" the inbred baron asked.

Ethan smiled, but with little humor. "As long as you remember what Horse was supposed to tell you," he said simply, gesturing to the sec men.

Riley dismounted and pulled Jak off his horse. He was hoping to catch the albino off guard and to make him fall: Jak was never off guard. He slid easily off the horse, his elbow shooting out and catching the sec man on the way. For the third time that afternoon, Riley hit the ground with his face damaged.

Horse sighed. "You dumb fuck, Riley. You never learn, do you?"

Jak ignored the glare that the blond sec man gave him from the ground, fixing his attention on Ethan.

"You've got a half-hour start, so I'd run if I was you," Ethan murmured.

Jak shot him a look of pure venom and turned, disappearing into the woods at an easy pace, determined to map out his territory rather than rush.

"Now, gentlemen, I suggest we proceed to the best vantage point. Horse will lead the way," Ethan said

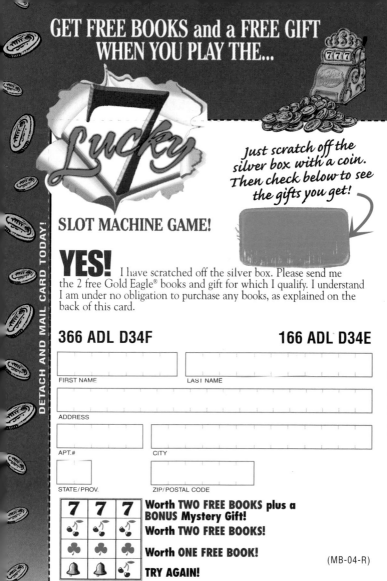

GET FREE BOOKS and a FREE GIFT WHEN YOU PLAY THE...

Lucky 7

Just scratch off the silver box with a coin. Then check below to see the gifts you get!

SLOT MACHINE GAME!

YES! I have scratched off the silver box. Please send me the 2 free Gold Eagle® books and gift for which I qualify. I understand I am under no obligation to purchase any books, as explained on the back of this card.

366 ADL D34F   **166 ADL D34E**

FIRST NAME   LAST NAME

ADDRESS

APT.#   CITY

STATE/PROV.   ZIP/POSTAL CODE

7	7	7	**Worth TWO FREE BOOKS plus a BONUS Mystery Gift!**
🍒	🍒	🍒	**Worth TWO FREE BOOKS!**
♣	♣	♣	**Worth ONE FREE BOOK!**
🔔	🔔	🍒	**TRY AGAIN!**

(MB-04-R)

DETACH AND MAIL CARD TODAY!

The Gold Eagle Reader Service™ — Here's how it works:

Accepting your 2 free books and mystery gift places you under no obligation to buy anything. You may keep the books and gift and return the shipping statement marked "cancel." If you do not cancel, about a month later we'll send you 6 additional books and bill you just $29.94* — that's a saving of over 10% off the cover price of all 6 books! And there's no extra charge for shipping! You may cancel at any time, but if you choose to continue, every other month we'll send you 6 more books, which you may either purchase at the discount price or return to us and cancel your subscription.

*Terms and prices subject to change without notice. Sales tax applicable in N.Y. Canadian residents will be charged applicable provincial taxes and GST. Credit or debit balances in a customer's account(s) may be offset by any other outstanding balance owed by or to the customer.

brightly, gesturing to the sec chief. "This should be quite an interesting day's sport."

J.B. DIX WAS LAID OUT on a stretcher. It had a folding wheel attachment that was made of light aluminum and fiberglass, as was the frame. It had obviously been salvaged from the same place the Pleasantville scavengers had found the cultures that were causing this problem, and Mildred was for once thankful that Bones had taught his search squads well. The wheels could come in useful, and give them a greater speed and mobility than if they had opted to carry J.B.

For that was their plan. It was more than an even bet that Ethan would want to chill J.B., and he wouldn't want it to be from the meningitis becoming full-blown, thus risking an epidemic. This didn't give Michaela enough of a time frame to get to the ruins, find what she wanted and get back. It didn't give J.B. enough of a time frame to recover sufficiently to defend himself even if she did. But it did give Mildred and Michaela enough uninterrupted time—if they were correct—to get a head start on a mercy run to the ruins.

The two women were busy packing what little supplies they had for the run, both medical and in terms of food and water, while the Armorer slept fitfully. Mildred checked her ZKR and turned to Michaela.

"Checked your arms?"

The young healer shook her head. "I don't have a blaster. I hate the things."

Mildred raised an eyebrow. "Nice thought, but not practical, especially now. You do know how to use one?"

Michaela shrugged. "Guess so. Everyone does, don't they?"

Mildred sighed and took J.B.'s Uzi from where it was stowed on the stretcher with his other belongings. She tossed it at the spiky-haired girl, who caught it awkwardly.

"Ever used one of those?" she asked. Michaela shook her head. Mildred moved over to her and showed her how to load, reload, set to single or continuous shot, and sight on the SMG. She stood close to the girl, her arms around her as she guided her hands over the metal of the blaster. While she took in everything that Mildred told her, Michaela also felt a thrill run through her as their skins touched.

"Okay, we set?" Mildred asked, moving away and finishing her own preparation. Michaela nodded, trying to stop herself from trembling; both from fear and from lust. Despite what she was feeling, this was just not the time and place.

Mildred went to the front of the hospital and recced the street outside. A single sec guard lounged against the stoop on the building's veranda. He looked bored and inattentive.

Good.

Mildred found it astoundingly slack that Ethan would leave her with all her inventory and J.B.'s to boot, and with such a lack of sec to guard them. But then again, he wasn't used to people going against him, and he had wanted to bluff the companions into believing that he was speaking the truth.

Oh well, hopefully he'd learn just a little too late.

One guard on the front, seemingly uninterested. Mildred moved from room to room, checking at every window for any signs of a guard. Unbelievably, there were none. Not even at the rear of the building, which would be an obvious first point of weakness in event of escape.

It crossed her mind that this was a little too easy. Could it be that Ethan wanted her to make a break, so that he could legitimately chill her? But to what end? As baron, he could do what he liked, so why make an elaborate ruse of everything? No, it had been down to his own arrogance, and nothing more. He hadn't expected her to attempt any kind of an escape, but to wait for J.B.'s alleged regular booster.

Fuck him and his arrogance.

Mildred returned to where Michaela was waiting by the stretcher.

"There's only the one lazy guard out front. We'll take John to the back, I'll make a quick area recce, then we'll move out. Okay?" Except it was more of an order than a question. Michaela nodded, and they wheeled the Armorer to the rear of the building.

Mildred cracked the door, then drew her ZKR. Holding the pistol muzzle down with both hands, ready to lift and sight at the slightest provocation, she darted out into the alley at the rear of the building, running lightly to each end of the alley to check for movement of any kind.

The area was deserted. Mildred hurried back and indicated to Michaela that all was clear.

The women lifted the stretcher down the back step of the hospital and set it on its wheels. Mildred had made sure that they were well-greased, and they moved easily and quietly on the dirt-packed ground. They ran the stretcher to the end of the alley, and a look of surprise came over the young healer's face when Mildred turned to the left.

"What are you doing?" Michaela whispered. "The old city is that way," she added, gesturing to the right and the ville wall, visible over the low buildings.

"We're not heading there direct," Mildred replied in a low tone. "Think about it—how are we going to get past any sec there with J.B. in tow? No, we need a little help with that, and we made need a little help getting around that city."

Michaela said nothing, but gave Mildred a questioning stare.

The black woman grinned broadly. "Listen, sweetie, who has Ethan's implicit trust and so wouldn't get suspicion from any guards…and who knows more about the ruins and old tech than anyone else? I think that old bastard Bones may be more than a tad useful, one way or another."

"But he'll be vidding the hunt, like he always does," Michaela almost blurted loudly, realizing what Mildred intended.

"Then we'll just have to hope we're quick enough to catch him before he leaves." Mildred shrugged.

"And if we're not?"

The grin returned. "Then we go to Plan B."

"What's Plan B?" Michaela asked, perplexed.

"I don't know—I haven't made it up yet," Mildred replied with a chuckle that made Michaela's blood run cold.

Chapter Nine

Bones fiddled nervously with the screwdriver in his left hand, trying to balance the vid camera in his right while he screwed the battery pack into position. During the time he had spent repairing the old tech he had used the electricity supply that was fuelled by the gas-powered generator Ethan had given him for his sole use. The camera had been damaged during the last hunt, and it had taken the old man some time to get it repaired. Ethan wasn't the most understanding of men, and so Bones had stalled for time when the baron had asked him if it was ready. He had hoped that he would be able to fix the problem without having to incur Ethan's wrath by telling him of the delays.

It was a delicate balance: Ethan's threats and the possibility that he may find punishment before the hunt, against a certain chilling—and possibly a painful one—if it wasn't fixed by today and the baron discovered this. It was a tightrope that the old man was loath to walk, but just lately Ethan had been getting far too intoxicated by the power and wealth that the hunts and the old tech had brought to him. He was starting to make plans to build an empire. Bones had shown him some old vids that he had taken from a house in the ruined city. Most tape had decayed over the time since skydark, if it hadn't been eradicated in the nukecaust, but some, hidden in dark corners of old apartment blocks and offices, had survived by fluke.

There were some vids that showed what life was like before the nukecaust. It seemed like a land of milk and honey to the old man, with limitless jack and tech to make life easy and comfortable. But there were some that seemed eerily prophetic of what life was like now, as if ancient seers had made these vids to warn the people of what could happen. In some of them, barons—not called that, but barons all the same—had taken over great tracts of land using that which they had plundered from the past. They ruled with a cruelty and a ferocity that was legend in their time. And they faced enemies like the ones Ethan was using for the hunt. Enemies who would wipe them out and restore a kind of justice.

Ethan used these as a kind of template for what he wanted. He would come with Horse and sit in Bones's house, watching these vids and telling Horse that this was how it would be.

Bones had no idea what the sec chief thought of this. The dark man stayed impassive, made only the noises that Ethan wanted to hear. Why not? That was exactly what the old man did, as well. It was easier that way; but it became harder as Ethan's ideas became more and more inflated, like his ego.

What if these people he was using in the hunt were like the ones on the old vids? Those sent from the gods, almost... Those sent to bring him down and to restore some kind of natural justice.

Not that the old man necessarily believed in natural justice. He need only to look around. But what if it was there? He stopped fiddling with the battery pack and tried to remember a word that he had read recently. One that went back to old legends in the mists of predark, before there was any tech at all to record these things. What the hell was that word?

Nemesis.

Yes, that was it. What if these people were like those on the vids. What if they were nemesis?

That would be trouble. For everyone. Mebbe that was why Ethan had hit on the idea of using hypnosis and making them hunt one another. If they did that, then they wouldn't be able to band together as they seemed to usually, and turn the hunt back on the baron.

The hunt… Shit! Bones looked at his wrist chron. Ethan always gave him times according to the chron, as he spent so long inside working that he couldn't track time by the sun. The trouble was, his eyes were getting so bad that he had to squint heavily at the chron. It was a vague worry at the back of his mind that if his sight got much worse, his usefulness would cease. Yes, Ethan wanted him to train people in using and repairing old tech, so that would give him a little longer. But, the truth was, once the people were trained, then, bye-bye Bones, time for you to buy the farm. You're no use, and you know far too much.

Time was getting on. He had to get this vid fixed and get over to the forest, meet with Ethan and the barons. He fumbled the screwdriver, cursed to himself and tightened the last screws.

MILDRED AND MICHAELA had wheeled J.B. through the back streets of the ville with little difficulty. Whatever else she could say about Ethan, she had to admit that the man believed in keeping the ville living conditions as good as possible. Ironic that such cleanliness and order was built on blood and horror—a blood and horror that was shared by most of the inhabitants, as they all seemed to be clustered over by the sec compound, waiting to see what happened.

That was okay. It meant that the two women and the prone Armorer were able to make swift and unimpeded progress. In next to no time, they were outside the house in which Bones lived and in which Doc had first learned the secret of Pleasantville. Mildred did a quick recce, scouting to see if Bones was still in the house, and if so, where. She gave a triumphant grin when she saw him through the window, trying to repair something that looked like an old camcorder. They'd always been a problem when they were new, back when she'd lived in the twentieth century. And it looked like it was the battery pack that had screwed him over, making him late.

Some things never, ever changed. And right now, she was suitably grateful for that. She backed off to where Michaela was hiding with J.B. and explained that they were in time to catch the old bastard, and that she would go in alone. "You stay here and keep watch on John."

"You'll be all right?" Michaela asked anxiously, trying to keep her concern for the object of her desire under control.

Mildred looked at her oddly. "Sweetie, if I can't handle Bones, then we may as well give up now." And before Michaela had a chance to form a reply, Mildred was gone.

She reached the back door of the house in a matter of seconds and tried the handle, careful lest it make the slightest noise. She couldn't believe her luck that it was unlocked. What was it with the people in this ville? They seemed to have nothing in the way of security consciousness. Maybe that was why they let Ethan get away with so much. To live in this kind of security in these times would encourage you to cut a lot of slack for a baron.

Still, all the better for her. She entered the house silently, careful for any noise she may make: it was unnaturally quiet inside and the lack of covering noise from outside wasn't doing much to provide her with cover, either. She slipped through the kitchen and the back rooms until she was standing in the door of the main lounge area, where the old man was still bent over the camcorder. He wasn't working on it, but rather as staring into the distance, seemingly lost in thought. Then he checked his wrist chron, muttered to himself and secured the battery pack before switching the camera on to record. Mildred had held her ZKR muzzle down as she'd walked through the house, but as he began to arc the camera, she felt an irresistible desire to ham it up. She raised the ZKR, sighting him.

BONES ALMOST DROPPED the vid camera when Mildred came into view, and she broke the silence, her voice seeming unnaturally loud in the silence of the room. From seeing her in miniature in the viewfinder, she was now revealed in full size in front of him.

"The hunt's under way. Won't Ethan be pissed at you for being late?" she asked in a neutral tone.

"Not half as pissed as he will be when I don't turn up. And I've got a feeling that I won't be turning up," the old man replied with a resigned sigh. "Look, d'you mind if I sit down?" he added, seating himself without waiting for an answer. He put the vid camera on the table and took a pocket handkerchief from the breast pocket of his coat, mopping his forehead with it, then taking off his glasses to polish them. He was squinting so heavily without them that Mildred figured he was almost blind. She couldn't tell, but she would bet that it was cataracts. Something that she could have done something about, once.

Curiously, she felt sure that he wasn't going to reach for a blaster, or a weapon of any kind. He had a resigned air about it him that made any such thoughts absurd. But she didn't lower her ZKR.

Bones put his glasses back on and stared at the blaster. "That's not really necessary, y'know," he said sadly. "I'm not armed, and to tell the truth I've always been a crap shot anyway. You could snuff me out before I had a chance to even get the safety off. But I can understand why you're doing this. I suppose you'll be wanting to stop the hunt and get them back to normal."

Mildred furrowed her brow. "Normal?"

Bones grimaced. "You're not going to like this, then, but don't chill me out of anger, that's all I ask. I'm not crazy about the idea, either. But there's no telling Ethan when he gets an idea into—"

"For God's sake," Mildred cut across him. "You're as bad as Doc. Just cut to the chase and tell me what you mean."

So Bones haltingly told her about the hypnosis, diverting along the way to tell her how he discovered the secret on one of his expeditions. She cut him short on this.

"What you're saying is that Ryan, Krysty and Doc are now hunting Jak, and they won't rest until he's bought the farm, or they have."

"That's about the size of it," Bones agreed. "I'm not there to vid it because Ethan thinks that'll be bad for anyone watching, looking to buy a hunt. He just wants the action. Ironic, in a way. If not for that, you wouldn't have caught up with me. I thought you knew about it, and that's why you're here…or is because of J.B.?"

"What do you know about that?" Mildred questioned.

Bones shrugged. "Only what you've figured out. He's been keeping him alive to use as a tool, and now he's got no use for him. And the only way you can get him better is to go into the old city. You got Michaela with you?" Mildred nodded. Bones shook his head. "She's a good kid, and she doesn't like Ethan. She'll be a good guide. But I'm guessing you wanted the best."

"You're right."

"Well, I don't know if I still am. Old and blind, lady, old and blind. But Ethan'll flay me alive for missing the hunt. You've got a blaster on me right now, and I read this old saying once about being hung for a sheep as a lamb. Didn't quite grasp what that meant until now."

He stood slowly, holding his hands palm up and away from his body.

"No tricks, no nothing. I'm not armed, and if you don't feel happy with that, then—"

Mildred didn't know whether to trust him. He

seemed to be too keen to get out of Pleasantville, a mite too quick to join forces with her. He had to have read that in her expression, because he chuckled.

"I don't blame you for being uneasy. It must seem like a rapid change of heart, especially when you consider I kinda had here everything I always wanted." He looked wistfully around the room. "But they're only things, when all is said and done. And if Ethan's gonna buy me the farm anyway, I wouldn't have 'em for much longer… And speaking of longer, if we don't get it together and get the hell out of here, we're not gonna have any kind of head start on the sec who'll be chasing us." He fixed her with a beady stare that was accentuated by the thick lenses of his glasses. "You're gonna have to let me come with you or chill me. And you must've wanted me to come with you, otherwise why are you here?"

Mildred shrugged. It was a fair point. She just hadn't expected him to acquiesce so quickly. Maybe this damn place was making her too paranoid, and the sooner they got the hell out, the better it would be.

"Will we need weapons in the old city?" she questioned.

"It'd be preferable," Bones answered with a shrug of his own.

"Then grab something, and we'll get going," Mildred told him.

The old man nodded and disappeared from the lounge for a moment as Mildred holstered her ZKR. Was she taking a chance in trusting him? Maybe, but right now, there wasn't much choice. By the time these thoughts had passed through her head, Bones was back with a small Vortak precision pistol, the like of which Mildred had rarely seen, and a 14-shot Glock, which seemed to be the favored blaster of the ville. He noticed her looking.

"We had a trader once who paid Ethan for a hunt with a cache of blasters he'd uncovered. All Glocks. And the ammo, it must've been some kind of old arms dump he'd stumbled on, or even a Glock factory for all I know. Weird, though…" he mused as he stowed the Vortak in a holster strapped to his calf, and shouldered a bag into which he placed the Glock and the spare ammo. "Still, doesn't matter now," he added brightly. "Let's get out of here."

It was all Mildred could do to suppress a smile at the implied notion that it was her holding them up. They left the house through the back and, after a brief recce, made their way across to where Michaela was waiting with J.B.

"Where have you been?" Michaela whispered, her nerves palpably showing. "I've been shitting myself in case someone came by. I hardly know how to use this thing, and if it brought a whole other load of sec around us—"

"Quiet, girl," Mildred said, placating the extremely frightened healer. "It seems that our friend here has his own reasons for wanting to join us, so that should make things easier now we've taken the time to have a few talks about it. Better to waste some time now than run into trouble later."

Michaela grunted and eyed up the old man with more than a hint of suspicion. Bones noted that, and a wry grin crossed his face.

"Hey, you kept quiet about not agreeing with Ethan so you could keep your job and your hide. Ever cross your mind you weren't the only one doing that?"

Mildred was on one knee, checking J.B., who was muttering softly and incoherently in his sleep. "Never mind the recriminations," she said with a note of anxiety in her voice, "we need to get moving. Bones, you know this place better than just about anyone, I'd guess. What's the best route out for avoiding any trouble and moving quickly?"

The old man sucked in his breath. "Those two don't necessarily go together. There are some points where there isn't much of a guard, and one or two blind spots. But with him on a stretcher they aren't practical."

"Then give us something that is," Mildred snapped.

"I will if you let me think," he returned quickly. "It's not as easy as that. Ethan keeps this ville sewn up a lot tighter than most people know, but seeing as it's the hunt, if…" His face lit up with a cunning grin as he realized something. "Yeah, this could be good. But we'll have to hurry," he added.

Mildred took one end of the stretcher gurney while Michaela grabbed the other. Bones waited, barely patiently, then set off, gesturing them to follow. Neither woman had the slightest idea what he had in mind, but they had no option but to trust him at this moment.

Bones led them through a maze of streets, pausing at every intersection to check that there was no one in sight, and gradually the wall around the ville became more and more visible, until it took up the whole of the horizon and they were virtually beneath it. It loomed up over them, seemingly daunting and impossible to scale with the stretcher.

The three of them, with J.B. barely conscious on his stretcher, stood at the end of an alley. In front of them was a stretch of bare earth that led to the wall, which was about fifteen feet in height and composed of scavenged brick, rock and lumps of reinforced concrete that had been somehow jammed and joined together to form a seemingly impassable barrier. Lookout posts along the wall were manned by SMGs mounted on tripods. Mildred couldn't make them out from this distance, but she suspected that they may be old Thompsons, working on belt or drum ammo that had been traded from somewhere.

The important point was that the posts were empty.

"Knew it," Bones rasped, his breathing coming heavy where he had exerted himself. "Ethan's putting on a big show for big jack, and he's pulled everyone over to the hunt. See, this isn't as big a ville as he'd like everyone to think." He grimaced as he sucked in more air. "If we can get up the wall, then we'll be fine. There's no chance of anyone getting back yet, it's far too soon," he added, checking his wrist chron.

Mildred studied the wall, and then looked at Michaela, Bones and the prone J.B. The young healer was wiry, but her strength was an unknown quantity. Mildred had no doubt that she could make the climb on her own...but with the stretcher? That was a point of some contention. Mildred knew that she would need help with it, and Michaela was essential if they were to get J.B. over the wall. And then there was Bones. She no longer had any doubts about the old man's sincerity, but looking at him—standing against the wall of a house, blowing hard and red in the face after such a short trek—she very much doubted if he could get over the wall under his own steam. Frankly, she'd back Doc over him any day; and Doc was always the wild card in such circumstances.

Bones caught the look of apprehension in Mildred's face and gave her a sly grin.

"You didn't think I was gonna make you climb that and haul your man here after you, did you?" he asked. "Come to that, you didn't think I was up to doing that myself?" He paused, savoring Mildred's discomfort as she tried to decide whether she should answer. He preempted her. "Listen, d'you really think that there's only the one gate in and out of the city? How stupe would that be? Especially as the old city is behind this wall— on the far side of the gated wall—and we're always bringing stuff back?"

"There's another way out?" Michaela asked, voicing the confusion Mildred was feeling. "But we always—"

"Yeah, I know," Bones cut in. "You kids are always risking climbing the wall and, to be honest, the sec ignore you 'cause they used to do the same thing. You get cut some slack here, after all. But that's not what I mean. Y'see, in order to get things into the ville and not have to risk riding them around the walls, and also to have a little something up his sleeve if ever we came under attack, Ethan had a tunnel constructed under the wall. Only the salvage squads know about it, and they keep quiet because they don't want to incur the baron's wrath."

"And you know about it, too," Mildred said. It was a statement rather than a question.

Bones tapped the side of his nose. "Who taught these fuckers all that they know?"

"Well, stop talking about it and lead us to it." Mildred sighed. She could hear the faint sounds of the cheering crowds from the far side of the ville and was aware of the uneasy feeling in her gut that told her not only was there very little time to waste, but that the sounds were those of her friends in peril. She'd feel cleaner, more useful, once they were out in the old city, making some kind of progress.

All this went through her mind in the split second it took Bones to beckon them to follow him.

The old man led them off at a tangent, cutting across the open ground until they reached the area underneath one of the gun emplacements and lookout posts. He slowed as they approached the wall, Michaela and Mildred wheeling J.B. as quickly as possible across the rough ground. They avoided jarring the ailing Armorer as much as possible, but there were still a few rough patches of ground that made him moan as his body was jolted on the gurney.

Bones was waiting for them to catch up, a sly grin on his face. He was standing in front of an area of concrete that spread out around the base of the emplacement. It seemed solid enough, but there was something about the arrangement of dirt covering it that seemed to Mildred's eyes to be almost artful. It took her a few seconds to realize that, unlike the rest of the area around, this section of concrete was covered by dirt that carried no human or animal tracks, suggesting that it had recently been recovered to make it blend in.

A smile similar to the old man's flashed across Mildred's face. "Nice," she said simply. "Very nice."

"I thought you'd appreciate it," Bones replied as he bent and pulled at a seam in the concrete floor, barely visible through the layer of dirt. The slab started to lift, and the sweat started to bead the old man's forehead. "Guess I'm not as strong as I used to be," he gasped. "Someone give me a hand."

Mildred stepped forward, first casting a glance at Michaela so that the healer should know to keep an eye on the old man, just in case. It wasn't that Mildred didn't trust him, just that the air of paranoia about Pleasantville was still infecting her. She stood beside Bones and locked her fingers under the ridged edge of the concrete. It was heavier than she had expected, being a good two inches thick, and she was a little surprised at how far he'd managed to lift it on his own. Together, they heaved, muscles straining to get the slab up.

Then it gave way in a sudden lack of resistance, and the momentum they had built up made them both topple backward into the dirt. Mildred cursed loudly and rolled out of the way of the slab, thinking that it would fall on top of them, and was surprised to see that Bones stayed where he had fallen.

"Move, you dumb old coot," she yelled, for a moment feeling exactly as if she was talking to Doc.

"Ta-da!" Bones said by way of reply, laughing and holding his arms aloft as the slab stopped about two feet from his face. He wriggled out from beneath its shadow and got to his feet, dusting himself down. "Guess I forgot to add that it was hinged," he said with a disarming mildness. "You wouldn't have been so worried about me then, would you?"

Mildred bit back the angry reply that sprang to her tongue. This was no time for playing games. She walked over to where the slab had now formed a hinged trapdoor. It led down a shallow slope that doglegged into a tunnel about five feet high and four feet wide, the earthen sides shored up by timber and concrete struts.

"It's safer than it looks," Bones commented, taking in her expression of doubt. "We've used it for a long time, and worked out how small we could make it and still get all the old shit we wanted through there. That way, if anyone on the other side found it, it wouldn't give them that much in the way of access, and all we'd have to do is fire the damn tunnel."

Mildred looked down into the narrow depths. Certainly, anything that was in there if it was fired wouldn't last for long before buying the farm. A shiver ran down her spine when she thought that she, Michaela and John would be down there in a moment.

"What about light?" Mildred asked, shaking off her fears to address the practical issues. "And where does it come out?"

Bones looked thoughtful. "Torches, usually old ones we've charged from generators—I figured out how to recharge old predark batteries a long while back. Can't use naked flame, it takes the oxygen out too quickly, and the smoke is a killer. No ventilation, see?"

"So do you have a torch?" Mildred asked, knowing that she and Michaela had no such items.

Bones shook his head. "Didn't think to pack one. I

was a little surprised by you, after all. But don't worry, it's not a tunnel of great length, and there are no branches. You're not likely to get lost down there," he added wryly. "And don't tell me you're afraid of the dark."

Mildred glared at him. "Not funny, Bones. We've got a sick man to transport, and the last thing we want is any of us stumbling on roots or rocks and twisting an ankle. So if this tunnel isn't that long, tell me where it comes out."

Bones held up his hands placatingly. "Whoa, sorry. Guess I'm just a little shocked at myself for doing this. As to where it comes out—just on the other side of this wall is a five-hundred-yard zone that was cleared to provide a lack of cover for anything or anyone that may want to sneak up on the ville wall. On the edge of that zone is the remains of an old building that was razed to mark the end of the zone. The cellar is still intact, and the tunnel comes out into that cellar. The entrance is disguised on the old ground floor of the building. If you want to know for sure how far we're going to have to go in the dark, I'd say to add on another couple of hundred yards as it doesn't go straight, and we need to get past the wall from this side."

The old man's tone had switched and become more serious as he discussed the obstacle they faced. Mildred listened intently. They'd have to hurry to get out of sight before the sec guard returned to the wall on this side of the ville, but at the same time too much haste could lead to an accident in the darkness. It was a hell of a distance to cover in the dark, with a sick man on a stretcher.

"What about the entrance on the other end. Think it'll be like this one?" Mildred asked.

Bones looked thoughtful. "Didn't expect this one to be so stiff. It suggests there hasn't been anyone going into the old city for some time. Mebbe we'll have to really put our shoulders to the other end to open it. Should be like this one, though. Get it past a certain point and it'll give with its own momentum."

Mildred wasn't looking forward to this one little bit, but it had to be done. She went over to Michaela, who was tending to J.B. The Armorer was muttering to himself, twisting and turning on the gurney, evidently in some distress.

"I think we need to get the hell out of here and make a run for it," Michaela said in a low voice as Mildred approached. "I don't like the way he's going. I reckon that we don't have much time on this score, even if Ethan's thugs leave us alone for ages and don't realize we're gone."

Mildred made a cursory examination of J.B., and agreed with the spiky-haired healer. They'd have to move now. She explained about the tunnel and where it would emerge. Michaela listened intently and didn't seem pleased with the prospect of the darkness. Mildred added, "We don't want to risk the wheels on this thing in the dark, so as soon as we get into the tunnel, we'll have to carry John."

Michaela took a deep breath. "Okay, let's do it," she said with an attempt at an encouraging smile that did nothing other than betray how little she was looking forward to this part of the journey.

The two women wheeled the gurney to the entrance

of the tunnel, and with the barest glance to scout the ground to the bottom of the dogleg, flipped up the wheels and carried J.B. down into the darkness. Bones waited for them to reach the bottom, then followed, tugging at the slab.

"Here it comes!" he yelled as the weight of the concrete slammed the slab back into place, disturbing a small cloud of dirt and dust that made him cough before darkness fell upon them.

There was an eerie silence as the women stood still at the mouth of the tunnel, the only sounds breaking the quiet being J.B.'s soft moans and the pattering of Bones's footsteps as he came down the incline toward them.

Mildred looked around, desperately hoping that her eyes would adjust to the gloom and that there may be some small source of light to just outline shapes. But there was nothing—the faintest whisper of breeze, the movement of air, but nothing more. Not even the scurrying of rats.

She felt a sudden and overwhelming sense of claustrophobia wash over her and a desolating sense of loneliness, which was absurd considering that she was in the tunnel with three other people. The thought that they may be trapped down here, and no one would find them, made the bile rise in her gorge and she had to swallow hard. She didn't usually react this way to the darkness and she realized with a start that it was because she felt the weight of responsibility on her. John—even though he didn't know it—was totally reliant on her right now, and she had these two Pleasantville citizens who had abandoned all protection from their baron to aid her.

And then there were the rest of the companions, pitted against one another. How could she help them, being the only free member of the group...?

She shook her head, trying to clear it. First things first: get out of here and get John better. Then deal with the rest as it arose.

"Hey, are we moving or what? I'm getting a little antsy down here," Bones piped up from the rear. Obviously she wasn't the only one affected by the pitch-black of the tunnel, which gave Mildred a little boost. She was at the front end of the stretcher, and she gave a decisive nod, not that Michaela or Bones would see it, but it made her feel better.

"Let's move," she said calmly. "But stay as alert as you can be down here. We don't know what the floor is like."

She began to pace out the floor of the tunnel, each foot gingerly coming down, testing for breaks in the surface, bumps and rocks and uneven potholes in which she could twist, sprain or break an ankle. The floor was surprisingly smooth, worn down and hard-packed earth forming its base. She had no idea how close the walls were to her, but once or twice she found herself veering away from a straight line and bumping into them. She couldn't tell what was happening behind her. She knew that Michaela had to be following directly behind at a steady pace and with surefootedness, as the stretcher kept up with Mildred's speed, its weight and balance steady. But there was no other way of knowing: no one spoke, their breathing was shallow and barely audible, almost as if they were afraid to use up the air in the tunnel; and it was pitch-black.

The walls and floor of the tunnel smelled musty, where the air was stale. But there was also a richness underlying it, from the dampness of the soil as they traveled below the sun-parched surface, hitting where the water table began. The old timbers also carried their own smell, beginning to muster and rot as the damp earth worked on them. It became almost overpowering and Mildred's head was filled with visions of being trapped down here, the panic beginning to rise again.

She bumped into a wall in front of her. The tunnel floor was heading upward, and they had hit the dogleg at the other end. Trying to suppress the cry of relief she wanted to give, Mildred spoke as calmly as possible.

"We're at the other end. Bones, get the hell up here and help me open the tunnel."

She put down the stretcher and heard the old man shuffle past until she could feel rather than see him beside her.

"Should be just up… Yeah," he said, reaching out to touch the concrete slab. Mildred felt it as she, too, reached out. It was cold and unyielding.

"Push on three. One, two, three…" she gasped, putting effort into the push and hearing Bones grunt beside her. The slab was unyielding for a moment, and a cold dread clutched at her guts. Then, before it had a chance to take hold, the slab gave way, springing open to let daylight flood in. She screwed her eyes against the painful intrusion, then turned to see Michaela doing likewise, standing over J.B.

"Stay here a moment," Bones said quickly. "I'll just have a look to see if the sec guards are back on the wall. If they are, we'll need to be careful. If not, we can just go for it."

And before Mildred had a chance to speak, the old man had scrambled out of the mouth of the tunnel and was on his way, using the lower level of the old cellar floor and the surrounding rubble as cover. It seems he had taken her imprecations for speed to heart. Which, looking at a sweating J.B., wasn't a bad thing.

And let's face it, she thought, whatever came next couldn't be as irrationally scary as the tunnel. Whatever the ruined city had in store, at least it'd be an enemy she could see.

Chapter Ten

As Ryan, Krysty and Doc watched Jak being taken from the sec compound, they each felt an inchoate rage rise within them. They wanted to rip him limb from limb for some imagined ill that they couldn't bring back to mind, but that ruled their instincts and senses. Each of them strained against the bonds that kept them tied to the stakes, and each yelled incoherently at the departing albino and his sec guard.

Ethan watched them from back up on the stand, where he could also hear his customers make wagers and argue about the merits of each side of the contest. He was pleased. There was a lot of jack riding on this hunt, and he had little doubt that it would be a success as he watched the three outlanders almost rupturing blood vessels and tearing off their own limbs to get at their former comrade.

"Gentlemen, may I suggest that we take our leave?" he queried as Jak, accompanied by Horse and Riley, exited the compound on his journey to the forest.

"Sounds goods to me. The sooner we get out there, the sooner the fun begins, right?" one of the traders asked, chuckling.

"Exactly," the baron stated before leading his guests to the horses that had been supplied for them. As they mounted, he called over to him a man-mountain of a sec guard, with a face heavily tattooed with a spider's web. The man had been chosen as Horse's number two for the hunt mostly for the reason of his size and strength. "Tracey," the baron began as the man lumbered to him, "keep a close watch on your wrist chron and give us half an hour. Then you bring these scum out to the starting point. Horse told you where that was, right?" He waited for the sec man to nod before continuing. "I want you to be real careful with them. They're raging, and they may be hard to handle. They'll want to get straight after Jak, and we don't want that, right?" Again, he waited for the tattooed man to nod dumbly, signaling that he had taken in the instructions. "Good," Ethan said finally. "Now, there's one thing. I want the big bald guy sent to the farthest sec post on the wall. I want him nowhere near the action, okay?"

Tracey wasn't the brightest of the sec guards, although possibly the strongest, and he furrowed his brow, trying to understand the connection between the two sets of instructions. He knew that it was wrong to question the baron, but...

"Why?" he asked. "I mean, sir, I know I shouldn't ask, but what do I tell him if he asks?"

Ordinarily, Ethan would have exploded at such apparent insubordination, but there was an ingenuousness about the tattooed man's face that suggested he was asking from a genuine concern over what to say if asked. It was a mark of the baron's good mood on this day that he didn't shout and rant at the man, but gave him an answer.

"There's some sympathy between the big man and

the albino. I get the feeling that he doesn't approve of this hunt. But he's too good to throw away, so I want him where he can do no harm. Tell him I want the wall defended well because there may be an attack with the number of barons and traders we have with us today. Tell him I have had information."

"Have you, sir?" Tracey asked, a note of anxiety creeping into his voice.

Ethan grasped the man's shoulder and resisted the urge to laugh. Such innocent stupidity in someone so large and dangerous. It seemed incongruous, to say the least. "No, son," Ethan said gently, "it's just a story to keep him away from the hunt."

The tattooed man seemed to think about that for a second, then smiled a little and nodded. "Yeah, I see, sir. I'll do that."

"Good." Ethan clapped him on the back. "Now bring me my horse and we'll be going."

Tracey rounded up the horses for all the guests and for the baron, and watched them leave, checking his wrist chron and working out when he had to release the three prisoners to take them to the forest. Then he looked up with a grim expression on his face and walked over to fulfill the second part of his task.

"That's stupe," the bald sec man said bluntly when Tracey gave him the baron's explanation.

"Are you arguing with Ethan? 'Cause it's not me saying it." Tracey bristled. He hadn't expected to be questioned and he wasn't sure what to do.

The big man thought about it carefully before answering. "No," he said finally. "I'll do it. But it sucks, and you know it."

Without another word he turned on his heel and set off for the gates out of the compound, not looking back.

Tracey scratched his head and looked at his watch. Still a lot of space before the hands on his chron, which were formed by the hands and arms of a black mouse in red shorts, which usually made him chuckle, but not today—reached the point where he could let loose the three prisoners.

Shit, he preferred it when he was taking orders rather than giving them. There was less to worry about, then...

THE HOT, chem-hazed sun beat down on the compound, mercilessly hitting the three companions as they struggled almost nonstop with their bonds. The sweat poured from them and they hadn't been given anything to ease the thirst and dehydration that was building up within them. Jak had been gone for some time, and it seemed to them, in their frenzy, that they would never be able to track him.

Eventually, Tracey and a team of sec men walked over to them. They were carrying large knives to sever the bonds that kept the trio bound to the stakes, and chains with which to bind them once more until they had reached the hunt site. Following on the heels of the sec party were women with salty food and buckets of water. They also carried small canteens of water for the companions to carry on the hunt, something that had been denied to Jak.

"Take them down, and be real careful," Tracey directed the sec party, before adding to the companions, "Okay, listen up. We're going to let you off in the woods. Don't go all crazy on us and try to get away, 'cause that won't work. You'll get to rip the little guy to shreds, but first you gotta eat and drink, get some water and salt back in you. Then we're gonna take you to where he is. So you be calm now, or else we're gonna have to hurt you, and we don't want to do that. D'you understand?" he added in a slightly plaintive tone, seeing the wild look in the eye of each person, and wondering if they could even hear him.

In truth, it was difficult for his words to penetrate the perverted and corrupted consciousness of each of the companions. The hypnosis, the constant draining heat of the sun, and the loss of salts, minerals and water from their bodies had left them in a state where everything around—each stimulus—came to them as though it were through a red mist: a mist of pain and nonunderstanding, where every nerve fiber screamed for an action they couldn't take.

Inside their heads, each was playing out a scenario where they hunted and chilled Jak. Their minds were filled with twisted images of the wrongs he had done them to incur such wrath. And all of these were filtered through the pain caused by the constant straining against their bonds and the mental anguish of that small part of their minds that still screamed that they were wrong to feel this way.

The sense of Tracey's words filtered through—perhaps to this small part of their consciousness—and they each stopped writhing and straining against their bonds. Blank-eyed stares were all that greeted him as he tried to look into their faces and he whistled softly before directing his men to cut them loose, reminding them to be real careful.

The sec party stepped up to the stakes, three to each companion. Even though they were obviously weakened by the heat and their exertions, they still had the strength of the crazed, and in front of those Pleasantville citizens who were still watching with interest, Tracey didn't want the men he had been put in command of to fuck up.

On a count of three, and like a well-oiled machine, one sec man sliced the bonds at arms and legs with precision strokes of his razor-sharp machete, carried for that purpose. As the companions fell limp for a second, the blood-drained legs and arms not quite receptive to the brain's command, the two sec men on each side, equipped with the chains, grabbed the person and secured them so that they were effectively hobbled.

Tracey watched and nodded appreciatively. So far, so good. If Horse got a good report about this, then he may not get stuck with as many shitty tasks as he had in the past. That was all that concerned him: getting it right, and getting better tasks in the future. He didn't care about what was happening in the hunt or to the three people in front of him. Why should he? As far as he was concerned, they wouldn't worry about him.

Chained, the three companions were then fed and watered by the women who had followed the sec party. At first they were resistant, as though they didn't know what was happening, and it was some kind of bodily invasion. But then the need for salt and water took over and they followed instincts that told them to eat and drink. They all partook hungrily of what was offered, and were clamouring for more when, at a signal from the tattooed sec man, the women pulled back.

Tracey looped the canteens of water over their necks personally. "Now, this is for when you're on the hunt, chasing the little dude. You've got to save this...I hope you can understand me," he added to himself, noting the animal quality that still haunted their eyes, seeming to make them distant from what was going on.

"Bring the horses up, it's time for us to get going," he called to the other side of the compound.

There was a horse for each companion, and they were to be escorted by two sec men each, with Tracey heading the party. He looked anxiously at his wrist chron. The mouse's black hands and arms were almost in the right place.

"Okay, get them mounted," he shouted to his men.

The companions were pulled to their feet and led to the horses. They didn't try to resist the sec men, as though they had—in some way—taken in what had been said to them. But trying to get them astride their mounts presented problems of its own. With their hands and feet effectively shackled, it was hard for each of them to get their bodies up. They were still dazed from the heat and the sudden effects of the food and water on their blood sugar, and were pliable when the sec men tried to get them on the horses, but it was no good.

"It's a fucking stupe idea, Tracey," one of the sec men said finally. "They ain't gonna get over the backs of these horses. Look at the chains on their legs. No way are they long enough to let them get a leg each side."

"Aw shit," the tattooed man cursed as he came over to look. It was true. The length of the chain wouldn't stretch across the backs of the beasts. "Okay, sling the fuckers over on their bellies."

"You sure about that? It ain't gonna look good when we reach Ethan and the payers when they come like that."

"It's that or nothing." Tracey shrugged.

He saddled up and mounted his own steed, signaling to the sec guard with him to follow on, bringing the horses with the three hunters flung across their backs. The entourage left the sec compound to the cheers of the remaining crowds, with the man in charge feeling uncomfortably aware that they didn't look quite as heroic as the baron would have wished.

For all three companions, the time spent on the backs of their mounts passed slowly and in a haze of discomfort and pain. Doc vomited heavily as the jarring of the horse made his stomach rebel. Krysty was in a semiconscious state, her mind slipping in and out of strange and disconcerting dreams, and Ryan was aware only of a throbbing in his head, as though the pressure had built to such a pitch that the only way to vent it would be through his empty eye socket.

As the sec party bearing the hunters approached the forest, Tracey held up his hand to halt the parade.

"What's wrong?" queried one of the sec to his rear.

"Look at them," the tattooed man said in disgust. "If we ride up with them like this, Ethan'll have our hides. We've got to make them look like they can do the business. Right now, they just look like a bunch of stumblebums."

"Yeah…" the talkative sec man replied slowly. He wasn't sure what his tattooed boss was talking about, but looking at the so-called hunters slung across the backs of their mounts, he could take a pretty good guess. "What d'you suggest, then?"

The tattooed man dismounted and walked back to the three hunters. "They don't look like they're gonna make a run for it, do they? We unshackle their legs so they can sit on the horses properly, we clean up the old guy, and we douse them down, try to wake them up a little. They've gotta look good, if nothing else."

The rest of the sec party could only agree. None of them wished to incur the wrath of their baron, and so they all pitched in to help. The three companions were taken down from the horses, the chains to their legs unlocked and removed. All three of them found it difficult to stand at first, as their muscles were cramped and starved of oxygen and blood from their awkward positioning on their mounts. Doc was covered in caked vomit, which was already starting to harden and dry out under the chem-covered sun. He was doused in water and rubbed down with rags, his rambling ravings ignored as two sec men cleaned him up.

Ryan and Krysty seemed to see the world around them through a mist. They recognized each other, and they could see that Doc was being cleaned up, but what they couldn't tell was why. There was only something in their heads that kept dragging their thoughts back to Jak, and how to chill him.

They stood, looking as though they were a million miles away, swaying slightly where their muscles were still returning to normal. Tracey looked at them and sucked in his breath. He'd better liven up the fuckers, and pretty damn quickly.

"We got spare water, other than their canteens?" he asked the assembled sec party. There was a general assent. "Douse them," he ordered. "That might wake them up a bit."

The shock of the cold water as it hit all three of the companions in their faces was as effective as the tattooed sec man had hoped. The mists seemed to clear before their eyes, and their senses were shocked into some kind of normality.

"Do that again, and I'll drop you where you stand," Ryan snarled at the sec man in front of him.

"Y'know something, One-eye? I'm actually kinda glad to hear you say that," Tracey said with an audible relief. "You was all kinda out of it, there. You know why you're here?"

"Of course we do," Krysty snapped. "We've got to find that treacherous little fuck Jak, and make sure he buys the farm."

The tattooed sec boss turned to his sec companions. "Yeah, it's worked okay," he said as an aside.

Turning back to the three companions, he continued. "Look, I'm real sorry if y'all kinda pissed at me for what's just happened, but you were all a little bit—" he gestured to his head "—which I guess is that little shit's fault. We're taking you to where the hunt for him is taking place. Then you get to find the fucker. Sound good?"

"Lead us to him, dear boy, lead us to him," Doc muttered, shaking his head to clear it further and sending a spray of water from his straggling mane of white hair.

Tracey smiled to himself. The other sec men looked at him in amazement. Considering how stupe he was, that was a pretty amazing story he'd just told the hunters. They weren't to know that he had been briefed earlier by Horse, in case of such an eventuality. And no matter how dumb he was, he had a good memory, parroting the story he had been fed almost word for word.

The sec party remounted and led the hunters on toward the area where the baron and his paying guests were awaiting their arrival. The three companions, their clothes drying rapidly in the sun, were now erect and alert, ready to begin battle. They would arrive at the appointed spot looking lean, mean and ready to fight. Only their hands were chained, and these would be freed in front of the hunt party. Already they looked keen for action, the hatred blazing in their eyes.

The tattooed sec man breathed a mental sigh of relief. No one would know how they had traveled most of the distance, and no one in the forest had seen them dazed, confused and slung over the horses. Appearances were everything, Horse had drummed into him.

And they looked just fine...

JAK LAUREN HAD KNOWN that he had very little time when he had been set loose by Horse and Riley, in front of the coldheart bastards who were paying jack to pit him against his friends. What time there was, he had to use well. He didn't want to chill Ryan, Doc and Krysty, but unless he could find some way of breaking the hold Ethan had over them, then that was the way it would have to be. It wouldn't be easy, but it would be a necessity.

But first, Jak felt compelled to try to make them see sense. And if he was going to do this, then he would have to use all the cunning and hunt skills that he possessed to trap them. While keeping this out of the view of the party who were paying to watch the hunt.

Ethan and his guests had assumed that Jak would make a straight run for it, to try to put distance between himself and his pursuers. They planned to follow the other three. As a result, they didn't track his progress through the forest, and so were unaware of his actions.

On being set free, Jak had made a straight run until he was sure that he was out of earshot and out of view. Then he had stopped and climbed a tree overhanging the path he had taken. The foliage was less dense there and it would be an obvious route. He listened and waited for a short time, but there was no indication that he had been followed in any way.

He didn't wait as long as he would have wanted. There wasn't the time and he knew that any of his actions from now on would be compromised by the fact that he had to hurry. He was battling time as much as he was battling his erstwhile friends.

Jak slipped down the tree and doubled back, taking care not to tread exactly the same ground. He came within view of the hunt party, talking idly among themselves while they waited for the hunters to be delivered to them. They were placing bets on how long it would take him to be caught, and discussing with some animation the ways in which they thought he would be chilled. Jak smiled coldly, his hard eyes glittering. He'd remember some of the things they said, and just mebbe use them against these bastards if he got the chance.

They would be there for some time, and they seemed disinterested in what he was doing. Good. That gave him the freedom to put a few plans into operation.

Jak left them and moved silently back into the forest. He was aware of the smell of animal life all around him. Most of these were small birds and mammals that offered no threat, but he thought of the bald sec man's warning about the mutie raccoons they had encountered before. If he could locate their dens, then he could use that to his advantage.

It wasn't difficult for someone of Jak's skills and instincts. The creatures were basically nocturnal, so they would be at rest in this heat. That would make them particularly bad-tempered when roused; it also made them easier to track right now. Following his senses, Jak headed for an area where the smell of the animals was strong and there were less traces of other birds and mammals. The raccoon muties would scare away any other life that came near, so the absence of any scent and noise other than the raccoon was a giveaway. Their dens were set into mounds of earth, burrowed deep beneath the shade of a crop of stunted trees. Jak smiled to himself, marking the spot mentally. He could lead his pursuers here, stir up the beasts and get behind the inevitable battle.

That was one trap. He would need more.

Jak moved in a semicircle around the area where the hunt party was waiting. He didn't want to go too deep to give anyone too much room in which to lose themselves. They would expect this from him, but his plans ran to the contrary. He didn't want to lose them, he wanted them all close, where he could track their movements. Rather than run, by waiting and planning, he was turning the hunt on its head—they may think that they were hunting him, but in truth the reverse was the case.

At an angle approximately three o'clock to where the hunting party waited unawares, and almost 120 degrees from where the mutie raccoons slept in the daylight, Jak found a small hollow. It was a dip in the earth where the tree roots formed a web of potentially fatal consequences. Anyone tripping or getting caught in this web could seriously damage their leg or ankle, rendering them vulnerable to attack. The thing that stopped this hollow being a deadly trap was that the root systems were in full view to anyone approaching, being uncovered.

Jak had time to change that. As quietly as was possible, he ripped tree branches covered in leaves and armfuls of grasses from the surrounding area, covering the root system as best as possible. It wasn't a perfect trap, but he didn't have the time to perfect the camouflage. It was covered and the foliage overhead darkened the hollow. Someone chasing him at full speed wouldn't hopefully have the time to think before charging straight into the trap. Even if they were suspicious, it would at least slow them.

Two traps laid, but three companions to stop. Jak's brain worked feverishly. He needed at least one more trap, and quickly. The problem was that the woodland presented him with very little in the way of ready-made traps and he didn't have the time to spend on constructing something a little more useful. Ideally, he would have liked to use one of the denser crops of trees to hide a net trap that he could lead one of the companions into, but that would necessitate the construction of a net, and although he could find the makings of one easily enough, he didn't have the luxury of time necessary to make the net from these raw materials. He needed something in the natural landscape that he could turn to his advantage rapidly.

It was then that his heightened senses told him that

the hunting party was being joined by others, which must mean his erstwhile friends who were now programmed to hunt him down.

Jak's mind worked rapidly. The area of densely wooded forest where he would have built the net trap was also home to a sudden steep incline with loose shale and a treacherous path underfoot. He knew that from his recce; his enemies wouldn't. Ryan or Krysty would be able to cope, Doc perhaps less so. So he would try to lead the older man into this section of the forest and use this trap on him. The tree roots would be good for snagging the Titian-haired woman, who always wore the silver-tipped cowboy boots that were usually good on rough terrain, but were spectacularly ill-suited to such a treacherous underfoot environment. And the mutie raccoons were something he would keep for Ryan. The one-eyed man was the strongest of the three, and as such would need the trap that sapped that strength the most, leaving him vulnerable.

Jak gave an almost imperceptible shake of the head, his stringy white hair, matted with sweat already, barely moving around his scarred white face. It didn't make much sense to him to be thinking of taking out his old companions in this way, but he knew that it was a necessity. They would certainly be out for his blood.

He moved back toward the spot where the paying hunters were waiting for their sport to arrive. Without the benefit of Jak's highly attuned senses, they were unaware that the second half of their entertainment was approaching until the sec men and the companions were almost upon them—by which time Jak had positioned himself so that he could observe their arrival, and take stock of what condition they were in. As far as he was concerned, the most important thing—in fact, that on which his success in staying alive depended—was to separate the companions almost from the off, so that he could take them in a series of one-on-ones. Mebbe that wouldn't be possible. He hoped it would be, as it would make his task that much easier.

From his vantage point, he assumed an almost preternatural immobility to avoid detection, waiting until they came into view.

"AH! ABOUT TIME, TOO, but I think you'll find it's been worth the wait," Ethan commented as Tracey led his small party into the clearing where the paying guests were waiting along with Horse and Riley.

The dreadlocked sec chief cast an eye over the three companions. They were erect in their saddles, their legs free but their arms chained. They looked alert, wide-eyed and ready to hunt. But the dreadlocked man smiled humorlessly as he noted that there were barely dried water stains on their clothes, and that Krysty's mane of Titian-red hair was darker at the ends, a little matted where it had been wet, was still damp, and had tangled in the backdraft of their journey. He suspected that they had been in a less than presentable state until they had reached the edge of the forest, and that the stupe sec man had done the one thing he was good at—following orders carefully. Certainly, unless you looked hard, you couldn't tell that they were anything less than a hundred percent fit and ready for action.

The sec chief wasn't to know that Jak was hidden on the edge of the clearing, taking in everything that the sec chief had; noting the same thing, which gave him a little edge the hunting party would know nothing about.

Baron Ethan, on the other hand, was completely immune to these nuances and saw only what his customers saw: three bright-eyed hunters, ready to chill.

"As you can see, gentlemen, they're in fine fettle, and I'm sure that you would all like to make private wagers on which one of them will take out the albino."

"Wagers for which you will no doubt act as banker, Ethan—for a small charge," one of the traders commented. The words caused the party of barons and traders to laugh uproariously. Ethan joined in, but with a self-deprecating air that paved the way for his next comment.

"Of course, you may have intended that in jest, Rowan," he said to the stocky, tough-looking trader, "but you raise an important point. I will be taking no part in this hunt, and my jack is already secured for supplying the entertainment. If I did act as banker, then it would insure a certain impartiality, would it not?"

The trader he had addressed as Rowan gave him an astonished look that bloomed into a smile accompanied by a full-throated chuckle. "You old bastard! You're right, of course. The last thing we want to do is fall out and fight among ourselves over a little jack. But it would take you to turn that to your advantage. Still," he added, addressing the other barons and traders, "I figure that we wouldn't be here without Ethan's ingenuity, so if the dude wants to make a little more on the side, who are we to begrudge him?"

Laughingly, the others agreed and argued over who they would place their money upon to be the one to make the actual chill. Horse and Riley watched with a detachment that could only come from being outside the action.

"I don't care about any of this, I only hope the little fucker gets the one-eyed bastard," the blond sec man murmured in an undertone to his chief.

Horse bit his tongue to suppress his amusement. "C'mon, Riley, wouldn't you rather that One-Eye makes it through in one piece so that you can have another go at him—or mebbe you don't think that you could take him down?" he added after moment's thought.

The blond glared at his chief through narrowed eyes. "You know I could, if I wasn't taken by surprise. Anyway, are you telling me that no matter what happens we get to chill all the fuckers?"

"You don't think that Ethan's gonna turn them all loose after what's been going down, do you? As soon as the hunt is over, we have to mop up whatever's left— whether it's Whitey or One-Eye or the woman or the old dude, or any combination of them. They've all bought the farm, it's just that they don't know it yet."

"What about the black woman and the other guy?"

Horse smiled, but it stopped at the eyes, which were cold and hard. "I don't think they've got anything to worry about anymore."

Riley gave a low laugh. "I think I'm gonna enjoy this even more than I was before," he muttered.

Neither man was to know that they were being observed. Jak was positioned in the foliage so that he could see and hear everything that was going on in the clearing, and this discussion had particularly attracted his attention.

There was nothing he could do about Mildred and J.B. They were on their own, and he trusted Mildred to be smart enough to have already worked out that something in Ethan's plans had been a lie. If any one of them could haul J.B.'s ass out of trouble, and get him better to fight against the enemy, then it was Mildred Wyeth.

No, Jak's concerns were based solely around the hunting party in the clearing. The fact that it was no longer chill or be chilled, but all chilled whatever the outcome, changed everything. He would take out the friends turned against him if he had to in order to survive, but if he was going to buy the farm anyway, then his imperatives changed.

Jak wondered about the hypnosis. He had seen Ryan hypnotized before, by the beautiful Katya Beausoleil, who had wanted to take Ryan from his companions to use for her own pleasure. A similar thing had happened with the evil witch queen Jenna, wife of Baron Alien, when a rogue nuke had nearly ended their tenure on the earth. Each time, the one-eyed man had fought an internal battle that had ended with his true self eventually surfacing. Jak had no doubt this could happen again. The question was, would it take longer than Jak could afford?

Similarly, he and Krysty had fallen under the spell of a mutie leader who had wanted to unite all muties in the Deathlands against those who carried no mutated genes. For a while, they hadn't been themselves, until they had broken free of the mind shackles. So he knew that Krysty had the strength to break out of a hypnotic hold. Once again, it was a matter of time.

As for Doc— The man wasn't as old as he seemed,

his apparent age caused by the stresses of being trawled twice through time by the whitecoats of the Chronos section of the Totality Concept. In the same way, his mind had been twisted and distorted in such a way that his grasp of the every day could sometimes be tenuous. So, once again, it seemed possible that the hypnosis may only have a tenuous hold. It came back to time, once again...

Meanwhile, Ethan was ordering Tracey to release the shackles on the three companions.

"We get to hunt yet?" Ryan asked as the chains were stripped from his wrists, much to the amusement of the assembled spectators.

"In a short while, Ryan, my friend," Ethan answered him, using tones that would have been more suitable for speaking to a child—although in many ways this was the level to which hypnosis had reduced the companions. "Just trust in me..."

The one-eyed man didn't answer, merely replied with a stare that was inscrutable. Ethan felt a flicker of worry. Did the gaze of that one cold, diamond-hard orb mean that Ryan was beyond understanding or that he was putting up a front and would turn at any minute?

For the first time this day, the baron felt uncomfortable. This hunt meant everything to him: the beginning of a new era in sport for the ville, and a new era of expansion, bringing in more and more jack, increasing his power base in this region, and mebbe even across the whole of the Deathlands. There was so much riding on this that he didn't want anything to go wrong.

His fears were allayed by the reactions of Doc and Krysty as they were released. Both were itching to get to the hunt. They were agitated and expressed desires to get out there and chill.

"I say we release them one at a time, and they go for the albino as individuals rather than a group," said the inbred baron, his soft palate distorting the words. "Makes the wager a little more interesting—and we follow our favorites, yes?"

The others enthusiastically agreed.

Chapter Eleven

"I've never been so glad to see a stretch of asphalt in my life," Mildred gasped as they turned a corner and came upon a road that was long and unencumbered by any blockages.

"It will be a relief," Michaela echoed breathlessly as she joined Mildred in setting up the light aluminum wheel supports of the stretcher gurney, allowing J.B. to touch the ground once again.

Mildred massaged her aching forearms. "Who would've thought it could be such a pain carrying a stretcher over a few bits of rubble."

"A few?" Michaela grimaced. "It feels like we've lapped this damned city at least twice."

"Yeah, well, you know who to blame for that," Mildred murmured, inclining her head toward Bones, who was still walking in advance of them. She whistled and the old man stopped and looked back, peering through his thick-lensed spectacles.

"Come on, come on, we don't have time to waste. You yourself said as much," he called peevishly.

Mildred shook her head. "Get back here," she yelled, waving him toward them. "We've got a few things we need to do before we go any farther."

She could almost hear the old man sigh as he trotted

back, and not for the first time she thought about how like Doc he could be. For a second, it crossed her mind that Dean would have found the old man amusing, just as he could find Doc a source of humor as well as affection. But she dismissed the thought almost immediately. There were more pressing concerns to be dealt with.

As soon as they had emerged from the tunnel mouth, they had been up and running, almost literally. Bones had given the all clear, and the two women had snapped the wheels on the gurney, lifting the Armorer to take his weight as they made their way into the ruined city.

The rubble at the fringe of the ruins had been built up by Ethan's sec men to form a kind of wall that would keep anything in the city at bay. The ruins that had occupied the now cleared space between the ville walls and the area where the tunnel emerged had been piled high to form this barrier, and although it may give a sec army led by intelligent humans cover from which to mount a siege, all it did for any hostile wildlife or muties like stickies was to provide a platform they would have to scale before being silhouetted against the sky as easy targets for the blaster posts on the ville wall.

The rubble barrier formed in this way extended for about a hundred yards. It was uneven and treacherous underfoot, and as Bones sped across it, Michaela and Mildred found it difficult to keep a firm and even footing while keeping J.B.'s stretcher level. Their progress was slow, and there was an anxiety that grew within Mildred's breast: on top of the rubble, hands occupied with the stretcher, they were easy targets for anyone that may return to the blaster emplacement before they were clear of the area. They were also easy pickings for any-thing that may lurk within the ruined city, waiting to at-tack. Teetering over the rubble they were a slow, prone target for anyone or anything.

In theory, Bones should be acting as lookout and point for them, covering them with his own blaster. But somehow, Mildred doubted if the old man would be much good. He was too far in front, and seemed ab-sorbed in his own activity to notice what was happen-ing behind him. It was almost as though he had rediscovered his own youth in skipping over the ruins like a child. Mildred had no wish to rob him of this. In fact, it may be useful to them as they got farther into the ruined city and were directed to the old medical labs. But she could wish that he would be a little more con-siderate at this stage.

She couldn't even call out to him to get him to come back to act as point man. There was a deathly silence over the ruins and every footfall sounded loud and dis-ruptive as they progressed in a haphazard manner over the rubble.

Mildred had cast a few glances back toward the walls of Pleasantville, and could see that the emplacements were still empty. She had tried not to think of the hunt, but the knowledge of what was occurring weighed heav-ily. When she had J.B. back on his feet, they would go back for their comrades. And if vengeance needed tak-ing, then there would be no questions asked or quarter taken.

It was hard to stop to take a look back at the ville, as Michaela had always been at her heels, head down, pushing onward and muttering to herself to give her the courage to keep going. The young healer had no stomach for danger, but was pushing herself to her limits. While this was noble in one way, it did make Mildred a little anxious as to how soon it would be before the girl would snap.

They were over the rubble barrier and down onto the streets of the old city in what seemed like slow motion. But once they were there, Mildred was able to breathe easily, without the tightness of tension that had been constricting her chest. Still they had to carry the stretcher, as the old roads were strewed with rubble and debris, making it impossible to pilot the gurney and make any kind of progress. But at least the ground underfoot was surer and they were able to move more swiftly.

Bones was away from them, taking a definitive path. There was little doubt that he knew where he was headed, but Mildred was concerned that they would lose track of the old man because of his sudden spurts of speed. He was around corners before they had a chance to catch him, darting back only to hurry them on. He seemed to have no sense of caution about the terrain and its possible perils, only a desire to move quickly.

Mildred, on the other hand, had her hands full metaphorically as well as literally. There was a blanket of silence over the ruins and little indication that any muties—either human, stickie or animal—lived in the rubble. Neither were there any birds overhead, or the distant sound of birdsong. In fact, it was as though nothing were alive in the ruins; nothing wished to live here. And Mildred knew from bitter experience that this usually meant that there was danger of some sort. The wildlife of the Deathlands was hardy and adaptable, and for it to shy away from an area meant that it could sense danger with a surety few humans possessed.

Sooner or later, that danger would make itself known. And she wanted to be ready when it did. So her relief when they hit the plain old blacktop, uncluttered by debris, was powered by more than just her relief at resting her aching arm muscles.

Bones turned back and came toward them as they rested momentarily. "I thought you were in a hurry," he snapped. "This is no time to stand around idling."

Mildred grabbed him by his jacket as he came within range, bunching the material in her fist as she pulled him up against her. "Listen, old man," she snarled, patience at an end, "there was an old saying—'the more haste, the less speed'—and it's never been more true. We're tired, we need to get rid of the cramp and lactic acids in our muscles so that we'll be of some use if we have to fight, and I want you to stop acting like a little kid and tell me where the hell we're going."

She let the old man loose suddenly and he stumbled backward, looking at her with a mixture of surprise and fear, his eyes large enough without the magnification of his spectacles.

"There's no need to be like that," he said mildly, composing himself. "You only had to say…"

Mildred gritted her teeth. Hell, Doc Tanner was never this bad.

Michaela looked around at the remains of the buildings along the road. Most were three- or four-story blocks made of brownstone that had been ravaged by the chem storms, the shape of the building facades eaten away, glassless windows gaping emptily down at them. The ground level of each frontage had once been a store of some kind, the interiors now devoid of anything that would give clues to their previous life. The damage looked as though it had been caused by fire, and was unlike any they had seen so far. It also looked recent, which was a cause for concern.

"What d'you reckon did that?" Michaela asked nervously, indicating the storefronts.

"I don't know, but whatever it was, it wasn't very friendly," Mildred mused.

"Do you know anything about this?" she asked Bones.

The old man shook his head. "Doubt if it was any of our people," he said after some consideration. "We haven't really used this part of the old city—nothing here that's worth the taking. And firing the old buildings is too stupe for even the dumbest of the sec that get sent here. What if it caught and spread through the whole of the ruins? All our scavenging would be gone."

"I was afraid you'd say that. That means that someone—or something—else is responsible for this. We'd better keep our eyes and ears open. Triple-red and stay frosty, and let's hope we don't have to carry John any farther. The longer we can keep him on wheels, the easier it'll be to defend ourselves."

"I'll second that," Michaela murmured, checking the blaster that Mildred had given her back in Pleasantville; it seemed a lifetime ago, although in truth it was no time at all.

Sobered by the thought that something unknown

may be lurking in wait for them, Bones kept closer to Mildred and Michaela as they began to pilot J.B.'s stretcher gurney along the blacktop. In the distance, Mildred could see the skeletal remains of tower blocks and skyscrapers, like rotten teeth in a skull as they brokenly thrust their jagged shapes into the afternoon sky.

"How the hell do you manage to salvage anything from here?" she asked the old man as they progressed through the old streets. "It looks like it's been totally destroyed by the nukecaust."

Bones allowed himself a small, indulgent smile. "You'd think that, wouldn't you, to look at it," he said. "But a lot of the damage was either on the taller buildings or on the area surrounding when bits of them started to fall. This city developed in a little more of a haphazard pattern than others in the old States." His smile grew broader as he noted Mildred's look of astonishment. "Oh, yeah, I know what this land used to be like. You didn't really get to see the vast amount of material I've amassed. You and your friends wouldn't recognize it. It must have been good to be alive in those times," he continued, little realizing how much Mildred would agree with him. "And I sometimes wish… But no, I must stick to the point. There were older areas of this city where the buildings had not yet been torn down and replaced with the tall ones like those." He indicated the ghostly skyscrapers with a gesture that was almost dismissive. "Buildings that were more attractive and must have been nicer to live in…but no matter. The point is that these smaller areas suffered less damage, and it's from them that the most amount of material has been saved."

"How did it survive?" Mildred pressed. "I've seen old cities with lower level developments that haven't yielded so much."

Bones shrugged. "Some of it is chance, and we shall never know. Some of it is because places like the old hospitals we're headed for were designed to withstand a nukecaust. They were low level, but reinforced, with basement levels that were almost miraculously untouched. And they have an unconventional power source."

Mildred pondered this. She couldn't work out the name of the old city they were in, as she wasn't sure of their exact location. Without a map, and knowing how the years of nuclear winter had changed the coastline, it was almost impossible. But out in the northwest, they were less likely to get a direct nuke hit, and perhaps it was possible that such areas would be developed as fall-back and support areas in the case of war. It was just a shame that no one had truly thought through the consequences of a nuclear winter.

She looked around at the devastation, made all the more stark by the silence in which it was shrouded. A shiver passed over her, as though someone were walking across her already dug and filled grave.

"Let's get to it," she said brusquely. "We don't have the time to be standing around here talking like a lot of fools."

Taking their lead from Bones, who set off at a more reasonable speed after observing how they had to steer the gurney around the rubble, Mildred and Michaela pulled the Armorer along the old blacktop.

The old man took the streets as though he had been

walking them all his life, which, in a sense, he had, as he had been exploring the ruins on and off from a very young age. His eyesight may not be as good as it once had been, but he still knew every twist and turn of the old city, and seemed to go almost onto an automatic pilot as he negotiated the ruins.

Mildred watched the surrounding wreckage as they progressed from the area of old brownstones to a development of squat, gray concrete blocks that looked scorched but otherwise untouched by the ravages of the years. Here, there was more rubble strewed across the sidewalks and roadway, and she and Michaela had to lift the stretcher to negotiate some parts of the thoroughfare. Each time they lifted the gurney, and were unable to lay hands on their weapons in a split second, Mildred felt ill at ease, and was relieved when they were able to put J.B. back down on the deck. There was something about the silence in the ruins that was ominous. All other ruins she had visited with the companions had been colonized, either by man or by wildlife of some kind. Why was this different?

But there wasn't much time to dwell on this as they moved out of the low-level buildings and into the central section, which consisted of the old tower blocks and skyscrapers. Here, the wreckage was strewed all over the streets, made worse by the passage of time, and it was so dense that they had to carry J.B. all the way.

"Hey, Bones," she snapped at the old man. "Do we have to go this way? Can't we skirt around this section?"

The old man stopped and looked back at her, a mild bemusement coloring his features. "But I thought you wanted to get there quickly?" he asked mildly. "The center of the old city is quite large, y'know. If we went around the edges, it would take more time than we have—or, at least, than you think we have…"

Mildred cursed to herself. The old man was right. If cutting across this central section saved time, that had been the imperative she had pushing home. But all the same, a creeping terror was inching its way up her spine. She was unaware of how long she had paused, until he continued.

"Look, what's the problem? There's nothing here to harm us. It's empty, for fuck's sake!" He threw his arms wide, as if to demonstrate. For a second, she almost expected some eldritch terror to rise up behind him, like out of some barely remembered horror movie in her previous life. But he just stood there, framed against the shell of an old skyscraper, surrounded by silence.

"Yeah, I guess you're right. Let's get going. Time is of the essence, after all, and I'm just… I don't know, just being bugged by the silence. Not used to it, I guess," she added as she picked up the gurney once more and followed the old man.

"Mildred, I'm getting worried about him," Michaela murmured to her as they followed Bones.

"No, he's okay, just a cranky old man," Mildred remarked over her shoulder.

"I'm not talking about Bones," the healer replied. "It's J.B. He's gone really quiet. Haven't you noticed?"

To her sudden surprise, Mildred realized that she had been so preoccupied with the silence around her that she hadn't noticed that John was now contributing to it. She cast a glance over her shoulder. The Armorer was lying still and silent on the stretcher, his lips parted as he breathed easily, a waxy sheen on his skin.

There was nothing she could do out here, no point in stopping. They could only carry on and hope for the best.

"Hey, I recognize this," Michaela piped up suddenly. "Yeah, I've been through this. We're nearly there, Mildred."

Mildred felt a sigh of relief well up within her. They had passed through the ruined center of the old city and were leaving the majority of old towers and skyscrapers behind them. They were now entering a neighborhood of blown- and burned-out old concrete low-levels, like the ones they had previously seen. Incongruously, in the middle of it all, an old burger bar, the golden arch still miraculously standing, though the metal was twisted and the yellow plastic scorched and melted from yellow to sienna to black in places. It stood at an almost jaunty angle, as though beckoning them.

"Yeah, I know that thing," Michaela yelled. "We're nearly there."

Ahead of them, Bones turned and grinned. It was satisfaction for a job well done. "Told you, didn't I?" he crowed. "Got you here, and pretty damn triple fast, at that. The hospitals are over there," he added, throwing out his left arm to indicate a series of concrete three-story buildings to Mildred's right.

What happened next seemed to take place in slow motion. It was incongruous, unexpected…and deadly.

As Mildred watched in sheer astonishment, a dark shape circled silently in the sky, moving from their rear until it was behind Bones, and moving in and down toward him. It was huge, with a wingspan of at least twenty feet and a squat, potbellied body, and enormous beady eyes that seemed to bore into them from a distance. It was covered with fur, the wings made of a membranous leathery substance rather than skin and feathers.

It looked like a giant, mutated bat. But even as Mildred tried to snap herself out of her surprise to take action, it seemed that completely incongruous questions were going through her head. Where had it come from? Why was it out during daylight? Why had no one told her about this creature? How the hell many more were there?

It was what happened next that shook her from this trance. The creature swooped toward Bones's outstretched arm, which still pointed limply, left hanging in his shock at seeing the creature circle him. He began to turn, his arm still meekly pointing at the buildings.

The giant bat swooped down on him, the outstretched wings cutting through the air as it angled its descent. The claws underneath the squat body came down and aimed with unerring accuracy, taking the old man's left arm in both feet. He screamed, high-pitched, almost inaudible, a combination of shock and pain as the claws dug into his flesh, tearing through the flimsy material of his jacket and suit. He stood firm, trying to pull against the flying monster, but all he did was give it better purchase with which to twist its claws. His arm rotated in the shoulder socket, the joint wrenched free as the burning pain of muscle and tendon being rended shot through him.

Mildred could hear Michaela turn away and vomit

with fear and disgust as the giant bat pulled the old man's arm free from his body, an obscene squelching rip sounding as the flesh and blood vessels severed, underlying the snap of the ball joint in his shoulder. The bat flew upward with the arm securely in its claws, a thin trail of blood raining to the ground. Bones stood stock-still in shock, the only movement being his mouth as he screamed, louder and longer than Mildred could ever remember hearing anyone scream. The shoulder spouted blood in rhythmic gouts, shooting out several feet onto the roadway around him. The scream dropped off as the blood stopped feeding his brain, pouring out of the open wound. He crumpled to the ground, collapsing into his own gore, dead before he hit from a loss of blood and severe shock trauma that stopped his heart from pumping what was left of his blood out through the gaping wound that had once been his shoulder and upper arm.

Mildred was suddenly galvanized into action. She pulled the Czech-made ZKR and whirled, taking a bead on the creature as it flapped away. Already it had some distance, and she refrained from wasting ammo. Chances were that its hide was so thick that it would need bigger ordnance than the 551 at this range to make an impression. Besides which, there was something else that caught her eye as she followed the creature's line of flight.

"Michaela, for God's sake, get it together," she snapped at the healer, who was looking in frozen shock at the corpse of Bones. "Two things—one, we need to get cover. Two, I need information from you, girl. In that order."

Michaela shook her head, mumbled "Sorry," almost to herself and picked up her end of the gurney. Mildred rapidly holstered the ZKR and grabbed her end, directing them toward the cover of one of the nearby lower level concrete buildings. It was an office front with the windows and doors blown out on the ground, although remnants of glass remained in some of the windows on the second and third stories.

Mildred heaved a sigh of relief as they gained the shelter of the building. The doors and windows were too small for what she had seen outside to get near them. For the thing that had made her decide not to fire and to get to cover wasn't the giant bat flying away with Bones's arm still dangling beneath its belly. Rather, it was the sight that greeted her at the bat's destination. Around the top of one of the ruined skyscrapers were several more of the creatures—perhaps seven or eight, it was hard to tell—circling rapidly, obviously agitated by what had happened below.

When they were inside, Mildred led Michaela to the second story, so that they could get the best view possible of their new enemy. The rear of the building faced the skyscraper that seemed to act as the creatures' nesting area. Mildred helped the girl lay the gurney down in the far corner of the room, as far away as possible from any potential danger, then led her to the window. They could see the creatures circling the ruined skyscraper, their orbit growing larger. One broke away and swooped down over the building, making them both duck and cover.

"Shit, girl, what the fuck are they? And why the hell didn't anyone mention they'd be around?" Mildred yelled.

"I don't…I don't know… I…" Michaela couldn't tear her eyes away from the glassless window and the sight of the giant bats circling the area of the building.

"What do you mean, you don't know?" Mildred yelled at her again. Michaela didn't answer. Her eyes were riveted to the outside and she couldn't do anything but gaze helplessly at the danger beyond.

"Dammit, girl, I really need you to snap out of this, and now." She grabbed the healer by the shoulders and turned her so that she was facing her. "Snap out of it, and now!" Mildred commanded, backhanding the girl across the face and knocking her to the floor with the force of the blow.

Michaela picked herself up, blinking. She wiped at the corner of her mouth with the back of her hand, looking wonderingly at the smear of blood that had accrued where Mildred's blow had split her lip. She looked at Mildred, and then began to cry in choking sobs that made her body shake.

Mildred stepped across and held the young woman. "It's okay, sweetie, it's okay. I shouldn't have hit you quite that hard, but I had to do something. I'm going to need you to be really on the ball if we're going to get out of this in one piece." She stepped back a little, holding the young woman at arm's length. Michaela looked directly into Mildred's eyes.

"Sorry—I really lost it, there," she muttered with a feeble attempt at a grin. "It's just that I've never seen anything like that before."

"Now that's one of the questions I needed answering," Mildred replied gently. "Never?"

Michaela shook her head. "I didn't know there were

creatures like that in the city. I don't think anyone does."
She shivered as she thought of Bones—the expert on the
old ruins—crumpling to his chill demise.

"I guess that means you never come out here by
night," Mildred said rhetorically. "Thing I can't figure
out is why the hell they've been disturbed during daylight hours." Michaela looked at her with incomprehen-
sion, so she filled in the blanks. "Sweetie, bats like
that—though Lord knows they're usually a whole lot
smaller—are strictly nocturnal. So something must
have really rattled their cage to get them out when it's
still sunup."

"Mebbe it's us," the healer said softly.

"What do you mean?" Mildred frowned.

"We've come through the middle of the old city,"
Michaela explained. "For as long as I can remember, anyone who's come out of Pleasantville—whether they're
supposed to or not—has avoided the center. Not because
of those," she added, gesturing to the still circling creatures, "but because it's not really safe with all the old
buildings falling to shit all the time. Bones brought us
through the middle, taking a real risk. Guess he did take
in how important it was to move quickly, after all."

"Guess he did," Mildred said absently, this knowledge making her wish that she could have been quicker,
sharper, somehow done something to stop the old man
buying the farm.

But such regrets wouldn't solve their problem now.
The bats had them trapped and they were running out
of time.

"They're circling, but not coming after us," Michaela
said softly, looking once more out of the window.

"They're not stupid," Mildred answered, joining her. "They know that they've got us cornered. They also know that they're too big to get into these buildings and worm us out that way. I figure they'll just circle and wait until we have to come out. They don't need us for food, so they're not in any hurry. And let's face it, we've got more reason to move than they have."

Michaela cast a glance over her shoulder to where J.B. lay in the corner. "So they just wait until we have to come out, then rip the shit out of us in the open," she stated flatly.

"That's about the size of it. The onus is on us to move, and they're a whole lot bigger and more powerful than we are. They're also really pissed at us for encroaching on their territory. So unless we can do something to either wipe them out or to drive them away, then we're screwed and John's bought the farm…"

Michaela indicated the row of concrete buildings that was visible through a break in the towers. "The bitch of it is, that's where we've got to go. Only about five, ten minutes on foot at most."

Mildred zeroed in on the concrete structures and then took a long, hard look at J.B., still and waxy on the stretcher. "Screw this. If we've got to go, we're going to go down fighting," she rasped. "Come over here."

She led the young healer to J.B.'s gurney. Stowed beneath him were the bags in which he kept the companions' inventory, as well as his own weapons. Mildred hauled out the bags and spread them across the floor. She felt the weight of J.B.'s Smith & Wesson M-4000. A load of barbed-metal fléchettes through one of those mutie bats could do a hell of a lot of damage. And that was just for starters.

"You don't know shit about weapons, do you, sweetie?" she asked of Michaela, who shook her head. Mildred grinned mirthlessly. "Then pay attention," she said, chambering a round in the M-4000, "'cause you're just about to have a crash course in all-out combat."

Mildred emptied the ordnance bags and went through J.B.'s personal inventory. The M-4000, which she had slung over her shoulder, was the most immediately useful of his, but she also felt certain that his Uzi would also be useful if they could get some in-close shots at the creatures. There was plenty of spare ammo for both, and also spares for all the companions. She carefully parceled it up.

The Armorer had a plentiful supply of plas ex, as well as detonators and fuses. She was a great believer in plas ex, but in this situation could think of nothing that would make it of practical use.

Which left her with the grens. There were stun grens, gas grens and frag grens...

Mildred looked out of the window at where the giant bats seemed to be circling. Their nests were in one of the old skyscrapers. There was no way that she had enough explosive to bring it down—besides which, the pandemonium and wreckage would more than likely buy them the farm in its aftermath and it was way too high to attack with the grens.

It wasn't, in all truth, the ideal ordnance with which to attack an enemy that used the air as its medium of combat. The M-4000 would be effective if she could get a clear shot at the bodies of the bats as they swooped.

The Uzi, likewise, could do a lot of damage if it was used at a fairly close range: but the danger here was in getting that close. As for the grens, if they could time it so that the thrown grens detonated in the air, then the gas and stun grens could do them some good. The frag grens would definitely take out the enemy, but at the risk of those standing beneath the point of impact.

It wasn't going to be easy. Mildred gave Michaela a crash course in the blasters and the grens and then outlined her tactics. They were simple, of necessity, and they were also risky. Because there was no other way of handling the situation. If they tried to wait it out, they were chilled. If they didn't, then they could be ripped apart by the angry mutie bats. It wasn't much of a choice.

When Mildred had finished, Michaela was a deathly pale white. She was only too clear on the dangers, but knew that they had no choice in the matter.

"Are you ready?" Mildred asked her.

"No, but now is as good a time as any," she said with an attempt at a smile.

The two women gathered the grens and the ammo. Mildred gave the Uzi to Michaela, figuring that its relative lack of kick would make it easier for the in-experienced girl to handle than the M-4000, which had a greater recoil. They packed the spare ordnance on their bodies and stowed the rest of the armament back under the Armorer. Then, laden down with their combat supplies, they picked up the gurney and went back to the ground floor, leaving J.B. at the front of the ruined storefront. Mildred planted a gentle kiss on his forehead.

"Hope we get through this, babe," she whispered. There were many things she wanted to say, but somehow they seemed pointless when he couldn't hear. Pointless when she had to be hyped up to chill.

Mildred joined Michaela in the doorway of the store and they looked up at the circling bats. Pausing to try to take count, it still seemed to be somewhere between eight and ten. Four or five to one: not the greatest of odds. But they had the advantage of cover. Mildred pointed out the gaping entrances to the empty storefronts and told Michaela to use them whenever possible.

The two women exchanged glances and Mildred gave a curt nod.

The battle was on.

Moving out in opposite directions, they ran low and fast, keeping an eye on the skies above. Three muties were directly overhead, circling in a complex pattern and the women had waited until they were at their highest point before making their exit.

Two of the three bats immediately broke off and made for the women. Mildred turned and stopped dead, raising the M-4000 and sighting as the bat swooped lower. Sweat ran into her eyes and she ignored the sting just as she ignored the hammering of her heart. She waited as long as she dared, until she was sure that she could see the reflection of herself in the bug eyes of the mutie. Then she squeezed, letting fly with a load of barbed-metal fléchettes.

The load spread as it reached the bat, making her realize that she had fired early. But no matter. Some of the fléchettes tore holes in the leathery membrane of the wings, but most hit the creature full in the face and body. One of the eyes splattered as metal ripped the surface, and blood spurted from the furry body as the barbed metal ripped out chunks of flesh and fur, twisting and turning as it traveled into the mutie's innards, splintering bones and mincing organs.

It let out a high-pitched, almost inaudible shriek as the life began to ebb from it as fast as the rain of blood that poured from its wounds onto the road below. Its momentum picked up as it lost control of its flight and it plummeted into the earth, landing with a thud that almost knocked Mildred from her feet as she sought to escape its path. She also had her eye on the third mutie, which was following its stricken mate.

Meanwhile, Michaela was finding things a little more difficult.

The bat that had homed in on her turned in the air to achieve the right arc for its approach and as she ran and fired, her inexperience with the Uzi meant that her first burst of fire went wide of the mark. The bat swooped lower, its claws extended, ready to pluck her off the ground.

She was saved by the fact that she wasn't looking where she was going. Stumbling over rubble on the old sidewalk, she fell to her left and the bat's claws skimmed against the shoulder of her jacket, ripping into it. She yelled in pain at the plucking of her flesh and also at the jarring blow as she'd hit the old blacktop road. The pain and fear cleared her mind of any anxiety and the pure rush of adrenaline focused her completely as she rolled and came up firing. The aim was wild at first, but she hit the creature with a burst, the Uzi shells ripping into the creature's rear end as it tried to turn, making it fly into the side of a concrete building as it yelped in pain, losing all sense of direction.

Michaela got fully to her feet, ready to face anything that these muties may throw at her.

Mildred, on the other hand, was hoping that there wouldn't be much else. She was faced with the third bat, heading toward her at speed. She racked another shell into the chamber and fired, but this time the bat had learned from its companion and veered away as Mildred fired. A few of the fléchettes hit the membranous wings, but the majority sailed high, wide and harmless.

"Jesus help me," she muttered as the creature whirled and came back. This time she made no mistake. She waited and let fly when the bat was too close to veer away in time. The fléchettes ripped the front of the creature into shreds of flesh and bone and a spray of blood that hit her in its full stinking glory. Mildred moved out of range and puked bile, spitting it out and clearing her eyes so that she could see where the next attack would come from. Michaela moved over to her.

"Three down. Looks like they're using whatever brains they have," she said breathlessly, indicating with her Uzi to the distant tower. None of the muties had followed directly the three that had attacked them; they were circling, ready to make a move.

Two of them moved away from the tower orbit and began to fly toward the two women.

"Listen, I've got an idea," Mildred said hurriedly. "Come on."

She led Michaela back into the storefront and took one of the canvas bags containing ordnance from beneath the Armorer's gurney. She emptied it and put a selection of gas, frag and stun grens inside. Leaving the bag open, she kept one frag gren in her free hand.

"Cover me when we get outside. If they're going to take us two at a time, then they'll wear us down. But they might just have screwed themselves," she added with a grin.

The women went out into the open as the bats approached, Mildred with the M-4000 over her shoulder, holding the bag and the lone gren. The women stuck together, making the bats head in one direction.

"Wait till I break for it, then try to take out the one on the right," Mildred instructed. Michaela nodded curtly.

The bats homed in on them, and as they got so close that the women could almost smell them, Mildred suddenly took off, running along the sidewalk while keeping an eye on the mutie following her. It peeled off and as it did Michaela let rip with a burst of Uzi fire that tore into the other mutie, dropping it.

"Come to Momma," Mildred breathed, pulling the pin on the frag gren and slipping it into the bag. "If this doesn't work, I love you, John," she added to herself.

As the bat's claws reached for her, she arced the bag so that it snagged on the claw while throwing herself out of range, hitting the ground hard in a roll and coming up with the M-4000 off her shoulder.

"Drive the bastard back, but don't hit it," she yelled, loosing a charge wide of the bat. Michaela also fired high and wide.

The spooked bat flew back toward the tower.

"Hurry, you bastard," Mildred whispered.

The bat reached the tower as Mildred counted. As she and Michaela watched, the creature seemed to disappear in a mist of gas, blood and exploding flesh. The frag grens spread their deadly load around the tower, into the other circling bats, causing havoc. The top of the tower crumbled in the impact and shock wave, and the sound that reached the women, a fraction of a second later, was deafening.

"Quick, inside," Mildred said, hustling the shocked Michaela back into the storefront as the dust and rubble washed over the road.

They took cover, trying to breathe through the clouds of dust that blew over them. They waited for the dust and noise to subside, then Mildred stood and walked to the storefront, looking out into the distance.

"Shit," she whispered, "I think we've seen the last of them."

Michaela joined her. She stared openmouthed at the gap in the sky where the tower had stood. There was no sign of the bats.

"Come on," Mildred said, turning away, "we've wasted enough time."

Chapter Twelve

Jak was encouraged by the idea that the hunt party wanted his erstwhile companions to hunt him individually. It would make things a hell of a lot easier for him if he could lay a few false trails and take them one at a time. Ryan, Krysty and Doc, however, had other ideas.

"You want this to be good, right?" the one-eyed man asked, addressing Ethan and his guests. "You want a good show, and you want the little fuck nailed as much as we do, right?" He waited for Ethan to assent before continuing. "Then we each get an individual crack at him, and you follow who you favor, but we don't act independently."

"What do you mean?" Ethan questioned. He sniffed the hint of a trick, and was momentarily worried that he was about to be double-crossed. It was the look of bloodlust on Ryan's face that persuaded him otherwise.

"I mean, we know what Jak's like. You just let things ride, and he could hide out here forever. No," Ryan added, shaking his head to emphasize his point, "you want us to nail him, then you let us call the tune."

Ethan cast a glance at the assembled hunt party. One of the barons looked dubiously at Ryan, but the others seemed interested.

"Go on," Ethan said cautiously.

"We know how he works, and we know what he's likely to do," Ryan said softly, "and I'm telling you that the best way to get him is if we go in and form a pincer movement, driving him into a channel so that he has very little option on where to run."

The inbred baron smiled. "That's an interesting idea, One-Eye. That way we get to follow our favorites, and we have more guarantee of an end result."

"You'll get that, I can guarantee it," Ryan said decisively.

Jak, sequestered under the cover of trees and shrubbery, decided that he had heard enough. If that was the way that they were determined to play it, then it would pay him to get some distance between himself and them: find a place where he could plot their courses and cut them off before they had a chance to pin him down.

Swiftly and silently, Jak moved from his cover, moving backward into the woods, keeping an eye on the clearing. His heavy combat boots were lighter than air on the treacherous blanket of leaves, bracken and branches beneath his feet. One wrong step could give away his position.

Jak never took a wrong step. He was always surefooted, and he moved out of his position and into deep cover without making a sound…so it had to have been some kind of mutie sense that made Krysty whirl so that she was facing in his direction. He could see her, squinting into the darkness of the forest, and he knew that she couldn't see him. At the same time, he was certain that she knew he was there.

Ryan and Doc turned to her, noting the way that her sentient curls had tightened around her head.

"Jak?" Ryan asked brusquely.

"Not sure, lover," she replied, shaking her head slightly. "I can't swear to it, but I'm sure we were being watched, and from over there…" She indicated the spot where Jak had been hiding until a few moments previously.

The hunt party exchanged glances, not knowing what to make of this.

"Trust her, gentlemen. If Krysty tells you he was there, then you can bet your life—or his—that he was," Doc directed at them. "I suggest, friend Ryan, that we begin the pursuit."

As if to emphasize his words, Doc unsheathed the sword from his silver lion's-head cane, the finely honed blade of Toledo steel catching the light with a wicked gleam.

Ryan unleathered his SIG-Sauer and pulled the panga from its thigh sheath. "That sounds good to me… Let's go. Doc, take the left. Krysty, follow your instincts and go where he was. I'll take the middle path, cut the little fucker off. As for you," he said to the hunt party, "you'd just better hope that you can keep up."

Jak didn't hear their words, as he was now out of visual and aural contact, and had turned to run swiftly through the forest, checking his .357 Magnum Colt Python as he went. It was fully loaded, and he wouldn't hesitate to use it if he had to, but he was only too pleased to reholster it. Stealth would be one of his greatest weapons, and it wouldn't make great use of the cover the forest gave him if he loosed off the Python at the first opportunity. It was a heavy-duty handblaster and the noise it made would only serve to attract attention and notify anyone of his position. No, it was the knives he had secreted in his camou jacket that would be his greatest asset.

Jak moved over the ground as though he were floating just above it, barely seeming to touch the surface. It meant that he would make little noise, not giving away his position. It also meant that he could hear what was happening behind him, as the three companions moved into the forest followed by the crashing of the hunt party, still mounted. They would be easy to locate, although this had the disadvantage that their noise could obscure the movements of Ryan, Krysty and Doc—the real danger.

Jak had been hoping to lead Ryan to the raccoon nest and Krysty into the hollow trap, but he realized that this may have to change if he had to counteract a pincer movement. It would be whoever was nearest getting caught in each trap, which made things a little more difficult. Still, he reflected as he shinned a tree to get an overall view of the forest to his rear, who had ever said it was going to be easy?

From his vantage point, he could see that Ryan was moving in a straight line through the trees, which would take him directly past the hollow trap and the raccoon set without touching either. Krysty and Doc were flanking him, striking out in semicircles to hem in the territory in which they hoped to trap him. At their current trajectory, it would lead Krysty past the raccoons and Doc past the hollow.

Behind the three companions came the hunt party, which had also split into three, with Horse and Riley shadowing Doc and Krysty respectively as sec for the interested hunters, and Ethan himself riding shotgun for those who would follow Ryan.

Jak figured that he was safe from an attack by the sec or the hunt party, at least until he had taken out the three companions. If their favored hunter lost out in the pitched battle, then they would want to follow Jak onto his next fight, and maybe try to win back jack they had lost on the initial combat. Sick fucks. Still, if it kept them from attacking him to begin with, then he guessed that it had to be counted as an asset. If Jak had any notion of what irony may have been, he would have appreciated the situation as such; as it was, he just determined to take care of business.

The three companions were moving slowly through the undergrowth, not wanting the albino to slip past and attack them from the rear. He sat up his tree and watched for a little while longer. There was no doubt that he would still want to take out Doc first of all. The albino concentrated his attention on the old man, breathing reduced to a shallow minimum as he focused his attention on studying Doc's movements. Jak had to forget that this man had once been his friend. Now he was nothing more than another piece of prey.

Doc had his LeMat in one hand and the sword in the other. He was using it delicately to carve a path for himself. He looked wild-eyed and disheveled, and although he was hopped up by the hypnotism, Jak could almost smell the undercurrent of fear coming off him. Even in this altered state, Doc was still aware that Jak was a younger, fitter, better fighter. If he wished to make the chill and avoid his own demise, he would have to act swiftly and decisively.

Which would also make him jumpy, prone to move at the slightest stimulus. Jak judged the distance between the old man and the hollow where he had baited the trap. It had the added advantage of being just a little too narrow for the hunt party to follow on horseback…and somehow, Jak couldn't see them wanting to dismount and risk themselves. They would be content with watching from a distance.

So Jak's main task was to guide Doc into the trap and deal with him.

He slipped down the tree, set on a course of action…

"SEE, I FIGGER that the old man will have the drop on Whitey because he has the experience," the trader who had bet on Doc explained to the inbred baron, who had opted to follow Doc. He hadn't bet any jack on the old man, but was sure that he would see him chilled, and that was excitement enough. His money was on One-Eye, but he figured that the albino would opt to take out the old man first.

"I can't agree," the baron replied. "I think the albino will be too quick."

"Speed ain't everything," the trader said wisely, shaking his old and grizzled head. "See, the albino ain't gonna want to use a blaster in case it draws attention to him. But the old guy ain't got any such worries."

"And you're sure that the old man's aim is true?" the baron mocked.

"Have you taken a look at that blaster of his?" roared the trader. "Shit, son, you don't need to be accurate. If he lets loose with that, just be glad we're behind it. It'll skin anything within a hundred-yard radius!"

Horse listened to the two men ramble on, and not for the first time wondered what the hell he was doing nursemaiding a pair of blood-hungry idiots—albeit idiots that had given his boss a whole shitload of jack for the privilege. He had a few concerns of his own, and they didn't concern Doc or Jak. Ethan hadn't said anything back in the clearing, and the excited hunt party hadn't even noticed, as far as he was aware, but Horse was wondering what the hell had happened to Bones. Part of the deal with these hunts was that they were recorded on that old tech of his. Ethan used those tapes to advertise and sell the hunt to potential customers. This one was a primo example of the sort of thing Ethan wanted, and he'd been looking forward to getting the old man to record this. But he hadn't shown up. No explanation, no nothing, just hadn't shown.

Horse knew that Ethan would be pissed about that, and would want the old man's hide when they got back to Pleasantville. Ethan wasn't a man to be crossed. But that wasn't what worried the sec chief: Bones had always been totally loyal to Ethan, whether through fear—like so many—or because he was grateful for the role that the baron had found him, enabling him to keep indulging his passions at a time when most barons would have found him little more than a useless and annoying old man.

Bones wouldn't just blow off the baron for nothing. So what the hell had stopped him showing up? Was there something going on back in the ville that the dreadlocked sec chief should know about, should be attending to?

Horse listened to the inane chatter of the two men

riding in front of him, and looked beyond them to the old man stalking a path through the forest. Was this all there was to being head of sec in Pleasantville? Nurse-maiding greedy hunters and old fools on pointless chases?

So it was that when action exploded around him, Horse was in no position to respond.

JAK HAD BEEN WATCHING Doc as he moved toward him. The old man was no fool, but Jak knew that he was no great hunter, either. The albino was only too well aware that he would be able to sneak up on Doc and put him out of commission. What worried him was if the men behind took it upon themselves to break their agreement with Ethan and take some part in the action. So he figured it would be a good idea if he could get Doc away from them and into the hollow where he had laid the trap earlier.

All he had to do was tempt Doc into following him.

Jak flattened to his belly and pushed through the undergrowth, ignoring the insects and small mammals that he disturbed and the prickle and scratch of the bracken and tough grasses. He moved lithely, barely disturbing anything other than the area immediately around his torso, making no noise—at least, nothing that could be heard above the rustle of the old man and the accompanying riders as they moved toward him.

Jak circled slightly so that he would be able to attract Doc's attention from an angle, making the old man turn and thus be less likely to attack immediately. From his position at an acute angle, he could see—as he raised his head—Doc scanning the area around him, the

LeMat and the swordstick raised expectantly. Silently, he took one of his leaf-bladed throwing knives from its place of concealment, balancing the weight in the palm of his hand. He squinted through the darkness caused by the overhanging canopy of foliage, figuring out the distance between Doc, the three riders and himself. Then he grinned, and swiftly and silently raised himself onto his knees.

With a minimal swing he sent the leaf-bladed knife spinning through the air, its speed and momentum building with each turn as the energy contained in his arm action became fully realized.

Doc didn't see it coming. It was a blur of white metal, catching the briefest of reflections as it carved the air in front of his nose, the sudden chill of its backdraft noticeable, making him start. With a dull thunking, it embedded itself point-first in the trunk of a tree to his right.

Before the noise had even had a chance to die in the air, Doc had whirled. He caught sight of Jak, still on his knees, and fired the shot chamber of the LeMat without hesitation.

Jak was pleased with his aim. He hadn't wanted to take the old man out right here; rather, he just wanted to attract his attention and make him follow. He hadn't expected Doc to turn and fire without aiming, and that fraction of a second lost almost cost him his life.

The LeMat sounded large and evil as the explosion of the chamber broke the silence of the forest. Horse kept a tight rein on his own mount, but was secretly gratified to see the startled baron and trader both have trouble containing their frightened horses.

Doc yelled in frustration as the LeMat went off, knowing that his own frazzled nerves had made him fire before he was ready, wasting the chance to take proper aim. The shot went wild, peppering the foliage for a wide area, chilling small mammals and birds that got in the way.

Jak hit the ground sideways, unwilling to flop forward to meet the hail of shot head-on. He felt the hot blast of flying metal above him and the sting of some pellets hitting his upper arm, elbow and face as he fell. The warm blood on his face tasted salty as it trickled from his temple to the corner of his mouth, the tang suddenly making him aware that he had to move, and quickly. He was lucky that he had gotten down quick enough; unlucky that a few stray pellets had hit him. At least he knew he had the old man's attention. And if it wasn't occupied reloading the shot chamber, then he wouldn't want to waste the ball chamber unless he had a clear shot. Either way, it gave Jak a fair chance to lead him into his trap.

Jak sprang to his feet, risking a quick glance in the direction of the hunters. In the briefest of looks, he could see Doc wildly scanning the area before him, moving forward over the scrub, while Horse and the two hunt guests tried to control their horses.

Jak realized that the explosion of the LeMat had to have been close enough to take the edge off his hearing—or else the shock of being hit in the head by the pellets had traumatized his ear—as he hadn't heard Doc begin to move noisily across the scrub. He also realized that Ryan and Krysty would have heard the percussion pistol's detonation and would now be headed toward the source of the noise, seeking to narrow his channels of escape.

The albino turned and ran, moving toward the area where he knew the horses would be unable to follow and where he had laid the first of his traps.

Jak moved quicker over the ground than Doc, and, glancing back over his shoulder, he saw that he was moving away from the old man too quickly, putting too much distance between them. He had to slow slightly if he was to stand a chance of getting the old man where he wanted him, even though it went against every instinct that was screaming at him to run with three riders and an armed man at his rear.

Jak looked back and saw that Doc was beginning to gain a little ground. Excellent. Now to lead him into the trap. Jak ran toward the narrow hollow, making sure that Doc was close on his heels, although not close enough to snap off an accurate shot on the run.

The albino, fleet of foot, bounded down the slight incline that led into the hollow, opting for the narrow corridor of trees and disappearing into the gloom. Had Doc been his usual self, he would have wondered why Jak had been so ostentatious in his choice of path and why he had chosen a way that seemed so restrictive.

But Doc wasn't his usual self. The hypnosis had overwhelmed him with the feelings of hate it had inspired, and the intensity of those emotions running around his head had tipped the balance of sanity and madness. Doc was following, and acting on blind instinct, but he wasn't exactly seeing what everyone else could see.

"Shit!" the trader explained as he saw the albino disappear into the trees. "We'll never be able to follow the little bastard in there!"

"The little savage isn't as stupe as I thought," mused the inbred baron, ignoring the irony that he probably was as stupe as the trader and Horse thought he was, for that remark alone.

"We can try to ride around," the dreadlocked sec chief yelled, "see if we can catch up with them on the other side."

The trader snorted. "Not much use when the real action's probably gonna take place in there, and not on either side," he moaned.

"There's fuck all we can do about that," Horse snapped back, "but if both of them come out the other end, then we'll need to be there to follow them."

The baron and the trader exchanged glances. Neither liked the tone the sec chief had used, but both were prepared to ignore it as they knew he was speaking the truth. With a gesture of agreement, they joined the sec chief in riding a circle around the crop of trees, leaving the two companions within.

As soon as Jak had entered the hollow, he had made sure that he had leaped over the covered tree roots and had bounded up one of the trees so that he was overhanging the treacherous path beneath, waiting for Doc to enter. He stilled his breathing, his muscles rocklike and immobile as he almost immediately melted into the shadows of the hollow.

Doc blundered after, the swordstick and the LeMat waving in his hands, trying to control his momentum on the downward slope, lest he trip and fall. Little did he know that was what Jak had in store for him.

"By the Three Kennedys," he swore. "The darkness, the darkness…"

The world around the old man was plunged into a sudden gloom where shadow had substance and substance was only shadow. There seemed to be shapes that loomed out at him from nowhere, then dissipated as insubstantial phantoms. Branches hit him in the face, cutting into his flesh, whipping at his eyes, and he had no idea of where they came from. They were invisible enemies that struck at him from nowhere, when he least expected it.

Doc tried to concentrate, to keep his mind focused on what he was supposed to be doing, but the fears of unknown and unknowable things that seeped up from the primordial subconscious made him lose all sense of perspective. He stumbled, slowing suddenly, whimpering as he looked rapidly and helplessly around him.

Ironically, all Jak's work in preparing the trap and covering the roots with ferns and leaves was wasted. Doc didn't even look down as he stumbled forward, his feet catching in the twisted root systems that comprised the floor of the hollow, boots snagging and ankles twisting as his forward momentum wasn't matched by the movement of his entangled feet.

For one brief, intense second Doc was pulled back to full awareness as the searing pain shot up his calf, then he was pitched forward onto his face, making a surprised noise as the air was expelled from his lungs, the LeMat and the swordstick clattering from his grasp onto the floor of the hollow.

That one second was enough.

Jak was down from the tree before the old man's

weapons had even hit, one of the tiny throwing knives in his fist, ready to sever the old man's windpipe and slice through his carotid artery. Jak would be merciful and make it quick if it was necessary for his survival.

Doc felt his mane of white hair grabbed and tugged, his head pulled backward at an almost impossible angle, his neck taut so that the artery, veins and Adam's apple stood out. He felt the coldness of the knife before it even touched his skin.

"Jak, wait," he gasped in a strangled breath, eyes bulging in fear. "Wait, hear me out."

Jak paused. He had one knee firmly planted in the old man's back, his head held securely, and the knife at his throat. He could hear the horses at the other end of the hollow, so he knew that they were alone. And there was something about Doc's tone that was familiar and comforting, as if the old man had regained something previously lost.

Jak lessened his grip on the old man's hair slightly, allowing him a little more slack with which to gain his breath and speak a little easier.

"Make quick," Jak said softly.

"Insanity has saved many a man from madness," Doc said somewhat obliquely, with a rasp to his voice where Jak's grip had taken its toll. "I fear that, perhaps, mine own brush with the obloquy of the unsettled mind has somewhat dulled the desired effects of friend Ethan's dastardly tactics."

"Sound like old Doc," Jak whispered in his ear. "Don't understand fucking word. Make easy…"

"A fair point, a fair point," Doc agreed, "but somewhat hard to do when one is facing a certain end and is trying to marshal one's thoughts. Jak, let me put it like this. I have long since faced up to the fact that my mind has a tendency to wander, and that I am, indeed, a mad old coot, as Dr. Wyeth has been known to charmlessly describe me. In short, I am prone to what we could call, without fear or favor, bouts of madness. Would you agree?"

Jak grunted his assent, but didn't loosen his grip any farther. "Make quick," he reiterated.

"It is true to say that I wanted to see you dead when I was standing in the sec yard. Indeed, even when I fired at you a few moments ago, I wanted most dearly to see your demise. But something has happened to change that. Coming into here, I was terrified—almost literally out of my mind, I think—and when I fell, then things began to change. Pieces of a jigsaw puzzle that fit together in your head."

"Losing me, Doc," Jak said shortly. "You saying you not want me buy farm?"

"Yes—no—I mean I did, but no longer. Something has wiped clean the pernicious influence of Ethan's hypnotism."

"Why believe you?"

Doc shrugged as best he could under the constriction. "There is reason in the world why you should believe me," he said softly. "No reason except that it is the truth, and yet I do not know how you could test this without putting yourself at risk."

"Then mebbe I should. Quicker, better fighter…only way get me is with blaster. Mebbe I should put to test…"

Jak let Doc loose and stepped back. The old man

struggled to his feet and turned to face the albino, who was now standing a few feet back, knife in one hand, the other dangling loose and empty. He stood, impassive, watching while Doc picked up his swordstick and the LeMat.

"This is most trusting of you," Doc murmured.

The albino shrugged. "Figure could still take you. Anyway, everything say to me truth."

Doc allowed himself a crooked smile. "That is nice to know. So I shall warn you to cover your ears. This may be a little loud in here…"

With which, Doc turned and loosed the shot charge of the LeMat toward the far end of the hollow, to where the horsemen would be waiting, and away from Jak. The sound seemed to blot out all other senses, and Doc then yelled, a blood-curdling scream, into the void.

"What the fuck—" Jak began. But when Doc turned and smiled at him, that crazy-old-man grin that he had seen so many times, all Jak's instincts told him that whatever it was that had snapped Doc back to normal, it was no fraud. This was the Doc he knew so well.

"Just to put them off the scent, dear boy." Doc grinned. "They will be expecting some kind of firefight or fight to be going on in here, so why not give them that? Besides, it'll buy us some more time to talk. And we need to, believe me."

"Yeah, and you'll do most," Jak said with a rare smile from the eyes. "Glad I not have to chill you, Doc."

"So am I, dear boy, so am I," Doc returned with an involuntary shiver. "But this still does not solve our big problem. How do we get out of here without arousing the suspicion of the riders, and how do we deal with Krysty and Ryan?"

"That two problems, Doc. First one simple. They're that end—" he pointed to the far end of the hollow, where he had heard the riders travel "—waiting for you to come out winner, or for me to run with you chasing. So we do it that end—" he pointed to the way they came in "—and if you just follow me, then we can lose them. That's one problem."

"Sounds reasonable," Doc agreed, reloading his LeMat as Jak spoke. "Although I must confess that my first impulse is to go and put a load of shot through those coldhearted scum for making me feel as I did."

"Later, Doc," Jak said with a grim nod of his head. "Save for when sweeter. First get Ryan and Krysty back."

"Which may not be as easy as it was with me, I fear," Doc mused. "Oh the perfect irony of it. My insanity saves me from doing something insane. But they are quite sane, and so the hypnosis may have bitten deep into them. It may not be so easy to shift as it was for myself."

"Chance have to take." Jak shrugged. "If chance four of us kick shit out of Ethan and his sec, much better than two."

"I have to say I admire your reasoning," Doc said with his tongue resting firmly in his cheek. "I would love to show Ethan a thing or two about being on the receiving end of one of his schemes. But that will have to wait. First thing is to actually get to Ryan and Krysty."

"Not problem," Jak replied. "As soon as heard first shot, bet changed direction to move in here."

"In which case, we'd better get moving, dear boy," Doc mused. "We need to try to capture Ryan and Krysty."

"Leave to me, Doc. Not want to make hunters too suspicious."

Doc shook his head. "No," he said in a considered tone. "No, I think it would be best if we approached them together. At the moment, they feel that we are all against you. They feel that because it has been implanted in their minds. We have to undermine that, to make them see that you and I are now fighting together—just as we all did, and will again."

Jak shrugged. "Mebbe so, but got to do that and stop Ethan's sec seeing it and firing on us."

Doc clapped Jak on the shoulder. "Ah, dear boy, did anyone ever tell us that it was going to be easy? But the harder the struggle, the greater the prize. Now run, dear boy, run as swiftly as the wind, though not so fast that I cannot keep up," he added with a wry grin.

"Okay, let's go," Jak said.

The albino took off for the opening to the hollow through which they had both entered, being careful to avoid the covered root systems. Doc followed, wincing at the pain he felt in his ankle and calf from the fall he had taken. It hurt, but it wasn't enough to slow him, and he hoped that he would be able to keep up with Jak.

Jak came out into the light, running for a crop of trees on the far side of the path where he had first ambushed Doc. It seemed a little self-defeating to head back that way, but there were tall trees that he could climb to find Ryan and Krysty's position; and they wouldn't be expecting him to double back as they closed in on the hollow, following the sounds of Doc's LeMat. This would buy Doc and himself just enough time to formulate some kind of plan. Which one of the companions would they tackle first, if they had the chance? For surely they couldn't take them both on and expect to come out of it still standing.

He looked back over his shoulder and could see Doc chasing after him. The old man was limping slightly from his injury, but was gamely keeping pace with the albino. As Jak looked back, so Doc, too, cast a glance over his shoulder to see where the hunters were. They were barely visible, circling around from the far end of the hollow. The baron and the trader were excitedly yelling at each other, their words lost over distance. But it was noticeable to both companions that Horse, bringing up the rear, was silent. The dreadlocked sec chief wouldn't be easy to deceive as they put their plans into operation.

Jak and Doc against Ryan and Krysty would be hard enough, Doc's relative weakness evening the score, if not turning it in their pursuer's favor. But Jak and Doc against Ryan, Krysty, and nine mounted and armed men? That was putting them in a ridiculous situation.

Jak sprinted across the relatively open patch of ground, flinching when he heard the ball chamber of the LeMat detonate behind him, but unable to resist a wry chuckle when foliage in front and the left of him fell victim to the shot. If Doc wasn't careful, his deliberate misses would become a little too obvious.

Jak reached the cover of the trees and took a running leap at the tallest, grabbing an overhanging branch and hauling himself up into the upper reaches. He watched

Doc reach the cover, and put down an arm to help the older man as he struggled, unable to get a sufficient push from his injured leg.

As Doc settled in the canopy cover beside him, Jak gestured for him to be silent. They sat and watched as the three horsemen entered the cover, the baron and the trader cursing as the lower branches hit out at them when they passed through.

"Where have those tiresome beasts gone?" the inbred baron asked. "This is really too bad. It's not turning out quite as I would have hoped."

"They must have cut through quicker than we can. They're on foot," Horse said placatingly. "Let's press on through there," he added, indicating a channel through the trees, "see if we can pick them up on the far side of this."

"That's if they don't double back again," the trader muttered.

"Not likely. They're on a straight chase this time. We can't make that kind of mistake again," Horse said firmly, unaware of the two men above his head and the unintentional irony of his words.

Jak and Doc stayed still until the three horsemen were out of earshot, and then the albino moved swiftly and silently into the top of the tree. Doc waited patiently until he descended once more.

"Ryan is at three o'clock, Krysty at seven," Jak said. "He has more cover, but she's going to be easier to take because we can use the raccoons."

"Pardon?" Doc questioned, wide-eyed.

Jak laughed. "Surprise had for Ryan, but things not gone to plan. We use them to run the horsemen away, give us time with her."

Doc shrugged. "Dear boy, I am currently in the dark, but I will trust your judgment. Lead on, and just tell me what you require me to do."

Jak dropped through the branches to the forest floor, followed by Doc. This wasn't going to be easy, but if anything was to aid them, then speed would be of the essence.

Chapter Thirteen

After the dust had settled and the noise had retreated into the hollow ringing of complete silence, it took Mildred and Michaela a few seconds to gather themselves and make their way across to the gray concrete buildings that held the key to getting J.B. on his feet.

The ruins of the old city were still and quiet, with nothing to hinder their progress or to sidetrack them into unnecessary wastes of time. And yet it still seemed as though they couldn't move fast enough over the rubble-strewn streets. It was only a five- to ten-minute trot with the gurney, but still it seemed to Mildred that it took so much longer. She was aware of the sun above them sinking slowly as twilight began to fall. She was aware of the still and quiet from the waxy-skinned Armorer, even his fever-induced ravings now stilled as he entered into the next stage of his infection.

Time seemed almost like a solid, palpable thing. There was so little of it, and with each step she was aware of thin slices being shaved from it by the razor of entropy, slowly reducing the block left until it would be reduced to nothing, or an infinitesimally thin slice that could be infinitely subdivided forever on a subatomic level, but would mean very little in the harsh reality of the ruined city, where J.B. would buy the farm and she and Michaela would succumb to the first stages of the now infectious disease. And as for the others, out wherever they may be, hunted by Ethan's men and those who had paid him.

Mildred gritted her teeth and shook her head, cursing to herself. Dammit, if she thought too long and hard about all this, it could make her as crazy as Doc. Come to that, some of the things that had just been going through her head had been as crazy as some of the things she'd heard him say over their time together. She hoped he was doing okay, that all the others were, and that she would have a chance to see them again.

That was why she had to keep going, to forget about anything else except putting one foot in front of another as she and Michaela made their way across the ruined sidewalks and blacktopped streets to the old hospital buildings.

"Second one along—the basement's through a strong room door at the back," Michaela gasped from behind Mildred as they approached the trio of buildings. The girl sounded breathless, tired. Mildred became aware of the fast pace she had been setting, expecting the healer to keep up, and a pang of conscience pricked at her. But then again, there wasn't the time to be nice.

The two women, J.B.'s gurney suspended between them, made their way through the burned-out frontage of the building. Mildred could see that at one time it had been the reception area of a private clinic or research facility. The remains of office furniture and sofas for clientele still littered the front of the building, while the bleached-out remains of framed prints either still hung—by some miracle—on the walls or lay on the floor.

"No one's bothered to tidy up lately," Mildred remarked. It drew a small chuckle from the healer.

"After Bones first found this place, it wasn't long before Ethan stopped anyone except himself, Bones and a few trusted sec men from coming here. Even I've only been here once, when Bones showed me where they got the stuff I was using in the ville. Truth to tell, I don't think he was supposed to have even done that."

Mildred refrained from comment, but she was glad that the old man had sometimes broken the rules, and for all his faults she wished for a moment that she had been able to do more to try to save him when the bats had attacked.

"Through the back, over on the left," Michaela prompted, breaking Mildred's train of thought.

As they entered the rear of the facility, it was obvious that this was the area that, predark, the public hadn't been meant to see. There was little left of any note, but Mildred could see that this had been sparse and functional, desks and spaces where old computers had been looted. And, away where Michaela had directed her, there stood the vast metal door that guarded the entrance to the basement and the labs themselves, where the real work had gone down.

The door had once been painted to match the walls, but where they had merely faded over the years, the paint had eroded and peeled from the door, leaving the metal exposed with only a few flakes to note its previous color. The lock mechanism was hidden in the doorjamb and lintel, with only a keypad to the left to indicate how the door was opened.

"You know the code, I take it," Mildred commented as they approached.

Michaela made a noise that suggested she didn't. Mildred turned to her, her eyes flashing angry. "Then what—" She stopped when she saw the sly smile on the healer's face.

"You won't believe this, but it doesn't need one. The lock is broken. All we've got to do is open it."

Mildred couldn't quite believe it would be this simple, that the sec door designed to guard the labs from prying eyes could be so open now, so accessible. She lowered her end of the gurney onto the carpeted floor, covered in dust and debris, and put her hand on the handle of the door, resisting the temptation to even reach for the keypad, which she did almost as habit.

The handle gave easily and the heavy door swung open on a well-oiled hinge.

"I wouldn't have believed it," Mildred whispered. "Especially as everything else down there still seems to be working," she added, noting that the hum of the air-conditioning, the dim glow of the lights and presumably the freezers, were still working.

"Bones reckoned that the generators were something special to have worked this long after skydark and well protected down here, but that the door must have had some heavy trauma during skydark that fused the mechanism."

"But it's so untouched," Mildred said in awe. Most places, she would have expected it to have been long since looted.

Michaela shrugged. "Like I told you, once it was discovered, no one came here on the orders of the baron. And before that, well, I guess no one really looked, 'cause it just seemed to be an empty building."

Mildred shook her head. She was damn sure that she would have had the curiosity to look, but maybe they just didn't breed them that way in Pleasantville.

"Come on, let's get to it," she whispered, suddenly aware once more of the passing of time.

The two women picked up the gurney and walked down the narrow stairway that led into the med labs. As they reached the bottom, Mildred whistled long and low. The labs extended the length of the block and carried on beneath all the buildings that surrounded the upper office through which they had entered. Lit by overhead fluorescent tubes, the floors were covered by functional polyvinyl flooring, on which had been laid a number of workbenches with sinks and fuel outlets. Many of the benches still had retorts and test tubes seated on them. Some of the floor space was partitioned off for offices or secured lab areas, and sec locks on the doors indicated the degree of danger that they may represent.

At the far end from the entrance stood the freezers, behind gleaming metal doors with sec locks that were still blinking LED displays above their keypads.

"You know the codes?" Mildred asked on seeing the locks.

"Oh, yeah," Michaela assented, "I know those."

"Then what are we waiting for?" Mildred said perfunctorily, not wanting to get into this argument. There wasn't the time, not now.

She and Michaela carried the Armorer the length of the med labs and into one of the side offices, setting him down gently.

"Now let's get to it," Mildred murmured, leading Michaela toward the freezers.

The spiky-haired healer stood at the sec door and punched a six-figure code into the keypad in front of her. There was a hiss of air as the seal on the door cracked, and the handle gave under her hand. The heavy metal door, thickly insulated, came free as she tugged and Mildred looked over her shoulder to the riches within.

Metal compartments lined the walls, leaving a metal floor space large enough to work in, with a metal table in the middle. The lighting overhead was harsh and functional. Mildred moved past Michaela and studied the drawers. Inserted in a slot on every drawer was a small piece of card with a name or a chemical formula written on it. Some were in blue ink, some in black. Obviously, they were changed as the contents of the drawers changed, and she was a little surprised to see that not only were they as bright and unfaded as on the day they were written, but also that they were handwritten, not computer printouts. It was a small reminder of the people, long since gone, who had worked here before the nukecaust. People who had lived at the same time as her, knew the same TV shows and records, drove the same cars…

A pang of—not nostalgia exactly, but a sadness for things past—went through her; for something she missed, but hadn't time to think about; for people who she may even have dealt with in her time as a hospital intern, in her previous life.

"Mildred, what is it?" Michaela asked gently, touching her arm.

Mildred snapped out of her trance and began to scan the cards on the metal drawers once more. "It's nothing—nothing that we've got time for right now," she said, not wanting to enter into an explanation that would take too long and raise too many questions.

It took her a few moments to find the drawer she required. Holding her breath, praying that Ethan hadn't taken all the supplies of the virus, she gently opened the metal drawer, which gave easily on its tempered metal runner. Inside there were six spaces in a padded interior for small bottles, four of which were empty; but two were occupied. Mildred carefully removed one of the bottles and read the label. It seemed to be the right stuff, but there was only one way to be sure.

Moving quickly and assuredly, as though Michaela weren't even there, Mildred headed into the main body of the lab and went to one of the benches. There was a microscope on it, which she tested to see if it was still working.

"You know where everything is in here?" she asked. And when Michaela assented, she went on, "Prepare me a slide of this," holding out the bottle.

She waited while the young woman moved around the lab, preparing the slide, which she then mounted under the microscope. Mildred focused and saw the culture that she recognized so well.

"That's it," she said simply. "Get me a hypodermic and needle. The sooner I get this done, the better."

She watched impatiently while Michaela prepared a hypodermic and then handed it to her. Mildred examined the contents, flicked it, then released the trapped air. Without a word, she moved into the office where they had left J.B., and knelt over him, rolling up his sleeve, then flicking a vein. She double-checked the hypodermic, took a guess at how much he would need as she had no real way of knowing, and then plunged the needle into his arm, praying that she had guessed right.

She straightened away from him, letting his arm drop, and noticed that Michaela was watching her, biting her lower lip.

"What now?" the young woman asked.

"Now we just sit and wait," Mildred replied, trying to keep her tone neutral. There was nothing else she could do.

MILDRED CHECKED HER WATCH once more. It would be dark outside by now, and she wondered how the other companions were faring in the hunt. Even if John recovered from the antidote, and she hadn't been too late, it would still take him some time to recover from the effects of his illness. The three of them wouldn't be much good, and she wasn't even sure if she could count on Michaela. The healer had been as good as her word so far, but it was a big step from running away into the old city to fighting against her baron.

Mildred moved uncomfortably. Right now, Michaela was asleep, her head resting on Mildred's stomach, whimpering to herself at some bad dream. The young woman wasn't used to the kind of activity and adrenaline rushes that a trip to the ruins with Mildred had turned out to be; come to that, the good Dr. Wyeth could have easily done without some of the excitement, but that was irrelevant. The point was that Michaela was exhausted and when Mildred had told her that all they could do was wait for J.B.'s crisis to pass, all life seemed to have drained from the young girl.

The two of them had settled themselves in the corner of the office, Mildred with J.B.'s Uzi close at hand, just in case they had been followed in any way. It was unlikely, but she hadn't come this far to get caught out at the last. They had then eaten some of the self-heats that were always carried by the companions. Michaela had protested at how foul they were, not used to the artificial taste of the food. But she had still eaten every last scrap. She was too hungry to go as far as turning down the chance of food. After she had washed the taste away with some water, she had felt a torpor creep over her. As they had settled in the corner, sleep had gradually drifted over her.

Mildred let the girl slump down onto her, not knowing how comforting it was for the young healer to be against someone for whom she held such a passion. There was nothing that she could do right now, so why not let the girl rest?

But now she was starting to get a cramp, and she was also starting to get the itch of impatience. She needed to get over to J.B. to see how he was doing. Slowly she edged out from under the sleeping woman, holding her head so that it didn't fall to the floor with a thud. She used her bundled coat as a pillow, and laid Michaela's head down gently on it before getting painfully to her feet, the cramp making her wince as the circulation restored itself to her lower limbs, and going over to where J.B. lay.

She crouched, ignoring her protesting muscles, and checked his vital signs. The Armorer had been quiet since she had given him the antidote, and he was still silent, the only sound being the slight whistle in his breath as he continued to respirate deeply and evenly. His pulse was strong and even, moving a little fast, still, but slower than before.

All the signs were that the effect of the antidote was positive, but there was no way of being sure until that time when he opened his eyes. His temperature was down, but that could just be because he had entered a later stage of the illness. Hell, he may even have infected her and Michaela. No, that was unlikely. The worst thing was not knowing whether she had overdosed him on the antidote, or whether the disease had already had a chance to damage his brain, impair any of his functions.

She let his hand drop, where she had been holding it for his pulse, and looked away from him. If it was too late for J.B., then what could she and Michaela do against a whole ville?

She was suddenly aware that she was holding J.B.'s hand again, but she couldn't remember taking hold of it. In fact, it was the Armorer who was gripping her hand, not vice versa.

Mildred looked down at him, the astonishment plain on her face.

"Dark night, and I thought you'd be pleased," the Armorer whispered wryly, his voice just a dry, cracked husk.

WHEN MICHAELA WAS ROUSED from her dreams—dreams where everything was nice and normal, and she hadn't seen a man ripped apart by giant bats and she hadn't fired at them and seen their innards splatter over the ground—she panicked. Mildred wouldn't be rousing her unless there was danger, and through her sleep-clouded eyes she was aware of a third figure standing in the small cubicle.

A third figure… She groped clumsily for a blaster, knowing that this had to be danger.

"Whoa there, calm down," Mildred said soothingly, restraining her. "Look…"

Michaela's eyes adjusted to the light and to wakefulness, and she was astounded to see the Armorer standing in the room. He looked a little unsteady, still, but the point was that he was conscious and on his feet.

"It worked?" she mumbled dumbly.

"Doesn't feel like it, but I guess it has," J.B. answered her, his voice still harsh and cracked. Mildred handed him a canteen and he drank thirstily, almost choking on the first mouthful where his throat was so closed.

Michaela was now fully awake and on her feet. "How are you feeling?" she asked as she moved toward him, poised to check his vitals and clicking into healer mode.

J.B. stepped back and held up his hands. "Hey, Millie's already been through that routine."

Michaela looked at her questioningly.

"His signs are good and he seems to have made a pretty good recovery—pretty miraculous, considering I didn't know how much of that shit to pump into him. Could easily have bought the farm," she added with a sly glance at the Armorer.

"Thanks, I'll remember that," he said dryly.

Michaela was beside herself and didn't know what to say. A tumble of emotions and thoughts ran through her, and she wasn't sure how she felt. On the one hand, she felt happy for Mildred that J.B. was now on his feet, and she was glad as she was sure that they would need his smarts, even if he was still weakened by the virus. But she could also see how happy Mildred was and a small part of her realized that she could never say anything about how she felt for the woman. Still, if nothing else, her emotions had given her the impetus to break from her fear and to change her life. Although whether that was a good thing, as she stood with just two other people against a whole ville, was open to debate.

Her train of thought was broken by the Armorer's next words.

"We've got a lot of work to do, and not much time. So we need to get to it."

"What do you mean?" Michaela questioned. "You're not in any fit state to do anything just yet. It's only a matter of minutes, probably, since you came around, and—"

"Whoa, calm down," Mildred interrupted, gesturing to placate the worried healer. "Listen, I hear what you're saying, but you don't know John Barrymore Dix, and you don't know what a stubborn son of a bitch he can be when he gets going." She exchanged a wry smile with the Armorer before adding, "Anyway, he's got a point, damn him."

"Which is?" Michaela demanded.

"Which is that we've got no time to waste. Dark night, you think I wouldn't rather rest up a little before taking on those coldhearts? Of course I would, but I'll be nuked if I'm gonna sit here and let that bastard Ethan get his own way after what he's done to the others…and what he did to me."

"So Mildred's told you the whole story?" Michaela asked with a tremble of trepidation in her voice. When J.B. nodded, she added, "And you trust me, after hearing it all?"

J.B. gave her a crooked grin as he took off his spectacles and polished them. "You're here, aren't you?" he said simply. Then he replaced his spectacles and assumed an altogether more serious air. "Okay. So as I see it, we've got two problems. One is to get back into Pleasantville and deal with any opposition we may encounter. The second is to get Ryan, Krysty, Jak and Doc back with us, hopefully all of them and hopefully not under hypnosis. Don't know how likely the second thing is, but the first…" He looked Michaela in the eye before asking his next question. She felt herself quiver under the intensity of his gaze: whatever answer she gave, he would know it to be the truth. But what was the question? He continued. "You've turned against Ethan and you've told Mildred you were silent for a long time. Question is, how many others are there like you?"

It was some moments before she answered, considering her response very carefully. "I couldn't say for sure. For instance, I didn't know Bones felt the way he did until he actually joined us willingly. But one thing I do know—there are a lot of people who are very frightened in Pleasantville. Ethan's gotten worse with each year, the power and the jack making him more ruthless and his schemes weirder and weirder. I think he's gone crazy, but no one dares to tell him. And I don't think I'm alone. Sure, everyone probably put on a good show when the hunt began, turned out like it was a celebration, but they were scared. I've been there myself, and I haven't dared not to show. I know I'm not alone. I just don't know how not alone. And I don't know how many you could rely on to join in a fight."

The Armorer considered her words for a few moments, then split his face in a big grin. "Shit, we've had worse odds than that before now, right, Millie?" he asked Mildred. When she nodded, he continued. "All we've got to do is outthink the sec men, and if they leave the walls unguarded when they've got prisoners, then you can bet anything you want that they're dumb bastards. I figure we've got a fighting chance."

"Yeah, but not right now, John," Mildred said. "It's still dark out there and you're still weak. Try to catch a couple hours' rest until sunup, and then we'll head for the ville. The last thing I want is to get lost in these bastard ruins because we can't see where we're going."

J.B. eyed Mildred suspiciously. "Bullshit. Dark is the best time to attack, and I'd bet that Michaela could find her way back to Pleasantville. But if you're that concerned that I get some rest before we set out, I don't reckon there's much I can do."

The Armorer lay on the floor and eyed the gurney on which he had been carried to the labs.

"Tell you one thing, though…bet you're glad you won't have to carry me back."

THEY GRABBED a few hours' rest. As fitful and full of frustration though it may have been, it was necessary before they set out for the ville. It also allowed the sun to rise. Michaela worried about the kind of reception they would get; Mildred worried if J.B. would be fit enough, sharp enough, so quickly to tackle any trouble they may run into; J.B. tried to rest, feeling how weak his body was compared to his normal strength and vitality, but all he could think of was how useless he'd been, how he'd lain there while Mildred and Michaela battled muties, and how the others were out there somewhere trying to chill each other because of one man's greed. That was enough to keep him from resting.

So it was that, in their own manner, they were all relieved when their chrons told them that it was sunup on the surface and they could begin the trek back to the ville.

"How are you feeling?" Mildred asked J.B. as he checked his M-4000 and Uzi before arranging the ammo and gren supplies about his person, ready to carry them.

"Okay," he answered briefly before catching her eye and cracking a grin. "Okay, yeah... I've felt better, I'd be lying if I said otherwise. A bit weak and shaky, still, but I figure we can't wait much longer. Thing is, I know I'm not my usual self, and I can allow for that."

Mildred nodded. She knew the man well enough to realize that this degree of honesty in such matters was no front and that he would be as good as his word. And a J. B. Dix who was only partly fit was still more use than most people would be in a combat situation.

A frown crossed his features as he checked the gren supplies. "Dark night, Millie, how many did you use on those bastard muties?"

"If you'd seen them, John, you'd understand," she

answered wryly. "Now stop moaning. We've got some ground to cover."

The three of them left the labs, keeping alert as they ascended the stairs to the ground-floor level of the offices and then out onto the sidewalk of the deserted city.

J.B. whistled as he got his first look at the ruins. Mildred stopped, momentarily wondering if anything was wrong, until she realized with a start that this was the first time he'd actually seen the landscape through which he'd been carried the previous day.

"It's pretty awesome—and pretty damned quiet," he whispered.

"I figure that the bats scared everything else away."

They set off across the ruins, heading toward the walls of Pleasantville and going back through the areas they had traversed the previous day. They took the same route as it was convenient, but—aware that they may have been followed—they were strung out in a line, with Michaela nervously sandwiched between Mildred and J.B., who was on point.

It was deathly silent. The only sounds were those made as they walked the old streets and sidewalks, the occasional clang of kicked or disturbed debris all that broke the silence. It would be easy to fall into complacency in such circumstances, but J.B. was determined that this wouldn't happen, and he made a habit of checking the storefronts of ruined buildings before allowing the other two to follow in his wake.

"Why is he bothering?" Michaela asked eventually. "There's no one there."

"But there might be—that's what matters," Mildred explained patiently.

THE TRIO WAS only five hundred yards from the no-man's-land between the walls of Pleasantville and the city ruins when J.B.'s caution paid off. He had gone ahead to scout a section of crumbling brownstones when he heard the noises from within the farthest shopfront. Diving into cover, he was just in time to avoid detection as three sec men walked out of the open building.

"I tell ya, there ain't no way that we're gonna find them if they're in here," one of the sec men complained. "I dunno why we're doing this."

"Because I say so, stupe," a tattooed sec man replied, hitting his companion with a backhand slap across the head. J.B. didn't know it, but this was Tracey, the man who had taken J.B.'s companions to their fate. Perhaps it was just as well, for if he had known, it may have been difficult to stay his hand and listen.

The third sec man was now out of the building. He was a huge, bald man, whose H&K looked like a toy in his giant fist. "Look," he said, sighing wearily, "what difference does it make anyway? You were told to chill the poor bastard, and he'll probably buy the farm anyway. There's nowhere for the black woman to go. And as for poor little Michaela... Can you blame her for running? Would you want to be handed over to Horse as a toy?"

J.B. narrowed his eyes. Dissension in the ranks. This could be good for him, in the long run. The Armorer also noticed the look of disbelief on the tattooed man's face.

"Fuck! I don't think I've ever heard you say so much in your life," he muttered, astonished, to the bald man. "You're not gonna go soft on us, are you?"

"Soft?" the bald man spit. "The way we live now

isn't soft? Using these poor bastards and only making jack for Ethan?"

"Shit, you'd better stop talking like that," the third sec man said, pulling his mane of black hair back from his face, his coat falling open to reveal a Glock and an M-4000 underneath. "That ain't gonna go down too well."

J.B. didn't wait to hear any more. It was enough that there was dissent, and it was enough that three men— all heavily armed, if his glimpses were any indication— were moving toward them.

The Armorer pulled back to where Mildred and Michaela were waiting in cover, and explained the situation. He hesitated slightly before mentioning what had been said about the spiky-haired healer.

Michaela winced. "Yeah, I'd say that was about right. You got a better reason to go down fighting?"

"Don't reckon so," J.B. replied. "But we'll have to be careful with these bastards. They've got a lot of hardware."

He began to outline his plan. When he had finished, he checked to see if Mildred—and particularly Michaela—understood what he had said. The young healer had a grim face, and he could tell from her brief nod of assent that she knew this was no longer about hiding. It was about taking the offensive.

"Okay, let's take them down, then," he said simply.

TRACEY LED HIS SEC TEAM to the junction of three streets. They were walking easily, with no sense of danger. The bald man was still moaning.

"I don't see why we can't just leave them to it."

"Because Horse wouldn't want that. Ethan wouldn't want that. Besides," Tracey added, "Horse wanted you on the wall. It wouldn't be too impressive if he knew you let them slip by, would it?"

"You know as well as I do that you didn't send me to the sec post until after they'd gone," the bald man replied angrily.

"Yeah, I know that and you know that," Tracey replied slyly, "but would Horse know that, or Ethan?"

"You little prick, you'll pay for that one day," the bald man muttered.

"Yeah, sure," the tattooed man replied in a mocking tone.

Their long-haired companion had stayed silent. Truth to tell, he didn't want to upset Tracey, who seemed to be in charge right now while Horse was gone, and he didn't want to upset the bald guy as he was terrified of him. Best thing to do was to keep quiet. Beside which, he was nervous out here. He frowned suddenly as the morning sun caught a reflection that gleamed from one of the buildings across the way. Must be an old piece of window…except all the glass had been blown out of the storefronts opposite.

"Fuck! Down!" he yelled, realizing that they were out in the open with no cover. He was torn between reaching into his coat for the M-4000 or using the H&K he already had to hand.

It was a fatal moment of indecision, for in the fraction of a second it took him to opt for the H&K, Mildred was able to sight and fire from her own separate position. Her Czech-made ZKR was a precision instrument and it was in the hands of an expert. An Olympic silver medalist in her predark life, Mildred wasn't one to make mistakes when it mattered. Her aim was true and the bullet drove straight into the long-haired sec man's forehead, chilling him instantly. He went down, the exit wound in the back of his head messier than the neat hole in his forehead, spilling brain and blood with fragments of bone onto the dusty road. As he fell, a reflex tightened his finger on the H&K, which was dropping in an arc. The fire sprayed around him, almost taking out Tracey, who leaped for cover, bringing up his own Glock to fire several rounds in the direction of the shot that had taken out his man.

But Mildred had already moved into deep cover. She was out of range of the answering H&K fire from the bald sec man and Tracey had no chance to sight and fore before his own battle was ended.

J.B. had moved across the area between Michaela—whose Glock had caused the reflection—and Mildred, and had circled behind the healer, so that he could come at the two sec men from a third position, just to their rear.

He had the back of the tattooed sec man as a perfect target. The M-4000 roared as a load of barbed-metal fléchettes was propelled through the air. He was close enough for the load not to spread in the air, and almost the full complement hit him in the small of the back, ripping flesh and splintering bone. It almost pulverized his spine and severed his body in two with a shower of blood and viscera. He was chilled and hitting the ground before his brain had a chance to register that he was no more.

Which only left the bald sec man, who had loosed one burst of covering fire before retreating.

J.B. was surprised when the bald man's H&K was thrown out onto the road, followed by a hunting knife and a Browning Hi-Power.

"Listen to me," the bald man yelled. "I figure you want Ethan down and your friends back. What happened to them sucked. I'm not the only one thinks that. Neither are you, Michaela. I'm coming out. Chill me if you want, but if not then I'm with you."

The bald man walked out into the center of the street, arms raised above his head, stepping over the corpses of his erstwhile comrades in arms.

There was a pause while the three people in cover considered that action. Then J.B. stepped out into the open, blaster pointed down. Mildred and Michaela followed.

"Well? My arms are starting to ache," the bald man yelled.

J.B. exchanged glances with the two women.

"Looks like there's four of us now," he yelled back.

Chapter Fourteen

It was a simple enough plan, although not as easy in execution as it may have sounded. To separate Krysty from her mounted shadows, so that Jak and Doc could have time alone with the Titian-haired woman, they had to take her past the den where the mutie raccoons were sleeping and loose the vicious beasts upon the armed men.

As Jak outlined his idea to make it happen, Doc gazed doubtfully from a treetop across to where he could see Krysty and her three horsemen making a line for the copse where they hid. Below them, Horse, the baron and the trader were still blundering around, looking for the two hidden men.

"You got it?" Jak asked finally.

"By the Three Kennedys, it seems simple enough, but I only hope I am agile enough to move at the speed you want. Remember, dear boy, Krysty is younger and fitter than I am."

"Yeah, but she still fucked up in mind, you're not. Edge is off her."

Doc was doubtful but resigned. "There is only one way for us to find out if this is so, dear boy. Let's do it."

Jak clapped Doc on the shoulder. It was a strangely reassuring gesture, despite the fact that the old man felt his balance wobble in the upper reaches at the force of the friendly blow. Both men shinned silently down the tree until they were on the forest floor and Jak made one final gesture at the direction of the path they would take. Doc nodded, his face set firm with determination.

Jak set off at an angle that would take his path across Krysty's, and Doc counted three before hitting the trail hot on Jak's heels.

The two men made a lot of noise crashing through the undergrowth, making sure that they trod on branches that cracked, ferns that rustled. Doc kept an ear cocked for sounds from the rear of their trail, and was gratified to hear that Horse, the baron and the trader had picked up on their direction and were following. Although he wanted to keep them at a distance, Jak had been adamant that they have the mounted shadows following them. That way, he and Doc would know exactly where they were.

Jak hit the open sward of ground that bisected the copse of trees and took off across it like a hare with hounds at his tail. Doc felt his chest tighten with exertion, his lungs seem to decrease in capacity with every breath as he sped after the albino, keeping him in sight as Jak veered toward the area where Krysty was on the prowl.

The albino was making a lot of noise, trying to attract attention to himself. Doc could follow his trail easily when they were back in the cover of foliage, and for a moment the old man wondered if Krysty would find this a little suspicious. But then he remembered the way he had felt before the hypnotic spell had cracked and he knew that the lust for Jak's blood would overcome all other senses.

Thus it was that, when he came across the woman, he was more than a little shocked. Especially as she appeared out of the undergrowth clutching her .38-caliber Smith & Wesson blaster and angling it in his direction.

"Hold it right there," she yelled, bringing up the blaster. Doc whirled to face her and the shock of being directly in line of the barrel made him freeze. "Doc!" she yelled, dropping the weapon to a safer angle.

"Madam, I thought it was the albino we were supposed to be hunting," he said.

"I heard the crashing, followed it and I thought—"

"Well, you thought wrong. He's already passed through," Doc commented, indicating Jak's direction with a gesture from the swordstick, "and unless we hurry ourselves, we will lose ground on him. I have already had a couple of good shots at him, but he is as slippery as ever. I think I may have caught him with some shot, though, so he may be slowed a little," Doc added, improvising to try to put her in a frame of mind where she could be more easily suckered.

Krysty smiled a cold, evil smile, with none of the humanity he knew was in the woman. Doc had to suppress a shudder at what he saw, not just for Krysty, but because he could see that until very recently, he had been the same himself. Ethan would pay for this.

It was a train of thought interrupted by the sound of approaching horsemen from two directions. They had to move now or get caught.

"Come, we are letting him gain ground," Doc yelled urgently, moving toward the path Jak had forged.

Krysty followed him without hesitation and together they plunged into a thick part of the undergrowth. Jak had deliberately chosen this path, knowing that the density of the undergrowth would slow the riders following in their wake.

Doc led the way, with Krysty hot at his heels. He knew what waited up ahead, but was a little unsure as to what form it took. He was apprehensive, to say the least, but had to trust to Jak's judgment.

While Doc and Krysty cut a swathe through the forest, Jak was already at the burrows where the raccoons had their warrens and dens. It was hardly identifiable as such, unless you knew what you were looking for. Jak could see the disguised holes in the ground that led to the underground nesting places and he noted that they had built these dens near water, a stagnant pond lying nearby.

A humorless grin crossed his scarred and otherwise impassive face as he heard Doc and Krysty approach. Behind them, and losing ground in the restrictive environment, were the horsemen.

Timing was now everything.

Jak waited until Doc and Krysty were coming into view, then took out his .357 Magnum Colt Python. But he had no intention of using it on the approaching hunters. He had a more obtuse use in mind.

The sun was beginning to sink and he could see that only about a half hour of daylight remained, which meant that the mutie beasts, who were basically nocturnal, were beginning to stir for their night's hunting. This was just the right time to stir some shit. They would be awake enough to emerge, yet not awake enough to move at their full speed, which should enable Jak the ability to expedite an escape.

Jak crouched in front of one of the closely set holes and thrust the barrel of the Colt Python into the darkness before squeezing the trigger. The booming of the large-caliber handblaster was subdued by the enclosed space, which acted as a baffle, and yet the shock wave from the shot seemed to make the ground ripple beneath his feet.

Moving swiftly, Jak took three steps to his right so that he could put the barrel down another hole, ignoring the yowling of pain, anger and fright that was already beginning to emanate from beneath the ground. He squeezed off another shot, with another muffled boom and a shock wave beneath him. The sounds of the raccoons grew louder as more of the colony responded in confusion to the intrusion, and some of those not damaged by the two shots began to make their way to the surface, to attack whatever had launched this assault on them. Jak intended to be well out of the way when this happened.

But first he also had to avoid being shot by Krysty, who had her Smith & Wesson leveled at him. Jak was already holstering the Colt Python as he turned to run and he trusted to Doc to give him cover.

The old man didn't let him down. Knowing that they would have to move quickly to avoid being trapped by the beasts, and that he couldn't let Jak fall into danger, the old man had been keeping an eye on Krysty. He saw her draw and take a bead on Jak, and chose that moment to make his own diversion.

Doc raised the LeMat, making sure that he would fire the ball chamber, and squeezed off a rapid shot before Krysty had a chance to fire. He contrived so that the ball would go well wide and high of the mark, and also that he was able to convincingly essay a slip on the greasy surface underfoot, where the edges of the pond had turned the otherwise dry earth into a mudball. With a surprised yell, Doc flung out an arm, ostensibly to balance himself. In fact, it was cunningly contrived so that he would catch Krysty as she took aim and thus ruin her shot.

The woman swore heavily as her shot went wide and low, digging up a clod of earth some twenty feet from the rapidly retreating albino.

"Doc, for fuck's sake!" she exclaimed.

"Mea culpa, my dear, but let's not waste time in recriminations," the old man replied hurriedly. "We have to move quickly."

He knew that Krysty would have to wait to berate him, as there was no way she could argue with his summation. Even as he spoke, the first of the giant mutie raccoons was starting to nose its way out of the burrow.

The two hunters skirted quickly around the area, intent on following the albino—although each for a different reason. They were quick enough to avoid the anger of the wild muties.

The half-dozen horsemen following in their wake weren't as lucky. Slowed by the density of the undergrowth, Horse, Riley and the four hunt customers they were protecting weren't able to catch up with Doc and Krysty before they were once more out of view. They did, however, come up against an army of mutie raccoons who were hungry for blood, hungry for revenge against those they thought had attacked them in their lair.

"Fuck, what are those?" one of the barons yelled, drawing his blaster.

"Trouble," Horse snapped shortly. "They're strong fuckers, don't let them get too close. Riley, defensive formation and back away," he ordered.

The blond sec man assented, his blaster ready. Like Horse, he was carrying an SMG, which he set to rapid fire. The two sec men got in front of the four riders they were supposed to be protecting and began to fire random blasts into the wave of attacking animals. The muties would normally have turned and hared back into their warrens at the onset of such a barrage, but they had a blind anger and terror that just drove them to attack.

"Back, quickly," Riley yelled over his shoulder. The barons and traders behind the sec men didn't need telling twice; they began to turn and retreat along the path they had just ridden. Horse and Riley followed, trying to back up their horses so that they could keep firing, keep the mutie raccoons at bay.

The creatures were driven on by their anger, more pouring out of the tunnels, climbing over those that had been chilled by the SMG fire, coming on toward the sec men. Horse and Riley staggered their fire, so that there was always lead in the air, even when one of the two had to stop and load a new magazine.

They pulled back into the woods, leaving the air filled with the stench of chilled flesh, blood and cordite. The raccoons emerging at the back were stayed by the smell of death that now formed a barrier of their chilled fellows between themselves and the retreating hunt party.

Horse and Riley finally stopped firing as they retreated farther down the path, the narrow way making it harder and harder to get a clean shot.

"Glad that's over," the blond sec man breathed when they felt they were safe.

"Yeah, but you know what? We've lost sight of the old man, the bitch and the little white fucker," Horse murmured grimly. "Who knows where they are now…"

JAK FOUND IT EASY to outdistance Krysty and Doc. The old man was deliberately getting in Krysty's way, making it seem as though it were his own enthusiasm for the hunt that caused his obstruction. The albino could hear the woman yelling abuse at the old man in her frustration, and Doc's muted apologies as he gained the necessary distance.

He had two things to do. The first was to attain high ground to see if he could ascertain where Ryan and his mounted shadows were at the moment. It was important that he keep himself, Doc and Krysty apart from the one-eyed man until the time was right. The second was to find space from which he could double back and unite with Doc in an attempt to sway Krysty's mind back to its old, and usual, state.

Jak could feel the ground beneath his feet move up on a slight incline and he figured that this was as good a time as any to make the first of those moves. He could hear his pursuers, and there was enough time for him to quickly ascend a tree to recce the area around. He picked the nearest trunk, glancing up and judging the height to be enough to take him onto the necessary high ground. With an ease born out of years, he shinned his way up the bole until he was hidden in the upper branches and their rich foliage.

It was getting hard to see now, as darkness was falling rapidly. But Jak's red albino's eyes were better suited to these conditions than to the harshness of bright sun, and it took but a moment for the pigmentless orbs to adjust to the reduced light. He could see the one-eyed man making his way through the undergrowth, traceable more for the three riders that followed than by his own trail. He was heading toward the area where the mutie raccoons were still snapping at the retreating party of horsemen. That should hold him up for a while.

Shifting in his perch, Jak could see Doc and Krysty getting closer. The old man was still in front, holding up her progress. Jak allowed himself a small smile. Time to get busy.

The albino moved toward them, using the branches of the trees to move from bole to bole, surprisingly weightless and quiet despite the heavy combat boots. He crossed over their heads without either noticing, Krysty too busy berating Doc for slowing her down.

With a lithe grace, Jak dropped from the trees at their rear, landing with a gentle thump on the forest floor. It may not have been enough for them to have heard him above their bickering, but Krysty's mutie sense more than compensated for that. Even in the darkness, Jak could almost see the hair suddenly tighten and curl closer to her skull. She stopped in midrant and turned toward him.

"You little bastard, you really thought you could fool me?" she yelled. "You really thought I wouldn't hear you?" She raised her Smith & Wesson, her finger tightening on the trigger, beginning to squeeze.

Jak stood impassive, even when the dark was filled

with the flash of the detonation and the noise of the shot being fired. He knew it would go high and wide. He had total faith in Doc.

The old man didn't let him down. Doc knocked Krysty's arm up with a blurted, wordless, sound of anger. She whirled in surprise and anger, and caught the old man's bony fist on the point of her jaw as he swung a haymaker at her. It was enough. Taken by surprise as she was and with no guard to speak of, the sudden and violent blow caused detonations of concussive sparks inside her head and she spun, unconscious before she hit the ground.

"Think that work for her like work for you?" Jak asked.

Doc looked up at him, not sure if there was a hint of ironic humor in Jak's otherwise toneless voice. "I would not think so. But it does, at least, prevent her trying to chill you in the meantime," he commented dryly.

The two men took hold of Krysty, Jak grabbing her ankles, and carried her off the narrow trail and into cover.

"Better bring her 'round quick. Not much time to waste," Jak whispered.

Doc nodded and produced the canteen of water that they had each been given at the beginning of the hunt. Pausing only to take a mouthful for himself, then offering to Jak, he poured the remains over Krysty's face. She spluttered and coughed as it went up her nose and down her throat, making her gag as it snapped her back to consciousness.

She opened her eyes, a sudden shock making them snap from hazy semiconsciousness to full alert.

"Doc! What—" she began as she tried to move up, only to find the old man pinning her shoulders while the albino had her legs secured.

"Krysty, listen to me, my dear," Doc urged in a low, crooning voice. "Think about what you are doing. Why are you doing it?"

"Because…dammit, Doc, what are you doing? He's there, the little fuck. You should have chilled him, you should have let me chill him."

"Why?" he interrupted, still holding her down. "Think woman, why are we supposed to be doing it?"

"Because…because…" Her head was spinning. It ached from where Doc had hit her so hard and it ached for another reason. At the edges of her reason, there were nagging tendrils of doubt. Why was she chasing Jak? Why was she so keen to see him buy the farm? Because he had… What, exactly? What was he supposed to have done? Who had told her? Told her… Shit!

"Ethan," she whispered, "he said—"

"He said we were to chill Jak," Doc interjected, aware of the urgency of the situation. "He hypnotized us. But he is not as good as he thinks. The hold is not that strong, not if you fight it. And you must. We still have to fight back and find Mildred and dear John Barrymore."

"Gaia," Krysty whispered in awe, "what has that bastard done?"

"Nothing that cannot be remedied," Doc whispered urgently. "But first we must get to Ryan, and bring him back."

"What about the riders?" she asked as they allowed her to sit upright. "Surely they're—"

"They got enough troubles," Jak snapped. "Not our problem…yet. First get Ryan."

"And I have no doubts that you know exactly where he is, dear boy," Doc muttered.

Jak assented. "Follow…"

RYAN CAWDOR WAS almost frothing at the mouth with frustration. He was hyped up to chill, and so far had seen no action. The initial plan to form a pincer movement had come to nothing, and as the darkness fell over the forest it became more and more difficult to follow what exactly was going on elsewhere.

Whatever it was, it was a hell of a firefight that he was missing. He had heard the LeMat go off a couple of times, and some shots that he could identify as Krysty's Smith & Wesson. There had also been some muffled reports that could have been the Magnum roar of Jak's Colt Python, followed by the incessant chatter of SMG fire and the sound of mutie animals like those he could remember encountering on their journey to the ville.

Ryan's head ached horribly and he felt confused when he thought of that. Jak had been with them then, so why had they not wanted to chill him? He had been their ally. What had changed, why did he feel the way he did?

It was hard for him to concentrate with these thoughts and also the comments of the riders on his trail buzzing around his head. The baron and the trader who were accompanying Ethan at his rear were less than pleased with the lack of action they were seeing and were blaming the one-eyed man. They were making jokes about his competence and asking if they could get their jack back if they saw no Jak.

In this confusion, it was difficult for Ryan to make the direction from which the hunt seemed to be preceding. He stopped for a second, trying to get his bearings.

It was then that he heard a single report that rose above the chatter of SMG fire. It was the Smith & Wesson Model 640: he would know that sound anywhere.

He turned in the darkness, trying to pinpoint the direction of the sound. It seemed to be over to his left, about two o'clock. Ryan took the Steyr off his shoulder and racked a shell into the chamber.

"Looks like One-Eye's finally looking to do some hunting," the trader to his rear commented with a sardonic air.

"About time," the baron agreed shortly.

Ethan held up his hand. "Please, please, I have great faith in Ryan," he stated, but not without a hint of sarcasm in his voice.

Ryan felt the beads of sweat on his face, felt his skin burn. There was something so very wrong with this, something that he couldn't quite put his finger on, something that was troubling him and stopping him doing the job as he should. But it wasn't... No, it just wasn't coming together. He turned and glared at the men behind him. He didn't like being watched in this way and was aware that there was something so very wrong with what was happening.

Hunt... That was what he needed to do. He needed to get moving, find his target. Identify and chill. From the sounds of mayhem that were echoing over the forest, he was sure that Jak was still alive and running. No one had managed to pin him down yet, even if they were on his tail.

It was time for Ryan to get in on the action.

With his target area identified, Ryan set off, carving a path into the undergrowth, heedless of whether Ethan and the other huntsmen would be able to follow. In fact, it would suit him fine if he was able to lose them. He could hear them, struggling in the confined spaces on their mounts, receding into the distance.

It would be just him and Jak: one-on-one.

"YOU SURE Ryan will come this way?" Krysty asked as they laid the trap.

"No other way he can get here," Jak answered firmly. "He heard your shot and I saw him head in this direction."

"It would, therefore, be a reasonable assumption," Doc commented dryly. "But what about the riders on his storm?"

"What?" Krysty asked in astonishment.

Doc shook his head. "I am so sorry, I do not know where that came from. I meant, what about the three riders shadowing him?"

"Too dense for horses. They fall back, mebbe have give up," Jak answered. "Now shut up and cover."

It was a simple enough trap, and also stood a very good chance of not working, but it was all that they could do in the short time that they had. There was only one path that could be followed through this part of the woodlands, and the bracken and grasses covering the woodland floor provided thick cover that, in some places, was almost ankle deep. Which was perfect for their purpose.

Across the floor of the forest, running through the grass and bracken, Jak had tied a rope at a four-inch height, between two tree trunks. The rope was improvised from material torn from his shirt and his concern was that it would rip under pressure, rather than trip whoever ran into it, which was why they had built the second part of the trap. This was more vicious, and was only a last resort. They wanted to stun and capture the one-eyed man, not injure him.

A line of Jak's knives, connected together by being pierced through the grain of a long, fallen branch, were laid across the path three yards past the rope. They were pointing up, and the three companions were smearing them with mud made from canteen water and dirt, then covering them with leaves so that they wouldn't be visible. The razor-honed knives would go through Ryan's heavy combat boots if he trod on them and stop him in his tracks. There was a three-yard gap to insure that if he fell at the first trap, he wouldn't fall onto the knives and be injured.

Jak raised his head, his sharp hearing picking up their oncoming friend. "Ryan, this way," he said shortly, gesturing for them to pull back into the shadows of the foliage.

"Lover, this way, he's this way," Krysty yelled as she went into hiding. If Ryan had any doubts about his direction, she should have settled them.

From their shelter, they could see him pound into view, his fierce, ice-blue orb blazing like a diamond in the restricted light. He was so hyped up that, if they couldn't break the hypnotic hold, they would have to chill him to stop him.

Hopefully it wouldn't come to that.

Ryan was scanning the narrow way in front of him, looking for some kind of sign. He caught sight of the knives, one blade just poking out of the mud and leaves enough to attract attention. What the hell was going on? Fireblast, if he'd been fooled in some way. Ryan tried to slow down, but he wasn't quite quick enough. His left foot caught in the concealed rope, the material stretching then ripping from one tree trunk, wrapping itself around his foot so that with every stumbling step he became more and more entangled. His momentum was such that he pitched forward face first.

He rolled onto his shoulder as he landed, aware that he had to fling himself to one side to prevent pitching into the knife trap. But on a path so narrow, this only sufficed to throw him against a tree trunk, his spine slamming against the hardwood, driving the breath from him. His head cracked against an edge of bark, glancing at the rounded edge of the wood. Stars exploded in front of his eyes and he found himself momentarily unsure as to who, where and what he was.

That moment was all the others needed. Rushing from their hiding places, the three companions swarmed over their leader, pinning him to the ground.

"Ryan, lover, it's me," Krysty yelled, her red tresses flopping into his face, filling his nose and mouth with her scent. "We need to talk—and you need to listen."

"He has had a blow on the head," Doc commented, "which has possibly put him in a more receptive mood.

Ryan, my friend, listen to me. We have been the victims of a most heinous trick."

"Must…must get Jak… All his fault…" Ryan whispered, his voice a dry, dazed husk as he fought to regain senses that were swimming wildly around him, a sense of nausea rising in his gut.

Jak tensed when he heard this, ready for the worst. He had a firm grip of the one-eyed man's legs, pinning him, keeping out of eyeline for the moment.

"What is all Jak's fault?" Doc pressed. "Tell me, my friend, what is it that he has supposed to have done?"

"Nearly…nearly got us chilled… Got us hunting… Lost J.B. and Mildred… Lost Dean…"

"No, no, baby," Krysty implored. "That was Ethan— the bastard who hypnotized us to hunt Jak. It's not us who want this, it's him. He's got Mildred and J.B. He's got us doing this. And Dean was gone before we got here. It was Sharona who took him, remember?"

Ryan looked at her, confusion and concussion battling for space in the ice-blue orb that refused to focus on her face. He knew that there was something wrong with what he was feeling, what he was thinking, but it was something that he found hard to pin down.

Ryan's head reeled with more than just the trauma of the fall. There were other things spinning around his brain, things that he was finding it hard to understand, to take hold of… He caught sight of Jak, the albino's head just visible as he held Ryan down. There was a sudden swell of anger within him, as though he would rise up and strike down the enemy; but this was suddenly replaced by a realization that the albino was acting in tandem with Doc and Krysty. They were together.

But surely...

"Fireblast! That sick fuck son of a gaudy whore!" Ryan exploded, his muscles knotting with the sudden rush of adrenaline, his strength—enhanced by his anger—enough to push Krysty and Doc away, so that his torso rose up, leaving only his legs pinned by Jak's own wiry strength.

The albino looked up, coming into eye contact with the one-eyed man, ice-blue orb meeting twin red needle points.

"We'll get the coldheart bastard for this," Ryan whispered to Jak.

The albino's impassive visage split into a grin and he released his grip. Ryan rose to his feet and grabbed the albino by the shoulders, his imposing bulk dwarfing Jak.

"Where is he? We'll get the bastard right now."

"That way," Jak said, indicating the direction in which Ryan had come, "and approaching fast. Figure we move quickly and we take them."

"Sounds good to me. There's nine of them, right?" Ryan questioned, and when the albino assented, added, "That's only two apiece with one unlucky fuck left. That's good odds in my book."

THINGS HAD ALL GONE terribly wrong. What should have been the finest hunt he had staged, and the one that would begin to attract attention from across the Deathlands as the traders spread the word on their travels, was rapidly descending into a farce. Ethan was aware that the trader and baron at his side were becoming more and more impatient as he tried to locate where Ryan had vanished. The trail he had taken was proving hard for horses to follow, and it seemed that the harder they tried to plow through the undergrowth, the more it wanted to fight back and prevent them making any progress. All three men were now covered in scratches and bruises, and the two riders accompanying the Pleasantville baron were making it clear that it was not for such things that they had paid their jack:

"Okay, okay, so we can't get any farther through here," Ethan snapped after yet another complaint. "Look, we'll pull back and circle around this copse, see if we can make it any easier from the other side. Anyway," he added hopefully, "if the albino has been chased from both sides, then we may get to catch the action as he makes a break for it."

The muttered comments of the two accompanying riders suggested that they didn't share Ethan's faith in getting some action. But they were tired and sore, and they welcomed the chance to pull out of the copse.

As the riders moved out, Ethan was astonished to see six horsemen heading toward him at a trot: Riley, Horse and the barons and traders they had been assigned to protect.

"What the fuck are you doing?" he yelled, not realizing that—although his comment was directed at his own sec men—it would be taken the wrong way by those who had paid good jack for a hunt they were not getting to see.

"What are we doing?" the inbred baron lisped. "We're being ripped off, that's what we're doing."

"Yeah," added the trader who had accompanied him. "We ain't seen shit yet. And I'll tell you one thing—if there's three of the fuckers in there after one little scrawny albino, no matter how good he is, they're not making much of an effort at it."

Ethan stopped and held up his hand for silence. He listened intently. The copse was dense, but not that expansive, and any sounds that emanated from within wouldn't easily have been deadened by the surrounding greenery. But he could hear nothing. To all intents and purposes, there seemed to be nothing going on inside. He would have expected some kind of activity, even if the albino was proving adept at hiding himself. After all, there were three of them in there after him.

That's if they were after him, still… It hurt Ethan's ego to feel that his hypnosis may have failed. So much so that he didn't even want to consider it. As far as he was concerned, Bones had taught him well. But then again, he'd never really had the chance to put it to the test before.

The baron looked at the two sec men and the half-dozen paying huntsmen. Riley and Horse were awaiting his cue, but there was no disguising the hostility on the faces of the men who had given him their hard-won and hard-earned jack for a spectacle that looked as though it had gone belly-up on him.

Ethan made a snap decision, without realizing the echo he formed with the four companions in the copse.

"Okay, people, there's been a little change of plan," he announced with a calmness that he didn't feel. How would they take what he was about to say? "It appears that the three hunters have turned on us, and are back with their little white friend. So instead of watching a hunt, I figure that it's about time that we got our blasters out and went on a little hunt of our own."

"You saying what I think you're saying?" one of the traders asked with a huge grin spreading across his face. "We've seen 'em try to hunt, and now we get to whomp the shit out of them ourselves?"

"I don't think I could have put it better myself," Ethan replied with a smile that belied the tension gnawing at his gut.

The half-dozen hunters whooped in exultation. Ethan calmed them with an imploring gesture. "Okay," he said, "if we're gonna do this right, then I suggest you sort out among yourselves who you want to hunt. Meanwhile, I'll consult with my men."

The hunters joyfully agreed and huddled their horses together to argue among themselves about their targets. Meanwhile, Ethan gestured Horse and Riley over to him.

"This is bad," he said quietly when they were with him. "This is very bad. Those four are shit hot and if we lose any of these guys, then our reputation is shit and we may very well end up in a war situation."

"So what do you want us to do about it?" Horse asked, his ambiguous choice of phrase making it clear he felt Ethan had invited trouble.

Ethan ignored it. He could deal with his sec chief later—if there was a later. "I want you to make sure you get in first, ahead of these idiots. I want those four scumfucks chilled meat before these boys even get near them. Do I make myself clear?"

Horse nodded. "Perfectly."

Riley smiled coldly, thinking of his score to settle with Ryan. "It'll be a fucking pleasure."

Chapter Fifteen

"Name's Stark, and I figure it's about time that all this stupe shit came to an end." The bald giant held out his hand, and J.B., despite catching Mildred's suspicion-filled glance, took it.

"You know who we are, and you know that Ethan wants us chilled. So why are you going against him?"

The giant shrugged. "Why not? I've always thought he was a little fucked in the head, and I know I'm not the only one—" he directed his glance at Michaela "—and I know some of us have reason to fear Ethan and his sec, especially Horse. Fear is what kept us down, and mebbe it's time to stop being frightened. Mebbe there's a whole lot more of us than we thought. Shit, I reckon that's the most I've ever said in one breath in my whole life," he added with a surprised shake of his head.

"Mebbe it was just the time to say it," J.B. commented, continuing, "If there are a whole lot, then we need to get them together, and quick. And we also need to sort out who's on our side and who isn't. We've got to get back into Pleasantville first, right?"

"Y'mean who in the sec will join us and who'll want to whip our ass?"

"It's the first priority," J.B. agreed.

"Leave that to me. I know them," Stark said simply,

with an air of finality and confidence that left J.B. in no doubt that this man could deliver on his word.

"John…" Mildred spoke quietly, beckoning the Armorer to join her. "Are you sure you're really up to this right now?" she questioned. "You had a terrific shock to the system, and there's no knowing how strong you are. You need to be—"

"Millie, don't worry about it," he interrupted her, "there's no point. We've got to do this, so I'll just make the most of it. Now, it's getting toward midmorning and I don't want to waste any more time. We don't even know if the others are alive out there. They may have chilled Jak and skinned him for Ethan's pleasure for all we know. Or he may have taken out at least one of them. Either way, I reckon they've had all night, and it's probably over by now. So we've just got to pick up the pieces as best and as quick as we can."

The Armorer gently kissed her forehead, then turned back to face Stark and Michaela, who were deep in conference. The two Pleasantville dwellers faced the companions as they came across the open space toward them. They had the air of people for whom a momentous time had come in their lives.

"We've been talking about who we think will be with us," Michaela began before either J.B. or Mildred had a chance to speak. "We've got a list, some with power, others with influence…but our big problem is going to be getting back into the ville to begin with."

"The blaster turrets are now manned," Stark explained. "Tracey—that was the fucker covered in ink that you chilled—was left in charge by Horse, and his orders were to man them all. Now, I know who we can count on, but until we get to the way back in, I won't know who's on what turret and how we can tackle this."

"I see what you're saying," J.B. said. "We need to get close enough to find out without being blasted."

The giant agreed. "Thing is, I can see only one way to do it, and you're not gonna like it."

The Armorer allowed himself a grin. "I think I'm already there. You have to look like you've captured us so we can get through the tunnel and past the sec. And for that, you're gonna have to handle all our weapons and link us together like we're prisoners…leaving us, mebbe, defenseless."

"Knew you wouldn't like it…"

"You've got to be kidding," J.B. said playfully. "I love it. I trust you if she does," he added, indicating Michaela. The spiky-haired healer looked surprised.

"You trust me?" she asked, incredulous.

"I'd trust anyone who helped save my life," J.B. answered simply.

Michaela nodded decisively. "Then we trust the big man, here," she answered.

Stark's plan was simplicity itself as he outlined it. He would lead them into view by the concealed tunnel entrance, so that they could be seen by the sec manning the blaster emplacement. He would be carrying their arms, with his blaster trained on them, and they would be tied together. He would explain that he had overpowered them after they had chilled the other two sec men and that he was bringing them back for Ethan to punish at his leisure. Then, once inside the tunnel, he would release them and return their arms. They would emerge on the other side ready for a firefight if the emplacement sec men were loyal to Ethan, and recruitment if they were among the silent dissidents that Stark and Michaela could identify.

They crossed the remains of the ruined city quickly, making good time until they were at a point where they would start to become visible to whomever manned the emplacement across the wasteland.

Here they stopped and Stark collected their weapons and ordnance, slinging the heavy blasters and bags across his broad shoulders as though they were nothing. He then took the chains that he and the other sec men had been carrying with them to link and carry back the chilled corpses of the escapees, and threaded them through Mildred, J.B. and Michaela. It looked as though they were secure, although in truth it would take but an instant for them to shrug off their supposed bonds.

"Just one thing," Mildred said as they tried to get used to moving with their upper bodies temporarily restricted by the heavy chains. "Isn't it going to look kind of odd that you managed to get all three of us trussed single-handed?"

Stark shrugged. "If they stop to think about it. So we have to move quick. Anyway, you think of anything better?"

Mildred kissed her teeth. "Guess not, not at such short notice."

"Then let's do it before they figure it out, as well," the bald giant muttered.

The three chain-entangled, so-called captives shuffled out from cover and into sight of the blaster emplacement. Stark was close at their heels, his blaster trained on them, to insure that he was seen to be in control, so that they would not be fired on.

There were two men on the emplacement, both looking bored until the four people came into view. Then, with an almost comical spurt of activity, they sprang to attention, one training the mounted SMG on the group, the other shouldering a Lee Enfield .303, the idea being to back up the SMG's spray'n'pray fire with some sniper shooting for accuracy, should the need arise.

"It's okay," Stark yelled. "I got some meat to bring home."

"Where are the others?" the man with the rifle returned, his tone harsh and edgy.

"Chilled, like these will be after Ethan's finished with 'em."

"Thought your orders were to just finish the fuckers," the rifleman said with a suspicious edge to his tone.

"So they were," Stark replied amiably. "But seeing as they did so much damage, I figured that the baron may want to attend to matters himself."

"Sounds like a good call to me," the man behind the SMG replied. "Put the fucker down, J.T.," he said to the rifleman, "and let 'em through."

He stepped away from the SMG. The rifleman lowered his Enfield, albeit unwillingly, and allowed them to pass forward to the concealed tunnel entrance.

Even though they were pretty sure that they couldn't be seen from the emplacement once they were in front of the concealed entrance, the three "prisoners" allowed Stark to keep his blaster trained on them while he opened the tunnel entrance with one hand. Once they were inside the enclosed, dank space, he shut the door and lowered the blaster, producing a flashlight from a pocket. The beam was diffuse enough to illuminate a fair portion of the enclosed space. They could see that the other end of the tunnel was still safely secured.

"Good thing they haven't sent a welcoming party," Mildred commented as she slipped her chains. The other two followed suit, while Stark grunted to indicate he had something to say. He was, however, incapable of speech at that moment, as his mouth was occupied in gripping the torch while he shrugged off the "captured" blasters and ordnance to return to J.B., Mildred and Michaela. That wasn't as easy as it sounded, as he was a big enough man to almost fill the tunnel and he found that the movement of his arms within the enclosed space was difficult. But eventually, he had shed his load and distributed it to those from whom he had initially taken it. This done, he took the flashlight from his mouth.

"Okay, listen now. The guy with the rifle—J.T.—is a jumpy little fuck, and he's Horse's personal whipping boy. And yeah, does he love it. He's right behind Ethan, and he'll want to mow us down as soon as we come out. So we need to take him out straightaway."

"What about the other one?" J.B. asked.

"Eddie's a sweetheart," Michaela said before Stark had a chance to speak. "He's one of us, definitely."

Stark gave a lopsided grin that seemed strangely out of place on his otherwise grim visage. "That's one way of saying it, I guess, but yeah, trouble is, we come out shooting, he's gonna shoot back if only to protect himself."

"So we need to stop this J.T. from firing on us without alarming Eddie…should be simple," Mildred said with a sardonic edge to her voice.

"Think it just might be, actually." J.B. grinned, then outlined his simple plan before urging them to move toward the ville end of the tunnel. When they had reached the far door, leading up to the trap beneath the emplacement, J.B. signaled to Stark to go on ahead. The big man nodded and took his cue.

"Hey, I can't see a fucking thing down here," he yelled through the partly open trap, "come on, one of you give me a hand. My flashlight is fucked. Someone—c'mon, give me a break…" He continued when there was no reply forthcoming.

Then he heard Eddie's voice. "Gimme a second, big guy."

"No, Eddie, you stay at the emplacement," Stark returned quickly. "Horse would flay you if he found you deserting it."

"Heh, too right." J.T. snickered. "Much as I'd like to see that, I ain't gonna be party to that. You stay here, Eddie—I'll help the fat bastard with those scum."

"Nice guy, J.T.," Mildred murmured contemptuously. "I'm sure a shitload of people will miss him when he's gone."

They waited for the sounds of the rifleman clambering down the emplacement and scurrying across the ground to reach the other side of the trap. It opened suddenly, letting in the blinding light of early morning.

"Would've thought a big bastard like you could manage two outsiders and a pussy eater like her." J.T. giggled. It was to be the last sound he would ever make.

"You always did say too much," Stark commented dryly as he used the time it took J.T. in insulting them to reach out one hamlike hand and wrap it around the sec man's throat, squeezing beneath the carotid so that the little man nodded out from lack of blood and oxygen to the brain. When he was unconscious, Stark let his grip loose and took the man's head in both hands, twisting viciously to break his neck while he was unconscious.

"Wish I could say I was sorry..." Stark murmured as he let the lifeless J.T. drop to the ground. "Now for Eddie..."

The big man walked out into the light, so that he could be plainly seen from the emplacement. Eddie looked down on him with a puzzled air.

"Where's J.T.?" he asked, unable to keep the nervous quiver from his voice.

Stark smiled. "Eddie, you don't want to worry about that little shit anymore. He can't rat on anyone, now."

"Listen, what's going on here, 'cause I don't like the sound of this. And another thing, where are the three prisoners?"

"They're not prisoners, Eddie," Stark said simply. "We're the ones who are prisoners. Let me ask you something, do you really like what goes on down here?"

"You know the answer to that," Eddie replied guardedly. "But we don't have any option, do we?"

"Don't we? You know how many there are like us? You thought about what we could do if we all got it together."

"Mebbe I have. But that's not going to happen, is it?"

"Isn't it? You just come down here and talk about it."

From their place of concealment, the Armorer and Mildred watched with apprehension. The big guy was taking a hell of a chance, and he would be mowed down if Eddie had the slightest doubt. But no, the nervous sec man left his post on the emplacement and came to talk with Stark.

Rapidly and concisely, the big man told Eddie what had happened in the ruined city and how sick he was of Ethan's ways. He explained how he and Michaela had figured out there were enough dissidents to mount a revolution, and there would be no better time than now, while Ethan and Horse were both out on the hunt.

"Guess it figures," Eddie said at length. "But we're gonna have to move pretty quick, and there'll be a lot of folks who'll not be too happy if they know that two of the outsiders are involved."

"We won't be," J.B. said, stepping out of the shadows and into view. "I'm not in any fit state yet to be running around, and there's no way we'd expect any of your people to trust me or Millie. This is totally down to you guys. But what we can do is help you make your plans—at least that way we'll feel like we're being useful."

Eddie chewed on his lip thoughtfully. "Three of us and a whole ville to cover—yeah, guess your help would be necessary," he agreed.

"Good, then let's get to it," J.B. said, "there's no time to waste."

Eddie gestured them to join him in the emplacement. There was enough cover for Mildred and J.B. to stay hidden, while its height enabled Eddie, Michaela and Stark to get an overview of the whole ville while they planned. Plus, it would look less suspicious to any pro-Ethan sec men if Eddie was still visibly on watch.

Once they had attained the height of the emplacement, they began to go over the names of those they knew they could rely on. It was a considerable list.

"There isn't going to be time to get around to all of them," Michaela said despairingly. "How are we going to manage this?"

"Simple." J.B. grinned. "Look, you all know these people. Who are the ones that you know will be most committed? Go to them first, and then when you go to the next person on your list, give them a list of their own. That way you can hit several people at once and before you know where you are, you've got an army."

"That's all right as far as it goes," Eddie muttered, still gnawing nervously on his lip, "but we've got to hit hard, before those loyal to Ethan get a chance to crush us. From what we know, they've still got the blaster power and the sec advantage."

"Then you hit them first, and you hit them hard— and in ways that they don't expect," J.B. explained. "Look, I'm still off balance from that shit Ethan pumped into me. I feel like I could sleep a week right now. But if there's one thing I do know, it's how to plan an attack." He grinned more broadly than before. "You tell me where they're based and I'll give you a plan."

The Armorer then sat back and listened to Eddie, Stark and Michaela reel off facts at him. Places and people that would have been a blur if not for the fact that they were able to use the height of the emplacement, and the resulting panorama of the ville it afforded them, to point out key locations.

It seemed to J.B. that the problem would be in securing the armory and the sec compound. The majority of the dissidents that would unite against Ethan were from outside the sec force, and there were also a number of unconcerned residents who would go with the flow of combat, easily switching their allegiance to whoever had the upper hand. To stop a long and costly pitched battle, and to draw the uncommitted to their cause, J.B. knew that he would have to devise a plan that would secure these two key points.

"Tell me again who you have on your side and where they are," he said, narrowing his eyes as he was told once more, following the lines that could be drawn between the small groups of dissidents and where they were clustered. As he drew up these lines, an idea began to form in his head.

"The key is to keep the recruitment a secret until the moment you strike. That's kind of made easier by the speed you'll be moving at. But otherwise you'll have to keep away from key areas." He indicated spots in the ville where there were clusters of Ethan supporters. "Get some of your people to contain those areas, and leave the sec compound and the armory until last. Keep your best fighters for those. The important thing is to cut off attack from your rear, or support reaching those two areas."

Stark nodded. "So we surround pockets of support and then pincer the armory and sec compound, using the cover of the surrounding streets, and then hit hard and fast with fighters who really know their business."

J.B. nodded. "Exactly. People who aren't great fighters can use the other areas to their advantage in the containing operation, but for the two main targets you need good runners and accurate, swift combat experts. Do you have those?"

Stark grimaced. "Mebbe not as many as I'd like, but plenty who'll be willing to take a chance. There are people here who've been waiting a long time for this, even if they haven't realized it before today."

"Okay." J.B. nodded once more. "Guess me and Millie can't do anything more than just sit here and watch. And you'd better get moving. Whatever has happened out there on the hunt, you can bet it won't be long before Ethan and Horse are back."

Stark nodded and clapped his hand on J.B.'s shoulder. He didn't have to say anything.

The big man and nervous Eddie started to descend the emplacement to ground level. Michaela lingered a moment, caught in two minds before hugging Mildred.

"Thank you," she said, risking a gentle kiss on Mildred's cheek.

"What for?" Mildred asked, astonished.

"For setting me free, one way or another," Michaela replied before following the two sec men down into the ville.

"What was that about?" Mildred questioned softly, almost to herself.

"You tell me," J.B. replied, bemused by Mildred's confusion.

But there was no time for this matter to be pondered any further. If they could take no active part, as yet, in the revolt, they could at least study its progress from their secure bolthole.

Both Mildred and J.B. maneuvered themselves into positions where they could see across the ville, but couldn't be observed from below. Both had blasters in their hands in case sec men sympathetic to Ethan should want to relieve or check on the men they thought were manning the emplacement.

There was nothing to do now except wait and watch. It would be the most frustrating thing of all.

From their vantage point, they could see the three Pleasantville rebels split up and move off in different directions to begin rounding up their army of dissidents. The trio managed to steer clear of the areas they had identified as hot spots for Ethan's supporters. They disappeared into three separate dwellings and it seemed like an age before they all emerged once more, this time with three companions. All three were armed, and Mildred recognized one of them as Angelika, the trader in cloth who had settled in the ville and with whom Krysty had been billeted. As Mildred watched, the striking woman tied her distinctive multicolored hair extensions in a drab scarf, so that she was less inclined to stand out in a crowd. The woman had a Glock slung over her shoulder on a short strap and she appeared to be speaking in an animated manner to Michaela, who had recruited her. After a brief discussion, the two women parted company and headed off in different directions.

Meanwhile, Stark and Eddie had begun their own recruitment, and as the numbers of people doubled with each separate visit, it was easy to see a pattern develop across the ville, as the lines of dissidents grew, flowing out in a spiderweb pattern across the streets. As more and more were recruited to the cause, it seemed an inevitability that those who supported Ethan would know something was happening.

"Dark night, I haven't felt so useless for a long, long

time, and I hate it," J.B. whispered as he watched the action unfold in front of him.

Mildred grasped his arm. "It's better this way, John. We can get down there and join the firefight once it starts, but right now we'd only be likely to alert the opposition. We've got to have patience."

"Yeah…" J.B. didn't sound too convinced, but he knew that Mildred was right.

Meanwhile, down in the ville, there were a number of fighters gathering together to tackle the armory and the sec compound. Stark, Eddie and Michaela had managed to marshal a considerable force to tackle the two targets, and had encountered little, if no resistance. This was partly because they had been careful to approach the right targets and partly because the level of support for Ethan hadn't been as high as they'd suspected. Those who would follow the baron were complacent, and this complacency was enabling the rebels to grow in number.

J.B. and Mildred kept watching as the forces divided and gathered around the two areas that were marked for attack. There had been little resistance thus far: a couple of dissenting voices had been swiftly and silently stilled so as not to alert the sec forces. Most of the activity had been away from the center of the ville, and the rebels had been able to recruit without causing too many ripples in ville life.

But time was running out. There were now two forces gathered at the strategic targets, and by their sheer size alone they would be noticed by the still unsuspecting majority of the population.

BACK IN THE NIGHT, a few hours before, the four companions clustered in the wooded copse plotted their revenge against the horsemen that roamed the open space beyond.

Ryan was seething as the full realization of what had happened hit him. J.B. had possibly bought the farm, Mildred had maybe gone the same way, and the four of them gathered in the woods had nearly ripped each other into pieces at the behest of one man's greed.

"Jak, you reckon Ethan will have realized what's going on by now?" he asked of the albino.

"Be triple stupe not to—and Ethan not triple stupe."

Ryan nodded grimly. "That's just what I was thinking. From now on we have to assume that the horsemen will be out to hunt all of us. They've got firepower that is mebbe the same as ours, but not superior. And they've got the horses, which'll make them faster over open ground."

"But not in here." Krysty smiled. "So we take them on here. But Horse and Ethan will have worked that one out for themselves, so how do we get them in here where they'll be vulnerable? They'll be quite happy to wait out there for us to come out."

"Ah, yes, those two reprobates will be contented with such a course of action," Doc commented with deliberation. "But can you see those who have paid to see blood having quite such a long fuse? I'm sure that I cannot."

"Doc's got a point." Ryan grinned. "I figure that the best thing we can do is hit their vulnerable spots. That blond asshole riding with them wants my blood, so I'll give him something to think about. As for the coldheart bastards who've paid… Let's offer them their jack's worth and see how they react."

But the first thing that needed to be done was for the outside of the copse to be recced. While Doc and Krysty stayed in the center, Jak and Ryan set out to the east and west respectively, intending to skirt the edges of the forest to see where the riders were and any formation they may have adopted.

The copse itself was about five hundred yards in diameter and about seven hundred yards in length, forming a rough semicircle that spiraled at one point into an oval. It was large enough for the companions to successfully contain themselves from outside interference, but small enough to provide a group of horsemen with difficulties in maneuvering. Which was precisely why Horse and Ethan were keeping their increasingly impatient riders on the outside of the copse.

When both had finished their circuits, they returned to where Doc and Krysty awaited them.

"Well?" Doc asked impatiently. "What news from nowhere do you bring for us?"

"Say stupe things," Jak muttered, "but know what mean. On the west, six riders. Ethan, blond man, four others. Ethan split into two threes, each patrolling north and south end woods. Moving slow, triple-red, but not getting much. Four who pay big jack to see us fight getting restless."

"Good." Ryan grinned mirthlessly. "That's what I like to hear. The more impatient those fuckers get, the more likely they are to make mistakes, rush in instead of thinking."

"What about your side, lover?" Krysty asked.

"Just the three riders. Horse, some guy with no chin and a fat bastard who looks like a trader. He's keeping them tight to the center, so they can rush either end of the woods in equal time."

"Stupe not keep even numbers much as possible." Jak shrugged.

Ryan nodded. "Yeah, but what do you expect? Horse and Ethan haven't got that much combat experience and not that much smarts, either. Ethan wants to keep the customers happy, but with only one sec man for each pair, there's little else he can do."

"So what's the best way to hit them?" Krysty questioned.

Ryan grimaced. "Soon, more than anything." He looked up through the leaf and branch cover to where the sun was rising and the sky was beginning to lighten. "In this cover, one of our best assets was the dark. Now it's morning. I figure we need to move fast, make the most of what's left. I figure the best thing to do this...."

HORSE WAS UNEASY. The two riders with him were champing at the bit more than their mounts, eager to get into the copse and hunt down the four targets.

"Come on, man. Ethan told us we could have a crack at the fuckers," the fat trader complained. "So why are we still here? Why don't we go in after them?"

"He has a point, you know," the inbred baron added. "We've paid Ethan a lot for this, and it hasn't been everything that was promised...in fact, I'd say it's been nothing that was promised."

Horse could feel his patience stretched to the limit. "Look," he muttered through gritted teeth, "those are good fighters. I know those woods. If we take horses in there, then they have the advantage of speed and space, and they'll chill you before you have a chance to draw breath. If we wait until they come out, then we have the advantage over open ground. They can't stay in there forever."

"How do you know they won't just sit it out?" the baron asked.

Horse shot him a glance that was undisguised venom. "Because we've got their friends hostage back in Pleasantville, and they'll want to get them back. So why go in and risk a chilling when they'll be coming out? And why don't you just shut the fuck up and wait?"

The baron glared at him, outraged. "You impudent bastard. I'll report what you said to Ethan. You're not supposed to talk to us in that way..."

"I'll talk how I fucking like," Horse snapped. "Out here, you don't mean shit. My job is to keep you alive, and if the least that takes is harsh language, then you're fucking fortunate."

The trader chuckled. This didn't sit well with the baron, who snapped at him, "And you can shut up, as well, you fat fool. What have you contributed to this little campaign beyond hot air and your vacuous views?"

"You fuck-witted chinless freak, you talk to me like that and it won't be the fuckers in there that I'll be hunting," the trader snarled, drawing a Glock and waving it toward the woods before pointing it at the baron.

Horse winced. This was the last thing he wanted. Just when they were supposed to be on triple-red to cover any flight by the trapped prey, the hunters were squabbling among themselves and mebbe even chilling each other.

"For fuck's sake," Horse yelled, trying to keep his tone as neutral as possible, but knowing that he sounded pissed off and ready to leave them to it. "We've got more important things to do than fight among ourselves, okay? We need to keep calm."

The fat trader glowered at the sec chief as he lowered the Glock. "Yeah, well, mebbe you shouldn't start things by being so fucking mouthy in the first place."

"Yes, you should remember who you are," the baron agreed.

Horse sighed. Being put in his place by these two was all he needed, but at least they were united once more in their slanging of him.

Unfortunately for the sec chief, this brief respite meant that they had all dropped their guard for one brief moment.

That was the moment for Jak to strike. The albino had been silently watching them argue, waiting for the exact moment when, for that fraction of a second, they were all distracted, and all at rest.

Jak stayed in cover, and from his concealed position pulled two of his razor-honed, leaf-bladed throwing knives. Balancing one in each palm, he took aim and loosed the first, which flew straight and true into the left eye of the inbred baron. He gave a brief, strangled cry of shock before the momentum of the knife carried the point up into his brain and shut down all his motor functions. He didn't even feel himself fall sideways from his mount, a piece of chilled meat before he even hit the grass of the plain.

The second knife followed in less than the blink of an eye. It was headed for the fat trader, and in that briefest of moments he turned slightly to where his instincts—blunted by age and indulgence, but still retaining a vestige of what had once been needed to survive on trading routes—told him the knife thrower sat.

He didn't even have enough time to raise the Glock before the knife hit him in the side of the neck. It was slowed by the layers of fat and muscle that protected his carotid artery, but not enough to prevent the tip of the knife nicking the tough tissue that comprised the artery wall. The pressure of the blood within, pumping around his fat body, was enough to rend the nick, to enlarge it and cause the artery wall to rupture.

This took a few moments—moments in which the trader fired his Glock into the ground as shock made him squeeze the trigger; moments in which he lost his balance and toppled backward, falling from his mount and catching his foot in the stirrup, ending upside down on the turf with his lifeblood erupting from the suddenly rupturing artery.

His horse panicked at the sudden fall of its rider and rose up on its back legs before hitting the turf at a gallop, heading north and dragging the trader behind it. It would have hurt like hell if the fat man had still been alive, but the gouts of blood spraying from the neck wound and leaving a showered trail of rusty red on the dry grassland in the wake of the galloping mount were testimony to the fact that he was beyond caring.

Horse swore loudly and pulled his own Glock, firing four shots into the area of woodland he identified as the attacker's territory. The foliage was devastated by the heavy-caliber blasterfire, but to no avail. Before the second knife had hit its target, Jak had already begun to move away from his position and move to his left so that he was at an angle of sixty degrees to the last rider.

Jak was unhappy that Horse had fired and that the trader had loosed a shot before his demise. The point of using knives had been to keep the attack silent, so that it didn't attract the attention of the riders on the far side of the copse. He wanted them to stay in position for the other companions. That was blown now and he could only hope that the shots hadn't preempted their attacks.

But if silence was no longer an imperative, Jak wouldn't have to stick to knives. Horse was beginning to spur his mount to move toward the area where he had fired and was angling the steed to use it as cover, slipping from the saddle so that he was shielded by its body.

Jak cursed to himself again. If he had moved the other way, Horse's tactics would have been futile and he just would have presented Jak with an open target. Unfortunately for Jak he was slipping out of view.

It would have to be one shot and it would have to be good. Jak slipped the Colt Python into his palm so smoothly that it was up and aiming before his finger had even the time to curl around the trigger, tensing to squeeze.

He had a fraction of a second to sight and fire as the sec man's body disappeared behind the body of his mount. It would have to be a head shot, the most difficult of all.

As Horse began to sink behind the body of the galloping animal, Jak squeezed and the loud report of the Magnum round boomed through the woods and across the plain.

The dreadlocked sec man flew backward, away from the galloping animal, which now set off on a new direction, completely freaked and scared by the noise and the spray of warm blood, bone and brain tissue that had splattered over it. Jak's aim had been true, and the sec chief's head had split like a ripe melon, the entry wound of the large-caliber bullet around his nose and eyes devastating enough, but as nothing compared to the exit wound that took away the back of his head.

Horse was chilled before he even fell halfway to the ground.

Jak kept the Colt Python in his hand and turned to where he could hear the sounds of combat from the other side of the copse.

Time to check out if they needed help.

WHILE JAK HAD TAKEN the side with only three riders, Ryan, Krysty and Doc had opted to take on Ethan, Riley and the four paying hunters. Ryan had a particular score to settle with the blond sec man, and although he was the consummate warrior, and would never allow his feelings to overcome his sense of strategy and combat, he would enjoy paying this debt, and wasn't about to let it up lightly.

From their recce, the one-eyed man knew that Riley and his two hunters were at the northern end of the copse, while Ethan had taken his riders to the south. He sent Krysty and Doc to deal with the Pleasantville baron and his charges. There was only one stipulation.

"I don't care if you chill those coldheart bastards with him, but I want Ethan alive. Blow the bastard's arms off to stop him shooting if necessary, but he can't buy the farm. We'll need him if we're to have any chance of getting J.B. and Mildred back. That's why I want two of you to take them out. Try to separate him from the others."

Doc and Krysty nodded. In the heat of combat, it wouldn't be an easy task to stick to, but both knew the importance of keeping the baron in the game. He was their ticket to their friends. As they left Ryan and set off for their target, they knew they would have to be more vigilant than ever in a combat situation.

Ryan, on the other hand, had no such compunction. All he had to do was eliminate the threat that the three horsemen represented, and he was going to enjoy it.

He was able to move swiftly through the forest and kept noise to a minimum, which was easy as the bracken was cushioned by the grasses and leaves beneath the trees.

Ryan pulled up short of the border, keeping in deep cover about a hundred yards from where the three horsemen kept an agitated watch. He could hear them talking among themselves…talking when they should have been listening. That gave him an invaluable edge. As he carefully unslung the Steyr from his shoulder, opting for sharp-shooting from cover, he listened to them and was heartened by their unease and the level of dissent between them.

"What the fuck are we doing hanging around here when we should be out for those assholes' blood," one of the riders complained.

"Yeah, we've paid for some action and we should be seeing it," the other said, emphasizing his point by jabbing a finger at the blond sec man.

It amused Ryan to see the man's obvious discomfort as he answered, "Look, guys, I know you're the customer, and all that shit, but you don't know what those woods are like. On foot, they've got the advantage."

"Then why don't we go on foot?" the baron asked.

Riley shrugged. "Dunno—I just do what Ethan says, okay?"

Ryan allowed himself a grin entirely devoid of humor. The truth was that Ethan knew the companions would easily take out the hunters if it came to a battle on the ground. It was just that the sec man couldn't admit this to the hunters for fear of offending them. The dictates of jack… It was darkly amusing.

Ryan sighted on the baron first. The blond sec man was set apart from the baron and the trader, and the one-eyed man had opted to snipe those two first, leaving his preferred target until last.

It was then that the one-shot blast of the Glock came from the far side of the copse.

"What the fuck?" Riley yelled, jerking his horse in the direction of the sound.

The reactions of the other two riders weren't as sharp, to their fatal detriment. Ryan squeezed off the first shot from the Steyr almost synchronous to the distant sound of the Glock and it caught the baron full in the chest, throwing him backward off his mount, the shell piercing his thick clothing, skin and flesh as though it were nothing, severing muscle, tendon and blood vessels before hitting the breastbone and shattering it.

Beside him, the trader was frozen in shock, slack-jawed as he watched his erstwhile companion fall backward to the ground. This inability to react to attack was to seal his fate. It took the one-eyed man less than a blink of his single eye to shift the Steyr the few inches to sight the trader. He was side-on, gawping at the falling baron, and he presented a slightly more difficult target to chill with one shot. If Ryan tried a body hit, then the man's arm and shoulder would take the brunt of the blast, and so lessen the chances of a clean chill. So it had to be a head shot. But for that to work effectively, Ryan had to be quick, clean and accurate.

As the sound of Horse firing at where he thought Jak was drifted over the copse, Ryan loosed a second shot from the Steyr. The trader stiffened as the shell penetrated the side of his head, taking him under the ear and by the cheekbone, drilling a neat hole that emerged on the other side as a wider, more ragged wound, the brain and bone in between having been pulped by the shell and its shock waves. He stiffened only momentarily before slumping down over the neck of his mount, falling sideways and underneath the suddenly frightened animal.

"Shit! Fuck it!" Riley screamed, wheeling his panicking horse in a circle, trying to bring it under control as it responded to his nervous twitches with some confusion. He could hear the firefight from across the copse and could see the two men chilled in front of him, but he had no idea of where the fire had come from and was anxiously scanning the darkened woods, searching for a sign.

Ryan allowed himself another grin. This was going to be more enjoyable than it should be. One shot from the Steyr took the horse out from under the sec man, and Riley hit the ground with a bone-jarring thud, just about managing to throw himself clear of the chilled horse.

The last thing he needed was to be crushed or trapped beneath it.

Riley came up with his Glock in his hands, scanning the forest and arcing the barrel of the blaster so that he could get a wide spray of fire if he had the slightest indication of any movement. The adrenaline was running through his veins and he suddenly felt alert.

But not alert enough. As he stood there, Ryan picked one knee as a target and put a shell through it. Riley screamed as his leg gave way beneath him, and he tumbled forward, the Glock falling from fingers nerveless with the sudden agony that shot through him. Ryan broke cover and ran toward the sec man.

Riley swore as he saw the one-eyed man trot into the open, the Steyr held across his chest as he jogged toward the prone sec man. He tried to reach for the Glock, but Ryan leveled the Steyr and put a shell through the blond sec man's arm.

Riley squealed, the pain from his arm and his leg almost too much to bear, the world coming to him through a red mist, his ears singing with the pulsing of his own nervous system. He looked up to see Ryan standing over him, but could do nothing except croak hoarsely.

Ryan stood over the blond, the Steyr almost touching his temple. Ryan looked down and figured that it was a vendetta hardly worth pursuing now. It would be kinder to put the man out of his misery.

One shot and Riley's misted eyes clouded over for good. Revenge didn't feel sweet, it felt nothing. Besides, there were more important matters to attend to. Ryan turned to see Jak headed out of the copse.

"Okay?" the albino asked. At Ryan's nod, Jak added, "Let's get others."

KRYSTY AND DOC approached their targets with caution. Doc looked up at the rapidly lightening sky and wanted to say that they should hurry, but he kept a hold on his tongue, knowing that he should only speak when absolutely necessary.

Ethan and his two hunters were clustered together, the Pleasantville baron in the middle—just where they didn't want him. Krysty sidled up to the old man and whispered urgently, "I'll get Ethan away from those two. You use your blaster and just take them out as soon as Ethan is clear."

"Whatever you say, dear lady…"

He watched Krysty disappear into the shadows and checked the load on his LeMat. The shot and ball chambers were both loaded, ready for use. It was true that the antique blaster could, if the two riders were close enough, take them out with just the shot load. But how was Krysty going to lure Ethan away? He smiled to himself, he would just have to trust her ingenuity.

Krysty would have been touched if she had known of Doc's faith in her abilities, for as she stealthily obtained a new position in the woods, away from Doc, her mind was racing, trying to come up with some way in which she could separate Ethan. She drew and checked her Smith & Wesson blaster, and racked her brain for some plan.

Fate was to come to her aid. As she got into position,

the first of the shots from the far side of the copse could be heard. Ethan was immediately alert and she heard him tell the two hunters to stay, but to be calm and triple-red, as he reined his horse and moved at a trot toward the north, where he had left Riley and two riders. The reports grew more frequent, and it was clear that a firefight was in progress on two fronts. Ethan pulled his blaster and turned to speak.

Doc cut off his words before they had a chance to be spoken. With the two hunters isolated from the Pleasantville baron, Doc took his opportunity. He loosed the shot charge from the LeMat and the deadly hail of metal spread over the distance between himself and the two riders, cutting into the flesh of the horses and of the riders, a fine mist of blood spraying everywhere. The initial wounds weren't fatal, but were more than enough to down the horses and their riders.

Ethan was frozen with shock. His world seemed to be crumbling around him. Krysty was about to make it crumble a little further. She took aim and squeezed off a .38 slug that hit the baron high on the upper arm, making him drop the Glock. The shock was enough to make him tumble from his horse.

To secure the advantage, Krysty had to leave cover. She ignored the downed riders to her right, trusting Doc to mop them up. Her concern now was that Ethan, hidden by his startled mount, would be able to regain his blaster before she could put him any further out of action.

She ran toward the horse, keeping her blaster at waist level to squeeze off a low-angle shot if necessary.

To one side, Doc also emerged from the woods. He

loped toward the fallen hunters, LeMat in one hand, Toledo steel blade unsheathed and in his other hand. The two hunters were groaning softly, near to buying the farm from their wounds. In his mercy, Doc cut their throats with the blade.

Meanwhile, Krysty approached Ethan, who was now visible where the horse had bolted, exposing him. He had struggled up into a sitting position and was trying to reach for his blaster, despite the bleeding wound in his shoulder.

Keep him alive, Krysty thought as she brought up one silver-tipped cowboy boot to connect with his jaw. Unable to raise his wounded hand, his other too far away from his face in the short time he had, Ethan was an open target. There was a look of disbelief on his face as her foot connected, before the impact knocked all consciousness from him.

As he lay on the ground, Krysty set to staunch the blood flow from his wound and binding his shoulder. She was still doing that when Doc indicated that he could see Ryan and Jak approaching with three horses, which they had rounded up on their way. Doc had also managed to secure Ethan's startled mount and was calming it.

The sun was beginning to blaze down on them as they loaded the semiconscious baron onto one of the horses, taking a mount each for themselves.

"We've got our currency, now let's see if we can bargain with the bastard," Ryan commented tersely as he indicated they should ride for the ville.

Looking up at the sun, Doc estimated that it would be around midmorning when they came in view of Pleasantville's walls.

Chapter Sixteen

A shout went up from the walls as the companions came into view with Ethan draped over a horse, in front of Ryan, lying across the horse's neck.

"Triple-red, people," Ryan whispered hoarsely, fatigue and lack of water now beginning to affect him, as it was the others. "They probably won't like this."

The four companions pulled their blasters and were ready as the walls loomed larger. But the strangest thing was that up on the SMG emplacements, the people manning them were making no effort to take aim on the approaching riders.

"By the Three Kennedys, this is most strange," Doc muttered. "What can be occurring?"

"Reckon we're gonna have to keep going and find out when we get there, Doc," Ryan replied, unable to keep the note of surprise from his voice.

INSIDE PLEASANTVILLE, word spread like wildfire. The hunt was returning and it consisted of the four who had been the prey, with no sign of those who had paid or the sec men. But Ethan was there, disabled and as their prisoner.

The whisper spurred on the rebels who were clustered around the armory and the sec camp. Under the direction of Stark and Eddie, in their respective positions, the attacks were mounted. From their position on the far wall, J.B. and Mildred could see the battle commence. There were some sec men who were, like Stark and Eddie, sympathetic to the sudden swell of rebellion. The two sec men had known who they were and had sought their help. Pinned in, and with warning, the sec in the armory and the sec camp had little chance of fighting back, despite their superior weaponry.

The battle was swift and bloody, and seen from a distance seemed to be so simple. At each site, a pincer movement was put into operation, with a select few mounting a frontal attack, others taking the rear of each encampment, all covered by their lesser equipped compatriots, who had been carefully placed in cover.

It was noticeable from this distance that there was little resistance to the rebellion. All the fighting was concentrated on the two encampments and it was swift and bloody. The forces within each were almost overwhelmed before they had a chance to fight back. The onslaught was swift and well executed, with the rebels firing at will to take out any targets that presented themselves and directing fire toward the weapons stores, both to detonate and to prevent the sec within from getting fresh supplies.

Added to this was some dissent within the camps. At first, they were united in panic against the sudden attack, but that changed as they realized that it was their own people who were attacking. Some within weren't willing to fight, and when their fellow sec men refused to lay down arms they turned upon one another.

"Dark night, it's a mess down there," J.B. breathed

as he and Mildred watched. It felt strange to be observing a firefight of such intensity—the kind of firefight they would normally be in the thick of—as though it were some kind of game. For a second it occurred to both Mildred and J.B. that this was what it had to be like for those who had paid to see their friends hunt one another. A sick feeling overwhelmed them both.

"John, let's get down there to see what we can do. I reckon we're not going to be targets now," Mildred said quietly, trying to keep the thoughts of those she assumed chilled from her mind.

J.B. agreed, pausing before adding, "There's going to be a lot of shit to sweep clean."

THE FOUR COMPANIONS were still a little suspicious as they rode into the ville through a gate that was opened for them. They could hear a firefight in the distance, but here the atmosphere was strangely, eerily calm as they were welcomed by a small group of people carrying blasters at ease.

"You've got the baron, but what about the others?" asked one of the men who had been on the tower and had seen them approach.

"Bought the farm, all of them," Ryan said coldly. "And if you try anything, the same will happen to him." He prodded the semiconscious baron, who moaned softly.

"I reckon you could do anything to him and no one would give a shit," said an old woman, stepping forward and spitting at the prone Ethan. "He's told us what to do for too long. It's all change now, and it's thanks to you people."

"Us?" Krysty asked.

"Sure," the first man replied brightly. "You wouldn't know, would you? How could you? Your man and woman are with us. Stark and Michaela brought them back from the ruined city and they plotted to set us free."

Ryan cut him short. "J.B. and Mildred are alive?"

The man nodded. "Yeah. Dunno where they are right now, but word is everywhere that they're in the ville and helped plan the revolution."

"Where are Stark and Michaela?" Ryan snapped.

The man shrugged. "Dunno. It's chaos…but at least it's free chaos."

The small group of people began to cheer and laugh, suddenly intoxicated with events and ignoring the four mounted companions. Ryan indicated to them to ride on and spurred his horse through the throng.

"Where are we headed, lover?" Krysty asked.

"To the action," Ryan replied. "One way or another, I figure that's where we'll find J.B. and Mildred."

THE SEC COMPOUND was a mess. The air was filled with the smell of cordite and blood, and as J.B. and Mildred arrived, Stark and Michaela were standing in the middle of the devastation, speaking to the clustered fighters. There was an air of muted jubilation as exhaustion and the sudden realization of what had actually happened began to hit the people of Pleasantville.

"Spread the word," Michaela yelled over the crowd noise. "There's a new way of doing things. We'll have a meeting when this is cleared and everyone will get the chance to have a say on how the ville is run. We decide things by the majority from now on."

"No more oppressing others and using people. Fuck that, we're all sick of it, right?" Stark bellowed. "For the next few days, until we get ourselves straight, me and Eddie will run the sec—and by that I mean that we'll make sure cleanups are organized and patrols are mounted on the walls. Then we see how it goes from there. Michaela will return to the hospital, but she'll head up meetings. She's the smartest, calmest person I've ever met, and she'll see us all right. This thing of everyone having a say is her idea, and it sounds good to me," he added. He was about to speak again when he caught sight of the four riders as they were about to enter the compound. "Fuck! They're alive!" Without another word, he left Michaela's side and fought his way through the crowd to where the riders were being mobbed by the crowd. He reached Jak. The albino smiled and took the hand proffered by the bald man, which engulfed his own. "I knew you were the kind to make it back," Stark said quietly.

"Gaia! It's true! Ryan, Doc, look!" Krysty yelled.

Coming toward them, through the crowd, were J.B. and Mildred, astonishment written large on their faces, echoed by that of the four riders.

"How…" Mildred began.

"Could ask you the same," Krysty answered.

Michaela stepped forward to where the six companions and Stark were now clustered.

"No talking now," she said gently. "You know as well as I do, Mildred, that what you all need, what we all need," she added in a louder voice, "is to rest. This has been a momentous day. Tomorrow," she added with a steely edge to her voice, "we decide what to do with this coldheart."

She tapped the semiconscious Ethan, who responded with a quiet, exhausted grunt.

THE NEXT DAY saw the populace clustered around the sec compound, while the six companions, Michaela, Stark and Eddie stood within. With them, hands bound in front of him, stood Ethan. Despite his position the baron, now refreshed after a night's sleep and medical treatment for his wound, stood proud and erect.

The companions had caught up on each other's stories and were now ready to move on, but had agreed to stay for a while to see what the ville had in mind for their deposed baron.

Michaela spoke directly to Ethan, although her words were loud and directed at the crowds.

"For too long, you've ruled us by the hunt. It made our ville wealthy, but it became more than that. Its sadism and perversion infested your soul, and by extension the soul of our ville. We became obsessed by jack and chilling, even though we began with the idea to move beyond that. Well, I guess we will now. We don't want you, or what you stand for, and what you made some of us. We had to chill people we knew to get back to the right way of things. You're as responsible for those buying the farm as we are. So you've got one chance. From here, I turn you loose. You have to run through the streets to the ville walls. If you get out alive, you're free to go. But you'll be hunted every step of the way."

Ethan sneered. "You might as well chill me now, and you know it. That makes you no better than me."

"True," the spiky-haired young woman agreed, "but we are what you made us."

"Very well, let's get it over with," Ethan snarled, holding out his hands to her.

Stark stepped forward, a blaster in his hand. He smiled without humor. "Oh, no, I get to untie your bonds. You're not going to go for her, or you won't even get one step."

"You always were too smart," Ethan said flatly.

Hands cut free, the baron took one last, lingering look around at the people who had once followed him, then cast a venomous glance at Michaela before heading for the compound's gates.

He ran as though he meant it, but in truth he had to have known that he was doomed, condemned to a drawn-out execution that was a hideous parody of his own trade.

ETHAN TURNED LEFT at the gates, running through the streets and pursued by a baying mob that pelted him with stones. Michaela and Stark had forbidden the use of blasters, but they had said nothing about blades; the streets were also lined by crowds with knives who slashed at him as he ran past. The stones and rocks bruised and cut his back and shoulders, skimmed low and bit sharply at his knees and calves. His head, kept low, was also hit, and he staggered as dizziness began to overwhelm him.

The slashing from the sides ripped at his clothes and flesh, small cuts stinging, blood loss minimal from each, but cumulatively enough to add to his light-headedness. He had no idea where he was going, stumbling and falling, the ground hard and unwelcoming as it came up to meet him, his forehead clashing against concrete and tarmac, making his head ring and spin.

Ethan rolled onto his back, gasping for breath, eyes unable to focus, barely able now to hear the baying crowds that loomed over him, the hail of rocks and stones no longer hurting as a comfortable, numbing blankness began to wash over him. The world closed in, darkness turning it into a tunnel that closed to pinpoint, and then...nothing.

WHEN THE BARON'S chilled corpse had been taken away and the crowds dispersed, Michaela, Stark and Eddie followed the companions back to where they'd been billeted following their return.

A meal had been laid on for them, but none had an appetite to speak of. What had just occurred had left an unpleasant taste.

"Such savagery is not the way to start a new world," Doc commented softly.

"No, but perhaps it was necessary. To purge the old ways, it was right to get it out of our systems and to direct it at the man who was responsible for taking us that way. Drawing a line under it," Michaela explained.

"But you did not have to follow in the first place," Doc pointed out.

Michaela grimaced. "No, but that's what we'll have to live with, isn't it? Kind of a warning not to go back that way."

"It's not going to be easy," Ryan said.

"Nothing worthwhile is." The spiky-haired healer shrugged.

"Meantime, we've got something to ask you," Stark added, directing his comment to all six of the companions. "Running a ville is like making that old tech work.

Once you get the hang of it, and know how it fits together, then it's okay. But it's gonna be hard at first. Mebbe we need someone from outside who knows how it works, to show us. Would you do it for us?"

"Do what?" J.B. questioned, taking in his companions' bemused expressions.

"Help us run the ville. You're outsiders and have no vested interests," Michaela explained. "If you do this, then we can sort out what they used to call democracy while you stand apart."

Doc smiled. "It is a nice thought, but there can be no standing apart from democracy. Believe me, I know."

"Anyway, we have to keep moving," Ryan added. "It's hard to put into words. When we got here, I was fucked in the head, not thinking straight. We got into a mess because my son was gone, and that was all I could think about. I know he's alive, and mebbe the fates will let our paths cross one day. But dreaming won't help. I nearly lost something more here—my mind, my friends—and I've learned something from that. Mebbe we all have," he said, scanning the faces of his companions. "We belong together, and we learn together, because we're looking for something. And we all want it. And we've got to keep moving until we find it."

"But what is it?" Michaela asked.

Ryan thought about this for a moment, then said softly, "I don't know. Mebbe none of us do. Mebbe we won't know until we find it. But we can't stop until we have."

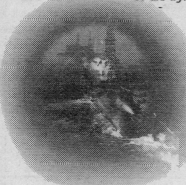

TAKE 'EM FREE

2 action-packed novels plus a mystery bonus

NO RISK

NO OBLIGATION TO BUY

THE DESTROYER

INDUSTRIAL EVOLUTION

GUESS WHO'S COMING TO DINNER?

Take a couple of techno-geniuses on the wrong side of the law, add a politician so corrupt his quest for the presidency is quite promising and throw in a secret civilization of freaky-looking subterranean dwellers who haven't seen the light of day in a long time—it all adds up to one big pain for Remo.

Book 2 of Reprise of the Machines

Available October 2004 at your favorite retail outlet.

James Axler
Outlanders

ULURU
DESTINY

Ominous rumblings in the South Pacific lead Kane and his compatriots into the heart of a secret barony ruled by a ruthless god-king planning an invasion of the sacred territory at Uluru and its aboriginals who are seemingly possessed of a power beyond all earthly origin. With total victory of hybrid over human hanging in the balance, slim hope lies with the people known as the Crew, preparing to reclaim a power so vast that in the wrong hands it could plunge humanity into an abyss of evil with no hope of redemption.

Available November 2004 at your favorite retail outlet.

GOUT31